'*An impressive novel from Hannah Mathewson. Rich and intricate world-building evokes a London that is both familiar and unfamiliar. The reader is swept into a world that is sometimes unsettling, sometimes terrifying, but always exciting.*'

JODI TAYLOR, AUTHOR OF *JUST ONE DAMNED THING AFTER ANOTHER*

'*Witherward is catnip for fans of complex characters and delightfully messy worlds. It delivers on a world of intricate factions and intrigue, without ever losing track of the vividly written living, breathing characters that are at the heart of it. This book broke my heart in the best ways.*'

A.J. HACKWITH, AUTHOR OF *THE LIBRARY OF THE UNWRITTEN*

'*Mathewson has delivered a dazzling, fantastical adventure where magic awaits you on every page, and nothing is ever quite what it seems. With a magnificent world I'd love to get lost in, intriguing magic, and a wide cast of dynamic characters you can't help but love,* Witherward *is a phenomenal and immensely fun debut that will leave readers wanting more.*'

ADALYN GRACE, AUTHOR OF *ALL THE STARS AND TEETH*

D1125723

Witherward

Witherward

HANNAH MATHEWSON

TITAN BOOKS

Witherward
Print edition ISBN: 9781789094435
E-book edition ISBN: 9781789094442

Published by Titan Books
A division of Titan Publishing Group Ltd
144 Southwark Street, London SE1 0UP
www.titanbooks.com

First edition: February 2021
10 9 8 7 6 5 4 3 2 1

This is a work of fiction. All of the characters, organizations, and events
portrayed in this novel are either products of the author's imagination or
are used fictitiously. Any resemblance to actual persons, living or dead
(except for satirical purposes), is entirely coincidental.

© Hannah Mathewson 2021. All Rights Reserved.

Hannah Mathewson asserts the moral right to be identified
as the author of this work.

No part of this publication may be reproduced, stored in a retrieval
system, or transmitted, in any form or by any means without the prior
written permission of the publisher, nor be otherwise circulated in any
form of binding or cover other than that in which it is published and
without a similar condition being imposed on the subsequent purchaser.

A CIP catalogue record for this title is available from the British Library.

Printed and bound by CPI Group (UK) Ltd, Croydon CR0 4YY.

For my parents, for welcoming me home

THE WHISPERERS
Whitechapel

LEADER: LORD JERICHO VOSS
MILITIA: THE STEWARDS

THE SORCERERS
The Heart

LEADER: HIGH SORCERER
LUCIUS
MILITIA: THE ENFORCERS

THE ORACLES
The Docklands

LEADER: THE SEER
MILITIA: THE ACOLYTES

THE ORDER OF
SHADOWS

GUILDMASTER: EWAN GRIMM

THE WRAITHS
The North

LEADER: LADY JOSAVIE WRIKE
MILITIA: THE BLADES

THE CHANGELINGS
Camden Town

LEADER: ALPHA HESTER
(WARDEN)
MILITIA: THE WOLVES

THE PSI
The Underground

LEADER: THE TRINITY
MILITIA: THE CLOAKS

I

THE CUCKOO
Cuculus canorus

A woodland bird found in Europe, Asia and Africa, the cuckoo is a symbol in many cultures of desire and longing. The female lays eggs that match those of another species in colour and pattern, and deposits them into the host's nest.

I

Ilsa did not need to pick pockets any more, but some people deserved it.

And the heckler at her shoulder had it coming. It wasn't just that the boy looked hungry, and his upturned cap was nearly empty of change. Or that he was only trying to entertain, even if his card tricks were well worn. It wasn't even that, as a fellow performer, Ilsa felt his blushes every time the man booed.

It was that he was distracting her.

She had squeezed to the front of the small street crowd so she could be sure of anything untoward in the boy's technique. Rarely, once in a hundred days perhaps, she would spot something that shouldn't be. A man moving too quickly through a crowd. A girl who noticed Ilsa and Martha whispering about her from fifty paces away. A teacup hitting the café floor with a smash, then being whole a moment later.

It was hardly worth her vigilance, but if there were other people in London with peculiar talents, then they were to be found among magicians, and so Ilsa would scrutinise every single one.

This little magician was no older than ten or eleven, and his pack of cards was too large in his hands. His levitating card was clumsy, and its method on show, if you knew where to look. He made cutting the aces harder than it needed to be, but when it worked, the crowd didn't seem to mind.

But whether his next sleight of hand was standard, Ilsa couldn't be sure. The man to her right raised his hands to cup his mouth, and hissed loudly, obstructing her view and snagging her attention. For that, he was losing his wallet.

Martha sighed loudly; she was losing patience. But when Ilsa winked and indicated the man's fat pocket, a finger's breadth from her hand, the other girl's eyes twinkled.

For Martha, unlike Ilsa, was not a reformed thief – she was a practising one. She smiled sweetly at the couple behind Ilsa as she repositioned herself to obscure their view, and when she nudged Ilsa's elbow to indicate the all-clear, Ilsa dropped her hand deftly into the heckler's pocket.

Her fingers closed around a wallet, and without hesitation, she lifted it smoothly and softly, and deposited it into her own bag. A serendipitous spatter of applause from the crowd was distraction enough for the girls to slip casually to the side. They were nearly away when Ilsa's attention was drawn back to the boy, and the cause of the clapping.

He was performing a simple snap change. The three of spades was gripped between his thumb and forefinger. He snapped his fingers and it became the jack of diamonds. Ilsa could do the trick perfectly herself: the performer would hold one card hidden behind the other, and swap them when he or she snapped their fingers. But as Ilsa continued to watch, the jack of diamonds became the ace of clubs, then the seven of diamonds, then the king of hearts, and so on. As Martha tugged impatiently on her coat sleeve, Ilsa watched the boy produce eight, twelve, fifteen different cards, snapping his fingers again and again until nearly a whole deck had flashed by.

It wasn't possible. To hold even three or four cards as if they were one was a delicate enough act, but to manipulate that many with two fingers and thumb? With a crowd surrounding him on three sides? It was no card trick she had ever seen before.

Her breath hitched. Perhaps the boy wasn't ordinary. Perhaps he was like her.

The owner of the wallet now in Ilsa's purse was shifting as if he'd noticed something awry. Any moment now, his hands would go to his pockets.

"*Ilsa*," Martha hissed urgently, but Ilsa couldn't move. The boy finished his act by tossing the entire deck into the air and letting his cards rain down on the audience. She tried to keep her eyes fixed on a single card as it descended, but amidst the motion of the crowd as they patted themselves down and searched around their feet, she lost it – and all fifty-one others.

The realisation among the punters was slow, and met with nervous laughter. The cards had vanished. The crowd had seen them – heard them – fall all around, and now they weren't there. It was too unreal to be a trick, and not fantastic enough to be real magic.

Or so the crowd thought. Ilsa, on the other hand, had seen real magic. She had performed it herself. As the onlookers dispersed – Martha slipping away with them as their victim looked frantically about – Ilsa cornered the boy magician. He was scooping up his cap, in a hurry to leave, but she stalled him by fumbling in her bag and gathering some stolen change.

"That weren't just a card trick, was it?" she said. The boy blinked in surprise but didn't answer. His hands shook as he collapsed his tiny folding table. "I know it weren't. I know what you did." It wasn't true. She was mystified. But she could see her chance disappearing, and she was desperate.

"Please—" she began, but he was already running. If he vanished, she might never know, so she gripped her skirt in one hand and took off after him.

The afternoon matinees were letting out, and the West End streets were teeming with people. Ilsa couldn't move quickly, but neither could the boy. He took the first turn he came to, and as Ilsa rounded the corner after him, she saw him dash into a narrow alley.

She had been him once. She had hidden from both coppers and other thieves – not to mention pimps and drunkards – in the secret corners of these streets, and she knew that unless he planned to climb the wall and sneak into the Beringer Hotel, the alley was a dead end.

With soft breaths and softer footsteps, she approached the corner. But he must have heard her anyway, because he bolted from the alley and nearly escaped again. Ilsa snatched at his jacket collar, nearly missing, and yanked him backwards hard enough that he lost his footing. His folding table clattered on the cobblestones.

"—the bloody 'ell off me!" he yelled as he struggled.

"Who are you? Where're you from?" She stood him upright and shook him as though the answers might fall out. "I got some money. Please."

"Ilsa?"

Ilsa jumped and spun around, but she kept her hold on the kid. Martha stood in the entrance to the alley, gripping the wall for support, her cheeks flushed from the effort of the chase. Her brow was knitted in confusion as she looked from Ilsa to the boy she was accosting and back again. "What're you—"

Martha's eyes grew wide and she cut off just as Ilsa felt the boy slip from her grasp. She made to grab him – only he'd vanished as completely as his pack of cards. Her fingers clutched at nothing. The alley was deserted save for the two of them.

Ilsa didn't have time to process this; she knew what was coming next. She lunged for her friend and clapped a hand to the other girl's mouth before Martha could let out a cry. "Don't go bringing no coppers down on us, Martha. Not when I got some fella's wallet in my bag."

Martha made a smothered shriek of protest and pointed to where the kid had vanished.

"It's a trick," Ilsa lied. "Not even a clever one. I do it myself, every night of the show."

Martha wrenched her hand away. "That weren't no trick," she said, eyes sparkling with unguarded awe, and a hint of fear. "Madam Rosalie told me about beings like that. It was a spirit messenger! From the beyond!"

Ilsa cringed. She knew better than to discount such possibilities, but if Madam Rosalie was correct then it was entirely by accident, as the woman was a charlatan. Ilsa had told Martha so, and Martha had rolled her eyes and called her a sceptic. She couldn't guess how closely Ilsa had studied the medium. How she'd watched the woman's 'niece' – Ilsa had no doubt the girl was in the medium's pay – shift slyly in front of the trick wall of their parlour to let a draft gutter the candle flames at the precise moment. How she could tell from the set of Rosalie's fingers that she was guiding the planchette across the Ouija board as her guests gasped.

Martha's revered medium was one of the hundreds of dead ends Ilsa had reached in her search for answers. And while she hadn't ruled out the existence of *spirit messengers* or those who could build a bridge to the beyond, Ilsa knew that *she* wasn't communing with the dead. And that meant there was more magic in the world than the likes of Madam Rosalie liked to pretend.

Martha didn't miss the look on her face. "You still don't believe!" She pointed to the spot where the boy had vanished. "Well, what do *you* think just happened?" Then her gaze turned suspicious. "And why'd you take off after him, anyhow?"

Ilsa took Martha's arm and tugged her away from the alley, but she was just trying to buy herself time to put together a lie.

Martha was a confidante and a true friend; the first girl she had come to ally with when she moved in across the way from her in a bottom-of-the-barrel boarding house. Two years older than Ilsa, Martha had taken it upon herself to watch out for the new arrival, and had inserted herself into Ilsa's life the day she arrived.

"Where're your family?" she'd asked, poking through the sad contents of the carpet bag containing everything Ilsa owned.

"Don't have none."

"I'm an orphan too," said Martha with a grin so cheery that Ilsa could see right through it. She knew they were alike even before the other girl had plonked herself down on the narrow bed and shared her story. They had both lived on the streets; Martha after her mother had died, and Ilsa when she had run away from the orphanage where she had grown up. They had both picked pockets to scrape by, and been good enough at it to avoid the pimps. Those were the hardships she knew Martha could relate to, but the strangest of Ilsa's secrets? Those, she couldn't bring herself to share.

Because Ilsa had her own ideas about what they had just witnessed. Ideas she loathed but couldn't shake. They had been planted in her mind by the woman who had raised her, the matron of the orphanage Ilsa had fled from at the age of nine.

Devil's get, she'd called Ilsa.

Any desire to tell Martha the truth fled at the sight of Ilsa's memories. To the matron, mysticism and mediums were nearly the pinnacle of evil, second only to Ilsa – a child of the devil's earthly realm, told this back when she was too small to question what even the cruellest of adults said. She thought it was from the Bible, like everything else the matron subscribed to, but when she'd worked up the courage to talk to a priest, he'd known of no concept like the devil's earthly realm.

Ilsa knew she wasn't evil. She didn't go to church, nor study the Bible, and she cursed, and lied; and yes, perhaps she had stolen from a man that very day just to be petty, but those were the worst of her sins. And yet the suspicion that there was some truth in the awful things the matron had hissed at her – *Demon. Devil's get* – clawed at the back of her mind. At the heart of Ilsa's search for answers, it was the theory she needed to prove or disprove. For if there was no such thing as the devil's earthly realm, then what was she? And if there was... what was she *then*?

Martha was still waiting for an answer and Ilsa wanted to give her the truth, but every time she thought of confiding in her friend, the very worst possibilities reared their heads. Martha would tell and the wrong person would find out. Miss Mitcham would hear of it and track Ilsa down. Most of all she could not stand to think that Martha herself would be afraid of her if she learned the *true* nature of Ilsa's magic.

"Thought I knew him, was all," Ilsa lied, her heart heavy.

"Break a leg," said Martha a short while later when they stopped outside the Isolde Theatre. "The shop", they called it when they were pretending they had more respectable jobs. Martha's shop was the busy thoroughfares of Soho, where she stumbled into drunkards, batted her lashes, and helped herself to their belongings. "Oh lord, Ilsa. Let me fix your hair." She started pushing pins back into place around Ilsa's ears.

"I'll redo it inside. Yours is worse," Ilsa warned her. Their nearly identical golden-blonde hair often had them mistaken for sisters, but Martha's was finer, and right then it was bursting from its pins in a halo of wispy curls.

Martha snorted a laugh. "Ain't no one going to notice."

Ilsa knew Martha would forget about the boy. She would tell her friends she saw a spirit messenger, they would shriek and ask questions, someone would suggest a séance, and then the story would fall into myth like every other, to be recounted piecemeal by a friend's sister's husband's cousin next time something supernatural happened.

But pickpocketing came with real dangers, like the gaol. Ilsa squeezed Martha's hand and kissed her on the cheek. Every time she saw her off, she wondered if this was the night she wouldn't return. She had tried to get her work at the Isolde more than once, but the manager, Mr Johnston, must have suspected her for a thief, or perhaps even a prostitute, because he found her "unsuitable". Instead, she persuaded Martha to take scraps from her plate on the weeks when she couldn't afford meals at the house. They managed that way. They were both better fed sharing two plates a day than they had been as street urchins.

"Be safe, Martha," she said. The other girl shot her a weak grin and hurried on down the street. When she had vanished in the crowd, Ilsa swallowed her fears for her, went into the theatre and slipped backstage.

2

Ilsa could put Martha out of her mind, but the boy who had vanished from between her fingers was not easily forgotten.

Her years of chasing clues had helped her recognise when she needed to charm someone. She was usually sweeter; asked better questions. But she had panicked.

She could make herself disappear if she wanted to, but not into thin air like the boy had. Nor could she vanish a pack of cards. Perhaps the boy would have known nothing of who she was or what she could do, but Ilsa ached to be sure. Seventeen years was too long to wonder.

She hurried into the makeshift dressing room in the hope of letting Mr Blume in on her encounter before they went onstage. Blume – or The Great Balthazar as he was known professionally – was Ilsa's exception; the one person in the world who knew her secret. In the five years they had been working together, he'd never treated her like a monster. Ilsa recalled the matron of the orphanage's nails drawing blood from her arm as she was dragged to her punishment, and felt a rush of affection for the once-great magician.

He was trying to straighten his ascot when she entered, but he was only making it worse. The half-empty bottle of scotch on the vanity in front of him told her why. Ilsa sighed.

"Here, sir. Let me." She pulled up a stool in front of him and started fixing his ascot, his waistcoat, his hair. He'd had enough practice at holding his liquor. He never stumbled or swayed, and if she could make him presentable, only the slurring would give him away.

"I saw a boy disappear today," she said as she smoothed his collar. His pale blue eyes narrowed.

"A magic trick?"

"It weren't no magic trick *I've* ever seen," said Ilsa, and she told him about the impossible snap change; about confronting the boy and seeing him vanish. "I was holding him by the shoulders, and then I was holding air. Just like that." Above them, the variety show they shared the billing with was wrapping up. A comedy duo descended from the stage and Ilsa paused until they passed. "You ever seen anything like that?"

Blume must have seen hope on her face, and Ilsa saw her answer on his. He believed in real magic, for he had seen things too, but he shook his head.

Deflated, she ducked behind the screen and changed into her costume. As a twelve-year-old, she had worn little trousers with a red tailcoat and top hat, like a miniature ringmaster in a circus. But as she'd turned into a woman, Mr Johnston had insisted on tighter, shorter, more provocative attire: a satin bodice, with a bead skirt barely touching her thighs, and a plume of red feathers hiding her bottom. It was thoroughly indecent, and Ilsa was glad. Anything to distract from what she was really doing on stage.

As she fastened her garters and helped herself to a finger of Blume's scotch, he wondered aloud about the disappearing boy.

"To be that young," he said. "Do you think he was born with his talents, as you were?"

"Yes. He must've been." She had more questions than she did answers, but of one thing Ilsa was sure: she'd had no say in what she could do. Yes, she had practised her talents to master them, but she would never have suffered the way she did as a child if she'd been given a choice.

"In any case, he must have practised," said Blume quietly. Below stage was beginning to fill with other performers. They were all preoccupied with shop talk and props, but Blume still lowered his voice and leaned closer – close enough that Ilsa could smell the whisky on his breath. "Perhaps with a teacher of sorts. This card trick you speak of... if you don't mind me saying, Ilsa dear, you had no such technique at his age."

She didn't mind him saying. In fact, she was thinking the same thing. She had been performing magic "tricks" on the street when Blume found her, but without an ounce of the young magician's finesse. If the boy had been trained, there had to be others. Her heart raced at the thought. "I'm gonna find him after the show. I got to."

Blume nodded, and mumbled solemnly. Not out of drunkenness, but to spare her feelings. He knew, as did Ilsa, that in a city of millions, the odds of rediscovering one boy – one *disappearing* boy – were as slim as the likelihood that his debts would ever be paid off. But it was the first hint of real magic Ilsa had seen in months.

*

As The Great Balthazar took the stage, Ilsa slipped into the back of the auditorium, the noise of applause and the flare of the theatre lights providing cover. Not that anyone ever noticed the magician's assistant's entrance. Ilsa's talent made sure of that.

23

"Good ladies and gentlemen! Thank you for gracing me with your patronage this evening, my fine, fine guests." Balthazar let out a long, contented sigh, and that was the moment Ilsa realised he was a sentimental drunk tonight; the worst kind. "Almost sober" was best, of course. "Surly" gave him an enigmatic stage presence if they were lucky. But "sentimental" unsettled the crowds. It didn't fit with the awe and mysticism they expected of a magic show. His greeting was met with a thick silence.

"I hope you have joined me tonight with an open mind. A courageous mind! For you may find yourself entertained, but you may also feel *fear*" – Ilsa held her breath as he conjured a flame with the gas lighter hidden in his coat sleeve, and breathed again when the trick played out safely – "*trepidation*" – that was Lighting's cue to insert red filters – "and dread." He slipped the trick knives from the hidden pockets of his tailcoat and threw one, then the other at the wheel he would later strap Ilsa to. "There is danger on this stage, be assured. But, thank God, I have only slaughtered two assistants this year."

He was improvising, but Ilsa took that as her cue. As the audience laughed half-heartedly, she transformed. A force pressed in on her from every angle and shrank her; the pressure almost too much to bear, but over in an instant. Her skin prickled sharply as feathers erupted from it. Her hands blunted, her elbows pivoted grotesquely, and she spread wings.

The first time she had finally become a bird, Ilsa had been nauseated by the feeling. Eight years later, she had grown to appreciate it. It was the proof of what her body could do, a pittance of a price to pay for a thing so powerful: her freedom. Her power to cheat the laws of the universe at their own game.

As Balthazar raised a large black cloth like a bullfighter, she soared, unseen, to the ceiling of the auditorium, and prepared to make her grand entrance over the heads of the audience.

"Allow me to introduce my current partner in crime while she is still breathing. My dearest Ilsa, where are you?"

She swooped to the stage, straight at Balthazar and his outstretched cloth. Darkness descended when the material fluttered over her tiny dove form. But she was no longer a bird. The audience gasped when the fabric fell on the figure of a woman – gasps that turned to riotous applause when the magician swept the cloth away, and Ilsa raised her arms triumphantly and beamed her biggest smile into the blackness beyond the lights.

As far as they would ever know, it was the second most astonishing magic trick in all of London.

The first was yet to come.

3

Delivery was everything. Even with The Great Balthazar's impossible illusions and show-stealing assistant, they would never threaten the box-office of London's best magic shows. They were the one act in town every critic agreed on: awkward and lacklustre, Balthazar's days were numbered.

And it meant Ilsa's were too. She was regularly offered better pay by better magicians who hoped to lure both the captivating assistant and Blume's methods onto another stage. Little did they know, Ilsa *was* his method. Not only that, but she was all the charisma and allure of his act. She was everything that kept him on the billing. Blume needed her, but the real reason they would go down together was this: Ilsa would go back to picking pockets before she told another living soul what she could do.

She held a smile on her face and feigned gusto, as always, as The Great Balthazar fumbled and slurred his way through the set. He drew belongings from his top hat and returned them to their bemused owners in the audience; things Ilsa had slipped from their pockets in the foyer. He sawed her in half. He made her "vanish", and she would become a mouse, and scuttle unseen to the other side of the stage to reappear. Ilsa's skills let them perform the illusions in a way no other act could: over and over in rapid succession. She would bounce around the stage and the auditorium like a rubber ball. It was her favourite part of every evening.

They ran through their mix of standard magician's tricks and real sorcery to middling applause, but as the audience sensed the big finish looming, the excitement in the auditorium crackled. This was what they came for: *the* most unforgettable magic trick they would ever see.

As Balthazar began his monologue about mystic teleportation, Ilsa hid herself beneath a hooded cloak and shifted again. Rival magician's spies had been known to crop up in the corridors as Ilsa was getting into position, and so they enlisted some of Mr Johnston's men as sentinels. One acted as a bodyguard to the cloaked, anonymous figure who climbed from below stage to the door of the box. He left her at the near end of the corridor, while another stood guard at the opposite end. When Ilsa was alone, she shed the cloak, and underneath she wore The Great Balthazar's red beard and gangly limbs; his straight, proud nose and his finely wrinkled skin.

She straightened her white gloves and smoothed her emerald waistcoat. It took a great deal of concentration to shift her clothing, but this too, she had perfected – it was better than leaving a duplicate of Blume's costume lying around the dressing room. Then she took the compact mirror from her breast pocket and checked her accuracy. From a distance, blanched by the spotlight, the minute twitches that cursed all her borrowed faces would be invisible. Nevertheless, she massaged her jaw in a futile attempt to smooth them away. The twitching aside, it was perfect.

All apart from the eyes. Blume's were blue; Ilsa's were not.

It had taken a lifetime to perfect, and a great deal of observation, but Ilsa could perform magic on every other part of her body. She could grow her hair until it trailed along the floor.

She could fatten herself until she was too heavy to stand. She could – and it was a point of pride – be an anatomically correct man, thanks to threepence, a fellow street urchin named Tom, and a deal that would have cost her one hundred Hail Marys back at the orphanage.

But whether she was The Great Balthazar, Queen Victoria, a dove, a bloodhound, or a ferret, her eyes were always stubbornly, distinctively hazel.

Ilsa tucked the mirror away and was listening for her cue when she felt a prickle on the back of her neck. She spun around, stomach plummeting, expecting to find someone behind her – but the corridor was deserted. She peered this way and that, listening hard, but even as she proved to her eyes and ears that she was alone, another sense told her otherwise.

Ilsa knew when she was being watched. It was something one learned fast when swiping coin purses and pocket watches on crowded streets. Yet even as the hairs on her neck stood higher, the uncanny surety growing, she was unprepared when she finally saw him. He appeared in the corner of her vision as he emerged right from the wall: a man in a long black coat, with a flash of metal at his belt. In the sliver of time it took her to turn her head, he disappeared around the corner with the speed of a bullet leaving a gun.

Another child of the devil's realm. This time, Ilsa wouldn't miss her chance.

The audience gasped; Balthazar had fallen through the trapdoor in a cloud of smoke. Ilsa was meant to emerge in the box across the auditorium, but instead, she was chasing the stranger towards the lobby.

She didn't get far. As the tail of his long coat vanished through the first set of doors, Ilsa caught a glimpse of her sentinel on the other side. He barely seemed to register what was happening. Perhaps he thought the flash of a coat zipping by was a new part of the act, but if Ilsa followed, too much would be revealed.

She couldn't leave the corridor looking like The Great Balthazar, and she couldn't leave the corridor looking like anyone else. The only way out was to finish the trick.

It had been less than ten seconds since Balthazar had vanished, but that was long enough for the auditorium to fill with murmured voices. She had already damaged their finale, so she returned to the door of the box, took a steadying breath, and stepped through as if nothing had happened.

*

As far as Mr Johnston was concerned, Ilsa wasn't part of the finale. As he lambasted Blume about the blunder, she stood silently to one side and felt the magician's quiet rage hang thick in the air.

His anger was stoking Ilsa's own, so much so that any guilt she might have felt for doing wrong went skittering away. He ought to see how it felt to see his livelihood fail through no fault of his own.

"This bloody farce of a magic show is poor enough as it is, Blume," spat Johnston. He was pacing about the dressing room as Blume sat at the table, his second post-show drink cupped in his fist. "If you had any respect for your standing engagement here—"

"I have every respect, Mr Johnston. These things happen in the theatre."

29

"They happen" – Johnston advanced on Blume and flung the tumbler from his hand. Ilsa tensed as it shattered against the wall – "when their performer is too sodding *drunk* to do any better! This is your very last warning, do you understand?"

Blume's eyes bore into Ilsa's skull as Johnston left. The unspoken tension that plagued their relationship was palpable. Both of their careers relied on the other, and it wasn't a comfortable state of affairs for anybody.

"What happened?" he said in a low voice, producing another tumbler from a chest near the vanity. "Where were you?"

"I'm truly sorry I was late, but we both know you got no right to be angry. This ain't the first time the show's got messed up, and I don't mean by me," said Ilsa, reining in her frustration as much as she could manage. It was difficult; losing first the boy, then the man in the long coat had shortened her fuse.

"No right?" he hissed. "Answer the question!"

Ilsa opted for a half-truth; he wouldn't be kind about it if she mentioned the boy again. "Someone got into the corridor. I din't see who. I was distracted. It won't happen again."

"A spy?" Ilsa shrugged dismissively. He didn't deserve to know. "And why didn't Bert see anything?"

"Did you ask him? P'raps he did." Blume narrowed his eyes at her, and she stared him down. "Before you go telling me to get my act together, sir, consider this: if that trick'd come off, it would've been the only solid note we hit tonight, and it would've been because of me."

"Because of you," he slurred. "Aren't we a team?"

Ilsa gritted her teeth, turning to gather her coat and bag so he wouldn't see. When she got to the door, she looked over her shoulder at him, then wished she hadn't. Blume was slumped low in his chair because he couldn't hold himself up. The expression she had taken for anger was concentration as he tried to keep a grasp on the conversation. Something part-way between pity and disgust dissolved her anger, leaving her tired. "You ain't a very good teammate, Mr Blume."

He called after her as she left, each cry more remorseful than the last. Ilsa blocked them out. He deserved to stew a while.

Most nights, when Ilsa left through the stage door, she ducked into the next alley and shifted into a man; the tall, brawny type of man who wouldn't have trouble walking home alone at night. But not tonight, because Martha was waiting for her outside the stage door, and a deep bruise was forming along her cheekbone. Ilsa's stomach lurched.

"Martha?" There were finger marks on her neck. Her lower lip was swollen, and had been bleeding. As Ilsa took hold of her, she started to tear up.

"Ilsa, I'm sorry. I didn't know where to go and my feet just carried me here." Her voice shook. "I didn't mean to bother you."

"Don't say that. You were right to come find me."

She herded her in the direction of home, and between her tears Martha told her what had happened.

"I thought it was a clean lift, but I'd only got ten paces when I heard him shout. I din't even look back. I just ran. He was drunk, and he was with his friends and... I should've dropped the wallet, only—" She let out a sob. Ilsa pressed her arm tighter around her and bit her cheek to hold in her anger. "Only I've had no luck all night, and I'm out of change, Ilsa."

Ilsa tried not to picture the scene – an alley, a group of men

31

and Martha on the ground, boots in her ribs – but it was all too familiar. Ilsa had taken her fair share of beatings as a street urchin, and witnessed plenty more. She remembered all the fates she had once pictured for herself – a knife in the gut; a brutish john who liked to make a woman hurt; shackles and the workhouse – and felt a pang of remorse for the way she left things with Blume.

As they reached the river, the buzz of Soho gave way to the lapping of water below the balustrade. The phantoms of ships' bells sounded faintly from downriver. Half a dozen seagulls cawed over the remnants of a heel of bread, scattering like shadows in a candle flame when they girls cut too close. Martha had cried herself calm, and Ilsa had just resolved to approach Mr Johnston about a job for her again when her companion froze in her tracks.

Ilsa followed her line of sight. The mist off the Thames was mingling with the smog, and through it four figures were lurking by their next turn. There was no doubt they were looking in the girls' direction.

Others might have brushed off their trepidation in that well-mannered way that got women into trouble, but Ilsa and Martha knew better than to trust in human decency. It was why Ilsa tended to disguise herself as a man when she walked home at night.

Gathering her wits, Ilsa steered them east to follow the river, but when she hazarded a glance over her shoulder, her heart started up a galloping rhythm. The four figures were following them.

"Is it them?"

"Can't tell," said Martha, picking up pace. "If we get across the bridge, there's a pub on the other side. We can hide in there."

But it was a long way to the bridge, and there was nothing but a deserted fish market along the way. If Ilsa had been alone, she'd have made herself a blackbird and flown to safety, but all they could do was try to lose them. It felt like having her arms tied behind her back, in a knot Ilsa didn't know how to slip. She kept hoping for the chatter of people trickling home from the theatre district, anyone who could help them, but the only sign they weren't alone in the city was the sound of footsteps twenty paces behind them in the smog. Ilsa's own feet threatened to betray her with every step; they were pounding over the slippery cobbles too fast, and not fast enough. Her breath came in jagged gasps, Martha's an echo beside her, the footsteps behind them gaining with every minute. The bridge was still invisible in the night when the shapes of two men were illuminated under a streetlamp ahead.

They had cornered them.

"Martha…" she whispered. If she were a wolfhound, could she take them all down before they hurt her friend? If she were a hawk, could her talons blind them quick enough? And if they did – could she trust her friend to keep her secret? Without her magic, helplessness seized her.

But Martha had survived as a human girl for nineteen years, and she dragged Ilsa under the cover of the fish market and into a maze of crates and pallets.

"This way," she murmured.

At top speed, they wove a random path through the market with their pursuers on their heels. A left, a right, another right, until they had obscured themselves deep within the warehouse. When they stopped, and held their breath, there were no footsteps nearby. "Let's hide in here," said Martha, and she pushed Ilsa towards a narrow gap between two stacks of crates. "You first."

Panic seized her in a crushing grip at the sight of the crevice. "No! I can't—"

But with a firm shove from her friend, Ilsa was between the crates, and her wits failed her. The stacks on either side pressed in and down on her like living things. She pushed further into the gap, hoping to find it open at the other end, but she was met with a brick wall. The air felt thin and hot. Her ribs were tightening around her organs like a cage.

A creak of wood. Martha's head snapped towards the sound and her eyes widened. Ilsa could see nothing, but there must have been no time left to hide; Martha freed her hand from Ilsa's and quickly slid an upended pallet across the gap between them so that Ilsa was hidden – and confined. Nausea swept over her. She thought up the most fearsome creature she could imagine, but she couldn't summon the form, not from this cage; her body couldn't shift when all it knew was how close the walls were. She was a heartbeat away from bursting from her hiding place in her own fragile skin when, between the slats of the crate, their pursuers came into view.

They were not men.

Their faces were almost unremarkable but for their eyes, which were pure, unbroken white. One had produced a strange sort of lamp, and in its glow their skin had a sheen to it, more like silk than sweat, and looked so bloodless it appeared silver.

"It's her, isn't it?" one said to their companion, who seized Martha by the arms, their fingers digging mercilessly into flesh. A third, a woman in men's breeches, seized Martha's chin. Before Ilsa could react, an arm restrained her from behind. Her whole body jerked in terror, then a gloved hand covered her mouth and someone pressed her tightly against them. It wasn't possible. There couldn't be anyone else in that tiny crevice. Her fear was playing tricks on her.

"Bastards!" screamed Martha, kicking against the one who held her. "Get your hands off me!"

"Yes, it looks like her," said the female. "Do it."

Helpless, hidden, immobile, Ilsa could do nothing as the third being unsheathed a blade, and dragged it across Martha's throat.

4

Ilsa tried to scream, but no sound escaped.

The woman was sprayed with blood as Martha died, and Ilsa stood paralysed as her friend twitched and collapsed onto the floor. She barely understood her captor as he brought his mouth very close to her ear and murmured in a low voice: "Disguise yourself."

She tried to twist out of his grasp but he gripped her too tightly. He wasn't a trick of her mind; some attack of nerves. Her mind fought even if her body couldn't. Did he mean what she thought he did?

"*Fast*. You can only fool them for a second."

She didn't have a choice. She willed herself into the disguise of Jeanie from her boarding house, who had deep brown hair and heavy freckles. Meanwhile, the four beings stood around Martha's body had become very still.

Her captor whispered to her again. "I'm going to let you go now. Stay silent if you want to live."

Slowly, he lowered his hand from Ilsa's mouth, and with a whisper of metal, drew a weapon. She barely kept from crying out as she pressed herself into the crates, as far from him as she could manage, but it seemed Ilsa wasn't his target. He slipped past her more easily than he should have been able in the tiny space.

"Something's wrong," said two of the others simultaneously,

and their stillness gave way to a flurry of agitated movement.

"We've been tricked."

"Where's the other girl?"

Four pairs of eyes suddenly swung to the gap where Ilsa and the stranger were concealed, but there was no time for them to attack. The stranger tossed aside the pallet that separated them, and slipped among the attackers so fast Ilsa did not see it. All she knew was that one minute they were hidden between the crates, the next, he had driven a long blade up through the woman's abdomen, and the pallet was clattering to the floor.

More blood mixed with Martha's. Before the woman even hit the ground, the stranger knocked down the second with a sweeping kick and kept him there with a knee on his chest as he buried a throwing knife in the skull of a third. No one had so much as drawn their weapons before the last one standing was gutted, and dropped to his knees. The stranger raised himself to his full height and sank his blade into the chest of the one on the ground, who flailed like a pinned bug before going still.

It was over in seconds. Ilsa squeezed through the gap and stumbled out of its reach, too stunned to run. She thought she had witnessed horrible things, but stood over five bodies – one of which was her closest friend's – she learned how innocent she'd truly been. Two hazel eyes, so like her own, stared up from the bloody ground. Ilsa's knees buckled and she sank against a crate.

"Put your disguise back on," said the stranger. He lifted one of the bodies like it weighed no more than a bag of flour, and threw it on top of another. He was piling them up; Martha lay untouched. "There'll be more if we're not fast."

Ilsa hadn't realised she'd slipped back into her body. It took so little effort these days to maintain another form, but shock could still jolt her concentration. She became Jeanie again.

"Wait here," he said. "Don't make a sound."

Before she could protest, he disappeared. Not like the little boy had, and not like she could, but in a way she recognised nonetheless. He was fast; too fast to see.

He was back before it hit her – his pace marred a little by a wheelbarrow full of bricks. It was the way his long black coat fluttered behind him as he came to a standstill that jogged her memory.

"You were in the theatre."

He glanced up from under his hood, and the light of the strange little lamp caught his features. He looked human; taller than most, and powerfully built, but human. He was young, his eyes were an unremarkable grey, his skin lightly tanned, and the hair that hung around his face was the same deep brown as Jeanie's. He was handsome, even – a model of normality. If she hadn't seen the things he could do, she would never know to fear him.

"I've been looking for you for three days," he said, and he lifted the four bodies one by one and placed them on the wheelbarrow. The one he had sliced across the stomach was spilling his organs as he was moved, and Ilsa retched once, twice, and emptied the contents of her stomach onto the blood-soaked ground.

When she lifted her head, trembling uncontrollably, the stranger was regarding her warily. "Gather yourself, please. If we're not fast, we will only be caught by the others."

That shook her enough that she clambered to her feet and

backed further away from the pool of blood seeping towards her. "Who are you?" she said, shooting a glance over her shoulder to find her best escape route.

"My name is Fowler, my lady. I've been engaged to find you." He had finished balancing his load on the barrow, cleared his throat and faced her purposefully. "I'm about to sink these bodies in the Thames. I'd like to do the same with your friend, but if you would rather I didn't, we can leave her here."

"Leave her?" A chill spread through her. Nothing made sense. "No."

"The water, then?" he said sceptically.

"No! We got to… I don't know, fetch someone." Ilsa didn't recognise her own voice, choked and thin as it was.

Fowler placed his hands on his hips and looked about in exasperation. "I see." He took a step towards her and Ilsa took two back, stumbling slightly in her hast to keep some distance and raising a hand like she could ward him off with it. But Fowler only crouched over Martha, and gently lowered her eyelids. When he looked up, his expression was gentle but serious.

"You need to come with me," he said.

Ilsa's incredulity manifested in a laugh. She shook her head fiercely. "I ain't going nowhere with you."

Fowler sighed, and as he got to his feet he produced a length of cord. "I was afraid you'd say that."

Ilsa realised what he meant to do the moment before it happened. In the space of a heartbeat, he stepped over Martha's prone body and pinioned Ilsa's wrists. She tried to yank them back but he didn't give an inch to her straining, and bound her with quick, deft movements.

"No," she said, her voice hoarse, even as she noticed he was tying a hobble knot. "Don't you dare—"

"I promise I'm not going to hurt you. But I fear you might try to take flight. Quite literally." There was a flash of humour in his eyes as he tied the other end of the cord to his belt, stashed the strange lamp in his coat pocket and took the wheelbarrow. Then he was walking swiftly back towards the river with his captive stumbling after him, and Ilsa saw her moment.

She had joined the theatre business with a dire, crippling fear of having her wrists bound. Like being confined, it was something a younger, weaker Ilsa had been too familiar with. But there was no room for such squeamishness in her line of work, and besides, no magician's assistant Ilsa knew had anything to fear from a hobble knot. Within three seconds, Ilsa had slipped her bonds and was running, not daring to look back.

She didn't get far. The stranger – Fowler – was before her again as though he had been blown into her path by a gale.

"Well, that was unexpected," he said. He might have found her at the theatre, but he clearly hadn't watched the show.

Ilsa turned on her heel, but she hadn't got five yards before he was on her again, an iron arm around her waist, her arms pinned to her sides. She opened her mouth to scream, but terror had robbed her voice of any strength: the noise she made was pitiful.

"Listen," he said in a reasonable tone; still, Ilsa struggled. "They told me you might not understand, so I am prepared to explain as best I can, but now is not the time. All you need to know is this: your friend is dead because they mistook her for you." As he spoke, he bound her a second time, but he'd learned from his mistake, and Ilsa's vision swam as she watched him tie a knot no magician would bother learning. "Their comrades already know a mistake has been made, and I can guarantee they're headed here right now. I've found you on behalf of people who care whether you live or die, and lucky for you, tonight is a rescue, not an assassination."

Martha was dead because of her? "I don't believe you."

"No. I don't suppose you do."

He gave a sharp tug on the rope, perhaps to demonstrate the knot's robustness, or maybe to remind her he had the other end, and then resumed his business.

They stopped at the river, by a gap between two moored fishing boats. Her captor guided her to sit against a nearby mooring post, and Ilsa didn't resist. She knew other tricks, after all, and while he was busy weighting the bodies with bricks, she went to shrink her hands. They refused to move.

Something else then. She thought up the form of a cat, but her body remained stubbornly Jeanie's. She couldn't even become herself.

Ilsa's panic rose, but it was the echo of an old panic; an old situation, in which her magic didn't come when she called it. She was back in the attic at the orphanage. The walls were closing in and her shackled hands were shaking; she could feel the promise of full control dancing at the edge of her consciousness, but couldn't grasp it. When her magic took her, a separation happened, the shifting feeling would hit her like an explosion and then she was something else. But it never saved her; she couldn't maintain it. Once, when she was seven, she had become a bird and made it onto the roof, then shifted back into her human body by mistake. It was snowing. She was naked.

But the day she escaped – *that* day she had cracked the code. For shifting wasn't something that happened in the mind; thinking would not complete the process. She wasn't supposed to *think* about the feeling; her body already knew what to do. A power inside her – a power she recognised from every accidental shift; that she could always hear but had never truly listened to – told her something she had known deep down all along; that her body was her own creation, not the tool but the material, and she could be whatever she wanted to be. The feeling overtook her, and for the first time she was an animal – a blackbird – by choice. To stay an animal, she just needed to remember what she already knew.

There by the docks, Ilsa didn't know it any more. Her focus was correct – she could feel the sensation rising in her body – but the power inside her wasn't answering. Her magic was gone. A panicked noise escaped her, and Fowler looked over.

"I'm sorry," he said, taking in her horror and the twisting, writhing efforts of her hands. "You won't be able to shift with those bonds on you."

Ilsa kept pulling on the cords that held her wrists. They were just leather; securely wound but fairly soft and pliable, and ordinary-looking. But the loss of her magic was in these bonds and not in her. Regardless of the source of her helplessness, whatever this man did next, she wouldn't be able to stop it.

Having weighted the bodies, he kicked them into the water as Ilsa tried to make sense of what he'd said. Somebody had sent him. The attackers had targeted her, or so it seemed. Martha was dead.

Martha was dead.

A sob escaped her. "They thought Martha was me?"

"So it seems. Your friend could easily be a Ravenswood."

A Ravenswood? "I... I don't understand."

"You often walk this way together?" he asked. Ilsa shook her head. "But *you* do, without her?"

"Yes." This was her usual route home, but if Martha hadn't come to the theatre that night, Ilsa wouldn't have seen her until morning.

"Then that's how the mistake was made. Oracles aren't easily fooled, but with a little spontaneity one can stay a step ahead of them." He dropped the next corpse, and Ilsa was spattered with Thames water.

"Oracles."

"Our friends here." He gestured to the last dead being before toeing him over the edge, followed by the barrow. "Let's go."

He drew Ilsa to her feet and took her by the elbow.

"*No*," she growled, looking over her shoulder at the dark fish market where Martha still lay. Fowler didn't answer her protest; he just lifted her over his shoulder and ran.

She was lucky not to vomit again. Between his inhuman speed and the abrupt halting every time he needed to look or listen, her innards couldn't keep up with him. By the time he dropped her unceremoniously on some wet slabs, she was bewildered, terrified and giddy beyond belief. The man wasn't even short of breath.

"You ain't of this world," she said. The truth of it chimed through her, rousing equal parts horror and excitement.

"No," he said. "But then, my lady, neither are you."

43

His words were a brief flash of ringing clarity; a moment of calm in perfect chaos, like the eye of a storm. The feeling dissipated when Fowler hushed her and drew his blade again. Fearing there were more Oracles – as he'd called them – nearby, Ilsa struggled onto her knees and forced her vision to right itself.

They had come at least a mile from the fish market. There was no one else in sight, but directly above them loomed the twin turrets of Westminster Abbey, and across the wide intersection were more buildings, some with lamps burning within. Ilsa didn't know what those buildings were, but surely if she could scream, someone would hear her.

"What would you achieve?" said Fowler, as if he had read her mind; perhaps that was another of his talents. Before she was fully on her feet, he had scooped her up again, and then they were in a tiny quadrangle. Shadowy cloisters surrounded them on all sides, and the abbey above blocked what little starlight penetrated the smog and the cloud cover beyond. With his long knife in one hand, Fowler withdrew the lamp he had claimed.

It was a luminescent stone, a little like a quartz crystal she had once seen in an occult shop. There was no flame, and no gas or oil to be seen. It surely hadn't been glowing in his pocket, but in his hand, it shone from within with a bright white light – enough to reveal a fountain in the centre of the quadrangle.

"Tell me where you're taking me," she demanded.

"Home." He raised the stone higher and shone it about the cloisters to be sure they were alone, then he approached the fountain and sank a gloved hand into the shallow water. "Your people tell me you have alpha blood, and you're in danger here.

A lot of it, I would wager, if the rumours are true."

Not a word of his explanation made sense, but the word *home* played on a yearning deep inside her.

"And the way to this place is in this courtyard?"

He was circling the fountain, and when his hand met with something concealed beneath the surface, he glanced up at her and almost smiled. There was a trembling, groaning sound of metal and stone shifting as he turned some sort of wheel beneath the surface, and Ilsa stepped back, out of the way of the passage opening in the ground beneath her. The head of the fountain itself was revolving as the slabs around it fell away like dominoes to become a spiral staircase leading down into the earth. When Fowler had completed a full revolution of the fountain, he was stood on the topmost step.

So, it was true. The devil's earthly realm was real, and here underneath Westminster Abbey was its gate. Ilsa heard a sound from the gaping, black entry – the hiss of a draft, or was it the whispering of a demon or ghoul? She didn't want to find out. "I won't go down there."

Her captor's jaw set, and he let out a slow breath. It was the only sign that she was trying his patience. When he spoke, his voice was patient and calm. "The portal only *appears* to lead down."

Still, Ilsa shook her head. With three slow strides, he came to stand in front of her, and took her bound wrists in his hands.

"I will be met with questions if I turn up in your quarter with a Changeling as a prisoner, so I need to untie you. When I do, I would appreciate it if you would not make me manhandle you down that staircase."

"Them things what killed Martha, and this evil magic you've

45

tied me with, and *you*." She was struggling to maintain some dignity amidst her fear. "P'raps I don't want to go *home* if where I belong's the devil's realm."

Fowler let out a breath that might have been a chuckle. "My lady, if I told you where we were going was a pleasant, safe place – a home to be proud of – I would be lying. But it is not the devil's realm. We call it the Witherward, and this, the Otherworld. And there are far worse horrors this side of the coin, believe me." As he spoke, he unwound the strange cords from her wrists until she was unhampered. The second they fell away, her power answered, swelling alongside a relief so intense that for a moment nothing else mattered. She tested her magic, turning her hair red, then fair, then dark again, the curls bunched in a shaking fist before her face so she could be sure; she could cheat the universe again.

When she could breathe she looked up to find Fowler had retreated to the staircase. She was free to make a break for it if she chose; he was far enough away that she could be out of his reach in time, high above the cloisters.

But he hadn't harmed her. In fact, he had saved her life. And now he was taking her to the people who had paid him to; *her people*, if what he said was true. Ilsa pictured the milky white eyes of the four who had ripped Martha's life away. She pictured more of them, creeping into the boarding house while she slept. Beings who knew what she looked like and where to find her. Fowler extended his hand to her and her instincts told her to take it. It didn't matter if she trusted him. She had never trusted another living soul, not completely, but her instincts had kept her alive all the same.

She took shaking steps towards the staircase and let him lead her down. As they descended through the portal underneath the abbey, she shed Jeanie's skin and became Ilsa again; the Ilsa who had never belonged in the world above.

II

THE GREY WOLF
Canis lupus

Native to the wilderness of the Northern hemisphere, the grey wolf – the ancestral canine of humankind's closest friend – is a social animal with strong familial bonds. They live and hunt in packs.

5

Ilsa fell.

Or at least she thought she did. After only a dozen or so steps, the dark stairwell shifted and her stomach lurched. It was like the feeling of being seconds from sleep, and then jolting awake as you fall off the edge of the world. Somehow, she landed on her feet.

She had taken several steps more before she realised they were ascending, and above them, around the bend, there was sunlight.

"You called this a portal," she said, her voice quaking.

"Slipping from one world into another is not as simple as geography," Fowler replied as they emerged into the same quadrangle they had left below – or above. Ilsa was blinded by the sun high overhead, and suddenly burning up, as if someone had opened the door of a raging furnace. A stupid, heedless fear told her this was not the quadrangle at Westminster Abbey; that she was dead and this was hell, just like she'd been promised. A metallic rumble split the air. Ilsa cast wildly about for the source, her eyes finally coming to rest on the clock tower striking one. It swayed before her eyes as the ground swayed beneath her feet. Was stepping through a portal into another realm supposed to feel like this?

As her eyes adjusted to the light, she saw they were surrounded. Eight or ten people had stirred at their arrival and closed in on them. They weren't armed, but their manner and the way they positioned themselves told her they were guards or soldiers. This was a whole other world – there was no telling the ways they could hurt her. "No," she said weakly. The fish market flashed before her eyes; Martha's blood leaving her, the crates pressing in on all sides.

Someone grasped her hand and pressed something into it. Ilsa willed her gaze to steady, and found Fowler in front of her, cool grey eyes on hers, a frown marring his brow. He was holding her fingers around a flask. "Drink," he commanded. "Get your wits about you."

The promise was tempting, but Ilsa tried to push the flask away. "I don't want it."

"The choice is yours, my lady, but the trials of this day are not yet at an end for you."

Ilsa tried to stop her despair showing as she took the flask, unscrewed the top, and sniffed. Scotch. She took a deep drink, then another. All she could taste was blood, but the burn numbed her throat, and as the alcohol started coursing through her, it promised to numb everything else, too.

Her escort turned to face the soldiers surrounding them and raised his hands.

"I wouldn't if I were you."

A man came forward, braced as if he might pounce at them. "What's your business here, captain?"

"I'm in the employ of Alpha Hester," said Fowler. He produced a folded document from the inside pocket of his coat, and added in an embittered tone, "I'd hoped she would be good enough to tell you."

The guard took the document from him, and as he read it, Fowler turned slowly and took in the other guards. Every man and woman he locked eyes with shifted their weight a little, but none faltered. Ilsa gripped the flask with white knuckles as she imagined witnessing another death match.

Whatever the captain's piece of paper said, it made the guard's head snap to Ilsa in red-faced astonishment. He turned his incredulous eyes on the captain, who nodded almost imperceptibly.

"Stand down," he commanded the others, and they all relaxed their stance. The guard handed the document back, and lowered his head to Ilsa in a bow. "My lady."

Captain Fowler plucked the flask off her and tucked it away. "This way," he said, and before Ilsa could raise any questions, he had rounded the guard and was heading for a door in the cloisters. Ilsa dragged herself after him, through a short passage, then another, and out onto a wide, bustling junction – the *same* junction.

It was London, yet this was not the city she had left behind in the night. The buildings were the same. The horses and carriages and people on the pavement were all identical. A young man was selling newspapers at the corner of an office building, and some of the men coming in and out were having their shoes shined by a man on the steps.

There were also two chimpanzees, little bigger than babies, wrestling on the pavement. Ilsa came to a jolting halt before them. No other pedestrians paid them any notice, and she wondered whether her mind had finally broken, or whether she had made a very poor decision in drinking Fowler's whisky. Not even the captain looked concerned; he was watching Ilsa's reaction with quiet humour.

A harried woman pushed her way through the crowd towards the chimps, scolding them as she approached. As she got close enough to make a grab for one of them, they both transformed into laughing human boys, and darted through the foot traffic away from her.

Ilsa found she wasn't breathing. Suddenly, she had an answer she had sought her whole life. She turned wide eyes towards the captain.

"Changelings," he said.

Yes. That is what he'd called her. A changeling.

"Welcome to Camden Town," said Captain Fowler, turning north, "the territory of the Changelings."

Ilsa was fast learning how little she knew, but if this London was like the one she had left behind, she knew its geography. "Camden's north of here."

"The borough, yes. The Changeling quarter that shares its name is vaster. Though it's small compared to all the others."

The Changeling quarter; the home of people like her. Ilsa's heart was hammering hard enough to break free.

They crossed the street and found a group of three more guards ahead. Each wore a red sash or neck scarf or armband, as had those at the abbey; a makeshift livery. They shot wary glances at the captain, even when he lowered his hood to appease them, and as Ilsa and the captain came level, the guards stood across their path.

"What business?" said one, as the others spread out to surround them. Again, they were all unarmed, but their tense, ready stance and squared shoulders were intimidating.

The captain scowled as he withdrew the document. "Read it

quick," he snapped. "At this rate, it'll be a miracle if we reach the Zoo by dusk."

The guard scanned the page, then returned it with the same astonished chagrin as the man in the abbey. "Apologies, captain. Take Whitehall. There are fewer wolves that way."

"We will." And they were on their way again, Ilsa taking two steps for every one of his.

Through the descending whisky haze, she tried to arrange her scraps of knowledge so they made sense – another London, an "Alpha Hester" who was looking for her – but each new piece of information only left her more at sea. "Wolves?"

"Camden's militia. Look for the men and women marked with something red."

A memory tugged at Ilsa – a wolf somewhere in her childhood – but she dismissed it. "Who'd they work for?"

The captain thought for a moment, then laughed mildly. "I suppose they work for you."

As far as understanding went, this was a step in the wrong direction. "Me?"

"While I said I would try to explain, there are some gaps in my knowledge about Camden business. You shall have to ask Alpha Hester who the wolves answer to these days."

Ilsa was trying to decide on her next most pressing question when a glaring difference between this world – the Witherward – and the other became apparent.

"There ain't no Big Ben!"

"Who?" He followed her line of sight. "Ah, the clock tower. The Otherworld have their parliament. We have the Trade House, the only neutral ground in the city."

Indeed, the missing clock tower was not the only difference to the Palace of Westminster. The building was similar, but it was like someone had taken the frame and finished it with bigger windows, steeper roofs and gilt moulding. It had an imposing stateliness that reminded Ilsa of religion instead of law, but certainly not of trade.

"What 'bout Buckingham Palace?" Ilsa asked. "St Paul's? The Tower?"

"Some of those places exist," said the captain. "Few serve the same purpose."

As they walked, Ilsa continued to spot Changelings in animal form. The frequent enormous wolves, she took to be the militia. Then there was a man who transformed into a monkey to climb a lamppost and find his wandering young son in the crowd. A woman waiting to board an omnibus was whispering seductively to a black snake draped around her neck. The driver charged her for two fares without batting an eye, but Ilsa struggled to look away.

She had never dared imagine a place where she could shift freely. In all the stories she had told herself about how she got her magic, she was an outcast. To find she was so very *normal* in this other realm was so hard to fathom, she was tempted to run the other way; back to the "Otherworld".

She attributed her fierce overheating to this anxiety – and the long walk. That is, until they reached the southern perimeter of Regent's Park, where the grass was lush and green, the trees were cloaked in frothy foliage, and the hydrangeas were in full bloom. The warmth suddenly made sense in a backward way.

"It ain't winter here, is it?" she said.

"When are we – early February? This is the hot season. We have a few weeks left before the leaves start turning." He suddenly snatched Ilsa's elbow and drew her closer. "Just keep walking."

She followed his line of sight to a figure among the pedestrians ahead of them, and her blood chilled. She was young, and frail-looking, but she had the orb-like, white eyes and sickly pallor of the beings who had slain Martha.

She did as the captain said and kept walking – partly because he was dragging her along even as she slowed, and partly because the girl looked so powerless. She swayed slightly as she stumbled along, and even with her empty eyes, it was clear she was nearly oblivious to her surroundings. Other pedestrians gave her a wide berth, or turned their faces like she wasn't even there.

They passed close by her, and she paused in the middle of the pavement and cocked her head to one side. Some kind of awareness had struck her; awareness of them.

"Keep walking," repeated the captain.

Ilsa did, but she watched the girl over her shoulder as they retreated. She tracked them with her empty eyes like she was following their scent. After a moment, she turned around again and stumbled on.

"Was that an Oracle?" said Ilsa.

"Yes." He released her arm.

"But I thought you said this was the Changeling quarter."

He shot her a look. "You ask tenacious questions for one in your position," he said, eyes travelling to the blood spatters on the hem of her dress: to her dishevelled curls and the lazy sway in her step. He offered her the flask a second time – perhaps an attempt to quiet her – but Ilsa refused it. Fowler put it away with a sigh. "It is the Changeling quarter, and it's wise to keep one's eyes down and hands at one's sides in another people's territory. Plenty would take you for a threat just for being there."

Ilsa looked over her shoulder. A man sneered and spat on the ground as he veered out of the girl's path.

"And Oracles can see your future?" Ilsa said, mining her knowledge of the occult.

"Theoretically, they can see anything that can be observed, regardless of time or space."

Ilsa wasn't sure what that meant. She only knew they had tried to kill her. "Ain't they dangerous?"

"Immeasurably. But whether they pose any threat is another matter. I assure you the weakest, most wretched beings you meet here will be Oracles. They have little loyalty, little capacity. The only thing they're good for is keeping the wrong people in power by falling to their knees for their precious opiates."

"What 'bout them four what attacked Martha and me?"

"Acolytes. The militia of the Docklands."

What did a militia force of Oracles want with *her*? And why had the very ruler of Camden thought to rescue her? Ilsa wondered if she'd missed a step – if the whisky had dulled her mind too much – but the questions kept coming to her.

"And what kind of soldier are you, captain?"

"A different kind," he said. "My faction is the North, but I belong to the highest bidder."

That was three types of soldier in one town. Ilsa sped up to get in his line of sight. "You know, this ain't looking to me like a better place than the one you took me from."

Captain Fowler sighed. His expression darkened and he said

quietly, "Granted, London is not what it was meant to be. Not yet. But I told you the truth."

"You told me your opinion."

"An opinion then," he said. "It is my *opinion* that we can not only live in accord but better one another. It's why we were put here together in the Witherward."

"In your opinion," added Ilsa. He shot her a look. "And on the condition you can stop attacking each other."

"We need only decide we want to," said the captain.

Ilsa looked back over her shoulder, but the Oracle girl had vanished around the bend.

"These acolytes. Why'd they want to kill me?"

The captain studied her meaningfully. With his hood lowered and the sunlight on him, Ilsa saw he was younger than she'd thought. "Revenge," he said solemnly. "They were provoked."

With that, he picked up speed again until Ilsa was trotting to keep up.

6

Ilsa never had the money to spare for transport. She loved to fly, though it was a strain, but a girl could miss a lot of hidden magic when she was up in the air, so Ilsa was used to traversing the city on foot.

But that was on a normal day. By the time they had been walking for an hour, the steadying effect of the scotch had burned off. She wasn't sure if she could really smell blood, or if seeing the floor of the fish market painted with it was irreparably burned onto her conscious mind. She was weak from tensing every muscle in her body. The day was hot, but she was dressed for a winter's night, and the heat made her feel like she couldn't breathe.

There was so much she wanted to ask, but every step took more energy than the last, and by the time they reached a grand white house set in the northeast corner of the park, she was swaying like the Oracle girl they had passed. Ilsa thought the place was different in the London she'd grown up in, but she was too disorientated to be sure.

Captain Fowler made his presence known at the gate while Ilsa slumped against the fencepost and closed her eyes. She was vaguely aware of words exchanged; of accusations by the captain as to why a carriage wasn't sent.

"If we had known you would traumatise her before you

even reached the portal, we would have. Couldn't you have hailed one?"

"I would never trust a hackney driver in the current circumstances, especially with a wanted girl under my protection. My fee?"

A heavy thump struck the ground too close. A shape blocked the sun that filtered through her eyelids. A huff of warm, wet air shocked her upright, and when she opened her eyes, it was into the maw of a humungous beast with black lips, ragged grey fur, and fangs as long as her fingers.

A scream Ilsa didn't have the strength to utter built in her throat. This was it. She had let her guard down but for a moment and this world was going to end her.

"For pity's sake, give her space," said a female voice, and the beast obeyed. It was a wolf, Ilsa realised, as it moved away and its whole face came into vision. Nearly as tall as her at the shoulder and with unnatural eyes for a canine – blue-green and too intelligent – but a wolf. Probably one of the militia. Still, her heart hammered on. Real wolf or sentient human, those jaws could have snapped her neck if their owner chose. Ilsa tried her best to hold herself upright as the shock rushed out of her as quickly as it had come, but she must have failed, as the next thing she knew, a girl with cold hands was pulling her to her feet and guiding her towards the house.

"Martha…"

"My name is Cassia."

She craned over the girl's shoulder. There were wolves everywhere; giant ones, most with scars and stories of violence etched into their fur, and all with their prying human eyes on her. And beyond them, on the other side of the closing gate, was Captain Fowler. He raised his hood, bowed curtly, and strode away.

*

She awoke slowly, and with a clear mind.

Nothing was wrong, even as she became aware of the soft, unfamiliar linens, and the violet hue of the light. She sat up in bed and tried to make sense of her surroundings. She was alone, and it was dark. The curtains were drawn, but around the edges, moonlight crept in. Everything appeared normal, if not familiar, except for the dimmest glow emanating from the sconces along the walls. But even that didn't alarm her. This, itself, was odd.

She tried to remember how she had gotten there.

There had been a bathtub, and a bottle of something that smelled of lavender. Ilsa had complained weakly, but a female voice had told her they needed to wash the blood off. But before that? A late summer's day. A beautiful clear sky. A park – Regent's Park – was right outside.

And a teacup, with a syrupy, magenta liquid inside. The steam had been a deep blue, and sparkled like starlight. The girl said it would ease her worries and put her to sleep. She had called it magic.

Ilsa had drunk it willingly – why?

Because of the fish market. Because of the Oracles, and the stranger in the hood, and…

Ilsa sucked in a breath like it was her first for days. Blood pounded in her ears. She wasn't in London. She had gone through a portal to the devil's realm. A world of Oracles and

61

swift assassins and beasts as big and as fearsome as anything Ilsa could become. So many of them.

And Martha. Martha was dead.

She wrestled free of the sheets and scrambled out of bed. Her feet hit the floor hard and she tensed, afraid someone would come looking, but a plush carpet had absorbed most of the sound and the boards beneath didn't protest. She was in the grand white mansion where Captain Fowler had left her, and as her eyes adjusted in the dim light, it was obvious.

It wasn't an ordinary room at all; it was the grandest room Ilsa had ever seen. Heavy, floor to ceiling curtains shrouded the windows on opposite walls of the wide space. They matched the sumptuous, floral pattern on the walls; in her human form, Ilsa could not have reached the decorative crown moulding at the top of them had she been wielding a broomstick. In the centre was the bed, big enough that half the girls in Ilsa's boarding house could have slept top-to-tail and would have considered themselves lucky. Its painted frame was carved in a pattern of vines and accented in gold leaf, like a wedding cake piled with soft linens. There was a matching bureau, a wardrobe, a dressing table, and silk-upholstered armchairs before a marble fireplace, empty of coals in the late summer heat. Above her, a chandelier blossomed from an ornate ceiling rose. It was unlit, and in the moonlight and the violet of the sconces it threw a warped, surreal shadow across the ceiling, like a nightmare looming over her.

As whatever she had drunk wore off, a chill went down her spine.

It was afternoon when she arrived – how long had she been sleeping? Was she a prisoner now? The thought made her nauseated, and she cursed herself for not considering it sooner. The night – or day – before had promised answers, but had it promised safety?

Only one thing was certain: she would not wait here to find out. She was in the Witherward now; she had answered the biggest question. There must be someone else in this city who could help her piece together the rest. Someone who had known her parents. Someone who hadn't *kidnapped* her.

Whoever had helped her bathe had put her in a nightgown, which wouldn't do. Listening hard and treading lightly, Ilsa scoped about for her clothes, but there was no discarded heap of fabric in any of the places she knew to expect. This wasn't the sort of room in which the occupant's only good dress lay folded over the end of the bed on every day but wash day.

So she tried the wardrobe, the hinges of which were mercifully silent as she pulled the doors open. But her clothes weren't there either. It was stocked with fine and pristine summer clothes; dresses patterned in forget-me-nots and pastel stripes; white muslin blouses with lace collars and sleeves. Ilsa pushed down the urge to wipe her hands first and grabbed the plainest skirt – pale blue with no bustle – and a blouse and hastily dressed. As she buttoned the skirt at her waist, it became clear it was too big for her, but before Ilsa could root around for something to belt it, the fabric tightened around her all by itself. Panicked, she grappled with the waist with shaking fingers, trying to rip it off before she was suffocated by whatever dark magic was working on the garment. But the skirt was already inanimate again – and a perfect fit. Tentatively, she put on the blouse, holding her breath as the sleeves and collar did the same. What kind of magic could make a garment shift the way a Changeling did? What if these magic clothes could also supress her magic, like the cord Captain Fowler had used to bind her wrists?

Well, she was about to find out.

Ilsa went to the window and made a gap in the curtains just wide enough to see through. She was on the first floor overlooking a garden. The shadows of shrubbery and ornaments stood like sentinels clad in black against a silver, moon-drenched lawn. Around the edge of the garden ran a wall, heavy with blooming wisteria and taller than two of Ilsa, but that didn't matter. She planned to fly clean over it.

She had unlatched the window and was about to pull it open, shift into a sparrow, and be gone from here, when one of the black sentinels unfurled.

Ilsa sucked in a breath. It was a wolf. As she watched, afraid to withdraw behind the curtain and catch the beast's eye, another came into view from directly below, so silent it could have been a trick of the light. So close. If she broke the absolute silence of the moon-touched garden with the beating of her wings, or if the window creaked, they would hear her and be wolves no longer, but birds on her tail.

Not the window then. If she could get to the ground floor, she could slip out and get as far away from the militia as she could before she grew wings. Ilsa unfurled her fingers from the latch and stepped away from the window with a slowness that belied her hammering heart, and as she turned to the door, she shifted. Her limbs pulled in towards her body and her skin prickled sharply as she grew fur. The breath was forced from her lungs as she was pressed down, down into the smallest form she could become: a mouse. It had served her well for sneaking in the past, including slipping under doors when she did not wish to be caught using them.

But Ilsa could not slip under this door. She struggled for a moment, head and shoulders wedged in the gap, paws grappling for purchase against the wood floor, but the space was far too small.

She became human again in a heap on the floor, panic rising with every moment, and looked wistfully at the fireplace. Another Changeling could escape up the chimney; in a space that small, Ilsa was as likely to suffocate from fright as she was to reach the top. Her chest tightened just thinking of it.

It tightened further as she got to her feet and wrapped her hand around the doorknob. She was leaving this room in her human form, or she was not leaving at all. The idea that they might have locked her in when she was capable of escaping in so many other ways had seemed pointless before, but now it was burrowing in Ilsa's gut like it wanted to tear straight through her. She couldn't be locked in, she thought as she turned the handle. She couldn't be trapped in here.

But the latch gave without a whisper and the door opened smoothly. Ilsa could have sunk to her knees with relief but instead she braced herself, waiting, ready to sprout wings should a canine beast barrel through the open door.

But the hallway beyond the chamber was deserted. It was a cavernous space, wider than any room Ilsa had ever lived in, and made bigger still by the darkness lurking where the paltry midnight light didn't reach, like the corridor might go on or up or outwards forever. Somewhere distant, a clock ticked on, but no floorboard creaked, no lights flickered. The household was sleeping, not guarding her like a prisoner.

Still, Ilsa kept her wits about her as she crept softly down the corridor. She rounded a corner, and the moonlight streamed in through tall windows, and revealed the rest of the house to be just as fine as the chamber she had woken in. It illuminated filigreed consoles, marble busts, and crystal vases of fresh flowers. A row of portraits faced the windows, of a size that made Ilsa wonder how a person could paint when they could only see part of their work at one time. Regal giants looked down at her from the frames, sometimes in twos or threes, faces sober and refined, each draped in a red sash like the tags worn by the wolves. They were all relations; the generations of a family immortalised. As Ilsa went from one painting to the next, each subject wore the ghost of the last in their features.

Every one of them made her uneasy, but it wasn't until she was very near the end of the gallery, where the last few paintings lingered in shadow, that her sense of the uncanny peaked.

She stopped before a portrait of a man and a woman; a plaque on the frame read *Alpha Lyander and Thorne Nyberg* and was dated eighteen years previously. The woman had a heart-shaped face and fair complexion. The artist had captured the way the light struck her thick, golden hair, and her hazel eyes had hues of caramel and vivid green. The man – her husband, Ilsa guessed – was also fair-haired, with a neat beard and moustache, and slightly sunken features. Ilsa's attention was wrested by his eyes; their shape, their pronounced lids, the familiarity of them. His mouth was familiar too. As she studied the painting, Ilsa put her fingers to her own lips to feel their shape.

But then, from the darkness in the corner of the corridor came a rumbling growl.

Ilsa leapt back, pressing herself against the wall as another wolf – no, something feline and blacker than night – separated from the shadows. The muscled contours of a gigantic body unfurled gracefully as it rose. A long tail uncoiled, whispering against the floorboards as it did so, like a cobra readying to strike. Ilsa was frozen like a rabbit, unable to think, the faces in the painting still muddling her mind.

The big cat bared its teeth at her as it stalked out of the dark, another low growl emanating from its throat. But then its human eyes – blue and unforgiving – took her measure in quick movements, and the teeth vanished. A second later, so did the cat, and in its place was the shadowed form of a young man.

"Oh," said the former panther. "I thought you were a Sorcerer."

Ilsa's breath left her in a rush of relief. Before she had a chance to raise her guard again, the boy turned to disappear into the shadows without another word.

"Wait! Where are you going?" she called after him. Ilsa saw him look over his shoulder, but she still couldn't make him out properly in the gloom.

"I prefer to contemplate the dead in solitude. You're here now. It ruins the ambience." His tone was callous and superior.

"I—"

"Apologise? I accept. Goodnight."

He made to leave a second time, and somehow, Ilsa found herself blurting the first thing that came to mind.

"I'm escaping."

He halted. Ilsa thought she heard him sigh. When he turned

around and emerged fully from the dark, the impression wasn't much better than being set upon by the panther. Cold, storm-blue eyes looked out from a face carved in sharp lines, like his sculptor had made the first rough cuts and found a cruel perfection worth preserving. His hair had probably been combed neatly back from his face at one time – it had the gloss of oil where a shaft of moonlight caught the inky-black strands – but that time was long past. He had harassed and overhandled it; swept it to one side and let it fall across his forehead. It made Ilsa think of raven's feathers, then of razor-sharp talons.

His hands were buried in his pockets, giving nothing away, and the cuffs of his wrinkled shirt were rolled up to the elbow. Whatever the hour, he hadn't slept yet.

"Escaping," he said, wearily.

Ilsa readied herself to shift; she wouldn't freeze a second time. "I'm a Changeling too," she said. "You can't stop me."

The tight set of his mouth relaxed into a smile. It was the kind a hyena might give its prey before it tore their gullet out. "You're in one of the most heavily guarded buildings in London," he said, strolling to the window and gesturing to the garden below. "I don't *need* to stop you."

Still poised to fight or flee, Ilsa approached the window and looked down, though she knew what she would see. More enormous shapes shifted in the dark like shadow puppets. He was right; she was surrounded by soldiers with fearsome magic. Even with her own talent to match, she didn't stand a chance of besting them.

Her sudden flash of helplessness must have been plain, for the boy who looked like a blade lost his humour in an instant and reverted back to bored. "You shouldn't be so easy to tease." His callous gaze went back to the garden, then to the park beyond. "The wolves aren't there to keep you *in*." Ilsa shot him a look, and he rolled his eyes and reached to open the window. "You can cobble together a bird of some description I trust? Since you *are* a Changeling too." He swept an arm in the direction of the open window, like an invitation. "Then grant both our wishes and be gone."

Ilsa hesitated, too overcome to grasp his game but sure there was one.

"No?" the boy demanded.

"For all I know, you want to see me torn to shreds by them wolves. You were baring your own teeth at me a moment ago — why should I believe a word you say?"

In a flash, Ilsa knew her challenge would not go unmet. He hardened like ice, the look he gave her as searing as it was cold. It took all she had not to flinch away.

"So you don't trust me," he said with another bitter smile. Ilsa missed the joke. "No matter. Come with me."

For reasons Ilsa couldn't put her finger on, she knew she couldn't be the first to relent, so when he turned on his heel and swept off down the corridor, she followed, trying to step lightly, quietly, as he did. Perhaps she could still turn this situation to her advantage; if she could parse some knowledge she could trust from this boy, it might aid her escape. If nothing else, she might discover what had brought him to that corridor, that painting, in the dead of night.

After several twists and turns, the corridor opened on one side to look down over a grand entrance hall, slightly better lit by the lamps burning low along the walls. Ilsa followed the boy down a wide staircase to a black and white marbled floor, so brilliantly polished that Ilsa felt as if she were looking down into its depths like a pool of clear, still water. Her companion peered warily around every doorframe as they crossed the hall and followed a passage to a set of doors leading to a terrace. Ilsa couldn't help noticing how he turned the handle and pushed the door wide with the unique muscle memory of someone who knew how not to make a sound; pulling the door tight against the frame as he turned the handle; gripping it by the edge as he swung it open.

He kept close to the wall of the house as he crossed the terrace, so Ilsa did too, stepping as he did until he crouched in a flower bed between a pair of blooming hydrangeas and beckoned her to join him. With nothing to lose and a surplus of curiosity, Ilsa lifted her skirts about her ankles and dropped to her knees in the flower bed beside him.

"You wish to leave and you believe the wolves will stop you. Fine. Then watch." He nodded to a shadowed corner of the garden and Ilsa followed his line of sight. She was prepared this time when a giant beast emerged from the shadows to prowl along the edge of the wall. The boy leaned close to her and spoke under his breath. "Ferrien keeps very regular time. He will complete every turn of the garden in just under two minutes, all night, every time he's assigned to this watch. When he rounds the east wing, this stretch of wall before us will be beyond his sights."

He gestured past Ilsa to a pavilion near the west corner of the house, beyond which a second shape was moving like a spectre.

With his other hand he produced an ornate silver watch from his trouser pocket and clicked it open. "Georgiana guards the west gate to the park. That lookout is a straight line, back and forth, and you'll catch her eye if you make your move when she's facing north." Sure enough, the wolf at the west gate changed direction and doubled back on herself, and it was obvious she would see anything that moved across the lawn between them. "You only need to pass that topiary monstrosity before you're in her blind spot, making your window of opportunity about fifteen seconds. Starting" – he held his watch so the moon shone brightly on its face and lifted his eyes to where Ferrien was disappearing behind the house – "now."

Ilsa held her breath. Looked from the corner where Ferrien had disappeared to the other wolf, Georgiana, stalking south with her back to their hiding place. She cast about her for another unseen guardsperson, but there were none. It seemed he was telling the truth; her way to freedom was clear.

But did she want it? Was it right?

"After me, then," said the boy, and quick as lightning he was gone, replaced by a raven as black as his panther form. He soared softly across the lawn, dipped over the wall, and vanished into the park while Georgiana at the west gate still faced away.

Ilsa got to her feet, then took to the sky. She pushed herself high then let gravity and the tilt of her wings send her swooping across the lawn and over the garden wall. She followed the raven as he swooped low over the park and landed in a copse of trees some distance from the house, where he leaned against an oak tree and waited for her. Ilsa transformed in the air and dropped to earth beside him, landing gracefully on her feet. She swung around, ears pricked, waiting to catch the movement of a wolf bounding towards them or the rustle of heavy paws crunching foliage.

There was nothing, but as Ilsa studied the scene, something else slowly dawned on her.

She had thought this place was different through the portal, and she'd been right.

"There ain't no zoo here."

Ilsa knew this corner of Regent's Park well. It was the site of the zoological gardens. She had sneaked in more times than she could count, as either a bird or a mouse, before shifting somewhere private and joining the patrons. Most of her more extravagant transformations – all of which relied on studying an animal in the flesh: the way it moved, its curves and edges – had been made possible by its inventory. It was dismaying to discover that what was such a wondrous place in the Otherworld was nothing but a big, white mansion in this one.

"Oh, there's a zoo," said the boy. "You're looking at it. The seat of Camden, some would say. Not quite what you're used to in the Otherworld, but rest assured, though there are fewer bars there are just as many animals."

The Zoo. Of course; that's what Captain Fowler had called it.

The boy pushed off the tree and started strolling back towards the house. "Now if this experiment of yours is over, I think I'll take tea. *Alone*. Oh, and don't *escape* in that direction if you still fear being seen. Make a straight line towards—"

"What are they keeping out?"

He stopped mid-stride and turned to face her. "I beg your pardon?"

"You said the wolves weren't here to keep me in. So what are they guarding this place from?"

It must have been a stupid question. He studied her a moment as if to gauge if she was serious.

"You know nothing of London," he said ponderously. "Do you?"

Ilsa folded her arms. "I know *everything* 'bout London. I've lived here my whole life."

He shook his head, the downturn of his mouth at once miserable and mocking. "Not in this London. For a start, it's not one city. It's six."

"Six?"

"Six peoples. Six factions. Six territories."

Ilsa swallowed. *London is not what it was meant to be*, Captain Fowler had said. He had failed to mention that acolytes, wolves, and whatever army *he* belonged to were only half the soldiers staking their claim to a part of it.

"Do you see those lanterns?" He pointed to a spot at the west edge of the park. It was so far away, and the shapes of trees and houses knitted together in similar shades of grey, but sure enough, half a dozen specks of light burned on; some stationary, others clearly held aloft by hand. "That's a guard point. It marks the boundary of Camden and the Heart, the Sorcerers' quarter."

"Sorcerers." Ilsa was struck with notions of enchanted castles and magical bargains. "Could a Sorcerer... move too quick to see, or step through a wall?"

"Stars, no," he said. He was warming to his role now. Ilsa feared it was her bewilderment that entertained him. Before she

73

could utter the question of what a Sorcerer *could* do, he turned and pointed past the house. "But a Wraith could. The faction of the North. They can pass through solid objects if they choose to. Walls, yes. Locked doors. Hence their name. Not to mention their formidable strength and heightened senses."

So that was how Captain Fowler had appeared from the brick when she was hiding in the fish market. He was a Wraith.

The boy turned ninety degrees again. "Venture east and you will soon reach a guard point to Whitechapel, the territory of the Whisperers. Mind readers. Thought benders. Don't let their lack of physical magic fool you, they are as dangerous as any of us. A Whisperer can make their victim forget their loved ones, their values, their self-preservation. Can make them crave violence, sex, *death* even. They can wipe a mind clean and refill it with whatever, and *whom*ever, they choose.

"Follow the Thames east and you will reach the Docklands, as I'm sure you know, expert that you are." He smiled wryly. "There you will find the Oracles. I understand you don't need me to warn you about *them*.

"And then there are the Psi. You can imagine the debates we enjoy this side of the portal. Which magic is most formidable? Which is mightiest in combat? Well, I favour the Psi. Their magic is psychokinesis. The ability to influence the physical with their mind." He laughed humourlessly. "One will stop believing in the superiority of Wraith strength or Whisperer manipulation when one has seen a person decapitated by the blade of someone who hasn't lifted a finger."

Ilsa balled her hands into fists to stop them from shaking. "And you've seen such a thing?"

He smiled. Perhaps it was the moonlight, but that smile was a vicious thing, unguarded and yet deceitful, like a fake smile painted on a wooden puppet. "Twice."

"And where do *they* live? The Psi."

"Let's just say we're surrounded by enemies on every side. That is what our soldiers are protecting the Zoo from: this city." He gestured around them again, somewhat wildly. Ilsa could tell he was reaching the crescendo. "It was founded on discontent and tribalism and it broke along those fault lines as it was always destined to do. Welcome to London, the city that orphaned you." His breath left him in a rush. He ran a hand through his already bedraggled hair as he added, quieter: "You were better off where you came from."

In the sudden hush that fell, he wandered away a little, almost as if he'd forgotten she was there. But Ilsa didn't mind. She too, needed to breathe. Her thoughts were tumbling too quickly over one another, like a barrel bouncing over stones as it rolled down a hill; if it didn't slow, it would break apart.

"So they really are dead, then?" she said, doing her best to sound collected. "My parents."

His eyes were black in the moonlight as he turned to her, but they seemed to grow darker still as it dawned on him. "You didn't know."

Ilsa opened her mouth to speak, but nothing came out. She thought she had known. She had been an orphan all her life, and though she hadn't rested without knowing where her magic came from, she had long accepted the truth that it meant being without a family. But the confirmation hollowed her out and whistled through her like an icy draft down empty corridors.

She shook her head. "I don't know nothing. Not who they were, or 'bout this place. Or magic."

The boy looked skyward and let out a sound halfway between a sigh and a groan. "Heaven, earth, and all the damned constellations," he said under his breath. "Well, now you do."

If that was what passed for sympathy, Ilsa would take it. A kind word or a gentle hand on her arm would bring on hateful tears. Tears of what, she wasn't sure. Bewilderment, grief, injustice; they all bled together and left her numb.

"You knew them? My—" *parents. My mother and father.* She couldn't make the words come a second time; they sounded too foreign. No one had ever been *hers*, and no one was hers still. Her mother and father were dead.

"Of *course* I didn't…" he began snippily, clearly struggling to adjust to Ilsa's absolute ignorance. His hands found refuge in his pockets once more, defensive. "I was an infant when they passed. My… my father was a lieutenant to the alpha, as I am now. Or *was*. I'm not sure any more."

"Your father – he ever talk about them?"

His unforgiving gaze snapped to hers. She had said something wrong. The wrongness of it flashed across the boy's face, torment so bleak Ilsa wished she could unsee it, and yet so brief she wasn't sure she had. He stared at her like she were a ghost, mouth open like he might speak, but he didn't.

"How'd they die, then?" She moved closer. She needed him to understand how important this was. "Tell me that at least."

"They won't like that you're talking to me," he said, almost to himself.

"Who?"

"The other lieutenants. I shouldn't be the one to tell you these things."

"Please." Ilsa hated to beg, but the word was out before she could stop herself. None of it was as she'd thought. She had imagined all sorts of scenarios leading to her being left at the orphanage, and most had involved her parents' horror at what they had birthed. Now that she was back in the world she had come from – a world full of magic – she knew this couldn't have been the case. She thought she would feel relieved, validated, but though her parents were truly dead, she understood less than ever why she'd been orphaned.

"I deserve to know why I was left at an orphanage."

He straightened, unable to hide his surprise. "You weren't left at an orphanage."

"I – I was abandoned," Ilsa said stubbornly.

The boy was shaking his head slowly. "You were hidden in the Otherworld to protect you. The day you were born was the day your parents were murdered."

Ilsa drew a sharp breath and wondered how it could hurt so much to hear of something she did not remember happening to people she had not known. "How?"

He ran a hand through his already dishevelled hair and looked about like someone – one of the lieutenants, perhaps – was about to catch them. Ilsa was compelled to look too, but there was nothing around them but an expanse of moonlit park. They were too far from the house to draw attention.

"Your mother thought she could tilt the needle towards peace. Before your birth, she gathered the faction leaders and proposed the Principles. They're... rules of engagement. Break the

77

Principles against another faction and their leader can retaliate as they see fit. Follow them, and you have the best chance of a peaceful life."

Rules of engagement. Just like on a battlefield.

"Each faction leader can govern their quarter as they choose, but they agree to enforce the Principles. And they did. The faction leaders signed and it was done." He laughed pitifully. "*Should* have been done. But there were dissenters. A small band of propagandists and enough hate-filled citizens to listen to them and be convinced that the Principles curtailed their freedom. The guard points, for example." He nodded at the pinprick lanterns at the west edge of the park. "The Principles say we must pass from one quarter to the next by way of the guard, and the propagandists said their leaders were trying to limit their movements. But there *was* no movement before the Principles. Approaching a border was like stepping into a warzone.

"The Principles said no one could use their magic beyond their own quarter. The propagandists said it was your mother's conspiracy to disarm the citizens of the other factions.

"The Principles said in writing that the faction leaders recognised Camden as the territory of the Changelings. And the propagandists said it was just the beginning; that if we were allowed a place in the city, we would grow our territory and our numbers until every other faction fell to us."

"That don't make no sense," said Ilsa, shaking her head. "Why'd they think it was some conspiracy? You said *all* the faction leaders agreed to them."

"*Stars*, that didn't matter! It was never about the Principles. When London was settled, we didn't yet exist. The last magic, they call us. Two thousand years younger than the Wraiths. One hundred thousand younger than the Sorcerers. The *legitimate* peoples of London could not tolerate each other, let alone us, but we were here anyway, and we were lost. Morgan Ravenswood united the Changelings, and then she won Camden for us with teeth and claws. With blood. Her family have been paid in kind ever since. Your parents were killed for the crimes of your ancestor and the desire to be better than her. They were…" he faltered, shook his head. His gaze found hers, tentatively, then shifted away again, finding a spot in the grass to address instead. "They were run into hiding. But they were found. The way I understand it, they had had a plan to hide you in the Otherworld since they learned you were coming. It was supposed to be temporary. Just until the unrest settled a little; a handful of years at most. You were supposed to be cared for there."

Cared for. "They din't leave me in an orphanage?"

"I don't know the details, of course. Like I said, I'm too young to remember any of this first-hand. But they had a friend in the Otherworld whom they trusted. Another Changeling. Lord Walcott, I believe his name was. He had agreed to make you his ward until it was safe for you to return."

"A *lord*?" Ilsa let out a miserable laugh, earning her a wary sideways glance. This life she had somehow lost; it was worse than simply *cared for*, which would have been enough. It was cared for by some wealthy Changeling lord, who would have fed her well and kept her in clean clothes and a warm bed; who would have told her what a Changeling was, and that she had had a mother and father who wanted her. The laugh that might have been a sob came again. "Where is he, then? This Walcott."

"Dead." He delivered the word as gently as he had the truth of her parents. "Smallpox. When you were still an infant. Not long after, Ilsa Ravenswood died of it too."

"I – beg pardon?"

Ilsa recognised the way he was watching her, like a spectator trying to work out the trick before the final flourish, and she knew before he spoke that he didn't have the answers. "My words exactly when we learned you were alive. No one had been in close contact with Walcott. I imagine they didn't want to draw attention to him, and to you. He would signal us that all was well, and then the signals stopped coming. When someone was sent to investigate, they were told you were both dead."

A noxious fear Ilsa didn't want to name crept into her belly. "By who?"

"Walcott's beneficiary. She was his housekeeper, I believe. He left her everything, including guardianship of you." *God granted me this house, child, and He'll have thanks for His grace, whatever He asks of me.* "She *said* she had nursed the baby herself until the end and was holding her when she died," he added slowly, purposefully. "I remember that specifically."

I will cure you of that demon inside you, as He wishes.

"What was her name?"

"I'm afraid I don't know," he said again. But he didn't need to know, because Ilsa did. She understood what had been done to send her life down the path it had taken.

The boy was watching her expectantly. "Do you know of her?" he prompted when Ilsa didn't speak. "Do you know why she said that?"

80

Yes, she wanted to say, but she knew the rest of the words wouldn't come. She knew she couldn't think on it right now, not with everything else she had learned. Magic, warfare, her parents' slaughter. It was too much.

"P'raps Ilsa Ravenswood *is* dead," she said instead, testing the way it felt and whether she could believe it. She wrapped her arms around her waist tightly. "P'raps I ain't her."

The boy shot her a probing look, black shadow and stark light throwing the crease of his brow into stark relief. "Come with me," he said. "That is, if you would risk stepping back into the house and being a captive once more."

Then he was a raven again, climbing high beyond the tops of the oak trees where he circled, waiting for her.

Ilsa looked around her at the silent expanse of Regent's Park. Where would she go, if not with him? This was where the answers she sought could be found. So she shifted and soared to join the raven; the first Changeling she had ever known, she realised with a pang.

They crept back across the wisteria-blanketed wall and swooped low over the lawn, then slipped in through an open window on the first floor and walked through the cavernous hallways in silence. He still hesitated at every doorway, listened before every turn. Ilsa realised in the dizzying torrent of questions answered, the mystery of this boy she had found lurking in the darkness had fallen to the wayside. She studied the sharp lines of his profile as he guided her through the house. He was too strange to be classically handsome; the set of his brow too solemn, the cut of his jaw and cheekbones too brutal. And yet...

He stopped abruptly, snapping her out of her reverie.

"I'll be made to pay when they find out we spoke, and I would have been hung, drawn, and quartered if you had flown out of here and disappeared again," he said, hands in his pockets, something of that riling superiority back in his features. Ilsa wondered if he'd caught her looking.

"You was never going to let me leave."

"You were never going to try. You say perhaps you're not Ilsa Ravenswood." He tilted his chin in the direction of something over Ilsa's shoulder, and she turned around. It was the portrait of Alpha Lyander and Thorne Nyberg. They were back on the spot where they had met. "I saw you looking at them. You knew who they were."

He was right. Without understanding why, she had recognised them instantly. It was their eyes; the shape of his and the colour of hers. Puzzle pieces that only fit together when Ilsa was added.

They were her parents.

"You already knew you belong here," the boy said.

You belong here. She felt those words hit her like a physical thing. A satisfying hurt. She knew she would remember hearing them again later when her mind and her heart caught up.

"So you were brought up in an orphanage." There was sympathy there this time, the subtle softening of his typically biting words. Ilsa nodded vaguely. "If it means a thing, your life – blessed or otherwise – is a remarkable stroke of fortune." He looked up at the portrait. "An hour later and you would have died with her." He turned to the window and gazed up at the stars, scowling like they had done him a grave insult. "Someone else might call it a miracle," he said ponderously. He shook his head and straightened. "The lieutenants will want to tell you everything in the morning. You should go back to bed."

And then he melted back into the shadows. It was only when Ilsa was alone that she realised she had never asked his name.

7

When Ilsa returned to bed, she did not believe she would ever find sleep. Her mind turned with thoughts of her birth, her exile, an orphanage in a grand old house. Self-pity weighted her down, and perhaps it dragged her under, as some hours later Ilsa woke a second time.

The fish market came rushing back. The quadrangle at Westminster Abbey, and the uncanny fountain that concealed a staircase to another world. The stranger in the black hood. Giant wolves.

And the shape of a boy in the darkness. Or was it a panther? Her slumbering mind had sent her phantoms bearing stories of her parents and her past before. But when she woke, the stories dissipated like smoke, broken apart by their own lies. Now, with golden morning light limning the drapes, her midnight discoveries seemed just as implausible and fantastic.

Only, there had been truth in them. Facts she recognised. Puzzle pieces that fit.

God granted me this house, child, and He'll have thanks for His grace...

Lord Walcott's former housekeeper was Miss Mitcham, the matron of the orphanage that used to be his home. The woman who had filled her childhood with torments she wished to forget. He had trusted her enough to leave her care of Ilsa, and kept her close enough that she had inherited his house and belongings. It stood to reason he had also made her privy to his magic. That was how Miss Mitcham had known what Ilsa was before Ilsa knew herself. Why she had been so intent on *curing* her.

And now Ilsa knew that everything she remembered suffering was only half of what Miss Mitcham had done to her. The matron had believed it her God-given task to rid Ilsa of her magic, her evil – and she had believed it so desperately, she had lied to keep her. She had faked Ilsa's death to the people who would have seen her safe.

Helpless anger seized her and she gritted her teeth against the threat of tears. Ilsa often tried to tell herself that the matron of her old orphanage couldn't hurt her any more. She was grown up. She was braver. And now, she was in an entirely different world.

But it wasn't true. Miss Mitcham hurt her every day. She had left a pernicious fear in Ilsa as surely as she'd left physical scars, and Ilsa could escape neither, no matter how well she hid them. She had been afraid of her magic her whole life. She had kept her true self from everyone but Bill Blume. She had woken in the night biting her pillow to keep from screaming in remembered pain.

There was hate and cruelty, and then there was Miss Mitcham, who could have wiped her hands of Ilsa and instead chose to steal what little her orphaned ward had left.

Ilsa buried her face in the pillow and found it wet. She hadn't held back her tears after all.

"Don't be alarmed."

Ilsa shrieked, and was on her feet before the cry faded. As her eyes swept the curtained chamber for the source of the voice, her fingers felt along the end table behind her and closed on something hard and heavy. She raised it above her head as across the room, a delicate female hand pulled back one of the drapes and the girl was illuminated.

She was beautiful – probably the most beautiful girl Ilsa had ever seen, and Ilsa worked in showbusiness. She was not much older than Ilsa, with smooth, alabaster skin and straight, raven hair tumbling freely down her back. She could have been made of porcelain, or marble; not just because of the delicacy of her features, but because of the way she held herself – with perfect posture and stillness. She looked dispassionately between Ilsa and the thing in her hand.

"What are you planning to do with that statue?" she said.

"*Hit you with it*, what d'you bloody think?"

That didn't garner much of a reaction, so Ilsa readied herself to demonstrate. The girl came towards her, until Ilsa could see sea-green eyes framed in long, dark lashes, and a distressed crease between them. There was an uncanny sadness about her.

"You are Ilsa Ravenswood, aren't you?"

Ilsa hesitated, the statue dropping lower. "I might be," she said. "I think so."

"But you are a Changeling, yes? The Wraith assured us he saw you shift. In your stage show. Did he not?"

Deny it, said an old instinct. *Devil's get*, rang the echo in her head. Tears of the agony her magic had caused were still fresh on her cheeks for this stranger to see, but things were different now. She had seen others like her. She was in a place where they shifted in the streets, unafraid.

"He did see it," she said carefully. "I can change. It's just

86

no one's ever called me Ravenswood. I was Ilsa Mitcham when I was a kid. Ilsa Rose on the stage. Ilsa Brown, if the police ask." Ilsa's weapon-wielding arm was growing weary, so she switched, and held the thing aloft with renewed vigour. "And who the hell are you?"

The girl studied her a moment longer, then drifted to the other side of the room and opened those curtains, too. Ilsa pivoted to keep the statue aimed at her.

"We already met, don't you remember? My name is Cassia Sims. You can call me Cassia," she said. "I couldn't sleep thinking what an ordeal you'd had. The Wraith said... your friend was killed." With the light pouring in, Cassia was looking at her differently. Ilsa realised why, and hastily wiped the moisture from her cheeks. At the mention of Martha, images of her needless death crowded Ilsa's mind, but she was beyond tears over her friend. The memory was still too biting. Too unreal.

"I was afraid you'd be distressed to wake alone," Cassia went on, hastening to continue as Ilsa opened her mouth to argue. "Yes, it's occurred to me now that waking... *not* alone is itself quite distressing. Forgive me. I hope we can start again." She unfolded and refolded her hands, fumbling a little, and Ilsa could no longer resist cutting in.

"What is it?"

"I beg your pardon?"

"You're scared! What's happening?" She tightened her grip on the statue, blood pounding, body bracing on instinct for new danger. "What are you hiding?"

"Hiding? No, I—"

"I ain't stupid! Are you here to stall me? Is someone gonna—"

87

"*I was nervous to meet you*," Cassia said in a rush, volume rising to meet Ilsa's. Her mouth snapped closed.

Ilsa dropped her arm: it was difficult to be coordinated and dumbstruck at the same time. "Beg pardon?"

The crease between her eyes returned, deeper than before. "You're Ilsa Ravenswood. You've been nothing but a sad story for seventeen years, and now you're here, and you're real. And you mean so much to" – she drew a short breath and recollected herself – "to the Zoo. And we waited for Captain Fowler for days. I've done nothing but wonder what you were like and what we would say to you and how in heavens we would explain." She grew quieter the longer she went on, until Ilsa was moving closer to hear. From the moment she'd seen the girl, she thought Cassia might be on the verge of tears, but now it appeared to be true. "I'm honoured to meet you, Ilsa. Thank you for coming."

Incensed, Ilsa resisted the urge to heft the statue again. "Well I weren't given much choice!" she snapped. "After my friend was murdered and the man what was sent to find me bound my hands."

Cassia paused a moment, her mouth open. "You make a fair point. We have a lot to answer for, I know. Let me take you to Hester. It's early, but… well, she won't be sleeping."

Cassia went to the wardrobe and produced a dress – white with a black ribbon at the waist and a high collar. "Let me help you," she said, unbuttoning the dress, but Ilsa would be damned if she was about to put her back to the girl. Cassia must have inferred this from Ilsa's sneer, as she tossed the dress over the top of the screen beside the wardrobe and retreated a respectable distance.

"You can put the statue down," she said. "No one will hurt you here, but should someone try, teeth and claws would be more effective, don't you think?" That delicate frown line appeared again. The rest of her face didn't appear to be malleable. "Or perhaps you're not a strong shifter. Did anyone teach you?"

Ilsa slammed the statue – a marble wolf, she noticed; always wolves, in this place – down on the end table and pulled the dress behind the screen. "I taught myself," she said through gritted teeth. "And I shift just fine."

Behind the screen she grappled with the dress, which had obviously been designed for a lady who had a maid to help her. Even a magician's assistant's flexibility, a pickpocket's dexterity, and the magic ability to grow her arms longer would not allow Ilsa to best the endless run of tiny buttons that fastened the back.

"Ilsa," Cassia said tentatively from very close to the screen, after several minutes had passed and Ilsa's sighs of frustration hadn't ebbed.

"Fine!" Ilsa snapped. "You can help."

Cassia came around the screen. As she fastened the buttons at Ilsa's waist, the dress magically cinched to fit her perfectly. Once again, Ilsa gasped in alarm.

"I didn't know what would fit when I ordered things for you, so I spelled all the garments to fit the wearer," Cassia explained as she worked, though it wasn't half an explanation enough. "But perhaps you noticed in the clothes you wore last night."

Ilsa warily turned her head, but she couldn't read the girl's expression any more than she could read her tone. Had there been someone watching the room after all? When Ilsa wanted to go unseen, she sometimes made herself into something very small. Her stomach lurched. How had she been so foolish? Cassia could have been in the chamber the entire time. Or perhaps, after all his reservations, that duplicitous boy had…

"You left them hanging over the end of the bed."

Ilsa peered through the gap in the screen. So she had. Cassia ducked her head purposefully, and Ilsa wondered if it was humour she was hiding.

"Where did you go?"

"I needed some air was all."

There was a long breath of silence. Cassia reached the final button at the neck of the dress and dropped her hands. "Did you pass through the gallery?" she asked.

Ilsa turned around. "Did I see the portrait of my parents, you mean?" Her parents who had tried to protect her; who would be angry for her if they knew of the lie that had changed the course of her life.

The sadness in Cassia's eyes compounded, and a conflict played out behind them. "I'm so sorry, Ilsa, but your parents—"

"They're dead? I know." Cassia opened her mouth. Closed it again. Ilsa thought it over a moment, but still wasn't sure why she chose the lie she told next. "I asked that Captain Fowler. He told me 'bout the factions and the Principles and all that. 'Bout how my mother and father was killed."

"I see," said Cassia, nodding absently.

Ilsa rounded the screen and made for the mirror to avoid any further questions. She was already lucky to have said something Cassia could believe. And she was lucky to have kept her tears in check in front of her.

"You're so much like your family." Ilsa stopped fussing with her hair as Cassia appeared in the glass behind her. "Your eyes…"

It was hard to drag her gaze from the beauty of the other girl's face to look at her own. Ilsa didn't think very often of her face. Appearance meant little when she could change it as she pleased. But now, as she looked in the mirror, she saw the woman in the portrait, dressed in a fine dress, standing in a beautiful bedchamber.

You belong here.

Doubt and dismay swelled in her chest, and she turned away.

"Have I got *any* relations here?" she asked, not daring to hope.

She must have caught Cassia in her own reverie, for she startled. If it was possible to upset the girl further, Ilsa had managed it; her eyes were glassy.

"You do," she said shakily, and let Ilsa reach the point of madness before she finished: "Hester is a cousin. Your second cousin, I think."

A cousin. The woman who had searched for her was her cousin – her family. There were names and faces, lives and deaths, all too big for Ilsa's paradigm. Her feet followed Cassia from the bedchamber and down the corridor, but her mind was in several other places; the orphanage, the portrait gallery, the room they were headed.

They reached a set of double doors, and Ilsa's nerves rivalled the first time she had stepped on stage. As Cassia knocked and waited for a reply that never came, Ilsa resisted bursting into the room, just to have it done with. Eventually Cassia took the handles and swung the doors open to reveal a long sitting room. Pre-dawn light was filtering softly through the high windows. It mingled with the lamplight to illuminate the feminine, pastel accents of the furniture and wallpaper – but the scent of stale smoke and rotting flowers spoiled the impression.

Across the room, a woman sat facing the window. She didn't rise, or even turn to acknowledge their presence; she just stared out into the gardens.

"Hester?" Cassia closed the doors behind them, and Ilsa followed her deeper into the room. "Ilsa has arrived." When Hester didn't react, she added lamely: "Here she is."

Hester spoke, her voice clear and commanding. "Fliss, move me nearer the couch."

As a tall, willowy woman with eyeglasses hurried from an adjoining room, Ilsa rounded the console between them, unable to resist the urge to get closer. Hester's wicker armchair had wheels. Fliss took the handles of the chair, pivoted Hester to face the room, and brought her closer.

And just like that, Ilsa was face to face with her family.

Hester regarded her with a bored, sardonic expression. She was not decrepitly aged, as Ilsa had foolishly imagined when she saw the wheelchair; thirty, perhaps. The resemblance she bore to Ilsa and her mother was less pronounced, but her eyes were the same distinctive shade. Her hair was caramel blonde – a shade darker than Ilsa's but identical in texture – her chin was pointed, and she had a high, broad forehead above narrow brows. She held a cigarette in a silver holder, and she took a long drag as she studied the new arrival.

"Ilsa, this is Hester Ravenswood, a cousin of yours and the Warden Alpha of Camden Town," said Cassia.

Ilsa wondered if a curtsey was proper, given the unfamiliar title. She did not perform one.

92

Hester cracked a smile, though it wasn't entirely friendly. "My lieutenants are always sure to remind me of the *warden* part. Thank you, Cassia."

"I was only…"

"You're Lyander's double, to be sure," she went on, heedless of Cassia's small sigh as she trailed off. Her voice had a ringing clarity that was equal parts compelling and intimidating. "Why don't you sit?"

Unsure if this was a request, Ilsa took a seat on the couch. Fliss was shooed; Cassia remained standing by Ilsa's shoulder.

There was a long silence while Hester watched her unblinkingly and enjoyed her cigarette. Ilsa met her stare, resisting the urge to seek direction from Cassia, who stood just beyond her sights.

"I din't know I had any family," said Ilsa eventually.

"Not a lot of it," replied Hester. "It's a shame you couldn't have come in December."

"I din't know none of this existed in December," she shot back, indignant again. "Why? What happened in December?"

Humour coloured Hester's features. Her gaze reached beyond the couch, to Cassia, and she raised an eyebrow.

"Ilsa only arrived yesterday afternoon, and she's been on an opposite clock," Cassia said. "Oren proposed we gather in the meeting room this morning and explain everything. Your presence is requested, as always…"

"And your presence in my chambers is deterred, as always, yet here you are." She took a long drag on her cigarette and Ilsa gaped, open-mouthed.

"Ain't you in charge?"

93

Hester laughed acerbically. "Only as a last resort, cousin dearest."

She made the endearment sound like a grave insult, and Ilsa recoiled. She looked to Cassia, whose mouth was pressed into a hard line.

This was so very far from everything Ilsa had imagined. She had a nauseating sense of things she had only just grasped spinning out of her control, and she reached wildly to grab hold again. "I ain't waiting for no meeting to find out what you ain't telling me." She pushed off the couch, gaze swinging between them. "I want to know why I'm here!"

"Damned if I know," said Hester.

Ilsa swallowed hard. Captain Fowler had said he was working for her, hadn't he? If she hadn't summoned her…

"Hester—"

"It's *Alpha* Hester to you, Miss Sims," Hester snapped, her expression suddenly fierce. "And this is some hour to be springing long-lost relations on me. Fliss! I'm tired."

Fliss reappeared and wheeled Hester into the next room. The door closed behind them without another word.

It had begun and ended so fast, and now Ilsa had family – this cold, hostile woman who had no time for her; who hadn't wanted her home at all.

A feeling Ilsa didn't want to name – hot, gutting, leaving her feeling exposed – set her lip trembling, and propelled her out of the room, Cassia hurrying after her. In the corridor, she took a deep breath, buried the awful feeling and replaced it with something stronger.

"That man Fowler said *Alpha Hester* paid him to find me!"

She gestured at the door Cassia was hurriedly closing. "That woman don't even know why I'm here!"

"Technically, Captain Fowler was hired on Hester's *behalf*," said Cassia, at a volume that alerted Ilsa to the fact she'd been yelling. "I was the one who arranged the contract."

Ilsa folded her arms and levelled a glare that dared her to go on.

"There was a messenger. They said Ilsa Ravenswood was alive in the Otherworld, and that the acolytes would kill her in three days' time. We didn't understand it at the time, but if there was a chance... well, thank the stars we acted anyway."

"We?"

"Hester's other lieutenants and myself. We've had to make all the decisions ourselves since the last attack. Since Hester was hurt."

The last attack? Was that what Hester had been referring to when she talked about December? How many attacks *were* there? And by whom?

Cassia glanced back at the door and beckoned Ilsa back towards the stairs. "It's only been six weeks, and she lost her ability to shift or walk and—"

"She can't shapeshift?" said Ilsa, and Cassia shook her head.

Ilsa's mouth fell open in horror. Her talents had caused her so much pain, but the only thing worse would be to know what it was like and have it taken away.

"My point is," said Cassia gently, "that Hester's not always this way."

"Just often," said an amused voice behind them.

Ilsa turned to see a young man with rich brown skin, classically handsome features, and a neat moustache. He was leaning against the wall, one wing-tipped shoe crossed over the other, and a cane topped with a gold wolf's head tucked under his arm. Everything about him – his cream three-piece suit, his gleaming gold cufflinks – was immaculate and spoke of wealth. He had pale brown eyes – weak eyes; a colour like dye faded in the sun – and they regarded Ilsa with a wicked glint from below a straw boater pulled low on his brow. Ilsa wondered at such a proper-seeming gentleman wearing his hat indoors, but perhaps the etiquette was different in the Witherward.

"Aelius," said Cassia, sounding relieved. "This is Ilsa. Ilsa, this is Aelius Hoverly, another lieutenant."

Aelius inclined his head to her and smiled, revealing impish dimples and perfect white teeth. "The wolves who witnessed your arrival have not oversold you. You are every bit as beautiful as your mother was."

Ilsa narrowed her eyes at Aelius and Cassia in turn. "And do them wolves also know why them Oracles tried to kill me?"

Aelius's eyebrows shot up and his smile grew wider. "The same fire too, it would seem." He turned to Cassia. "Shall I take it that Hester won't be joining us?"

"Careful, Aelius. That's *Alpha* Hester to you and me." This must have been a joke, because Aelius chuckled. "And thankfully, no. Where are the others?"

"Oren is taking breakfast. Young Master Whitleaf is, shall we say, heavily occupied down on the lawn—"

"That's… concerning," muttered Cassia.

"—and the eminent lord of self-pity is no doubt still abed. I sent a servant to aggravate him but we have ample time to take the scenic route down to the meeting room." He flashed another grin at Ilsa. "So let us show our newcomer around."

He gestured with his cane for Ilsa to walk with him, stepping around her purposefully so that he was on her right, and Cassia followed.

"Ilsa visited the portrait gallery in the night," Cassia told him. Ilsa might have been mistaken, but she sounded nervous again. "She also spoke with Captain Fowler and… Ilsa, what exactly did he tell you?"

Pushing her grief aside, Ilsa recounted what the boy had told her in the moonlight. The factions. The Principles. How her parents had died. How they'd thought her dead. But if Cassia had fallen for her lie, Aelius was not so easily fooled. As he listened, his gaze focused in on her until Ilsa felt like every evasion and twist of truth rang like a bell.

"This Wraith," he drawled when Ilsa was done. "He has quite the mastery of the facts. Which is especially impressive, given that some of them are highly privileged. Such a pity he's not a Changeling. I could certainly make use of a fellow like that."

Fearing she had stretched her lie past breaking point, Ilsa opted for distraction.

"What does a lieutenant do 'round here anyway?"

Aelius wasn't about to fall for that either, but he smiled knowingly and indulged her. "That entirely depends which lieutenant you ask, Ilsa my darling. Dear Cassia here is our genius treasurer. Oren is envoy to our people."

"And what 'bout you?"

Aelius grinned. "I am a merchant."

"What's being a merchant got to do with leading the Changelings?"

"I trade in knowledge. I barter for secrets."

Cassia cut in. "I think in the Otherworld, you would probably call it intelligence. And I'm not sure *merchant* is a good analogy, considering Aelius is banned from entering the Trade House."

Aelius, grinning wider, didn't even glance in Cassia's direction. Ilsa had the feeling he had counted on her to expose him; had baited her with his choice of words. She had known pickpockets like Aelius; boys and girls who wore their past sanctions like badges of honour. Trouble was, she had never known whether to admire them for it or check her pockets.

"What got you banned?"

"The unanimous decree of the faction leaders, my darling. In the days before I plied my trade for the Zoo, I did so for the highest bidder. And what better place to harvest secrets than in a fortress of iniquity like the Trade House." He sighed, as if remembering those days fondly. "For the harvest, the Changeling has the perfect bag of tricks, of course – a different face every day. But for the sale, I needed to be recognised in order to be trusted, and eventually, recognised I was." He flashed that grin again. "When one plays both sides, one is running down the clock. That is the game we play when we deal in deception. For years I made regular sales to regular customers, heedless to the way alliances were shifting and pacts were being forged. Enemies became friends and got to chit-chatting about their sources. Their sources were, of course, yours truly, and my game was up.

"Thankfully, no magic can match a Changeling's for running from the consequences of one's actions. A Wraith may excel at fleeing the scene of their crime, but they cannot cease to be the culprit altogether. I proved myself hard to identify and thus catch, and they were forced to settle for publicly banning me from a multitude of interesting places, including the Trade House, on pain of several flavours of torture and death, depending which lucky individual caught me."

"That's rough," said Ilsa, wrinkling her nose.

Aelius tapped her on the head with his cane; perturbed, Ilsa tried to duck out of reach, but she wasn't quick enough to stop him. "My sentiments exactly. However, where I saw defeat, your own ingenious mother saw opportunity. *Reinvent yourself,* she told me. *You've done it two dozen times a week for a lifetime.* Lyander didn't see the sense in wringing my neck when there were so many more interesting uses for me. So she spun me a line about duty and honour and, I must confess, hooked me with it. I've run the Zoo's, as we like to say, *communications* ever since. When Lyander was so brutally taken from us with most of her lieutenants in tow, Hester gave me the position I keep now."

Ilsa frowned at him. Her mother had been dead seventeen years, and Aelius didn't look old enough to have reached adolescence by that point. But then, Ilsa had gotten herself banned from plenty of places by the age of twelve, and perhaps Aelius had been equally precocious. Then again...

"Don't your face twitch when you change it?" said Ilsa, earning a curious glance from Cassia, but a slow smile from Aelius. "When I change mine, I get all these... little spasms."

Aelius shrugged. "An unavoidable fact of your magic, and mine, and that of every Changeling I've ever known."

"Then how d'you fool anyone?" She studied his profile, but

if he truly wasn't wearing his own face, like she suspected, there was nothing to give him away. "It's one thing me looking like I got some mad tic in the Otherworld. I bet here everyone and his mother's wise to it."

"But that's precisely what makes it so delicious!" said Aelius, bringing them to a halt. Cassia muttered something that sounded like *heaven and earth* and glanced longingly down the corridor as if plotting an escape. "Animals are all good fun, but changing faces is an *art*. Have you used a disguise before? Have you needed to pass for someone other than yourself?"

"All the time." Ilsa told him about the show; about how she would become The Great Balthazar for the finale.

"Oh, bravo! And tell me, how do you avoid detection by your enraptured spectators?"

"The lighting washes me out," said Ilsa. "We designed it like that on purpose."

"Lighting! The very first tool." Wearing a smile loaded with mischief, Aelius casually jostled the rim of his boater while stepping subtly to the right, out of the shadow and into the sunlight pouring in. And in the split second his hat was displaced and the sun shone on him, Ilsa saw it; the tremor just above his left eye. When he stepped out of the light and let the rim of his hat shadow his face once again, it vanished. If Ilsa scrutinised the spot, she swore she could see the twitches, but only because she knew they were there. "Know your lighting. It'll go a long way. Your angles too."

He turned as if to go back the way they had come, and brushed a thumb along his jaw, drawing attention to the twitch by the right corner of his mouth. Only for a second, before he turned around again and the weakness in his magic was hidden from view. Ilsa was astounded. He had chosen to walk on her right before the conversation had come up. He *lived* these deceptions; had probably been doing so for so long they were second nature to him. He saw her gaping open-mouthed, and flashed his perfect, false grin again.

"Misdirection is half the magic, Ilsa my darling."

Ilsa smiled. "I know a thing or two about that."

"I don't doubt it for a minute."

They walked on. Cassia and Aelius led her around the first and second floors while Aelius rhapsodised about the architecture and interior design – eighty of the very best builders had raised the Zoo in one hundred and twenty days; the stained-glass dome above the entrance foyer was an addition made sixty years previously; wallpaper in thirty-two custom designs had been commissioned from a famous decorator in a country Ilsa was certain did not exist in the Otherworld – but these weren't the sort of details she had secretly been hoping for.

"Begging your pardon, sir."

"Aelius, please. I won't abide *sir* and I certainly won't abide Mr Hoverly. That was my father, the less said of him the better." He winked and flashed his perfect teeth.

"Aelius, then. My mother." She paused at the feeling of those words coming from her lips. *Her mother.* "This is where she grew up, ain't it?"

"Not just your mother. Six generations of your family have lived here. The Ravenswoods have held Camden from this house for one hundred and thirty years."

Ilsa bit the inside of her cheek as she hesitated over her next question. "What was she like?"

Aelius's unstoppable grin softened. Cassia walked on ahead as if to give them some space. "Formidable," said Aelius reverently. "Don't misunderstand me, she wasn't a leader to instil fear. She didn't need it. Lyander was a woman who knew how to get her way and make her victim think it was *their* brilliant idea. She was a manipulator." He paused and glanced at her, as if fearing the word was too sharp. But Ilsa liked it. A manipulator could be kind, but she couldn't be trodden on. She liked thinking of her mother that way.

"Go on," she said.

"She was a quiet woman. She spoke less than any leader of people I've ever known," he said, and broke into a grin. "And I knew and bartered with them all in my independence. But I remember more of Lyander's words than anyone's. She made them *count*, you see."

"And my father? Did you know him, too?"

"Know him? I inherited my role from him."

"He was a spy?"

Aelius put a hand to his chest in a pantomime impression of offence. "He was a *merchant of secrets*, my darling. One of the finest I have ever known. He had all the talent in the world and not a care for it. That was why your mother recruited me. Thorne wished only to raise a family and play the devoted husband. And chess. The man was a deviously wicked chess player. He taught your mother and they wiled away many an evening in battles of strategy and wit."

They reached the main staircase. Beyond it, the corridor ended in a set of double doors even grander than the ones to Hester's chambers. Ilsa nodded towards them. "That another bedroom?"

"That," he said, fondling his cane and looking to Cassia, "is the largest chamber."

Aelius made no move towards it. Cassia did not even look.

"Well, can I see it?" said Ilsa. "I bet it's really grand, ain't it?"

Ilsa wasn't oblivious. As Aelius led the way to the room, she could read his reluctance. Cassia was the more unwilling. She hung back in the corridor as the others stepped inside.

It was, as Ilsa predicted, awfully grand.

They entered into a sitting room, where tall windows threw morning light over ornate furniture, and danced off the crystal chandelier overhead. An elaborate mantelpiece carved from dark wood dominated one side of the room, and flecks of gold in the Persian rug caught the light and sparkled like jewels. Ilsa was tempted to crouch down and find out if it was real – who was she to say rich people didn't weave real gold into their rugs, then walk over them like it was nothing?

Through a door was a study, with shelves of leather-bound, gold-embossed books ranged across one wall and a grand desk before the window – the kind at which a banker might count his fortune – and beyond that the bedchamber. A stately four-poster bed, carved with panels depicting all kinds of animals, filled the centre of the room, and forest green drapes and wallpaper transformed the space into some lush, wild jungle.

Ilsa inhaled the scent of furniture polish and the fresh gardenias that had been placed in half a dozen spots, and listened to the strange quiet that permeated the chambers. Aelius said nothing as she ran her hands over the fine fabric of the couch and the cool marble of a console; offered no history, pointed out nothing of interest. The rooms felt unlived in – cold from disuse, with a stillness in the air – and yet they were kept like some phantom occupant might have need of them at any moment. A quarter-full decanter of something stood dormant atop a liquor cabinet. The papers on the desk were undisturbed. And a chessboard – the pieces in the disarray of a game half played – rested on a card table by the window. It didn't take a genius to work it out: her parents had lived here. Had it been kept a shrine all these years?

If there was anything left of them in the suite, Ilsa didn't know how to recognise it. It was nothing but a reminder that her chances to know them had run out long ago. She let out a shuddering sigh and swept past Aelius.

"Where next?"

Aelius followed swiftly and closed the door behind them, and they made for the stairs.

As they descended into the grand, marbled entrance hall, a small black fox approached, as if it had been lying in wait for them. As it trotted towards them, it shifted into a young man in a dark suit, wearing a red militia armband around one sleeve. He spared Ilsa and Cassia a fleeting, stone-faced glance before leaning very close to Aelius's shoulder and speaking into the other man's ear.

The exchange lasted all of three seconds, at the end of which Aelius nodded once, and the young man turned back into a fox and dashed away. For all the pretence of secrecy, when he saw Ilsa watching, he grinned like he was taking to the stage.

"The wolves answer to the commander of the militia," he said coyly, "but the foxes answer to me."

"They spies or something?" asked Ilsa.

"Spies!" He waved his cane dismissively. He had put it to

half a dozen uses since they met, none of which were walking. Ilsa wondered if it was part of his act, a prop for distraction. "What is this preoccupation with spies? Spying is for sneaks and rogues. The foxes are connoisseurs of communication, Ilsa my darling. They sow trust and allyship among their contacts in other factions, and they reap information for the Zoo."

"Where I'm from, we call them spies."

Cassia didn't smile at that – Ilsa wondered if she was capable – but the look she shot Aelius was teasing.

They stepped out into the garden, onto the same terrace Ilsa had crept across the night before. At least, she believed it was the same. There were the hydrangea bushes they had watched the wolves from. There was the pavilion, and the west gate beyond. But the moon-drenched lawn and black shapes that might shift at any moment had given way to a riot of colour and life. She hadn't noticed how lush the grass was. There had been no bees and butterflies flitting among the flower beds. She hadn't even noticed the heavy summer scent of thousands of blooms mingling on their air. The events of the night before drifted even further from reality. It felt like a dream.

Feeling a pull to immerse herself in the summer beauty of the garden, Ilsa made for the steps leading down from the terrace, only for Cassia to grab her by the elbow and Aelius to block her with his cane.

"It's best to keep a safe distance," said Cassia apologetically.

Before Ilsa could ask what she was being kept a safe distance *from*, there was a loud hiss, and a plume of thick smoke rose up from behind some shrubbery.

"Something's on fire!" said Ilsa.

"We should be so lucky," Cassia muttered.

Something that looked like a cannonball burst from the shrubs and hurtled towards them. Aelius swore and dived one way, Cassia pulled Ilsa in the other, but nobody was fast enough. Ilsa ducked and covered her head, but Cassia threw up her hands like she could ward the thing away. And she could – the air around her set like ice. There was barely any change, but the boundary of whatever she had formed glimmered like the surface of a soap bubble, and when the projectile struck it, it burst softly, like a down pillow. A thin mist exploded from the thing and rained down, coating Aelius even as he tried to dodge it, still cursing. But Cassia and Ilsa stayed dry within the bubble.

When the mist had settled, Cassia lowered her hands and the air returned to normal.

"What the bloody hell was that?" said Ilsa, her voice an octave higher than normal.

"I can't say what the substance was," said Cassia, "but the disintegrating canister is something he invented when—"

"Not *that*! What did *you* just do?"

"It's on me," said Aelius, twisting to search his clothes and dabbing himself with a handkerchief. "Do you see it on me? Is it doing anything?"

"Oh, stars!" said a voice from across the garden. Ilsa looked up. A head had appeared above the bushes; just black curls and protective goggles. Then it vanished again, and a boy emerged, dashing across the lawn towards them.

"It's a shielding spell," said Cassia. "It's basic corporeal magic."

"Basic… *corporeal*…"

Aelius stopped his nervous dance and raised his eyebrows at Cassia. "You didn't mention that you're a Sorcerer, Cassia dear?"

Cassia laced her fingers primly. "Well, it didn't come up."

"Is everyone alright?" said the boy, bounding onto the terrace with a gait that wouldn't be out of place on a golden retriever. He bent double to catch his breath, hands on his knees, but when he caught sight of Ilsa, he straightened again, and his face broke into a wide smile. "Stars! You're her!"

"Ilsa, this is Fyfe Whitleaf, another lieutenant," said Cassia. "Fyfe, this is Ilsa Ravenswood."

Fyfe was young to be something as important-sounding as a lieutenant; a year or two younger than Ilsa perhaps but very tall, and slender. He had medium brown skin and unruly hair; though he had tried to tame it with oil, the black curls were falling freely around his sharp features. Now that his goggles rested around his neck, his dark brown eyes sparkled with warmth. He smiled with his whole face, and Ilsa smiled back.

"Fyfe," said Cassia, looking nervously at the spattering of moisture on the terrace. It smelled faintly of rhubarb. "Dare I ask?"

Fyfe scrubbed at his hair nervously. "It's, ah, a compound designed to bring about a spell of short-term memory loss. I thought loading it into some sort of projectile would make it useful for subduing skirmishes, that sort of thing." He looked back at the plume of smoke. Two wolves had appeared with buckets of water and were eying whatever was back there warily. "But apparently I need to work on the cannon."

"And, it seems, your formula," said Aelius, dabbing the last of the mist from his face. Fyfe opened his mouth. Closed it again. "I'm afraid it doesn't work, lad."

"Oh, it works. Not as I would hope, *yet*, but…"

Aelius's expression darkened. "What do you mean *not as you would hope*?"

Fyfe took a watch from his pocket and frowned at it. "Nothing serious. Just don't start anything important after eleven and be lying down at noon." He turned to Ilsa, his sunshine smile lighting up his face, and went on before Aelius had a chance to respond. "It's so good to finally meet you, Ilsa! Have they introduced you to Hester already?"

"Briefly," said Ilsa, folding her arms. "I din't get much chance to get to know her. What with her being 'bout as pleasant as sewer rats fighting over a cat carcass."

Fyfe's face fell. A ringing silence sounded among them. Ilsa knew she had spoken too freely before Cassia ever cleared her throat. "Ilsa, Hester is Fyfe's sister," she said.

Ilsa's stomach dropped. She felt the blood drain from her head in a dizzying rush. "*Sister?*"

Cassia hadn't mentioned any other relatives. And Hester and Fyfe didn't look at all related.

"Half-sister," said Fyfe flatly. "I'm not a Ravenswood. Hester and I shared a mother."

"Oh." Ilsa bit her tongue, for all the good it would do now. She tried to stammer an apology but Cassia hastily cut in.

"Fyfe is the lieutenant responsible for" – she looked to him and frowned – "bio… magical… chemistry?" said Cassia.

"Blowing things up?" offered Aelius.

"Innovation, I suppose." He turned to Ilsa. "Hester only made me a lieutenant because I begged to be one. She had to invent a role which required my, ah, unique strengths."

"Well that was… sweet of her," Ilsa said, hoping to make up for the last thing she said about Hester and fooling no one.

Aelius caught Fyfe's eye and chuckled. "Be careful of using language like that around the woman herself, Ilsa my darling," he said. "Accuse Hester Ravenswood of sweetness and I guarantee she'll show you how sweet she can be. Now let us find Oren and a pot of strong coffee."

He led the way back into the house. Ilsa followed behind, falling into step with Fyfe. An awkward silence stretched between them until Ilsa found the nerve to speak.

"I'm sorry 'bout what I said. It was awful of me."

Fyfe shook his head and managed a smile. "I know what she's like. It's as Aelius said, she never minded about being liked *before* she was injured and now… she'll be back to the *old* cynical Hester in no time. But she does have a kind side," he added hastily. "In her own way. She just doesn't show it to everyone."

Ilsa knew what it was to hide parts of oneself. Hester must have had her reasons. "Is she a good alpha most of the time?"

"Well, of course, she wasn't—" Whatever he had been about to say, he cut off abruptly. He chewed his lip and threw a glance at Cassia and Aelius who had gone on ahead. "She's an awfully good alpha, yes. Sometimes I look at her and I wonder what makes a person able to do a job like that. Is it something they have or something they forge themselves? If one could isolate it, what would it boil down to? I know human beings don't work like machines or chemical formulas, but I can't help but wonder." He shook his head thoughtfully. "And Hester was never even meant to be alpha. She was just the only one left when…"

"When my parents died," said Ilsa when Fyfe trailed off. That must have been what Hester meant when she called herself a last resort.

They caught up with Cassia and Aelius at a door with a plaque reading *Meeting Room*. As Aelius opened the door, Cassia paused, stiffening, and her gaze tracked across the entrance hall. Ilsa turned.

It took her a moment to recognise him in the light. The storm blue of his eyes was deeper. He wasn't as pale as she'd thought. But she recognised the perilous look in his eye and the tight set of his jaw. As he came closer, so did his air of roiling irritation.

"Ilsa, this is Eliot Quillon," said Cassia coolly.

Eliot spared her half a glance, quickly masking any surprise that Ilsa hadn't told Cassia they'd met.

"Charmed," he clipped, before he rounded on Cassia. That was gratitude, thought Ilsa, and she readied a contemptuous glare in case he looked again. "When I suggested you have a mercenary fetch her, Cadell Fowler is *not* who I had in mind." He made to swan past them into the meeting room, then apparently remembered a further gripe. "And by the way, what time of day do you call this?"

"Before noon," said Aelius, regarding Eliot contemptuously. "I doubt you recognise it."

Eliot adjusted his sleeve in an impressively dismissive manner. "I don't see the point in being awake just to be reminded that I'm not needed for anything, ever, until further notice," he said tonelessly, before sweeping past. Through the door, Ilsa watched him pull out a chair at the end of a long oval table and sink gracefully into it, as the servants laying out a tea service scattered like pigeons fleeing a cat.

Cassia shot Ilsa an apologetic look and ushered them into the room.

"It ain't that early, is it?" whispered Ilsa, leaning close to Fyfe.

Fyfe checked his watch. "It's just gone eight."

"But on the other side of the portal... it's late, right?"

Fyfe nodded enthusiastically. "It's eight o'clock in the evening. A remarkable quirk in the fabric between worlds."

"Right. So if I want to know what time I got to be back in the Otherworld, I just got to—"

"*Back*, my darling?" said Aelius. Everyone's gaze had snapped to her. That tiny frown between Cassia's brows had returned.

"For the show tomorrow," Ilsa explained. "Today's Sunday so the theatre's closed, but this time tomorrow I'm expected on stage."

"That's quite impossible," said a voice from the doorway.

Another man had joined them, and he closed the door with a resonating wooden click.

Ilsa turned to Cassia warily. "There's more of you?"

"Ilsa, this is Oren Tarenvale," sighed Cassia.

Oren carefully unhooked his eyeglasses from around his ears, folded them into his breast pocket and inclined his head at Ilsa. His mousy hair was greying at the temples, and exceptionally neat, like his tweed suit and starched white collar. He smiled tightly, but his eyes were kind, and his face was benevolent and mild, not that it did anything to favour Ilsa's first impression. She glared at him.

111

"And that makes everyone, at last," said Aelius. "As my pressing need for a spot of breakfast has provided us a deadline, let's be seated."

Cassia took the chair to the right of the head, Aelius beside her, Fyfe beside him. Oren drew out the chair opposite Aelius and motioned for Ilsa to sit.

"This seat usually belongs to" – he indicated Eliot, in exile at the far end of the table. The boy was running a finger around the lip of his teacup. He didn't appear to be listening. "Today, it can be yours."

He took a seat on Ilsa's left. The head of the table – Hester's place, she assumed – remained empty, but so did the place to Ilsa's right. Aelius had said this was everyone, but that couldn't be. Someone else was missing.

"Now." Oren had a notebook tucked under his arm, which he placed on the table, then he folded his hands and rested them on top in a precise and delicate motion. Ilsa couldn't be sure, but she thought she heard Fyfe sigh. Aelius's eyes went heavenward. "Before we start divulging all the sensitive details of our current situation to a girl from the Otherworld who is most likely a Changeling, who may or may not resemble the person we're looking for, and who could easily, in fact, be part of a deceit of some kind, don't you think we should at least attempt to establish her identity? We hired an outsider, after all – do we even have any way of verifying that Captain Fowler found her where he said he did?"

"You could ask me," Ilsa said through gritted teeth. "Or you could go take a look. P'raps my friend's dead body still marks the spot, depending what them other London constables are getting up to right 'bout now." Perhaps they were ogling Martha like a curiosity. Perhaps they were poking at her with pens, or having their dogs sniff at her clothing. Perhaps the newspapers were there. They would print that she was a common thief. Tears stung Ilsa's eyes, but she clenched her fists and held them back.

Aelius chuckled. "There's an idea, lad. Would this Other-worlder's body the captain spoke of be proof enough for you?"

"Actually," said Oren, lacing his fingers. He turned to Ilsa. "I was hoping you could tell us where you have been all these years. I went to find Ilsa Ravenswood myself, when she was about a year and a half old, and I was told she had died of smallpox some months previously."

"By Miss Mitcham," said Ilsa quietly. "Lord Walcott's old housekeeper."

Oren turned to Cassia, a question in his eyes. But the Sorcerer gave a small shrug as if to say she would tell him after.

"Precisely. And now it appears I was lied to," he said. "Do you have any idea why?"

The truth was on her tongue, but her breath wouldn't force it out. What right did they have to let those things happen and then interrogate her about it? "Because she ain't a good woman," she managed.

"She had the certificate of death to prove it," said Oren.

Ilsa turned on him. "I s'pose it was the St Genevieve Orphanage by the time you got there, weren't it?"

"That's right. She said she had been left the house in Walcott's will and had considered it her God-given duty to use it to help the less fortunate."

"And she had a bit of paper what proved a baby girl had

113

died in a house full of cold, hungry babies. I don't s'pect you'd understand, but it weren't all that uncommon, sir."

Oren nodded pensively. He didn't appear moved by the grim realities of Ilsa's childhood.

"There is a way you could prove your identity," he said. "When I smuggled Ilsa Ravenswood to the Otherworld seventeen years ago, she had with her a toy. Can you tell us what it was?"

Yesterday, Ilsa might not have been able to answer. She did not treasure any memories from her early childhood, and the more time passed, the happier she was to see them fade. But one had snagged since coming through the portal, first when the captain told her what the Changelings called their militia, and repeatedly since.

"It was a wolf," she said. She could see it in her mind's eye now. She had loved it once. She had never realised it was a clue. "A wooden wolf what rattled."

Oren's face was unreadable. "And do you have it?" Ilsa shook her head. "Why not?"

"I ran away from the orphanage," Ilsa said. She kept her voice even. "I escaped as a bird. I taught myself to shift enough that I could control it, but I din't know how to carry a thing with me, like I can sometimes do now, if I stick it in my clothes." Oren continued to study her, his expression inscrutable, and Ilsa felt her frustration rise. "If you don't believe me, you can go look for yourself. It's under a floorboard in the attic. I stashed it there, thinking I'd go back, only I never did."

"You were there," said Cassia. She was shaking her head. "When Oren was speaking to this woman… you were right there in the house?"

Ilsa nodded stiffly. "'Til I was nine."

"And what about when you left the orphanage?" asked Fyfe. Ilsa glanced up, and he gave her an encouraging nod.

"I lived on the streets for a while," she said into her lap. "I'd do magic tricks for change, like making myself disappear. Things I could do with my talents. Then a stage magician saw me at it one day. He was looking for an assistant. He'd wanted a young woman, I reckon, but he could tell I was doing something special. Something he needed."

It had taken months for Ilsa and Blume to build the tentative trust that led to his confession: that he may have been talented and charismatic once, before the drink, but he wasn't the secret of his own success. He had had a wife, a woman with peculiar talents different to Ilsa's. He never told Ilsa what she could do; he had kept his wife's secrets even after his drinking and gambling drove her away. But Ilsa knew her stage persona had been a mystic, and she had worn a scarf around her forehead when she performed. Whatever type of magic she had, it showed unnaturally on her face when she used it.

Blume had imbibed his heart with liquor rather than feel it break when his wife had run away. How much further would he sink if Ilsa didn't show up the following evening? If she squandered his final chance to salvage his career? If only she had known Captain Fowler would find her again, she never would have chased him when she should have been completing the finale. Then perhaps Blume would have had a second chance. Instead, she'd doomed him.

"Mr Blume paid his landlady to put me up in her flat for a few years," she went on. "When I was fifteen I moved into a boarding house. We've been performing at the Isolde nearly two years now. The Great Balthazar, the show's called. 'Course, now that you've taken me prisoner, he'll probably be fired."

She glanced at Eliot, wanting to catch his eye. He had made her think she was free to leave. His eyes were on his teacup, but the corner of his mouth twitched up into a sardonic smile. Ilsa balled her fists under the table.

"You are far from a prisoner here," said Oren, shaking his head.

"You told me I can't leave, din't you?"

Aelius chuckled. "Oren only meant if you want to *live*, Ilsa my darling. There are plenty more acolytes where they came from."

"And why? Why'd them Oracles try to kill me?"

Oren cleared his throat. "Because of something that may have happened four days ago. The Docklands – the Oracles' quarter – doesn't have a ruler as such, but the most senior among them is an appointed Oracle of exceptional power: the Seer. It's a sort of religious appointment, and in fact carries no authority. They are entirely at the mercy of the people and their wishes. Every Seer has an apprentice, who is to take their place should the Seer be found unsuitable. This apprentice, the Oracles tell us, has been kidnapped."

Ilsa remembered something Captain Fowler had said: *They were provoked.*

"Are you telling me that you… *kidnapped* someone?"

"Not us, exactly," said Aelius carefully. He toyed with the wolf head of his cane. "Our alpha."

"Hester?" said Ilsa sceptically. The woman recovering from a life-changing injury, who refused her duties and took to bed at eight in the morning, did not strike her as a likely suspect.

"Hester *was* our alpha once." Cassia's voice was little more than a whisper. "Her reappointment was an emergency measure."

"Our true leader is Gedeon Ravenswood," said Aelius. "The Prince of Camden. Your brother."

8

Her brother.

In Ilsa's endless imaginings, there were some versions of her story in which she had a sibling. They were invariably the worst versions; the ones in which her parents picked another over her. She'd done her best not to dwell on the possibility of a sibling, and so, she was unprepared for the news.

Unprepared for a lightness to come over her. It was like Aelius had told her something she already knew; like something missing had been put back. A brother fit the empty space inside her.

Quick on the heels of that happy yearning was rage again.

She turned on Cassia. So this was what she had been nervous of Ilsa learning. "I asked if I got relations here," she said quietly, hearing the quiver in her voice. "You din't say I had a brother." She shot a glare at Aelius. "You din't say nothing all the time you were showing me 'round."

Ilsa threw another look to the far end of the table, but Eliot appeared lost in thought, and he didn't catch it.

"They both had good reason," Oren interjected with a sigh. "It's not happy news. We decided we would discuss it together. We're sorry to say… he's disappeared. Over a month ago. We couldn't even be sure he was alive. Even now, we don't know that this was his doing. The group who visited to accuse Gedeon of the apprentice's abduction were incredibly hostile. They refused to answer most of our questions. We have no proof of what they're claiming and no reason to trust them."

"It's difficult to know what to believe when it comes to Oracles," Fyfe said gently. "They're capable of knowing everything, but so few do, and even fewer will be forthcoming. It conflicts with their beliefs to share knowledge with non-Oracles."

"They claim Gedeon found a way to penetrate the temple without being detected, which is a tall tale if ever I heard one," added Aelius sarcastically. Ilsa remembered something else the captain had said: that Oracles could see anything observable.

"It has put us in quite a predicament," said Oren. "We can't let all of London know that we're without our leader. Rumours abound, but a trusted-few wolves are taking turns impersonating him about Camden in order to stem them. We can't afford to look weak at a time like this."

"Because of the attack?" Ilsa glanced at Cassia. "The attack what hurt Hester?"

"The most recent in a string of such attacks," said Aelius. "You know the way of things around here, what with your perspicacious interrogation of young Captain Fowler." Ilsa was certain she saw him shoot a look towards the other end of the table and its occupant. "Our relations with our neighbours are less than friendly. The Changelings forced their way into this most minuscule sliver of London, and there will always be those who insist on taking it back. Our recent adversaries are a group of Sorcerers rebelling against their faction's alliance with Camden."

"So the Oracles are attacking *me* because Gedeon kidnapped their apprentice... whatever..."

"Seer," said Fyfe.

"… and these rebel Sorcerers are attacking *you* because they want more territory?"

Oren hesitated. He took his eyeglasses from his pocket and folded and unfolded them. "This isn't like the border wars we cycle through endlessly. Their target is the Zoo. They have tried to force their way in four times in as many months."

Ilsa took several deep breaths, but it didn't stop her head from spinning. A missing brother. A house under attack. She looked up and made eye contact with Eliot, who swept her face with an assessing gaze.

"And my brother's just disappeared? In the middle of all this?"

"Of his own volition," said Aelius. "Took a dozen wolves with him." He reached into the inside pocket of his jacket and produced a folded note. "One of them left this for his sweetheart, who is one of my foxes and brought it to me. It says they were under strict instructions from Gedeon to tell no one of their departure; that he had shared no details of why or where they were going and said nothing of their return." The last words hung over the table, their weight showing on every face. "My best guess is that he discovered something. Before he disappeared, he was devoting all his time to trying to find out what the rebels wanted from these attacks. It appeared an awful lot like they were searching for something, yet as far as any of us know, there's nothing in this house that could be so important to them. I believe Gedeon learned something of the true location of whatever it is they seek and has gone after it himself."

"And why'd he do that if he's got you lot?"

This appeared to strike a nerve with everyone. Cassia drew in a shaking breath. Fyfe chewed on his lip and sank into his chair.

"That," said Oren, "we cannot tell you. Gedeon and the wolves simply slipped away in the night." If Ilsa wasn't mistaken, Oren's gaze flickered to Eliot. "We're piecing together the evidence we can find, but for the most part, it's guesswork. Gedeon has made no contact. And now, this matter with the Seer's apprentice and this petty tit-for-tat. Unfortunately, he doesn't know you're alive. He doesn't know he's made you a target."

Aelius smirked. "Welcome to the Witherward, Ilsa my darling, where we measure our successes in blood spilled. Is it not enough to make a lady swoon from fright?"

Ilsa's head snapped up and she narrowed her eyes at him. "You forget I weren't no *lady* 'til yesterday. I ain't the swooning type." She pushed out of her chair, startling them all, but she needed to breathe, and she couldn't do it in this room with all these people telling her unfathomable things. "Am I excused? Or is there more you got to tell me? And think very carefully before you answer because I ain't got much patience left for things I din't know yesterday."

"Nothing springs to mind," said Oren levelly. "Though I hoped we could discuss some measures for your safety given that—"

"Oh, *earth and stars*," sighed Eliot.

All eyes swung to the end of the table, to the boy they were pretending wasn't there. Eliot's head was tilted back to rest against his chair, his eyes were closed, and he was massaging the bridge of his nose between a thumb and forefinger. He appeared mildly bemused to glance up and find everyone looking at him, like he hadn't heard himself speak.

Oren regarded him over the rims of his glasses. "If there is something you wish to add, Eliot, the floor is yours."

Aelius snorted. "Anything that might have slipped your mind, Quillon? Something pertinent to the whereabouts of our alpha and renegade wolves, perhaps?"

"You're wasting your time, Aelius," said Cassia.

Eliot sighed dramatically and rolled his eyes. "Imagine my surprise in finding there's no point in being me at this little get together after all," he said, unfolding himself from his chair and straightening the lapels on his jacket. His eyes landed on Ilsa, just briefly, then on the door.

And Ilsa understood. She had needed space, and he was giving it to her. A chance to slip away. A distraction. As Aelius made another snide remark about the hours Eliot was keeping, she skirted the table and softly turned the handle of the door. Then she slipped out into the hall and made for the stairs. She couldn't have explained it to the lieutenants, but she knew where she needed to be.

The smell of furniture polish and gardenias hit her when she stepped into the chamber she had thought belonged to her parents, and that uncanny quiet, like the room was holding its breath. Ilsa looked numbly at the papers strewn across the desk. The quarter-full decanter of liquor. These weren't her parents' chambers, kept as Lyander and Thorne had left them, like some sort of shrine.

Her brother had lived here. And now he was gone.

She sank onto the couch, her breath rushing out of her in a sigh. Gedeon had kidnapped an Oracle, in return the Oracles had tried to kill her, and somewhere in the middle was a messenger who had saved her life and brought her home. It felt like a cruel trick that she was only here because he was gone. That she was in his house, in his rooms, on his couch, and he still believed she was dead. Just another vicious twist of fate, like her mother birthing a healthy daughter only to die before she was a day old; like Lord Walcott contracting smallpox; like Martha dying for her blonde hair and hazel eyes. The unfairness of it pounded on the back of her skull, too much to comprehend.

Someone knocked on the open door, and Ilsa looked up. She didn't know who she was expecting, but she was surprised when it was Fyfe who entered. "I looked for you at your room," he said awkwardly. "Then Cassia told me you might be here."

He sidled closer, but didn't speak again. Ilsa didn't want to share, but her thoughts and frustrations built inside her until they spilled out.

"So that's it then? A cousin what don't care *what* universe I'm in and a brother what's gone, p'raps forever?" Ilsa laughed at her own self-pity. "It's funny. This time yesterday I din't have no family to speak of, and I thought it'd always be that way. I told myself it was better to think like that than have hope, you know? 'Cause it's the hope what'll kill you. And now, somehow, it don't seem possible but I'm... I'm..."

Disappointed.

It was vile and wrong and ungrateful, but it was true. Something had been taken from her in coming here, a possibility, and in its place had grown a deep and desperate wish, the hopelessness of which closed her throat. Tears came to her eyes as the wish rose up and engulfed her. It was a feeling she could never have imagined the day before. She was lonely for a woman she only knew from her portrait.

She wanted her mother.

"I s'pose—" The words came out as a gasp drowned in tears. She swallowed them down, but the waves kept coming. "I s'pose I really was still hoping."

Hoping to meet her mother. Her father. Hoping against hope that someone out there cared for her. And they had. But they were gone. So Ilsa sat on the couch in her missing brother's rooms and felt a grief seventeen years in the making. She cried until she couldn't see for tears and no lungful of air was enough.

She forgot she wasn't alone, and when she felt the couch shift, she opened her eyes, startled. Fyfe sat beside her, his handkerchief in his outstretched fingers.

"Gedeon calls me cousin," he said. "I know technically we're not related, but Hester's my blood and she's yours and Gedeon's blood. And some would say that makes us family. *I* would say that, also." He smiled shyly. "And I'll do my best to be a friend too, should you want one."

Ilsa tried to speak but couldn't find the words. Her tears dried up abruptly, stymied by surprise. Could it be that simple? Someone offered to be your family and you accepted? A cousin who wasn't a cousin was a thing she'd never thought to want, but her heart was lighter, joyous, even. It was the kindest anyone had ever been to her.

"I... thank you, Fyfe," she said, her voice hoarse.

He took her hand and placed it in his. "I'm sorry about what you saw happen to your friend. No one should have to see the people they love taken from them like that."

Ilsa wiped her eyes with Fyfe's handkerchief as another impossible wave of tears came over her. "She din't even know why they was hurting her. She was just afraid... and then nothing."

Fyfe was silent awhile, chewing his lip. "What do you believe in, Ilsa? I mean to say, do you think there's a, ah…"

"A heaven?" Ilsa tried not to recoil. *Devil's get. He'll drag you away to hell if I can't cure you.* "I know it don't say nothing in the Bible 'bout a second universe, so I'm inclined to believe none of it."

"Well, in the Witherward, all faith starts with the stars," said Fyfe shyly.

"The stars," Ilsa echoed, sceptical – though it explained Eliot's cursing.

"We believe our souls descend from above when we're born, and when we die, they return to the stars. And the stars see everything. *And* shape everything. And that would mean that, well, your friend has a hand in the direction of the universe now. So even though it hurts to miss the people we love, we're fortunate to have them up there, turning fate to point in our favour."

Ilsa turned it over in her mind. "That mean my parents are there too?"

"Everyone," said Fyfe. "Equally."

"And you believe it?"

Fyfe nodded in earnest. "Very much."

Ilsa wasn't sure she believed in Fyfe's faith, but she wanted to in a way she never had with the Bible. That a girl like Martha – poor, homeless, a criminal – was shaping the future alongside people as wealthy and powerful in life as her parents; it had a sort of justice to it.

"I think Martha would like that. She was always really bossy." Fyfe laughed, the relief at having helped clear in his features. "Fyfe, I think… I think I need to give speaking with Hester another go."

Yes, her cousin had been cold and dismissive, but Ilsa hadn't known what she was going through, and she'd been confrontational. If Fyfe could offer up his kinship to a near stranger, Ilsa could be kinder to her own blood.

"Would you like me to come with you?" asked Fyfe, standing and buttoning his jacket.

"No, s'alright. She don't scare me." She smiled and handed back the handkerchief. "Thanks again."

Fyfe smiled his whole-face smile again. "My pleasure."

*

Ilsa got lost in the maze of long corridors, but finally found her way back to Hester's chambers. It was her cousin's raised voice and the smash of glass that led her there.

She slowed in the corridor, straining to listen and ready to shift into a mouse if she needed, but she couldn't make out Hester's words. Somebody hushed her, their voice low and frantic. Ilsa realised too late that the second speaker was getting closer, and before she could shift or hide, Eliot opened the door.

He was looking back into the room, one hand on the doorknob. "There are worse things than you taking this out on me, Hester," he said. It was not the cool, uninterested Eliot from the meeting. This one sounded weary, nearly desperate. "To not even try would be one of them. You're not weak, but if you don't—"

"I do not need you to tell me I am not weak, you condescending bastard." Hester's voice was quiet, but she couldn't have been more fearsome if she was still shouting.

Eliot took a long breath. "My apologies," he said tightly,

and he stepped out of the room, slamming the door behind him.

It was only then he noticed Ilsa.

He stiffened, alarm flashing across his features before he could tuck it away.

"What was that about?"

Eliot's mask of easy nonchalance fell into place. He shot her a smile, less ghoulish in the light but still sharp as a blade. "That entirely depends on how much you heard."

Normally, Ilsa would have bluffed and seen where it got her. But she was distracted by Eliot's hand wrapped around something he had pulled from his pocket; the ornate silver watch he had had on him last night. His white-knuckled grip belied his easy smile. Eliot was already bluffing.

His grip eased as Ilsa failed to cobble together a lie. "In that case, it was nothing," he said. He slipped the watch back into his pocket and moved so he was squarely in front of her, a mere two feet away. He was taller than she'd thought, and she caught the scent of something fresh, like new linens.

"You didn't tell anyone we met." It wasn't a question.

"Neither did you," Ilsa shot back.

"No. If they knew I found solace in wandering the Zoo at night, someone would find a way to ruin it. Much like you managed to last night." He tilted his head. "But why didn't *you* tell?"

Ilsa had no idea. Perhaps she was so used to keeping secrets and hiding impossible truths that it was second nature to her. Perhaps she'd liked the idea of a secret she could share for once. Or, just perhaps, she was taken with something about Eliot Quillon.

She folded her arms. "You know, you're awfully good at being unkind—"

"Why, thank you."

"—but I'm *awfully* good at reading people, and you should know I see through you."

"Is that so?"

"You kicked up a storm 'bout answering my questions, but you answered them all the same, because you knew I needed you to. You got them all angry with you and put yourself in the firing line because you was the only one to notice I couldn't bear to be in that meeting room a minute longer. I don't know why you feel you got to play the villain." Ilsa closed the gap between him and flashed him a smile. "But I'm gonna find out."

A thrill rushed through her when Eliot took half a step back. His eyes roamed her face, something between hunger and trepidation shining in them.

"You shouldn't eavesdrop," he said, his voice quiet. "You might hear something you don't wish to."

He tore himself away with a backward step, then turned and strode down the corridor without another glance. When he disappeared around the corner, Ilsa looked back at the closed door of her cousin's chambers, the echo of smashing glass playing in her ears like Hester's vicious laugh. She raised a hand to the wood to knock – then lowered it again, and walked away.

9

Ilsa's old dress reappeared that same day; washed, mended, and folded on the bed.

She had no idea if magic was at play, or if it had simply been rinsed immediately and dried in the summer sun. She only knew the bloodstains were gone.

The sun crossed the sky as she sat in a stupor with the dress on her lap, running her fingers along the pristine hem. Not a trace of her friend's blood remained on the garment, but Ilsa knew she could never wear it again without thinking of Martha and every injustice she was served.

Martha had wanted to be an actress. She adored watching Ilsa's magic show whenever her friend could sneak her in, just so she could be near the lights, and the curtains, and the drama of it all. It was why Ilsa had tried desperately to get Martha into a paying position in the West End one way or another, whether it was the job at the Isolde Mr Johnston refused to give her, or chasing news of every open casting in town, but it was always a no. She was too skinny. She was too cockney; how would she deal with new material when she couldn't even read? Martha had been learning. She was trying her hardest. But there was no way up for girls like her.

Except discovering your long-lost family is rich, thought Ilsa bitterly.

Martha would have loved the drama of Ilsa's story; of everything that had happened to her since the fish market and the knife in her best friend's throat. She imagined finally telling Martha everything she had held back for two years; who she was, what her magic could do. She imagined telling her that they were heading off to another world, where they would sleep in a bed that looked like a wedding cake, and wear silken gowns, and eat cream teas.

Ilsa's tears had fallen onto her clean dress and soaked it through before she even realised she was crying. She wiped her eyes and looked up into the mirror above the dressing table, but her reflection wasn't there.

Martha stared back at her.

Her dead friend opened her mouth in a silent scream, horror filling her hazel eyes. As Ilsa grasped her throat, so did Martha. As Ilsa stood, the girl staring back at her stood too.

She had shifted. Somehow, while she was lost in her grief, Ilsa's magic had brought her friend to her, in its own macabre way. And now Martha stood before the ornate bed in beautiful clothes, just as Ilsa had wished. She could pretend, for one moment, that she wasn't facing this new life alone.

Ilsa forced a smile. She would see Martha happy again, one last time, and then she would put her to rest. But the smile didn't look right, and as she leaned closer to the mirror, she saw the flaws in the transformation. The nose was still hers. The brows arched in the wrong place. Reality descended, and with it, the foolishness of what she was doing.

Martha was dead. And even if Ilsa looked *exactly* like her, she couldn't bring her back; she could only produce a shade, a phantom. She could only torture herself.

Ilsa shook off the borrowed face. Her own was afraid and flushed from crying, dwarfed by the grandeur of the room around her.

Lost.

She had let her desperation sweep her up and carry her to a whole other world, with nothing but a fool's hope that things would be better after. But 'better' was an easy target to a girl who had just seen her dearest friend murdered. No one could mistake Ilsa's decisions in the hours since for well-thought-out ones. What if nothing was better here? What if the rebels attacked the Zoo again tonight and she was killed? What if they never found her brother and Camden crumbled without him? What if they *did*, and he was cruel and dangerous; a tyrant?

She gripped the dress tighter in her fists. She was trapped between two lives, and neither was right; neither was safe. Here, she had security in all the ways she'd wanted, and none of the ways that mattered. What she had carved out in the Otherworld was familiar, and hard-earned. It had a different kind of value. But would these people even let her have it back? If she put her old dress back on, and walked out the door and all the way back through Westminster Abbey, would they come after her? They said she wasn't a prisoner – that the wolves weren't there to keep her in – but not being a prisoner didn't make her free. Only choices made a person free.

Ilsa had to find out if she had any.

So the following morning, she dressed, did her hair, and matched a sensible black hat with a sensible black bag she found among the things Cassia had bought her. She had lost her own somewhere between the theatre and the portal. Then she put on a dark red winter coat and matching stole she had to dig from the back of the wardrobe, where they still resided in the box they were delivered in. It was early February after all, and no one had expected she would need them for months.

But where Ilsa was headed, they would be essential.

She found most of the lieutenants in the breakfast room. Cassia stood by the window, a cup and saucer in her hands and a contemplative look on her face. Aelius was entirely hidden behind a broadsheet, one leg crossed over the other, foot dangling in an immaculate shoe that looked like it had never touched earth. He was whistling a low tune off-key, and Ilsa wondered how no one told him to stop. Beside him, Oren was making careful markings in his notebook. His glasses were perched daintily on his nose, and his empty breakfast plate sat to one side, the knife and fork resting perfectly level with one another at a right angle to the edge of the table.

Eliot was, of course, on the other side of the room, as far as he could be from anyone. His eyes were closed, his elbow rested on the arm of his chair, and he had a teacup cradled in his fist. It was pressed to his temple like he could absorb its contents straight into his brain. The sun shone directly onto his face, highlighting the dark circles under his eyes, but when Ilsa stepped into the room, he blinked awake, like he had been waiting for her. He rubbed a hand over his face, a wry smile forming on one corner of his mouth.

"What an eye you have for colour, Cassia," he said.

Cassia was jolted from her thoughts. "What? Oh," she said when she saw Ilsa dressed in the coat she had bought, but then realisation dawned in her eyes. "*Oh*."

Oren glanced up distractedly. "If you mean to leave the house, I must insist you disguise yourself and one of the wolves accompany you," he said. "And it's important you don't leave Camden."

Aelius chuckled. "I think she means to go much further than the boundaries of the Changeling quarter, Oren my lad," he said, turning the page of his paper.

Ilsa took a deep breath, squared her shoulders, and reminded herself she was not asking for permission; she was issuing a threat. They would let her go, proving she was safe and among friends, or Ilsa was leaving anyway, whatever it took, and she wasn't coming back.

She would not be a prisoner.

"I'm expected at the theatre."

Oren blinked rapidly. "You still wish to go back to the Otherworld and place yourself at the mercy of the Seer's acolytes?"

"Wishing's got nothing to do with it. Girls what grow up in *orphanages* are lucky if they ain't in the workhouse. You learn to meet your obligations pretty quick with that hanging over you, and I got somewhere to be. So I'm gonna do the show 'til Mr Blume finds a replacement, 'cause it's what's professional. And" – Ilsa swallowed. She was about to push her luck – "and I'd be much obliged if you'd settle his debts for him. Seems you can afford it. And you are costing him a good assistant."

If pressed on the risk of her magician accruing *new* debts with old habits, Ilsa had a speech prepared for that too. She did not intend to abandon Blume with a little money and cross her fingers that he would finally get his feet under him. She wasn't leaving the Isolde until she had made him understand that this was a new start for both of them; a chance he couldn't squander.

Aelius waved a dismissive hand. "You can consider his debts handled, my darling, but" – his humour had vanished – "we're talking of *Oracles*. Don't you understand? Heavens, if I were an acolyte, I would already be at the theatre."

"No, it's *you* what don't understand! I messed up our finale. We got one more chance to stay on the billing or else Mr Blume's fired, and it'll be the last time. No one'll hire him no more and it'll be because of me. I ain't the only one with everything to lose." Even as she said it, she shivered to think of more Oracles coming for her at the Isolde, and a new, thudding fear hit her like a stone. "They'll know I'm going to the theatre."

"Of course," said Oren.

"And they'll know Mr Blume's there too?" No one answered, but Ilsa understood. The people who were trying to kill her just to settle some vendetta surely wouldn't balk at slaughtering Bill too. They had already killed Martha. "They'll hurt him, won't they? If they think it'll get me there."

"So you see why it's essential that it doesn't," said Oren. He addressed the surface of the table. "I am simply being pragmatic. It's unfortunate, but we must ask ourselves if it is our concern. You are safe if you stay here."

"Aren't you listening?" said Eliot, drawing contemptuous looks from every corner of the room. He rested his teacup delicately on his saucer and rose from his chair. "She's not staying. You said yourself, she isn't a prisoner. And she's right, the magician is in danger."

Aelius snorted derisively. "Oren's point remains—"

"Then damn you both," Ilsa growled, feeling her blood rise. "I'm going to find Mr Blume and I ain't asking for your help."

"You can hardly go alone," said Cassia. "I'm coming with you."

"As am I," said Eliot.

"Alright," said Oren. He didn't snap, nor raise his voice, but he quieted the room nonetheless. "But Cassia and I will be the ones to take you."

"Good call," said Aelius. He shot a suspicious glance at Eliot.

Eliot glared at Oren, then Aelius, and for a moment it seemed as if he would become a big cat and rip their throats out. The glimmer in his storm-blue eyes was one of unchecked malice. But then he smiled, a slow, seductive smile that transformed the hard mask into something as frightening as it was beautiful. He buttoned his jacket with quick fingers and inclined his head towards the group.

"Once again, it seems I've roused myself for nothing," he said. "Please do wake me when I'm *actually* needed."

Even over her fear, Ilsa felt the tension resonate between them all as Eliot stalked from the room.

Oren merely shook his head and led them out to find Bill Blume.

*

"We'll see you at the abbey," Oren said to Cassia when they had dressed for winter and gathered in the forecourt. "Be on your guard."

Cassia nodded – and vanished into thin air. Ilsa blinked stupidly at the spot where she'd evaporated.

"She's gone!"

Oren glanced up from where he was tucking his notebook

into his jacket and hooking his umbrella over his arm. "Good. Fly as close to me as you can. We should be safe within the borders of Camden, but if you see anything untoward – an arrow, a spell coming your way – turn right around and fly back here as fast as you can. Don't wait for me. What's your fastest bird?"

"Uh – I can do a falcon," said Ilsa. "I saw one in a bird show at the zoo once. The Otherworld zoo, I mean."

"Very good. Falcons it is, then."

Before she could ask about Cassia vanishing herself or what an oncoming spell might look like, Oren shrank, his feet left the ground, and he soared straight upwards in the form of a falcon. She followed in haste.

They dashed south, side by side, and Ilsa thought about the magician boy she had seen the day before. He had vanished into thin air just as Cassia had – that must have made him a Sorcerer too.

She wanted to tell Mr Blume. She wanted to tell him about a lot of things since they parted. The Witherward. The Changelings. How she was sorry for the finale. How she'd been thinking about family and whether it meant what she had always thought it did.

She finally had somewhere to belong, and suddenly the place she was desperate to be was back in the Otherworld, back at the theatre with Bill Blume. She didn't know how she'd bear it if he'd been caught up in this. Not after Martha.

When Oren touched down in the crowded street in front of Westminster Abbey, Ilsa made another circle overhead. She wasn't used to a world in which a falcon could transform into a man, and not a single onlooker would pay him any attention. Hesitantly, she dipped towards the pavement, and landed on her own, human feet. A man with his nose in the morning paper almost walked into her as she reappeared. He only tipped his hat and begged her pardon.

Oren replaced his glasses on his nose and looked her up and down. "You'd better wear a disguise," he said. "Just in case."

She became another girl from her boarding house – Eliza, red-haired and round-faced – and followed Oren towards the abbey.

When they reached the cloisters, Cassia was waiting for them. Like yesterday, the quadrangle was guarded by several wolves. But instead of surrounding them, they bowed their heads to Oren and Cassia, and stood aside to let them approach the portal.

"Would you like to take my arm?" said Oren at the top of the stairs. "The portal can be quite jarring until one gets used to it."

Ilsa took hold of the crook of Oren's arm. Again, they had only descended a handful of steps when the sensation of falling while standing still hit her. She gripped hold of Oren and kept walking, once again missing the exact moment they started heading up instead of down.

"You're a natural," Oren said, his eyes kind, like they hadn't just been arguing about whether to leave Blume to his fate. He had called himself pragmatic, but he meant ruthless, yet he was also a gentleman. Ilsa couldn't figure him out.

The sound of scraping stone came from above, then Cassia appeared around the corner. "The coast is clear," she said.

Oren raised his umbrella to shield them both before they were doused in rain and ice, and the three of them stepped into the dark quadrangle. Even expecting the winter weather and the dark hadn't fully prepared her. It had been so clear and bright in the Witherward.

Ilsa could just make out the time on the abbey clock. "The variety show will be ending right 'bout now. He should be at the theatre."

"Where?" said Cassia.

Ilsa gave her directions and the Sorcerer vanished again. Then Ilsa and Oren took off on wings into the freezing rain. In five minutes, they had made what was a half-hour journey on foot. Ilsa directed Oren to a secluded spot where they could land – in the alley alongside the theatre – and before they had shifted, Cassia was upon them.

"He's not here," she said. Panic leapt in Ilsa's chest. "I asked for the magician and they said he never showed up. They're giving people their money back." She shifted her umbrella and glanced over her shoulder. Sure enough, the crowds were exiting onto the street. "They said if I saw him, I should tell him not to bother coming back."

Perhaps it wasn't what she feared. Blume had forgotten his curtain call before, and Ilsa had always been there to run from pub to pub until she found him. But after what Mr Johnston had said, this was his last chance, gone.

Bill Blume wouldn't work again. His gambling and drinking had burned too many bridges. Ilsa thought about the big house in the Witherward, on the corner of Regent's Park. There'd be space for him. They couldn't refuse to protect the only friend she had left.

"Follow me," said Ilsa.

It was only two streets over, but the sleet was coming harder when they reached the street where Blume had a fourth-floor flat. Oren and Cassia were hesitant as they followed Ilsa inside, but everything appeared normal. The mewling of the landlady's fussy cat was coming from the ground-floor flat, where Mrs Holmes had cared for her as a younger girl. The couple who lived below Blume were shrieking at each other as always. But on the top floor, just under the rafters, all was quiet.

Ilsa followed Oren and Cassia's lead as they crept up on the door with soft, slow footsteps, listening as they went. When nothing presented itself, she became the girl whom Blume would recognise and reached for the knocker.

But then Cassia's hand shot out and gripped her arm, and she put a bone-white finger to her lips. Sure enough, light, quick footsteps were sounding from inside the flat, heading away from the door. A second later came the shattering of glass.

Bill.

"Stand aside," said Oren, and Cassia pulled her away from the door. The slender, ageing man reared up and kicked at the lock with more force than he looked capable of. The door burst open and Ilsa failed to stifle a sob. There was Bill: a gag tied around his sagging head, his arms fastened to a chair.

Oren made straight for the broken window and leaned out into the rain.

"They're getting away over the roof," he called, before shifting into a bird.

"Oren, wait—" said Cassia, but he had already disappeared in pursuit.

Ilsa was before her magician before she'd decided to move, his face in her hands. His eyes were open, but glazed. There was blood in his hair, on his clothes, and worst of all, on his lips. His skin felt cool – too cool. But it was a miserable night, and there was no fire. Ilsa was suddenly very cold too.

"Mr Blume? It's me. It's Ilsa." She untied the gag. "Mr Blume? Please wake up."

"Ilsa, I think…" began Cassia, but Ilsa wouldn't listen. She untied him from the chair and he slumped into her arms.

"Help me get him on the couch," she said. Heavens, there was more blood than she had thought. Maybe it was just the light, but it looked black where it had pooled on the floor around him. Black because it was old.

Cassia lifted his legs and they lowered him onto the couch.

"Why'd they do this to him?" Ilsa said, her voice cracking.

"To get you here," said Cassia. "To get… exactly this." She was distracted; her gaze swept the room. "If this was only one person, they must have expected you alone. I don't think this was an Oracle."

"Please wake up, Bill," said Ilsa weakly. She put a hand to his mouth to check for breathing and was surprised to find she was trembling.

"Ilsa, we're not safe here," said Cassia. "The acolytes will be coming. They'll know you've left Camden, and…"

There was a thud from below. Then another. Heavy feet were ascending the stairs.

"Stars help us." Cassia positioned herself squarely in front of the open door. "Ilsa. Look at me."

Ilsa dragged her eyes away from Bill. Cassia fixed her a fierce gaze. "Are you intimately acquainted with any predators?"

A sound of despair escaped her. Bill might be dead – was almost certainly dead – but their next threat was now on the floor below them and getting closer. She was going to be attacked again, and this time she needed to fight.

But how? All of her best transformations were for hiding or fleeing. She had tried some of the big animals she had seen at the zoo, but only for fun. She didn't have the practice.

Ilsa shook her head, doubt clawing at her. "I ain't sure I—"

They both started as the footsteps burst into the corridor with a crash, and Ilsa realised: there was no time to let grief cloud her mind, no time to form a plan. A survival instinct that had failed her among the crates in the fish market took over as a familiar electrical charge coursed down her spine.

A dog had teeth and claws. That would have to do.

The form, the figure, the mass and motion of a wolfhound only flickered through her mind for a moment before her body took over. She dropped helplessly to her hands and knees as her bones moved and changed. Her skin prickled as a coat of shaggy fur erupted from it. Her joints twisted, her legs elongated, her hands and feet rounded into paws. Her mind dulled at the edges; her senses honed. She poured all her strength into conjuring the largest, most powerful creature she could. When she was done, her ears reached Cassia's shoulder.

In the mind of the beast, Ilsa's rage and despair purified into something merciless and instinctual, until the bloodshed she was about to face felt almost *right*.

"They're Oracles. They know what you'll do," Cassia said. "Don't hesitate."

Then they appeared. Two pallid faces with dead, empty eyes filled the doorway. They were snarling, their teeth bared, and armed with pistols.

Before they could shoot, Cassia extended her hands and cast a shielding spell like the one she had used to protect them from

Fyfe's projectile. A bubble formed around her with Ilsa safe behind it. It repelled the Oracles' bullets with a sound like tin.

But more of them were appearing, and edging around Cassia's bubble. Two ducked behind the couch where Bill still lay and took aim at Ilsa. Just when she thought her only hope was to lunge and hope she was faster, their pistols flew from their hands with an explosion of light. Cassia's bubble had vanished, and she was aiming her palm at one Oracle after another, and firing something like lightning at their weapons.

So, that was what Oren meant about watching for spells.

But the Oracles were still coming. Eight all together had poured into the room and separated them.

Ilsa turned on one to find him moved already. Another made to lunge at her, but at the last minute targeted Cassia instead, and tackled her to the ground.

They know what you'll do, she had said. *Don't hesitate.*

They could see her every move before she knew she would make it.

Without a thought in her head she leapt at Cassia, caught the leg of the Oracle on top of her in the vice of her jaw, and pulled him off his feet. He went down with a thud, but he was only dazed for a heartbeat before he started to push himself up. Ilsa reared up and landed her front paws on his back. The second time his head hit the ground there was a crack, and the Oracle went limp. Without pause, she turned; a haphazard, sweeping movement to catch anything in her vicinity, and knocked another to the ground. She leapt at anything and everything that moved, lashing out with her claws. One Oracle was crushed when he charged at her, his momentum helping Ilsa throw him against a wall with her full weight. Another, she bit into at the neck, until she could feel hot blood spraying onto her tongue. Cassia wielded her magic ruthlessly. There seemed to be no limit to the speed with which she could let her spells fly. Some of her hits elicited cries, some sent weapons flying. One met its mark right between the eyes and he crumpled, dead, against the wall.

The last two Oracles fled. Or, at least, Ilsa had thought they were the last two. As she dropped onto all four paws, something leapt at her from behind, nearly buckling her. The Oracle dug his fingers down into her fur, to her skin. Ilsa thrashed and twisted, consumed by panic, but she couldn't shake him. She heard him unsheathe a blade.

"Duck!"

Cassia, stood over a body, was brandishing the dead Oracle's pistol at her.

Ilsa ducked.

Cassia fired, her arm steady, her gaze straight down the line of the barrel.

There was a clatter of furniture breaking as the Oracle fell. The gunshot – louder than she expected, and so close to her sensitive canine ears – shook Ilsa enough that she shifted, and as she fell to the floor, her own arms stretched out to brace her.

"Thank you," she gasped. The tang of blood coated the inside of her mouth and clung to her chin, hot and sticky. As a dog, it hadn't seemed so awful to draw blood with her teeth, but before she knew it she was running to the kitchen to vomit into a bowl. Cassia found a cloth and helped her get the worst of it out of her mouth and off her face. She had tucked the pistol into the waistband of her coat.

"We need to find Oren," she said. "We can't wait for him here. There'll just be more of them."

With an aching weight in her chest, Ilsa forced herself back to the couch and knelt beside her magician. "Bill."

The last time they had spoken, she had called him a bad teammate, but how would she know? He was the only person who truly knew her; next to Martha, the only teammate she'd ever had. They were supposed to see each other again that evening, when they would pretend like nothing happened, but be a little kinder to each other than normal.

But his eyes stared through her. His skin was colder still.

The blood had left him through several clean wounds in his chest and abdomen.

There would be no kinder words; not ever.

Bill Blume was dead.

"Ilsa, I'm so sorry."

A delicate hand rested on her shoulder, but Ilsa shook it off. The violence she'd already done suddenly wasn't enough. She wanted to leap out that window after Oren and track down whoever had done this.

But Cassia was right – they needed to leave.

"What 'bout…" *the bodies*. The scene was worse than the fish market. Ilsa had killed three of them; the one slumped against the wall, the one face down near the kitchen, and the bloodied mess by the couch. She stared unwaveringly at Cassia to keep from looking at them.

"I'm sure the other tenants are already fetching the police, what with the commotion. They'll take care of it," said Cassia. Her fingers grazed each of the Oracles' bodies in turn, then the couch, the table, the doorframe. Everything she touched rippled like heat haze and then righted itself. When she reached for Bill, Ilsa blocked her path.

"What are you doing?"

Cassia's eyes were sympathetic, but her tone was matter-of-fact. "It's a glamour. So no one will find anything unusual about this."

Ilsa gave a soundless, caustic laugh and stood aside. Why wouldn't a girl who could magic herself from place to place also be able to cast a *glamour*? All she knew was that she hardly knew anything.

When Cassia had cast her magic, Ilsa closed Bill's eyes, folded his hands atop his chest, and wiped the blood from his face. Was there something else he would want? A token for the afterlife? An instruction for the coroner? No; it was her, and not Bill, who was not ready, so Ilsa blinked back her tears and cast about the room. Bill's coat hung on a hook by the door, his paisley scarf draped over it. She had found the scarf in the auditorium, left behind by a punter, and had wrapped it in paper and given it to Bill for his birthday one year. As she took it off the hook and folded it small, she tried not to think of Bill hanging it there, oblivious to the fact he would never wear it again. She tried not to think of what happened after. Then she nodded to Cassia that she was ready, and with the scarf tucked under Ilsa's arm, they made their way back out into the street.

The sleet continued, but she no longer felt the cold. A different kind of numbness had taken hold.

The two girls stood side by side in the street, their third companion nowhere to be seen. In the dark and the sleet, no passer-by seemed to notice the gun, or the blood.

"P'raps they fought," Ilsa said. "P'raps…"

"Oren can take care of himself." Cassia nodded to the knife still in Ilsa's hand. "And they're not armed. I just hope—"

At that moment, Oren emerged from the alley. They ran for him. Cassia took him by the shoulders and looked him up and down. He was clearly unharmed, but there was something dull in his expression.

"Who…" began Cassia, but he shook his head.

"I couldn't look," he said quietly. "I couldn't stop them. They wouldn't let me."

"A Whisperer," said Cassia.

"A what?"

"The Whitechapel faction. They can read minds. Manipulate thoughts."

Ilsa drew a breath as Eliot's words came back to her. *They can wipe a mind clean and refill it with whatever, and* whom*ever, they choose.*

"They… got in your head?" she said, shivering.

"They were too quick. They had me before…" He trailed off, and reached a hand into his inside breast pocket. He produced a knife; unremarkable at first glance, and dull with blood. "Cassia, they dropped this."

Cassia took the dagger and held it delicately in both hands for them all to see. The light of a nearby streetlamp just illuminated a column of symbols along the hilt. They looked like the letters of a foreign alphabet.

Oren and Cassia exchanged a meaningful look.

"What's it mean?"

"It means this belongs to one of the Fortunatae," said Cassia. "It means we might know who's behind the Sorcerer rebellion."

For the second time in days, Ilsa was washing off blood.

She sat with her knees pulled up to her chin in a bathtub that was still magically steaming and clean after thirty minutes. It was a good thing too – Cassia knocked every once in a while, and Ilsa would tell her five more minutes. She needed the bath; needed to focus on nothing but the water hugging her, the solid sides of the tub keeping her from the world beyond.

But this time, when Ilsa dismissed her, Cassia let herself in anyway, only to hover hesitantly by the door.

"You gonna talk to me now?" Ilsa tried to keep the bite out of her tone and failed. Neither Cassia nor Oren had explained what the Fortunatae was, or what it meant. Every time she asked, they had looked at her pityingly and hurried her along. Truthfully, Ilsa knew she was only clinging to her irritation to stop other feelings from surfacing; to keep herself from thinking about Martha, and about Bill.

Cassia came and perched on the edge of the tub, her back to her. "You mustn't blame yourself for what happened to that man. It was our fault. Perhaps we couldn't have predicted what happened, but we ought to have been more prepared for everything the Oracles might do at least. But I promise, Ilsa, we shan't let anyone else you care about be harmed."

Ilsa made a mental list of the people she knew. The other girls at her boarding house. The performers from the variety show. If the Oracles looked at her life, was there anyone they would think to target the way they had Bill? The answer was all too clear. "There ain't no one else."

"Oh." Cassia lapsed into silence, and Ilsa couldn't blame her. What did you say to someone who had lost their last friend? Ilsa hugged her knees tighter to her chest and rested her head on them as she fought back tears.

"Will you stay?" Cassia said.

Ilsa looked up. Cassia was watching her hesitantly.

"You're not a prisoner, Ilsa. None of us want to keep you here against your will. But we *do* want to protect you, and we'll do everything we can to keep you safe if you stay. Besides, it sounds an awful lot like…"

She trailed off, but Ilsa knew what she meant to say.

"Like I ain't got nothing left to go back to."

Nothing left to lose. The desire to run – to put everything she had learned back in a box and close the lid – was still there, but Ilsa saw it for what it was now. She was afraid of feeling unmoored and out of her depth. She couldn't be the cleverest and the quickest in a world she knew nothing about.

She needed to learn. And fast.

"I'll stay," she said, "but I got a condition."

Cassia frowned, but nodded.

"I want to know about the Fortunatae."

"Alright."

"Right now."

"But…" Concern flickered across Cassia's face. "I thought,

149

with everything we've thrown at you – about Gedeon, the Oracles, our history…"

"You already tried to coddle me once and now Mr Blume is dead," Ilsa said, meeting the other girl's eye. "How am I s'posed to stay safe without all the information?"

Cassia looked away. For a moment she appeared to deliberate it, then she stood and fetched a dressing gown, which she brought to the tub and held open. "Well, when you put it like that, I suppose I ought to call for some tea."

*

Cassia must have remembered that Ilsa had skipped breakfast, as when the tea arrived at her room, it was accompanied by crumpets and jam. Not in the habit of refusing food, Ilsa buttered a crumpet, but the thought of it was churning her stomach before she could bring it to her mouth. Instead, she sipped the tea. She should not have needed warming up, what with the steaming bath and the summer sun beating down outside, but as the hot tea slipped down her throat, she felt her shivering abate. Her stomach welcomed it, as did her heart. She took another sip.

They were sat in the silk-upholstered armchairs in Ilsa's chamber, she was still wrapped in a dressing gown, a blanket around her shoulders. Cassia had also changed and washed off the blood. She looked tired, but nowhere near as shaken as Ilsa. Perhaps fighting for her life was a common occurrence for her.

"The history of the Changelings in London is long," Cassia said, warning in her voice. "And complicated."

Ilsa understood she was being given her last chance to refuse this story. Given what she already knew about the Witherward, and what had happened to Bill, she didn't expect it would be pleasant. But to know was better than to wonder. She nodded.

Cassia stirred her tea. "Everybody fights in this city," she said. "If it's not about borders, it's money or power, or some violation of an arbitrary code. And if we can't find reasons, we invent them. So you can imagine why we can't trust what the Docklands are saying about Gedeon.

"Every people can trace its origins back to the celestial event which formed them or gave them their unique magic. The original Oracles, for example, were the witnesses of the Blinding Light, a solar eclipse many thousands of years ago. The Wraiths fell to earth in a meteor shower." Cassia looked at her then, and the ghost of a smile brushed her mouth. "My ancestors evolved from the Ancients – elemental magicians – when they were touched by an aurora. We were the first of the modern people.

"And the Changelings were born under a red moon on the vernal equinox. The Shift, we call it. They transformed, from animals, across a vast swath of the Erro-Azian continent. But the epicentre was here. In London."

Ilsa had been enraptured by thoughts of celestial magic and ancient beings, but when Cassia paused, she remembered what they were supposed to be talking about. "What's this got to do with the Fortunatae?"

Cassia gestured for Ilsa to wait. "Five magics had founded London. They had always lived in separate quarters and already mistrusted one another. And then the Shift. Imagine it. Every single animal in the city – horses, dogs, cats, every bird, every bit of livestock – became a Changeling. In a single moment, the population was… perhaps ten times what it had been. It was cataclysmic, Ilsa. It destabilised any pretence of goodwill

151

among the factions. It ended the Sorcerers' rule. They call it the Century of Slaughter, or sometimes the Long Plague. Suffice to say after many decades the population righted itself. But they say *three* things brought London back from the Shift: slaughter, sickness... and Morgan Ravenswood.

"You know of her, of course. She led a bloody war to take Camden, mainly from the Sorcerers and the Whisperers. You can imagine what her legacy is beyond the borders. London never found even a false peace again after the Shift, and settling the Changelings in their own quarter brought some semblance of order, but the damage was done. The other magics had all the reason they needed to hate the Changelings as they hated each other. But even after decades of bloodshed, was there any moral high ground to be claimed over people who didn't choose to be there, who only wished to be allowed to stay where they'd been born?" Cassia's normally rigid posture was a little deflated. Her sad eyes stared intently at her teacup. "That's what the Fortunatae wanted: a justification. They're a secret society founded at a small college in Whitechapel – the Whisperer quarter – just after Morgan Ravenswood became the leader of the Changelings and made Camden your territory. There were fourteen of them at first, radical philosophers of five factions who believed that Changelings' origins raised an important question." She looked up. "Are you people who can change into animals... or merely animals, who are sometimes people?"

Ilsa stiffened. It was absurd, to hear her magic talked about like that. She had been animal, and she had been human, and she knew which she was inside. Only a person who had never known what it was like could think it a valid question.

"The members of the Fortunatae have little respect for your kind, Ilsa," said Cassia weakly. "But for centuries they were a society of intellectuals concerned with theory. Thinkers, not activists. And then a decade or so before the Principles were drafted, they went to ground. Someone had taken over as their head; someone they called the Sage. He had... new ideas. Plans of action." She drew a shaking breath. "When the Principles solidified in writing that Camden belonged to the Changelings, the Sage courted chaos and rebellion and manipulated it for the Fortunatae's means."

Propagandists. That's what Eliot had called them. She could picture it now; how easy it would be to rile members of every faction against the people who had brought about the Century of Slaughter.

"It's how they've operated before. If they are fuelling the fire of this revolt in the Heart, then they're after the same thing they wanted seventeen years ago: five quarters. Five factions. A London with no place for the Changelings."

Ilsa shivered. She understood what Cassia did not want to say, and when she forced the words past her lips, they were a whisper. "They killed my parents."

The Sorcerer shook her head. "Not just your parents. The Sage believed that if they ended the Ravenswoods' rule, Camden and its people would fall. They rallied enough of an insurgence against Camden that your family were forced to abandon the Zoo. They were hiding in a wine merchant's cellar in Soho when your mother gave birth. Oren was just a young wolf at the time, but your mother chose him to smuggle you to the portal. He left the cellar with you just in time."

Cassia's gaze was hollow. Ilsa couldn't find it in herself to urge her on. She could only wait.

"They killed seventeen that day. Your mother and father. Your mother's younger sister and her husband. Your grandfather. His brother, who was Hester's father. Two of your mother's three lieutenants, and nine wolves."

A massacre. Ilsa felt the bile rise in her throat and forced away the images. She had to put her teacup down; she was shaking again.

Cassia produced the dagger Ilsa had brought from Blume's flat, and held it across her palm. She pointed to the inscription along the hilt. Ilsa had not noticed at first, but the foreign letters were followed by a different sort of symbol, more intricate and pictorial. It was a cog, or sprocket, and contained inside was a head in cross-section, the brain outlined within.

"This is the Sage's seal. The Zoo never learned who they were. I shan't go into the aftermath of the massacre, but Hester pulled Camden back from the brink, and the Sage disappeared soon after you were born. As the years went on, it was assumed they had fallen from power. Only... this blade is newly made. Whoever it belonged to is still loyal to the person who killed your family."

The dagger had been cleaned of Bill's blood, but now it held new horror. It had belonged to someone who wished harm not only on Ilsa and her magician, but her whole bloodline and anyone allied to them.

Anyone Changeling.

Cassia shook her head. "I don't know how they knew about your friend Bill, or even that you were alive. But the timing.

It can't be a coincidence. Perhaps if we knew who sent that messenger from the Docklands…"

It didn't make sense that someone would warn both the Zoo and their enemies about the assassination attempt, but Cassia was right about one thing: it wasn't a coincidence. Bill was dead because Ilsa had been saved. Ilsa squeezed her eyes shut, but the tears came anyway.

Cassia studied her, her usually cold eyes flecked with tenderness. "I need to thank you, Ilsa. I think you saved my life when that man overpowered me."

"You saved mine too," said Ilsa, remembering the haunting image of her steely fortitude as she pointed that pistol. Then she remembered her own slapdash self-defence, and the Sorcerer's rapid-fire spells and shields. "Probably more than once."

"I've never fired a gun before," Cassia said, almost whimsically. "What violent things." She read the question on Ilsa's face. "My magic is… different. It doesn't truly come from the soul, but it feels that way to wield it. We Sorcerers are just conduits, in reality. We have the ability to channel and shape raw power. But our bodies love magic, and the magic loves us. It's intimate and sympathetic – friendly, you might say, at its core – even when it harms.

"But fire and metal. Holding that gun was a different kind of power. I don't think any Sorcerer can wield magic as brutal. One can dream."

Ilsa had to assume that was another joke, but the Sorcerer's expression remained grave as always.

Cassia let a long moment pass before rising from her chair to leave. "None of this will be easy, Ilsa, but it sounds as though your old life wasn't easy either. Now you have us to help you." She sighed. "But I do wish we were better."

Ilsa read the self-deprecation in her lovely face, and felt some tenderness for the girl too. For better or worse, she had nothing left to lose by falling down this rabbit hole. She didn't know what would become of her if she went back to the Otherworld now, with Blume gone. Her secrets, and thus her stage career, had gone with him. Suddenly, her grim history here was not what she wished to run from. She saw a path forward, away from the lies and hardships of her old life in the Otherworld, and the legacy of loss she had inherited in this one.

Cassia was nearly at the door when Ilsa stood, arresting her attention.

"I want to help find my brother."

Cassia's mouth opened in surprise, and a light sparked in her eyes. It dulled just as quickly as doubt appeared to set in. "That's admirable, Ilsa, but... how?"

"Gedeon thinks I'm dead, don't he?"

Cassia nodded. "He never had cause to question it," she said with a sad smile.

"And... the Sage. And the Fortunatae and this rebellion, they don't know I'm here, neither."

"We hope as much. Most of this city should never have known you existed."

"Then let me find him," Ilsa said imploringly. "Whatever it is Gedeon's up to, he thinks he's got nothing to lose. But things've changed since he went, and he don't know. If he knew I'm here and I want to help him... p'raps I can make him change his mind."

In truth, she had no idea how she was going to do what she was saying she would, but feigning confidence had made her hope. Ilsa wasn't sure she believed in Fyfe's stars, or any design that steered her course. But if she did, if there was meaning in all this, perhaps this was why she was here.

Cassia took Ilsa's hands. "It occurred to me too that you could change everything," she whispered. "Most days I don't dare to hope. We've tried so much already, but perhaps it's right that his sister should be the one to find him."

Ilsa offered her a smile, and Cassia returned it, though the cracks were showing at the edges. It was plain in her eyes that any hope Cassia felt was fading fast. She had more to say, but she hesitated, her gaze haunted.

"Gedeon would be furious that I almost got you killed today," she said carefully, and Ilsa wondered what she was trying to keep from her voice. "He's always been this way, really. It's why he left. He would always rather do things himself than risk anyone he cares for."

It might have sounded like a noble thing, but not the way Cassia said it.

"And what's he doing this time?" asked Ilsa.

Any softness in the girl's gaze hardened in an instant. "If you really wish to find out where Gedeon is, you should ask Eliot," she said tightly, then she let herself out, leaving Ilsa alone with her blood-soaked thoughts.

Ilsa's grief kept her from sleeping that night, and the peculiarity with the clocks didn't help. Around midnight, she gave up trying and slipped from her room, drawn back to the row of portraits in the long gallery where she had first laid eyes on her parents.

On this night, at this hour, the moon was at a different slant, and when Ilsa stood before the very last portrait – the one the shadows had kept from her the first time – she could see the face of the boy looking back at her.

He was a young man, really, at nineteen; captured here less than a year ago, she had been told. He wore a red sash, like the subjects of the many portraits she couldn't bring herself to look at yet, and his hair was a thick golden-blonde. He was very handsome, with strong cheekbones, lightly tanned skin, and an indefinable decency in his expression. The artist had captured a sharpness and strength of spirit in his hazel eyes.

Ilsa felt an entirely different presence stood in front of this portrait than the one of her parents. She wanted to reach up and brush her fingers over his brow, his hair, and along the edge of his jaw, like she might be able to feel the contours of a real face. Her brother, who thought her dead. She ached with wondering what else he had thought about her while she was busy not daring to imagine him. If she was ever going to know, they needed to find him, and Ilsa was going to be the one to do it.

Cassia had told her to ask Eliot. The only trouble was, this was the only place she knew to look for him. Perhaps he was up and wandering the corridors too, but in a house so big, at an hour so dark, what chance did they have of stumbling across each other?

As the thought crossed her mind, a burst of noise made her jump. Her first thought was that she'd been wrong; Eliot was here after all, about to emerge from the shadows and frighten her like last time. But then she recognised the sound for what it was: a swell of raucous laughter, coming to her from somewhere outside.

Ilsa crept to the window. Despite the hour, a ground-floor window at the corner of the east wing was illuminated, casting a swath of yellow light across the gravel path that ran by the house. As Ilsa watched, a second sliver of light appeared and widened as a door was opened, spilling two men into the garden. Not just men, Ilsa realised as they shifted. Wolves. They split off to their respective watches, melting into the night like shadows, but movement at the window told Ilsa there were more inside, and a sudden curiosity took hold.

It was a pitifully long time before Ilsa located the room; she could barely find her way around the Zoo in daylight. It wasn't until another burst of laughter echoed through the corridors that she was able to follow the sound down a narrow passage that ran by the kitchen.

She found herself at the door of a guardroom; a plain space with a brick floor and white walls, with a long table and benches in the centre. Three wolves were in the middle of a card game, but they dropped their hands and stood at the same moment that Ilsa entered.

She shot an alarmed glance behind her, expecting to find

Hester had followed her down there. But no; it was *her* the wolves were staring at as they stood to attention.

"What?" said Ilsa warily. They looked at each other as if deciding what to do, and Ilsa was suddenly unsure of herself. "I din't mean to intrude. I saw the light on is all."

Two of the wolves relaxed their posture. The third, a stocky young man with a mousy beard, looked Ilsa up and down distrustfully.

"Please, Miss Ravenswood, do come in," said the nearest. She had a rounded mane of tight black curls, black-brown skin, and she was dressed like a lady in a lemon-yellow gown, her militia sash around one arm. Ilsa had expected the attire of a soldier, but of course, there was no need for a soldier who could shift at will to dress any way at all.

"Yes, do," said the third, a man with russet-brown hair and freckles. He grinned at the wolf in the yellow dress as they sat back down. "I was about to take all of Georgiana's money, and I think I'd quite like a witness."

"You should be so lucky, Rye. Deal the next card. Miss Ravenswood..."

"Ilsa," she corrected. Miss Ravenswood still sounded like someone else.

"Do you want to play with us, Ilsa?" said Georgiana.

"But we're mid-game," blurted the bearded wolf who didn't appear to possess a smile.

"We can deal her in on the next round," said Rye.

"S'alright," said Ilsa before the other man could object again, though she *did* want to play. The card game, the moment snatched between other tasks, even the unpretty, functional

160

room; it reminded her of being backstage at the theatre. "I'll join some other time."

She addressed it to the bearded wolf with a smile; a threat to ruin his fun at some unspecified point in the future.

The wolves kept playing as Ilsa wandered deeper into the room. There were no weapons resting by the table – the wolves didn't need them – and the only thing adorning the walls was a schedule pinned to a board. Dozens of names filled in every watch over the course of a week.

"How many wolves *are* there?"

Georgiana glanced up from scooping her winnings into a pile. "Over a thousand in total, but ninety on rotation here. Others are posted to the guard points along the border, or the abbey, or they work the patrol."

"And do they all know 'bout…" Ilsa bit her lip and studied their faces.

"About the alpha being missing?" said Georgiana grimly. "Only at the Zoo. We've been sworn to secrecy." She made the word *secrecy* sound distasteful, and the wolves exchanged another look.

"And what 'bout them twelve what went with him?"

The bearded wolf raised his head. "What about them?"

"Why them twelve? Why not any of you?"

His scowl deepened. Ilsa had said something wrong. "Is there a reason you're concerning yourself with militia business?" he challenged. "They made you a lieutenant already?"

She jerked in surprise. No one had mentioned the idea of making her a lieutenant, nor had the possibility crossed her mind. Now that it did, she wasn't sure she liked it. What did she know of Camden that she could help lead it?

Georgiana interjected, sparing Ilsa from stuttering a reply. "Ilsa has joined the effort to look for the alpha, Selleck. Perhaps you ought to be accommodating."

The ask was clearly too high for Selleck, who elected to leave instead, tossing his cards down and throwing Georgiana, then Ilsa a distrustful glance as he made for the door.

Rye rubbed his neck and looked up at her apologetically. "Some of the wolves don't know what to make of you, Miss Ravenswood – I mean Ilsa. Secrets aren't good for morale, you see, and... well, some of the old guard knew of Lyander's pregnancy way back when, and they never told us you existed."

Ilsa didn't see how that was *her* fault. She'd known as little of it as anyone.

"And now the disappearance," said Georgiana, her shoulders stiff. "The truth is, no one has any idea why he took the wolves he did. Perhaps they were just his favourites."

She couldn't hide the bitterness in her voice and Ilsa couldn't blame her. Gedeon's wolves had to have known about the plan beforehand, perhaps for days, and had told none of their comrades. She had been so hung up on her missing brother, she had barely considered the fact that it wasn't just him, but thirteen of Camden's own who had betrayed them.

"I din't mean to suggest he had favourites or nothing. I'm sure there's a simple explanation."

Georgiana smiled. "I'm sure there is," she said unconvincingly. "Your bet, Rye."

Rye dropped a handful of coins onto the table between them, raising the bet.

After a moment's hesitation, Georgiana sighed and moved

as if to fold. Ilsa's hand shot out to stop her without her say so. They both looked at her in surprise, and Ilsa was forced to explain herself.

"He ain't got jack."

Rye's eyes widened as he stared at her, and Ilsa shrugged apologetically. Georgiana looked from Ilsa to Rye and back again. "How do you know?"

Because Ilsa had been watching. She couldn't help it. Years of playing cards with theatre folk, coupled with a deeply ingrained habit of observation, had made her a master of reading tells. Rye had folded his arms on the table, a tell-tale sign that he was trying not to fidget, whereas in every other round he had been still.

He was bluffing.

Of course, Ilsa said none of this in front of Rye. She knew better than to expose a player's tells to them when it could give her an advantage, and she fully intended to come back and take them both for all they had.

"Trust me. Play the hand." Ilsa turned away, before remembering one final thing. "Oh. Where can I find Eliot Quillon?"

Georgiana looked at her quizzically. "Second floor. Last door on the right of the north corridor."

"Thanks."

Ilsa was passing the kitchen when she heard Georgiana whoop and Rye swear, and she returned to her bed with a smile playing on her lips.

*

Eliot was evidently out of bed at night and loath to be woken in the mornings, so Ilsa waited until about breakfast time to be sure of catching him.

When she reached the last door on the second-floor north corridor, she rapped loudly, waited, then rapped again to be sure she woke him. There was no reply. She pressed her ear to the door and thought she heard motion from inside, but then again, it might have been the movement of her skirts.

"Eliot?" she called, her face close to the space between the door and the frame so that it echoed back to her and resounded in the wood beneath her hand. But there was silence from the other side. Tentatively, she tried the handle. The door was locked.

She crouched and put her eye to the keyhole. There was no key in the lock, but she couldn't see much, so with a furtive glance down the corridor, she shrank.

Becoming a mouse always began with the feeling of her arms and legs being sucked into her body, and a tickling in the rims of her ears. She shrank until she began to feel the sharp aching in her bones that told her she had reached her limit.

Nervously, mouse Ilsa squeezed into the gap beneath the door, praying for better luck than last time. Her head fit fine, then her shoulders and stubby mouse legs. This gap was wider; she was going to fit. She could see a shaft of light falling across Eliot's floorboards, dust motes dancing in it, the leg of a chair or a table just beyond – a shadow moving by the window? – but somewhere around her waist the gap got too tight. Ilsa felt her heart race when her first attempt to back up got her nowhere, but a moment's frantic scrabbling of paws ejected her back into the corridor.

Defeated, she changed again. Human height and with her field of vision expanded, Ilsa realised she was no longer alone. The door across the hall had opened and Fyfe stood on the threshold, black curls falling into his eyes, a cup of coffee in one hand. He was watching her and failing to suppress his amusement.

"Good effort, but there's no door in this house anyone can fit under."

Ilsa wanted to scowl, but there was nothing mean or mocking in Fyfe's words, nor in the way his face broke into a grin, and Ilsa was grateful it was him and not Eliot who had caught her. Instead, she took her frustration out with a kick to the door. "Well, seems obvious now you say it," she grumbled.

Fyfe nudged his shoulder into his own door and it swung wide. "This one's open." He beckoned her with a hand and disappeared inside, so Ilsa followed.

She couldn't suppress a gasp as she stepped inside. Fyfe's room was a study-turned-laboratory, laid out across a main level and a makeshift mezzanine floor – little more than scaffolding accessed by a mobile spiral staircase. Bookcases covered two walls, and ladders on rollers reached to the topmost shelves high above. Another wall housed a number of units like those a pharmacy or apothecary might have, with dozens of small drawers, each with a label in a brass brace, and there was a ladder for these too. Between them, the wall was plastered with maps, diagrams, mathematical equations, and papers in languages and symbols Ilsa couldn't read. A door on the other side of the room led to what appeared to be a bedchamber.

Several contraptions bigger than herself took up most of the floor space, but there was also a table crammed with glass beakers and jars containing liquids in vibrant colours – sky blue, violet, luminescent green – some connected with glass tubes; some producing steam; one sat on a wind-up apparatus that was revolving slowly so that the contents churned. More surfaces were piled with open books and yet more unreadable papers. A human skeleton, like Ilsa had once seen in a curiosity show, hung upright in one corner, but the space was littered with other vaguely macabre objects she couldn't identify. Above, on the iron mezzanine, was what Ilsa guessed was a telescope, though she'd never seen one in person, and above that, a domed glass ceiling revealed a view of the sky.

"What kind of scientist are you?" she said, failing to mask the excitement in her voice; the room was like nothing she'd ever seen.

"I don't think I'm any kind," said Fyfe, haphazardly scooping up armfuls of the books and papers that littered the floor. "I prefer to think of myself as an investigator. It's more broad."

As Fyfe made an effort to tidy that was more just shifting clutter into new piles, Ilsa inspected an alarming glass cube. The walls of the cube contained a pattern of tubes carved into the glass, and a greenish smoke flowed gently through them. Reams of copper wire surrounded a plate at the centre, above which a single oak leaf was held in the jaws of a clamp. "What's this do?"

"Ah!" Fyfe leapt over some of the debris, looking graceless with his awkwardly long limbs, and landed beside her. Ilsa didn't know if her excitement was feeding his or vice versa, but when he beamed his huge smile, Ilsa beamed back. "I've been experimenting with increasingly complex organic matter to see if I can cause another object to pass through it, the way Wraiths can become ethereal."

Fyfe opened a hatch in one side of the cube, took a pen from behind his ear and reached in to wave it through the leaf like it was nothing but a mirage.

"I haven't found a way to replicate their other skills yet, though. And this device is really only theoretical. I tried it with a feather and only succeeded in setting it alight."

"And what 'bout that one?" Ilsa pointed to an eccentric mess of copper and vulcanised rubber on a wooden platform. Within the main frame of the apparatus were a series of cogs and belts, a row of vials of emerald liquid, and two polished copper globes in a space at the centre.

"That," said Fyfe with a self-conscious laugh, "doesn't work, but the principle is the same. Transference. Harnessing the power of another people. It's *supposed* to extract a person's thoughts."

Ilsa took a large step away from the machine. "That sounds… painful."

"No, no, no! I mean psychically. It reads their mind."

"D'you mean like a Whisperer? Eliot told me they was mind readers."

Fyfe grinned his approval. "Exactly like that! A Whisperer can see inside your mind if you don't know how to keep them out, and they can manipulate it too. They can be quite dangerous." He flicked one of the vials of emerald liquid suspended between a set of tongs, and it made a delightful ringing sound. "See, I rendered this liquor from the brain matter of a Whisperer – already deceased of course. My theory is that I can channel its properties by running an electrical current through it."

Ilsa eyed him sceptically. "And that'll work?"

Fyfe rubbed his hair. "I don't see that magic and science are all that different. If a Sorcerer can manipulate pure magic to do

167

what they want it to, then perhaps there's a way for me to do so too."

It sounded like a big dream, a long shot. But Ilsa knew a thing or two about those. She'd never wanted someone else to succeed at something so badly. "But can Sorcerers... shift and read minds and that?"

"Well, no. They can channel magic in a limited number of ways. Through objects and substances, with words, or through their bodies – corporeal magic, they call it – but not the way you and I can." Fyfe laughed an awkward laugh. "Or you, at least. I'm, ah, not a very capable shifter."

"That why you're so interested in..." *what had he called it?*

"Transference? I suppose, yes. And no." He threw himself into an armchair and swung his legs over the side. When he continued, it was with a seriousness that seemed uncharacteristic. "The implications are so much more important. If I can replicate the way the other factions use magic, there's no end to the ways Changelings could defend themselves."

Ilsa felt the weight she was carrying press heavier on her shoulders. "You mean against the Fortunatae." Fyfe's head snapped up and he eyed her curiously. "Cassia told me 'bout them. 'Bout what the Sage did to my family."

"To my family too." Fyfe slumped deeper in his chair, and was silent a long while before he added, "Hester was there. In the cellar where the Fortunatae found them." Ilsa drew in a breath. Cassia had mentioned Hester's father, but not Hester. It hadn't occurred to her that the woman had seen first-hand the things Cassia described. "She was fifteen. Gedeon was two. She saw her father and her whole family die, one by one, to protect the place they were hiding, knowing Gedeon might cry at any moment and give them away. She lost everything, and then she was alpha, and she had to pick the whole of *Camden* back up and beat back the Fortunatae and the Sage. At fifteen! People used to tell me all about what Hester had done but it never *hit* me, not until I was her age. A week before my fifteenth birthday I was drawing up a design for rigged billiard balls so I could win a stupid tournament against Aelius and Cassia and Gedeon."

Fyfe buried his face in the crook of his elbow. "And now Hester can't shift or walk and it's my fault."

Ilsa made several incoherent sounds of protest before she settled on a response. "How could it be your fault?"

"The last time the rebels attacked, they came straight for my laboratory. She was helping me defend all this," he said, gesturing around him. "Some of my technology is decades ahead of what anyone else in London has achieved. Things our enemies would be attacking us for every *day* if they knew they existed. But it wasn't that. She could have had the wolves guard my lab if that was all it was. She had to be here herself because she knew I couldn't bear to let them tear it apart."

Ilsa pictured the woman she had met the day before, with her sardonic glare and hostile demeanour. Then she thought of the fish market and the fear that had held her in place as those Oracles took hold of Martha. Hester was spiteful, but she had saved Gedeon's life as her own was destroyed, and then risked herself again for her own brother. It was better to be spiteful, thought Ilsa, with a stab in the gut, than a coward. She had nothing to judge Hester for.

"That ain't your fault, Fyfe. You din't hurt nobody. Them

rebels did that all by themselves. 'Sides, I'd have done the same as Hester if it was me." Fyfe looked up in surprise. She gestured at the lab. "P'raps you'll save all of Camden with what's in here. Show me the rest."

Fyfe's cheeks pinked, and Ilsa was relieved to coax that smile back to his face. He obligingly followed Ilsa around the laboratory and explained some of his myriad inventions; a clock that told the positions of the stars; a locking mechanism designed to open only at the owner's touch. There was a canteen that stored liquids at a fraction of their former volume. Fyfe demonstrated it by pouring nearly a gallon of water into the ordinary-looking, hand-held canteen.

"The weight of the canteen stays the same," he said, grinning at the way Ilsa stared, open-mouthed, as he emptied it again in a seemingly endless stream. "And it keeps coffee perfectly hot! Should any desert wanderers prefer coffee to water."

Ilsa was also awed by an array of brightly coloured pellets that, Fyfe explained, released a smoke that inhibited the breather's magic for a limited duration.

"I call them dampeners. Hester calls them science weapons." He rolled his eyes in affectionate amusement. "Their effect is very short-term, and I'm still working on several varieties, but I've perfected these three. The yellow are for Sorcerers, the magenta are for Psi, and the dark blue are for Whisperers."

Fyfe's most recent invention was something he called a pocket forge. It was a complicated cylinder, one or two inches in diameter to fit in the palm of the hand, and made of dull metal. At one end was a cap with a switch on one side and a tip like a gas light. Fyfe held the pocket forge at arm's length and pointed the end away from them both. When he pressed the switch a fierce, violet flame roared from the tip, making Ilsa jump. Even Fyfe flinched.

"Watch," said Fyfe over the rumble of the flame, and he jabbed the pocket forge at a point on the desk before them. For a moment, nothing happened. Then the point where the flame had touched the wood caved in on itself, dropping charred wood to the floor below and leaving a gaping hole the exact diameter of the flame. As Fyfe switched off the device, Ilsa bent close to the desk. There were two dozen such holes, each above a pale mound of something that used to be wood.

"You melted it!" said Ilsa, awed.

"The pocket forge will melt anything," said Fyfe gleefully. "It will even melt through enchanted materials, spelled to be indestructible."

No wonder Fyfe held the thing so far from himself when he turned it on.

When they reached the corner shaded by the mezzanine, Ilsa found a pinboard with a map of London. Only, it wasn't London as she knew it. This one had been split up; coloured outlines divided the city into quarters labelled The North, The Heart, Camden Town, Whitechapel, and The Docklands.

"This is your London," she said as Fyfe joined her.

"It's your London too."

Ilsa jolted to realise he was right. *Her* London.

"And these are all the quarters?" she asked, running a finger along the coloured lines.

"As of right now," said Fyfe wryly. "I have it here to keep track of any changes to the borders."

"Who lives where?"

"Well, this is us," said Fyfe, indicating the quarter outlined in red. Captain Fowler had been right; the area she knew as the borough of Camden was about half of the Changeling quarter, which also encompassed the park, a thin sliver of land between Regent Street and Tottenham Court Road, and a chunk of Westminster at the southern end. It was small compared to some of the other quarters, and wedged in like an afterthought. "And Whitechapel is the Whisperers'."

Whitechapel, outlined in midnight blue, was also misleadingly named. In the Otherworld, it was a district far east of where they were, but the Changelings and the Whisperers shared a border. Their quarter stretched several miles along the river and went as far north as the Euston-Pentonville-Hackney Road line, sweeping around Victoria Park in the east.

"And then there's the Oracles. Theirs is the Docklands."

The Docklands were marked in green, and corresponded with what Ilsa knew as The Isle of Dogs – sure enough, the docks – and the area south of the river, as well as a stretch of the north bank.

"Oracles." Ilsa ran her finger along the green line. "And they see… everything, right?"

Fyfe nodded. "The past. The present. The future too, but that's more complicated. It's a formidable magic if the individual can learn to control it, and a curse if they can't. Imagine a library containing all the knowledge of the universe, but no index cards." Fyfe seemed to reconsider his analogy and frowned. "Then imagine someone is throwing the books at you. A lot of Oracles never master their magic, and it ruins their lives."

172

Ilsa nodded, though she wasn't sure she understood, and turned back to the map.

"The Heart belongs to the Sorcerers," said Fyfe, and he indicated the quarter outlined in gold; everything west and south of Camden Town. It was three or four times the size of the Changeling quarter. "It's a conceited name, but the Callicans were a Sorcerer empire." He caught Ilsa's nonplussed stare. "The Callican empire? They founded London?"

"The *Romans* founded London."

"Agree to disagree. And then the North. That's the Wraiths'."

The North was also very large. The black line of their southern border ran the width of the Heart, Camden, and Whitechapel.

Ilsa frowned at the map. *Let's just say we're surrounded by enemies on every side.* "So then, that means the Psi..."

"Ah." Fyfe reached above the pinboard, and unrolled another map over the first. This one was made of a very thin, semi-transparent parchment, and though it fit perfectly over the other, it barely resembled it at all. The river and roads were sketched in very finely, but another set of lines crawled across the city like a spiderweb. Instead of borders in red, blue, green, gold, and black, a single magenta line ran around most of the map. "The Underground. The territory of the Psi. These are their streets," said Fyfe, indicating the new set of lines, "and their homes are carved into the earth around them. Much of what's beneath us is hollow."

Ilsa had forced herself into the tunnels of the Metropolitan Railway a few times, and never stayed for long: that panic she couldn't name or control emerged when she couldn't see her way out, merely the thought of a whole people spending their lives in the Underground made her hot and dizzy right there in the lab.

"Don't they worry the whole thing'll cave in?" said Ilsa, but Fyfe only smiled.

"That's not a danger to the Psi." He smiled wider, his eyes lighting up with excitement. "They can move objects with the power of their minds. Those with the strongest magic can do incredible things. I've seen a Psi sketch a portrait without touching the canvas. A Psi man last year held a collapsing bridge together until the traffic got to safety." He scrubbed at his hair. "Of course, the bridge only came down because the Psi and the Sorcerers and the Oracles were fighting on it."

He straightened as if something had caught his attention, and glanced around until his eyes found the carriage clock on his desk.

"Stars! I'm going to be late." He bounded into the bedchamber, letting out a string of muttered curses as something clattered to the floor. A few moments later, he emerged in a clean shirt, and began collecting up books. "I'm sorry, Ilsa. I have a class."

Ilsa frowned. "What kind of class?"

"This morning it's geology, but I'm a student of, well" – he gestured around the lab – "everything, I suppose. I'm trying to get my bachelor's degree."

"Ain't you kind of young to be a university student?"

"I'm young to be a lot of things," he said with an unapologetic grin. "Precocious, Hester says."

As Ilsa picked her way through the maze of Fyfe's eclectic creations, she had to agree. "Alright. I'll come back when Eliot's here."

Fyfe halted his bustling and grimaced. "Ah, Eliot *is* here."

"*What?*"

"He's in his rooms. I wouldn't take it personally. He prefers to keep to himself these days."

Cassia was taciturn when she spoke of Eliot, Aelius was unashamedly rude, and Oren seemed loath to acknowledge him at all. But there was something different in Fyfe's voice. Ilsa thought it might be hurt.

Her own feeling was irritation.

"P'raps I'll stay here after all," she whispered. She put her finger to her lips, then gestured at the door, and hoped Fyfe would catch her meaning.

His stifled giggle told her that he did. "I'll show you out then," he said loudly from the doorway for Eliot's benefit. "You're welcome in my lab any time, Ilsa."

Then he pulled the door to with a theatrical *thunk*, only to open it again silently. His grinning face appeared in the gap and he winked at her, before disappearing down the corridor.

Satisfied that Eliot would believe she was gone, Ilsa chose a book, sat down in Fyfe's armchair, and settled in.

She didn't have to wait long.

About an hour after Fyfe left for his class, Ilsa heard the tinkle of china, and peeked around the doorframe to see a butler with a tray at Eliot's door. He must have rung for tea.

The butler knocked, a key rattled in the lock, and he was admitted.

Ilsa discerned the murmur of a voice rough and vulnerable with sleep, and forgot all of Eliot's hard edges and sharp words. She crept silently into the hall, where she became a mouse again, and pressed her little body to the skirting board right by Eliot's door. When the butler emerged, he pulled the door closed and Eliot swiftly locked it behind him, but Ilsa was already inside.

He turned at the sound of her shifting.

"Oh, heaven, earth and all the damned constellations," Eliot groaned. Vexed, certainly, but not surprised. Ilsa was disappointed.

"Morning."

"Well, please, do come in."

The corner room was large, but it had been divided in two by a partition wall. The bigger space was an office, and had an impressive amount of clutter for the sparseness of the room; the furnishings were minimal, the walls were bare, and no opulent rugs lay over the floorboards.

There were maps, however. A large desk and a lot of floor space had been given over to them. A vast map above the fireplace depicted a land Ilsa thought she knew. On studying it she realised that it vaguely resembled the British Isles. The large lettering above said they were the *Isles of Albia*.

The mantel beneath bore a layer of undisturbed dust, and in the fireplace was a heap of ash that must have been there since the colder months. Perhaps Eliot did not let the household staff in to clean, or perhaps they refused to venture into his lair. Either was plausible.

Through an archway was a rather slapdash bedchamber. The bed was pushed up against one wall, and bore no coverlet, no runner, no decorative pillows. The covers were rumpled, like Eliot, his shirt unbuttoned at the collar and his hair mussed up. She was suddenly a little bashful to be so close to Eliot's recently vacated bed.

If he noticed where her eyes were, he gave nothing away. He folded his arms and leaned against the doorjamb, a scowl on his face. She would have to play this right. She dropped her best smile and used her sweetest voice.

"Turns out I belong to a city I don't know nothing 'bout. Cassia said if I asked nicely you might be the one to show me 'round."

"Did she now." Eliot nearly managed to suppress a smirk, but his tone alone proved he didn't believe her.

"Well someone ought to," she pressed.

"Perhaps. But I have more important things to do than…" He made a vague gesture in the air that turned into rubbing his eyes. "Settle you in."

"You said you had jack to do."

He stilled, and looked up at her from between his fingers. "Did I?"

"You specifically asked to be woken when you was needed."

He rolled his eyes petulantly, like it was most unfair to use his own words against him.

"How am I s'posed to help you find Gedeon if I don't know—"

"*Help?*" His glare would have sent a more nervous person scurrying for the door. "You can't possibly help."

Ilsa drew herself up and folded her arms. "You din't think I'd spent my whole bloody life looking for my family to stop now, did you?"

Eliot didn't answer and Ilsa tamped down her frustration. She was well-practised in bending boys to her will, but this boy had no give. So she changed tack.

"Alright, Cassia din't say you'd take me 'round London."

"I'm shocked."

"She told me to ask you 'bout Gedeon."

He narrowed his eyes. "What?"

"You heard. The others act strange with you. You're in everyone's bad books, ain't you? Why?"

Eliot studied her, and smiled slowly. "Isn't it obvious? They think I know where their prince is."

"Do you?"

He blinked. "You're awfully direct," he bit out.

"What else was I s'posed to ask?"

"You want to know if I've been keeping a monumental secret from the people who rely on me, for over a month? You could have hesitated, just a touch."

178

"They believe it. And they know you better than me."

"Well observed," he said darkly. "You might have a knack for this sort of thing after all."

If it demonstrated a knack to note that Eliot hadn't answered the question, then perhaps she did. "And why'd they think that?"

Eliot shrugged away from the doorframe with a sigh. "Because of the wolves," he said. "I was their commander under Gedeon. I can't fault anyone for finding it suspicious that twelve of them vanished in the night and I knew nothing about it."

You shall have to ask Alpha Hester who the wolves answer to these days.

"Suspicious. Or incompetent. You *are* really young to be commanding anything."

Eliot drew up short and raised an eyebrow. "I see they didn't teach you manners in the Otherworld," he said.

Ilsa stood her ground as he prowled to within reach of her. That fierce gaze studied her, but she was gratified to see him fail to come to any conclusions.

"More to the point," he said in a low voice. "Cassia's not the only one who thought your brother told me everything."

He turned to the tea tray and poured a cup, but Ilsa had already seen his hurt.

"You ain't in charge of the wolves no more?"

Eliot lowered himself gracefully into a chair and raised his cup in a salute. "Hence my becoming a man of leisure. Hester's been admirably dedicated to her policy of refusing to lead us, but she made one exception when she used her authority to remove me from my post."

"Because she thinks you got something to do with this too."

Eliot's free hand slipped his handsome silver watch from his pocket and flicked the case open and closed. Ilsa kept her face impassive, but she was certain this time that she had discovered Eliot's tell. Whatever he said next would be a lie.

"She never approved of me in the first place," he said into his tea. "This matter was just an excuse."

So not about the missing wolves at all, then. She had believed him when he said the others thought he was involved in Gedeon's disappearance. She had believed it *before* then. But there was something else between Hester and Eliot. Her cousin had other reasons not to trust him, and Eliot knew what they were.

"And now you're idle," Ilsa baited.

He was silent a moment. Ilsa was reminded again of cards; of waiting for her opponent to lay his bet.

"Not exactly. I think I know a little of what Gedeon has been up to. Here." He rose gracefully and indicated for Ilsa to follow him to a desk, where several newspapers were splayed. "Shortly after Gedeon vanished, there was a raid on a chemist in the Heart. Then another. A week later, another." He lifted each story in turn and tossed them down in front of Ilsa. "Six in total. No money was taken. Most of the stock was untouched. Only vemanta was stolen. When the chemists replenished their stock, the raiders hit them all again."

"I never heard of vemanta," said Ilsa. "What's this got to do with Gedeon?"

"I'm coming to that. No, you wouldn't have heard of vemanta. Strange as it may seem, the flower we derive it from does not grow in the Otherworld, but I believe one can compare it to a poppy."

"Like opium, then."

"It's almost exactly like opium," said Eliot. "Available in any chemist, useful as a pain reliever or to help one sleep in small doses, but addictive. Do you know why someone would steal it all?"

Ilsa picked up the topmost story and scanned it. Smash and grab. Locks forced. Windows broken. It seemed Sorcerer shop keepers had sophisticated, magic ways of raising the alarm when they were robbed, but it had done them no good. The thieves were fast, knew what they were looking for, and vanished before anyone arrived.

"Someone with a habit?" said Ilsa. "I hear you're really sleepy these days."

Eliot grimaced. "That's some habit. And you don't have a very high opinion of me, do you?"

"I'm still deciding," she replied, staring at him straight on.

One corner of Eliot's mouth pulled up into a smirk. "You know what it means to be an Oracle, don't you?"

"Fyfe said something 'bout having books thrown at you." Eliot didn't have an answer for that. Ilsa shrugged. "I din't get it neither."

"An Oracle's magic is tremendously powerful yet impossibly difficult to wield. From the moment an Oracle is born, they See the whole past, the whole present, and the future as it will be at any given moment, of everything and everyone on earth, all at once."

Eliot paused, as if to give her a moment to consider it, and Ilsa was silent a while as she pretended to. "I still don't get it."

"Because you and I can never truly conceive of what it's like.

We experience time as linear, and our perception is fixed in place – it's limited to what information we can gather with our senses. Neither is true for an Oracle. An Oracle in Kensington, say, can See a kitchen of a lumberjack's cottage in Northern Tuman—"

"Where, now?"

"—not just in this moment, but in every single moment of time for as long as that cottage has stood. They can See the spot where it was built before any non-Oracle knew the place existed, when it was the feeding ground of creatures long extinct."

"If that's true, and they See *everything*, why ain't they running the show?"

Eliot smiled grimly. "Because they See it all at once, all the time, and they cannot shut it off. Imagine you're standing in a crowded room. You close your eyes and you try to pick out a single voice, no louder or closer than any of the others, and you try to focus on it. Imagine simply trying to hear your *own* inner voice amidst all the noise. Oracles call it the Glare. A blinding, indiscriminate deluge of space and time. For most, it doesn't mean power at all, it means madness."

"So what's all this got to do with vemanta?"

"Disorientation, sleeplessness, a loss of touch with reality. The hallucinations are the real kick in the teeth, if you ask me. As if it's not enough to be crushed under the weight of your Sight, flounder down there long enough and you won't even know which visions are real any more. It's no wonder so many of them choose to surrender their minds. Most surrender theirs to vemanta. Nothing dulls the mind, and thus an Oracle's magic, quite like it."

Ilsa had never been more glad to know so little. It staggered her that the Oracles could believe in the sanctity of a magic that was so… *broken*.

"So, Oracles robbed them chemists?" she said, puzzled.

Eliot smiled knowingly. "No Oracle with a pressing need for a fix is capable of a methodical, sustained operation like this, but Gedeon is."

Ilsa frowned at the papers spread in front of her again. The more she learned of her brother, the less honourable he seemed. "Why would he be stealing vemanta?"

"Control the vemanta, control the Oracles who need it. The Heart have had a monopoly on the city's vemanta supply for decades and it's made them very rich. They channel it mainly through their own chemists of course, to keep the money in the quarter, and sell just enough elsewhere to appease all the right people. These six chemists were all in the Heart. These" – he dropped another cluster of papers in front of her – "were in Whitechapel. Four more chemists, relieved of their supply. After the second lot of raids, they started redirecting their surplus there, and the same thing happened." He returned to his chair and sank into it. "An Oracle with a habit is a minute fraction as useful as a sentient one, but far cheaper to buy, and with time and the right incentive, most will magic up the answers one needs. I assume that was Gedeon's plan with these raids."

"But how d'you know it's Gedeon what's robbing these chemists?"

"Because I gave him the idea."

Ilsa narrowed her eyes at him. "So you do know where he is."

Her expression of scorn was mirrored back at her. "It's a years-old trick. I invented it when we were just boys and shared it with Gedeon. Create a scarcity of vemanta – block its sale, buy it up ourselves, steal it even – and win a little cooperation from some of the Oracles. We used it a couple of times, on a smaller scale, but Gedeon has gone all out this time. I'm positive this is his doing. If we can find where the vemanta is resurfacing, we can find him. There's a chemist somewhere in this city who has cut a deal with Gedeon, and their Oracle patrons are at his mercy."

Ilsa studied him, then the mess of research piled on the desk. Aelius thought he was sleeping past noon. "You ain't told the others this."

Eliot stilled. The pocket watch found its way back into his hand. Between his fingers, Ilsa spotted a fragment of an inscription: *your Athena.* "Do you trust them? Hester's other lieutenants."

Ilsa hesitated. She weighed her options, but Eliot's gaze – patient, expectant, and unambiguous – told her there was no point being coy. He knew she'd formed opinions. He wouldn't believe they were all good. "I think I trust Fyfe," she said slowly. Maybe she'd been pulled in by his kindness, but she could read his every emotion too easily to believe he could deceive her. The others... I ain't sure."

"That makes two of us," said Eliot, fingers tightening around the watch, and the hairs on the back of Ilsa's neck prickled. He was lying. "I don't need their help with this. Every strategy and scheme Gedeon has in his arsenal he learned from me, so I'm the one who knows how to react to whatever move he makes. The others... they'll want to find Gedeon their way; the way that's been failing since he vanished.

"Besides," he added under Ilsa's continued scrutiny, "there's

184

nothing I have to say that the others will hear from me right now."

The last was probably true. But Eliot wasn't telling her everything. Perhaps there was a reason for the others not to trust him, but if Ilsa was to figure out what it was, she needed more time with him.

"So," she said, "we just got to find which chemist."

"Very good," he drawled. "And how, pray tell, do we do that?"

Ilsa shot his condescension right back at him. "*Well*, in the Otherworld London, chemists make or buy their stock in bulk and decant it into tins and bottles and that. Then they put *their own labels* on the tins and bottles."

Understanding dawned in Eliot's eyes. "Tins of vemanta are usually stamped on the base, right into the metal. If it was packaged elsewhere, we should be able to tell." He gave her an evaluating look. But this time, when he shook his head like she was a puzzle, Ilsa thought it might be a puzzle he was starting to put together. "But there are too many chemists."

"Then we better make a start. His chemist is probably in Camden, right?"

Eliot was pensive. "It wouldn't be ridiculous to assume so. That's how we've done it before. A few likely shops come to mind."

"So?"

"So." Eliot put his cup down slowly, and stood. "No time like the present."

"Guess you're showing me 'round after all," said Ilsa, bouncing tauntingly on the balls of her feet.

Eliot swept up his jacket. He turned to look back as he prowled to the door and, to Ilsa's bewilderment, smiled at her. "Would you look how that worked out."

III

THE GREAT
WHITE SHARK
Carcharodon carcharias

Of the family Lamnidae, from the Greek lamna,
meaning fish of prey. Possessing a formidable sense
of smell, the great white can scent its prey from a
distance of up to three miles.

I 4

Eliot was adamant that Ilsa wear a disguise to leave the Zoo.

"But why?" she protested, arms crossed. "How are the Oracles gonna get me in Camden?"

The grand front entrance to the Zoo let them out to the north of the house, where Regent's Canal formed a moat. Two wolves – in wolf form, and fiercely large – guarded a bridge across it. Eliot led Ilsa into the centre of the forecourt; the same spot she and Oren had taken flight from on her last excursion.

"A disguise won't stop the Oracles from knowing you've left the safety of the Zoo," Eliot said. "That's not the point. The point is you look like a Ravenswood. You're the image of Lyander."

"So?"

Eliot's scowl deepened with each of Ilsa's questions. "I thought Cassia told you everything," he said accusingly, like her purpose was to rile him.

"*Clearly*, she din't."

Eliot ran an exasperated hand over his face. "Ilsa Ravenswood is a rumour, like Gedeon being missing. The news of your mother's pregnancy was guarded closely. There are no secrets in a city full of Oracles and Whisperers, but there's no need to hand anyone proof of what they think they know. Now…"

Before she could mention that she had already walked from Westminster Abbey to Regent's Park wearing her own face and that perhaps he was being overly cautious, Eliot shifted.

When Ilsa had passed through the portal and learned of other Changelings, she had also learned that the way each of them shifted was unique. Her own motion when she changed was smooth, and rolled up her body from her feet to her head. Oren would fold in on himself then burst abruptly into a new form. She had seen wolves around the Zoo who shifted like an avalanche and those who shivered into new skins.

Eliot was like lightning, so quick he made a *snap* sound. Ilsa had barely registered that the boy was now a hawk before he was above the house and away. She shifted herself and raced after him.

They flew south – Ilsa revelling in the warm air tickling her feathers and taking in the sun-bright city below – and landed on the street in Bloomsbury, where she became a dark-haired, almond-eyed version of herself.

"That why they hid me in the Otherworld? To keep me a rumour?"

Ilsa was ready for Eliot to complain of more questions, but it was worse when he didn't. Her tone had given away the hurt she couldn't help feeling when she thought of ending up in the orphanage. He gave her an opaque look.

"You know you were never supposed to be lost there," he said quietly.

Ilsa did know that. As easy as it would be, she could not blame anyone in the Witherward for thinking she was dead. The single architect of her years of misery at the orphanage was Miss Mitcham, and Ilsa hated that the woman could still cause her fresh pain, eight years on from her escape. The only way she would rise above it was to stop thinking of *supposed to* or *should have*. Nothing could be undone.

Eliot self-consciously straightened his jacket, his brow knotted. "I know. It doesn't help you," he said, unwittingly knocking her off-kilter. To have her thoughts exposed, and by a boy who was such a mystery himself, was an uncomfortable shock.

"Which way?" she said coolly.

Eliot's storm-blue gaze found hers again, and he looked like he might say something more, but he only inclined his head for her to follow, and started in the direction of Great Russell Street.

"I was a baby when your family was killed," Eliot continued after a few minutes' silence. His voice was tentative. "But I think hiding you in the Otherworld was the only choice your parents had left. Your mother had made a decision to protect her son and it ended up killing her. I suppose when she had Gedeon, she saw what he'd been born into with new eyes, and she realised London had two choices: to eat itself slowly until nothing remained for any of us, or find a way for each faction to mind its own business if it chose. That was why she proposed the Principles."

"Right, 'bout those," said Ilsa. "I read up on all the things you ain't allowed to do, and you're all doing them! The Principles say the factions can't have armies, right? But the Zoo's got the wolves, and the Oracles have got the acolytes. Captain Fowler's a *captain*, and he din't look like police to me."

"Law enforcement." Eliot tilted his head, as if indulging in a daydream. "What a quaint idea. The thing the faction leaders who drafted the Principles knew at the time – the thing your mother knew – is that they are an exercise in finding the loophole. Take the army rule. The Docklands acolytes are just that; they're dedicates. The Zoo invites wolves to join as members of a syndicate and earn a share of any profits we make in trade. There just isn't trust enough to lay down the law and rest easy in the knowledge that your enemies will keep to it. If the Principles were an iron-clad and binding rulebook, no one would have agreed to them." Eliot's expression darkened. "She was trying to create some order. And the Sage used it and twisted it to unite anyone who favoured bloodlust against her."

Ilsa's stomach twisted. She could see it now; the chain of events her own mother had started that led to her family's downfall. She had been trying to make a better world for her son. Eliot stopped in front of Edward Kelley's Dispensary and motioned her to follow him inside. "This is it."

There was a queue for the counter, but at a glance, it was obvious none of the patrons were Oracles. Was this a discouraging sign?

Eliot leaned over her shoulder to whisper as they waited. "Remember, we're just here to buy a tin of vemanta and be on our way. Don't do anything to draw attention."

Ilsa turned around, affronted by Eliot's insinuation, a few choice words on the tip of her tongue. At the same moment, the bell above the door jingled as a woman entered. The queueing patrons shuffled to make room in the small shop, squeezing together until Eliot was pressed close enough that, despite his best efforts, Ilsa felt the brush of his chest against hers.

Her breath caught at the unexpected shiver that skittered across her skin; her eyes met Eliot's at the moment she realised he had noticed.

Ilsa staggered back. Her heel caught the hem of her dress, and she would have lost her balance, but Eliot's hands shot out to grasp her firmly, warm fingers closing around her hands.

"Anything like *that*," he said roughly, eyes sliding to the woman who was tutting at their inappropriate display.

Ilsa huffed as she freed herself and turned to face the counter. It was hardly her fault the chemist's was too cramped. Far too cramped. And too warm. Warmer still when Eliot pressed close again and brought his mouth near her ear. "I thought magician's assistants were supposed to be graceful."

He was taunting her now; she could hear the cruel amusement in his whisper. She was about to risk a reprimand a second time when the person ahead of her stepped aside and they reached the front of the queue, where the sign on the counter was impossible to miss:

WE DO NOT STOCK VEMANTA
THANK YOU

Recovering, Ilsa placed her hands on her hips. Perhaps this was a lead after all. "There a secret passcode or something?"

"Don't," muttered Eliot, but she ignored him. The clerk was sweeping his gaze over her. He broke into a grin.

"For you?" he said, leaning across the counter. "Perhaps we can work something out."

Ilsa mirrored his body language and lowered her voice conspiratorially. "I can pay extra. Only, I heard there might be a supply surfacing somewhere 'round here."

"Stars," said Eliot under his breath, exasperated, and the clerk's eyes darted to him. Ilsa cursed inwardly. She didn't need to follow his gaze to know what he saw: hard lines, intimidating eyes, and a disapproving scowl. She'd bet he had his hands in his pockets like some common thug. The clerk straightened formally, any designs on her repressed, and shook his head. "Sorry, miss. Mr Kelley decided to run his supply down and wait out the burglaries."

Ilsa scrutinised him. "That the truth?"

He frowned. "'Course it's the truth."

"Fine. Thanks for your time, then."

She turned on her heel and made for the door, not waiting for Eliot to catch her up.

*

The second chemist Eliot thought likely was just north of Euston Road, in a glass-topped arcade near St Pancras Station.

"You'd think a Changeling boy'd be more suspicious of the way a girl looks," Ilsa said as they weaved through the shoppers in the arcade. "My right eye was twitching like mad and he din't even notice."

"He saw the way you look. I don't think he cared if it was your true form."

Ilsa lowered her voice. "But ain't everyone making them-selves prettier than they are?" She squinted at an attractive young couple, trying to ascertain if their skins were their own.

"Working girls, maybe."

"Know all 'bout that, do you?" She took his affronted expression as a no. "You telling me you're just less vain this side of the portal?"

"When everyone can have a perfect face, one starts to see the beauty in a normal one. Or a strange one, even. I'm sure even in

193

the Otherworld, beauty quickly loses its shine. Unfortunately for the likes of you."

Eliot's expression turned stony as he heard what he'd said too late, and Ilsa grinned. It was her turn to taunt.

"What's that 'bout my perfect face?" she said with exaggerated sweetness.

"That's what you took from that warning?" He countered quickly. "Wait a second." He glanced left and right, then pulled her around a corner so they were alone. "Take the disguise off a moment."

"You said I had to wear it."

"I know."

"You said not to hand no one the proof of what they think they know."

"Are you a parrot often? Just take it off."

Eliot's smile made her do it. She hadn't imagined the boy she'd woken that morning was capable of taking a teasing as well as he could dish it out, and yet her teasing had somehow coaxed a less cautious, more human Eliot from inside the monster, and she liked it.

He stood before her real face and looked at her straight on. *Really* looked at her, like he was deciphering a cryptic puzzle in the paper. Ilsa suddenly wasn't sure who was teasing whom. She didn't feel like the one in control.

"Your eyes are too big," he said after too long. "And you only have one dimple." He shrugged. "Your face *is* rather strange, come to think of it."

"Guess I'll take that as a compliment," Ilsa said, finding her voice had gone liquid and warm. She slipped back into her disguise. "You look like I'd cut myself on you, and that's just your normal face. Don't get me started on your smile."

Eliot did smile, in full force. He smiled like a boy who knew just how ferocious a full grin made him look. "And it serves me well."

*

They had more luck at their second destination, though they paid a premium for one of the stockist's very last tins. But once outside the shop, they examined the tin and concluded, to Eliot's renewed irritation, that it was the chemist's own.

"Alright, where else would he go?" said Ilsa.

"I'm out of ideas." Eliot rubbed his eyes, then looked skyward. "How many chemists in Camden? A dozen? Two dozen maybe?"

Ilsa nodded seriously. "I can flirt with that many shop boys if I got to."

Eliot continued to frown. "If we still don't have a lead once we've swept the quarter…"

"Then we make a new plan. Which way?"

Eliot nodded, but he didn't look reassured. "North. It's not far. We can walk."

They left the arcade and headed back in the direction of the park. Ilsa was glad to be walking. It gave her a chance to talk.

"You said something that night in the park," she said once she'd built up the courage. "'Bout when you all thought I was dead."

Eliot shot her a wary glance. "I told you, most of what I said was second hand."

"Right. Which is why I kept thinking 'bout this one thing. You said you remembered it specifically."

His paced slowed. "Oh. I told you that Walcott's housekeeper had said she was holding Ilsa Ravenswood when she died." Ilsa didn't have to ask her next question: how he knew. Eliot sighed and ran a hand over his face. "When we were very young, Gedeon asked about his family a lot. Hester was never his guardian officially, she was too young, but she's always made herself impossible to say no to, and she wouldn't have him coddled. He knew his mother and father had been murdered, and that he'd had a sister who died in infancy. But you know the way children can be when they develop a fixation, especially when they can sense a bigger truth. Gedeon was always pushing Hester or Oren over some minor detail of the story. It was such an obsession that it rubbed off on me too. At the ages of seven and eight, our main pastime was unravelling the things we hadn't been told about what happened to you all. It became a game." He hesitated. "Perhaps you don't want to hear this."

Ilsa was jolted. Why was he suddenly reluctant? "I asked, din't I?"

"But… alright. Eventually Gedeon and I wore everyone down. Hester's never talked about seeing your family killed and I don't think she ever will, but she allowed Oren to tell Gedeon everything he knew. I wasn't allowed to be there. I'll let you imagine how well eight-year-old me dealt with the exclusion, even though I knew Gedeon would repeat it all for me.

"I found him afterwards. There's a tree in the park with a perfect cradle at the centre of the branches. He used to fly up and hide there. I asked him what Oren had said and he told me. He skimmed over the details of the cellar and your family's deaths. Maybe it was too overwhelming. Most likely Oren had skimmed over them too, but I clearly remember thinking it was strange how he hardly dwelt on it. He was caught up with you.

"There was no kindness in what happened to your family," he said roughly. He spoke to his feet as he walked, overcome at the thought of that night the same way he was in the park when they met. "Perhaps that's why the fact someone had cared for you in your final days always stuck with Gedeon. Oren said Walcott's housekeeper had done everything she could to save you, and when she failed, she had held you and rocked you until you stopped breathing. The reason I remember it so well is because Gedeon remembers it. He's repeated it to me since, several times. When he hurts over his sister's death, he remembers that someone had some kindness for her and that he's grateful."

Grateful. The word gutted her. It was everything Miss Mitcham didn't deserve.

"And now it turns out every word of it was a lie," said Eliot with a brittle laugh. "It was false comfort."

Ilsa shook her head. "Comfort's never false," she said, even as fresh pain welled up and made her voice shake. She wanted to be a person who could be glad Gedeon had had comfort, even if it meant he'd had goodwill for Miss Mitcham. She *wanted* to be that person, but she wasn't sure she could. "Or p'raps it's always false. It's just how we choose to think of something, after all, ain't it? Comfort's in our heads."

Eliot was studying her warily. Ilsa could see him warring with his curiosity before he spoke. "After you left the meeting room yesterday, the others were wondering if perhaps she'd grown attached. That she told a foolish lie because she wanted to keep you for her own."

"There's an idea. Keep an orphanage open by making orphans."

Her tone must have given away just how wrong the theory was. Eliot grimaced. "I didn't think so. She told you nothing of magic or the Witherward, though she knew of Lord Walcott and your parents, and the portal." He looked at her bleakly. "It's like I said, children can always sense a bigger truth. If she had cared for you at all, she would have given in and told you eventually. But she let you believe you were alone. It was cruel. And the lie wasn't foolish, it was malicious."

Once again, the look he gave her brooked no argument. He had parsed the truth from the few reluctant hints Ilsa had shared and she couldn't take them back. If she had known he would think on it, she might have been more careful. Only, she hadn't thought him capable of caring.

"As *I* said," Ilsa replied quietly, "she ain't a good woman."

"No," agreed Eliot.

Fearing he might probe further, Ilsa asked something else she had been thinking on. "What was Lord Walcott doing in the Otherworld?"

Eliot raised his eyebrows. "Stars. Fleeing this mess? Making his fortune? I'm afraid I don't know that much about him."

"You weren't curious? Weren't it strange?"

Eliot laughed; a rare, unpoisoned laugh. "That a person might choose a life in another universe? That they might look at a portal out of here and simply decide to" – he threw up a hand in a gesture that dismissed everything around him – "step through it?"

"Are there a lot of them?" Ilsa said. "People from here living over there?"

Eliot was still disbelieving. He looked at her like he was trying to grasp her meaning. "It must seem a strange decision to you," he said eventually. "That anyone with magic would choose to live somewhere where it would be sensible to hide it. But that can be a benefit itself. Look what it did for you. You made a career of exploiting the Otherworlders' ignorance. A Wraith could be the best sportsperson while barely using their magic at all. A Whisperer could be a star detective without anyone ever knowing they could read their suspects' minds. Besides, some of them have no other choice."

"What d'you mean?"

"It's a convenient punishment for those who haven't earned death," he said. "We don't banish our undesirables from the city, we banish them from the world." His mouth twisted wryly. "Some punishment. You've been bad even amongst the terrible, here's your guilt-free pass to somewhere better."

"Don't be an idiot," said Ilsa. "People have got... *people*, you know. Families, homes, jobs. P'raps they don't want to be somewhere better. And why the hell should they, when their whole life's *here*?"

Eliot didn't reply. She didn't look at him, but she could feel his gaze; she could hear him drawing breath to speak then changing his mind.

"I did not mean that banishment itself isn't a bitter punish-ment," he said gently. "In fact, being forced into the Otherworld should hardly count. No law in this city means no true authority. If one wished, one could board a ship to the continent and slip back into this dimension there." Ilsa didn't miss how his gaze tracked east, as if he could see it if it weren't for the city around him. He was wistful as he added, "Paris has a portal."

"Let me guess. It's at the top of the Eiffel Tower." Eliot

looked at her strangely. "What, no Eiffel Tower?"

"There's an Eiffel Dam – I haven't heard of any tower."

Once again, this new information raised more questions than it answered. "You ever seen it?"

"*When* would I have seen it, pray tell? In one of the months when the Changelings haven't needed a militia force, perhaps?"

"Looks to me like the Changeling's militia force don't need you no more," Ilsa teased.

To Eliot's credit, he looked like he *tried* to resist glowering in response. "I hold out hope that this reprieve will be too short for a tour of the continent." His words made the claim, but his tone told another story. Eliot would see the continent, and probably beyond, on both sides of the portal if he could.

He slowed, something snagging his attention, and he smirked. "Look."

Ilsa followed his line of sight to a building under construction across the street. "That where we're going?"

"That's a building site, Ilsa. Just look at it."

Ilsa did. The building had been partly raised, its frame climbing five of six storeys and shrouded on all sides by scaffolding. The walls of the first floor were complete, and those of the second were under way. Above them, beams were being hoisted – albeit with impressive speed – but there was nothing else to see.

Except for the builders. The mechanisms of manual labour were nowhere to be seen: no lifting, no motion, not a trowel or shovel or hammer in sight. Instead, ten or fifteen men stood, sat, and lounged on the frame and walls of the building – doing nothing. And yet the work continued around them. Ilsa almost stepped into traffic to get closer to the ropeless beams floating upwards, and the self-assembling bricks as they piled on top of one another. The building was making itself.

"Is this sorcery?" she said, entranced.

Eliot laughed softly. "The Sorcerers can only dream of psychokinetic power like this. In their centuries of study, they have never been able to replicate what the Psi can do." *The Psi*. The dwellers of the Underground. "The work of these Psi builders is cerebral. Watch them. Watch their faces."

The nearest man was perched between a vertical beam and a diagonal one like a child in a tree. His leg swung casually, and his head rested on the wood behind him, but his eyes were focused. They followed a succession of bricks as they floated from a barrow and rested in the mortar of the wall he was building. Ilsa's eyes widened and her heart rate spiked, the wonder of it almost too much to bear.

The builder angled his head towards the sun, and a flash of white light reflected off his brow like sunlight on the ripples of the Thames. Ilsa got closer, and as the Psi man worked, a pattern of silver swirls pulsed across his brow, his temples, his cheekbones. It appeared inlaid, as if an artist had carved his skin and poured molten metal into the grooves. She turned her attention to another of the builders. He had similar markings, but his appeared as scars; he was not using his psychokinetic power.

"The markings exist from birth," said Eliot. "They say no two are identical."

Ilsa was barely listening any more. Something she had always wished to understand was falling into place. Bill Blume's wife had needed to cover her face when she performed.

Because she had been Psi.

A nostalgic grief wrapped itself around her, but there was comfort too. She suddenly knew her magician better than ever before, even though he was gone. She wondered what Blume would think if he could see where she was now, and that she had found the answers she'd been looking for.

Her parents had left plenty of things to learn about them too, and one of them was Gedeon. No, it didn't matter if they couldn't find this chemist in Camden. Ilsa would find a way. She had to.

"Ilsa?"

Her head snapped to Eliot, who was watching her with grim concern. She had almost forgotten he was there.

"It's nothing." She shook her head. "Let's go."

Their next destination was a shop called McCormick & Castor. In a coincidence she couldn't fathom, Ilsa knew it well, due to there being a duplicate in the Otherworld – a shop by the name of *McConnell* & Castor.

"It's called a weak spot," said Eliot when Ilsa voiced her astonishment. "The thinner the fabric between the two worlds, the stronger the similarities. London sits on a weak spot, and patches of it" – he gestured to the shop – "are weaker still. Then there are the portals, where the fabric breaks entirely."

"*Portals?* There's more than one?"

"There are five. Only the Psi don't have one in their quarter."

They were about to cross the street and enter the chemist's when an Oracle rounded the corner, and Ilsa tugged Eliot to a halt.

Ilsa recognised her; it was the girl she and Captain Fowler had passed on the street the day she arrived. Her fuzzy, violently orange hair formed a halo underneath her bonnet, and her sunken cheeks gave her the appearance of a ventriloquist's puppet; the clunky jaw too pronounced beneath the hollows. She was shrouded beneath a threadbare shawl, but still she trembled with cold. Ilsa knew enough working girls with a weakness for the pipe to recognise this as a symptom.

If the girl noticed Ilsa and Eliot, she thought nothing of them. Her gaze was on her hands, wringing at her breast, her chin tucked tightly to her neck. She stepped into the chemist's, and the door swung closed behind her, bell tinkling.

"Let's wait until she leaves," said Eliot, leaning back against the wall. "It's better if you don't get too close."

"Why?"

"An Oracle's visions of someone or something are stronger when that person or thing is close. Places, too."

Did that explain the way the girl had noticed her on the street the day she arrived in the Witherward? "But she's a vemanta user, ain't she? Don't that mean she's… living in the Glare or whatever?"

Eliot leaned his head back against the wall and closed his eyes. "That's exactly why it's best to keep your distance. A trained Oracle would be better able to suppress visions concerning the things or people they touched, unless they wished to see them. Suppressing their magic is the first thing Oracles learn."

Knowing what she did about the curse of Oracle magic, Ilsa found this unsurprising. She nodded at the chemist. "And she ain't learned that?"

Eliot grimaced. "It's ironic. One would think a people with such an unparalleled grasp of the mechanisms of fate would have less affinity for the self-fulfilling prophecy. The Oracles believe their magic is sacred, and those who can wield it are chosen by the gods. When an Oracle is born, another will See into their future and determine their capacity for controlling their magic. Those deemed to have little capacity – more than *half*, most likely including the girl in there – are forsaken. They're abandoned to a lifetime in the Glare. They're the ones who often turn to vemanta. If they're deemed to have adequate strength and mental acuity, they are taught how to *not* use their magic; how to amplify the here and now and minimise the Glare in the hopes of leading a halfway normal existence. Only if they're exceptional will they start to learn a specific skill. The acolytes, for example. They're trained in combat, so they learn how to concentrate on the immediate future and See their opponent's next move. It's an inexact science, of course. Every time they use their magic in combat, they change the fight."

"How?"

Eliot ran a hand over his face. "It's… complex."

"Try me," said Ilsa, folding her arms. "I ain't simple."

Eliot was quiet a moment as he considered it. "You and I can't act to change the future directly," he said slowly. "We're destined to take whatever course it is we're going to take, but if an Oracle Sees that course, they can try to change it. If their magic tells them you're going to lunge for their right, they can step left, but then *you* will react to the change they've made, you see?"

"I ain't gonna lunge for their right if it ain't there no more."

"Exactly. So as the acolyte steps left, the future changes. And perhaps they'll See that too…"

"But in the meantime, I've whipped them off their feet with my tail."

Eliot smiled. "So you see the bind. Fighting takes presence and concentration, and Seeing demands their focus is elsewhere, on the moment ahead. Yes, their magic can grant an advantage, but balancing the two introduces plenty of room for error." He laughed sardonically. "If you ask me, acolytes are fodder. They teach them nothing but combat, out of fear they could turn against them. When your militia's family are all poverty-stricken addicts because you refuse to care for them, you don't run the risk of arming them with the full strength of their own magic. An eternity of knowledge – past, present, and future – and all an acolyte knows how to See is the next few seconds.

"Of course, Seeing further into the future becomes even more fraught. There are countless Oracles out there making changes according to what they See, then others make changes to those changes and so on. Some are small, some have implications that stretch on for centuries. Those Oracles skilled in prophecy tend to spend their days studying what might have been and writing furious scripture about who among them should be allowed to act against the future.

"But among the most highly prized Oracles are the ones who study the present moment."

"What's so special 'bout that? I can see the present moment just fine and I ain't even an Oracle."

"You can see the present moment *here*," said Eliot. "Imagine the value of Seeing what the Sage was up to this very moment."

"Oh."

"Exactly. But the difficulties in using that type of Sight are manifold. Simply keeping their grasp on the thing they wish to See is a challenge. The present is in motion. It's much harder to stay focused on it than it is to look into the past."

"I'll say," muttered Ilsa, whose head was starting to hurt. She looked at the chemist. "So you reckon if I get too close, she might know her militia friends are looking for me?"

"It's a distinct possibility."

"That's unfortunate, 'cause I got an idea. Make yourself invisible."

He looked at her like she'd gone mad. "I don't know what kind of Changeling you are, but *invisible* isn't in my repertoire."

"Not like that. Watch me."

A couple of shops down was a greengrocer, and Ilsa concealed herself in the shadow of its striped awning, where she made herself invisible. It didn't take much; in both Londons, people in the street barely paid attention to each other anyway. She dulled the shine from her hair, leached the pink from her cheeks and lips, and made herself a couple of inches shorter. The rest was just misdirection, the kind she used on stage when she wanted the audience to look elsewhere. Hunched shoulders, eyes downcast, no large or sudden movements. Looking awed and confused, Eliot followed suit.

When the girl re-emerged from the chemist, empty-handed, she passed them like they weren't even there, and did not look around when they started following at a distance.

"I have no idea where you're going with this and it still feels like a bad idea," Eliot said under his breath.

"I got us this far, din't I?" Ilsa said in a whisper, as the girl made a right turn and descended the steps to a basement flat.

Even from street level, Ilsa knew where they were. No curtain hung in the front windows, but what looked like blankets had been strung up to keep out the light; the ramshackle door had a latch but no handle or lock, for ease of coming and going; and a beguiling floral scent with an undertone of human grime clung to the air.

This was an opium den. Or rather, a vemanta den.

She made to follow the girl down the steps, but Eliot stepped into her path. "What are you doing?"

"I'm going to talk to her."

Eliot laughed incredulously. "You can't go down there."

Ilsa crossed her arms to keep from punching him, and scowled. "I'll do what I please."

"Stars, Ilsa, you want to put yourself amongst a group of lowlifes whose leaders want you dead," he said, exasperated. "If anyone in there Sees that, we'll be surrounded. It's pointless anyway. Oracles are very superstitious, the pipe-smoking type especially. It violates the laws of their faith to share knowledge with non-Oracles."

"For one thing," countered Ilsa, "these *pipe-smoking* types ain't gonna know me from Queen Victoria. It's an opium den. And for another, going places what upsets you proper speaking, feather bed, afternoon tea rich folk is how *I'm* gonna to be the one to find Gedeon." With that, she turned into a blackbird, zipped over Eliot's head, and landed at the bottom of the stairs. "You coming or not?"

Eliot glared and prowled down the steps. "You know they speak in riddles?"

"Guess you won't be able to understand her then. Let me handle it." She lifted the latch and they slipped inside.

The flat was oppressively quiet, in a way that evoked the

muffle of thick fabric or heavy snow. Smoke hung thickly in the air. It curled in a shaft of light that reached for them from the end of the corridor, where a sheet imperfectly shrouded the back door. Low lights in red sconces guided them through a bead curtain and into a room carpeted with thin mattresses, most of which were unoccupied. Gedeon's raids must have disturbed the supply all over the city – just as he had intended.

Not everyone in the den was an Oracle. A black cat Ilsa took for one of her own kind was sprawled limply on a low couch, their tail twitching lazily. A Psi stared dreamily at a teacup that was revolving and bobbing in front of him, the saucer hovering below, while the whorls on his face glowed in pulses.

Crouched against the wall in the next room, defeated and empty-handed, was the girl. Even as Ilsa cast a dim shadow over her, she seemed oblivious to anything but her gnawing want. Brushing off Eliot's murmured objections, Ilsa smoothed her white skirt and slid down the wall until she was sitting next to the Oracle on the grimy floorboards.

Still, the girl barely registered her presence – until Ilsa unfastened her bag, removed the single tin of vemanta they had procured that day, and placed it on the floor between them.

Ilsa repressed a shiver as the empty orbs of the girl's eyes met hers. She had a rounded, upturned nose and a spattering of dark freckles.

Tiny pale hands snatched for the tin, but Ilsa was quicker.

"What's your name?"

"Lila Hardwick, miss," whispered the girl.

Such an ordinary name. Such an ordinary voice. "Lila, I—"

"You got a bargain for me," she cut in, furiously shaking her head. "No. No. Can't help." She gathered herself to get up, but the little cylindrical tin must have chosen that moment to make its siren call, and she froze, staring at it.

Ilsa wrapped a hand around Lila's forearm; gently, but she was ready to grip tight if Lila broke free of the vemanta's spell and tried to leave. "You know what I'm going to ask?" she said.

"Yours not to Know," she said sharply, her jaw tight, but she didn't struggle away. From the corners of the dark flat, several voices echoed her words, and a chill ran down Ilsa's spine. She decided to dispense with the preamble.

"Where can you get vemanta cheap? Tell me and I'll give you this," she said, holding forth the tin.

"Yours not..." Lila started saying again, but without conviction. She was looking at the vemanta with a fearful expression, like it was hurting her. "It ain't cheap. Not really."

"What's that mean?" said Ilsa, dousing any notes of frustration in her voice with sweetness and sorority.

"Yours not to Know," said Lila in a distracted whisper, and Ilsa blocked out the murmured echoes. Lila shuddered violently and started worrying her fingers along her shawl. Ilsa took her little hand in hers.

"S'alright," she said. "Could you tell me something I *can* know? Anything, and I'll give it you."

"They're paying with their Sight. My brother Freddie..."

This was it; what Ilsa needed to know. "Freddie's getting vemanta for cheap, in exchange for information? Yes?" Lila shot a nervous glance at Ilsa, then the tin, and back again, and nodded. "Where?"

"You don't know the city."

"Try me."

"You don't know it," whimpered Lila. She was such a pathetic thing that Ilsa nearly took pity, but when the girl extended a hand again for the vemanta, she pulled it out of reach.

"Lila, please."

"You know another place." Her eyes stayed trained on the tin. She was on the verge of tears. "You ain't from this world, or that world. You don't know the city." Her head snapped up. Her orb-like eyes fixed on Ilsa, and she could tell the girl was Seeing something. "There's a shop on Moorgate. On Marin Street."

At last, something Ilsa understood – and something she didn't. She loosened her hold on the vemanta, and with a determined burst Lila snatched it from her.

"But you named two roads. Is Marin Street *off* Moorgate?"

"Not the street, the station. I *told* you, you don't know the city." She stood shakily and edged away, the little tin pressed tightly to her breast. But she spoke again as she retreated, hateful venom in her voice.

"Yours not to Know."

15

She had been warned that Oracles spoke in riddles.

"Don't they mind 'bout finding the bloody Seer's apprentice?" she grumbled. "If they're so up in arms to come kill me over it, p'raps they should think 'bout helping me instead." She kicked a stone into the road with the soft toe of her new leather boots, and swore when it bruised her foot.

"There's little use in appealing to an Oracle's reasoning," said Eliot. He sounded smug. "The more incensed and frustrated you are, the better they feel they're protecting their knowledge."

Ilsa threw her hands up, though she wasn't oblivious to the irony of letting Eliot's words rile her. "But…"

"All we can do is try and make sense of what we have. Moorgate and that other street."

"You weren't listening?" cried Ilsa.

"You led us into a vemanta den," said Eliot. "I was a little preoccupied with the three wretched souls beyond your sight lines who were looking at you like your teeth or your hair might buy them some relief."

"Oh." She shuddered, mumbled a thank you, and kept her complaints to herself for the rest of the journey back to the Zoo.

They were just about to step inside when Eliot stopped her. "Ilsa." He glanced about to check if they were being observed. "We've been looking for Gedeon for weeks. I've tried to help but everything I've said and done has been met with nothing but suspicion from the other lieutenants. I've a feeling Hester's told them not to trust me."

"Why'd she do that?" said Ilsa before he could continue.

Eliot hesitated a moment, meeting her eye as if in defiance. "It's just a feeling. My point is, telling them anything we did or discussed today will only end badly."

From the way the other lieutenants were with Eliot, Ilsa could believe it. If they thought that he knew where Gedeon was, anything less than a full confession would read as misdirection.

"I ain't gonna tell them," she said, taking note of the way his shoulders relaxed and he smiled.

As they parted ways Ilsa wondered, not for the first time, if the other lieutenants were onto something. Whether or not Hester had warned them about trusting Eliot, nobody got that good at dodging questions without having something to hide.

*

Afternoon tea might have been a luxury entirely new to Ilsa, but she doubted she would tire of it any time soon. Very little had passed her lips in the aftermath of the scene in Bill's flat, and now she was ravenous. The strawberry jam she could barely look at the day before was disappearing on scone after scone.

Fyfe had joined her, and they sat at a table in the conservatory, which was surprisingly cool despite the sun beating down. The location was Ilsa's choice. On her tour of the house, she had been fascinated with the Zoo's very own tropical jungle under glass. Palms and ferns and plants she couldn't identify crowded together, climbed the walls, and otherwise vied to be more eye-catching than the next. A pond stood in the centre, with

212

red, orange, and silver fish circling beneath the surface, among banana plants that reached to the ceiling.

Hanging low above Ilsa's head and brushing up against her were dozens of waxy leaves bigger than dinner plates, and Fyfe laughed every time she was distracted by one.

"A lot of the specimens in here require a climate hotter and more humid than this," Fyfe explained eagerly, "but thanks to a combination of a chemical coating on the glass – my own creation – and an enchantment on the plants, thanks to Cassia, the conservatory stays comfortable whatever the weather and the plants thrive perpetually."

"You learn how to do that in one of them books?" said Ilsa, nodding to the stack of tomes Fyfe had brought with him.

"These?" He brushed a hand over the topmost book like he was petting a beloved cat. "These are on aerodynamics, astrology and Erropean history. I have some more classes after tea. I'm sorry to abandon you yet again."

"S'alright. Where are the others?"

"Cassia's negotiating dividends with the high-ranking wolves, since the militia have been working so much harder, what with the raids and looking for Gedeon. Aelius is probably pressing his contacts to try and find out who sent that messenger; the one who told us you were alive. Oren will be at the town hall. He usually hears petitions in the morning but he's awfully busy without Gedeon to make the final decision on anything, and Hester has left him to it. And Eliot. Well, we both know Eliot was in his room this morning. And then he was out with you."

There was a note of accusation at the end. She didn't think he'd meant for it to come out that way.

213

Fyfe cleared his throat and forced a smile. "What, ah, were the two of you doing?"

"He showed me 'round, is all," said Ilsa, taking a long sip of tea. Eliot must have been right about what the other lieutenants thought of him. "I said I wanted to see some Psi magic, and see what's different 'round Camden."

Fyfe nodded a little too much throughout her explanation, then became very interested in his cucumber sandwich, apparently out of things to say.

Ilsa would have steered the conversation into safer territory, but she was saved by the distraction of two wolves, identifiable as such by their red armbands, passing by the conservatory. Ilsa wondered why they were completing their patrol in human forms, until they came within earshot and she realised they were talking.

"Hester must be livid."

"I don't think it's like that."

The first wolf scoffed. "You don't really believe she'd step down quietly, do you?"

"Oh, stars no. I meant that I don't think they mean to give it to the girl. I hear she was some kind of street urchin."

"Well, I'd hope they wouldn't give it to her regardless. Some child from the Otherworld springs up out of nowhere and all of a sudden—"

Fyfe rapped his knuckles on the window and the wolves started. One man paled, the other – the one Fyfe had cut off – hid behind his comrade, giving Ilsa pause about the bravery of Camden's militia force. They mumbled apologies and retractions before escaping at nothing short of a run.

"Something I weren't s'posed to hear, I take it?" said Ilsa politely, though frustration was mounting. Was there something else she didn't know?

Fyfe rubbed his hair and frowned in sympathy. "They've been asked not to speak about you like that."

"Why? I *was* a street urchin," said Ilsa a little defensively. "I meant the part about Hester stepping down. What's that got to do with me?"

He hesitated. "Nothing, yet. It's just that there's a line of succession to being alpha. It was your grandfather, and then your mother, and after Gedeon it's… well, you."

Ilsa laughed. She couldn't help it. It was absurd enough that they had plucked her from her old life and transplanted her here, into a dynasty and a mansion. The idea that she could ever be in charge, simply because of who her mother was, was an absurdity too far. Then she thought again of the wolves' exchange and dread put an abrupt end to her humour. "Wait. No one's expecting me to actually…"

"Of course not!" said Fyfe hastily. "But it's come up, that's all. Stars forbid, if Gedeon never returned… but he will, and in the meantime Hester is just the warden. There's no rule that says that ought to be you, even if Hester hasn't… warmed to it yet. She will."

Ilsa wanted to ask if Hester could be persuaded to remain alpha permanently if there was a need, but the possibility was too distressing to utter. Gedeon *had* to come back, one way or another; it was the only solution.

Fyfe gathered up his books as Ilsa crammed a final finger sandwich into her mouth before leaving the conservatory.

"Are you ready for your lesson in Whisperer magic tomorrow?" Fyfe said, mischief sparking in his dark brown eyes.

Ilsa came to a halt. "Come again?"

"Cassia asked me to arrange a meeting with my astrology tutor. She's a Whisperer, and we hope she'll agree to teach you."

"Teach me to... read minds?"

Fyfe laughed, his whole face creasing. "To strengthen your mind against intrusion. It's an essential skill for those who can find a way to learn. Supposedly there are a handful of Whisperers in the city who will teach it, for a considerable fee of course, but Alitz is a friend."

"Have I got to have lessons for all the magics?" said Ilsa warily.

"If only such a thing were possible. Whisperer magic is unique in that it's of the mind, and so the mind can fight it. There's no protection against the other magics except our own."

It was a reminder Ilsa didn't need of the new dangers that had entered her life; things her previous fears and defences hadn't prepared her for. That gut-wrenching, blood-soaked feeling of being out of her depth settled in her stomach. She recalled the feeling of the Oracle leaping onto her back in Bill's flat. If the only protection was Ilsa's own magic, her magic needed to be up to the challenge.

"Fyfe," she said. "I need a really big mirror."

*

The ballroom looked like a jewel. The polished marble floor reflected the summer shades of the ceiling, which was painted to resemble the sky at sunset – oranges, yellows, blush pink. Accents in gold leaf caught the light pouring in from tall windows on two sides. The crystal droplets of the chandeliers dappled every surface with rainbows.

It was so fine, Ilsa wasn't sure she should be there.

But Fyfe had directed her to the largest mirrors in the Zoo, as requested. They stood either side of the fireplace and reached from the floor to just below the ceiling. Ilsa imagined the ballroom full of dancing couples in their finery, and how the mirrors would create the illusion that the party was twice as grand.

For now, it was just her. Which was a relief, since she was sprawled on the floor struggling to catch her breath.

She had shifted into a wolfhound a dozen times already, and each time she pushed the size of the beast a little further, milking every last drop of her magic, pushing her body to its very limits. Sweat misted her forehead and dampened her dress, every part of her hurt, and nausea was starting to descend, signalling that she had overdone it – and yet the improvements were minimal. She was a couple of inches taller and a few pounds heavier than she had been in the form in Bill's flat.

It wasn't enough. She had tried some other dogs – breeds built for power – but her magic couldn't compensate for their size compared to the wolfhound. With practice, perhaps she could make up a dog's shortcomings with skill, but she suspected the perfect animal wasn't currently within her range.

She climbed shakily to her feet, ruminating on the best way to fix that, when she noticed a second figure in the mirror.

Oren stood at the door.

"Are you well?" he said, peering across the ballroom at her through his glasses.

217

"Fine," said Ilsa, failing to muster a convincing tone.

Oren hovered awkwardly in the doorway a moment. His fingers toyed with the notebook he carried. Ilsa didn't know if his hesitancy was out of a wish not to disturb her, or the desire to avoid an encounter altogether, but eventually, concern must have won out, and he crossed the ballroom.

"I was just practising shifting, is all," said Ilsa by way of explaining her visible exhaustion.

"Ah." Oren pushed his glasses up his nose and looked her up and down again. "Any form in particular?"

"Some dogs. I've been trying to make strong ones. Dangerous ones." She shrugged in an attempt at nonchalance, but the memory of fighting for her life still plagued her. Her voice grew quieter. "I don't want to be a liability if I got to fight someone again."

Understanding crossed Oren's face. He nodded. "That's very prudent. Though I hope you know we don't intend that you will have to."

"I know that," said Ilsa hastily. "And I feel safe here, really I do. It's… it's just that…"

"It's just that everything is different here."

Ilsa nodded. "*So* different."

"And I have always counselled caution and preparation." He tucked his notebook into his jacket. "A dog is your preferred combat form?"

"My what?"

"It's a transformation you practise specifically for strength and skill in combat." He tilted his head to one side. "Perhaps you had no cause for such a thing in the Otherworld."

It sounded foolish, that Ilsa had barely used her magic in that way before. "It ain't that I never thought of shifting as a way to defend myself. I s'pose I just never knew the worst of what I'd be defending myself *against*. I din't know how strong I'd have to be. And dogs just ain't strong enough."

"Is there something else suitable in your repertoire?"

"I've done some bigger animals before. I used to practise a horse in the cellar sometimes when I lived with Mrs Holmes, but all they can do in a fight is kick. And I've tried some zoo animals, but they ain't no use in public so I never practised them. And when I don't practise, and I ain't looked at one up close in a while, I forget all the details."

"Alright," said Oren thoughtfully. "Why don't you tell me which animal you would like for your combat form."

Ilsa chewed the inside of her cheek. She had one on her mind, but what if it was stupid? "They got this leopard at the zoo in the Otherworld, right? 'Cept her fur is white and silver, instead of sandy."

"Ah. A snow leopard."

"Yeah. And she ain't all that big, not like wolfhound big, but she looks strong and she's got these really big paws. And I figure, maybe if I could do a snow leopard, but bigger…"

"Yes, I see," said Oren, nodding, and Ilsa breathed a sigh of relief that he didn't appear to find the suggestion ridiculous. "It seems appropriate that you would favour a cat. Gedeon and Hester both do."

Perhaps it was a small thing – she had seen Eliot as a big cat too; there was only so many powerful animals to choose from – but Ilsa felt a thrill at the connection.

"A snow leopard," Oren repeated to himself. He was rubbing his chin in contemplation. "Alright. I think I can…"

He tucked his glasses away, rolled his shoulders once, and shifted effortlessly into a larger than life version of the leopard in Ilsa's memory. He prowled slowly back and forth in front of her in a figure of eight; the perfect case study. Ilsa beamed.

There was an ease to Ilsa's understanding of anatomy to which she could only credit her magic. When she concentrated on the shape of an animal, the way it moved, she felt a flicker of the charge that entered her bones and let her shift. Apes, she understood best, followed by other mammals. Birds were harder. Reptiles gave her a headache, and she had never accomplished one.

Ilsa watched Oren make his slow figure of eight half a dozen times, then he sat on his haunches and let her come closer. Ilsa had seen the wolves behaving like humans, and she'd seen dozens of other Changelings in animal form the day Captain Fowler had brought her through the portal. She had even flown alongside Eliot and marvelled at the newness of being among her own kind. But it was another novelty entirely to stand so close to a leopard that was not a leopard, to see the wonder of her own magic before her eyes in a way she had scarcely dared to imagine. A smile played on her lips the entire time.

The leopard came to life in her mind smoothly, and when Oren jerked his head, halfway between a nudge and a nod, Ilsa understood it was her turn.

She shook off the aches and nausea of her previous attempts and felt her way into the form, letting go when she felt her magic take over. She pitched forward, landing on heavy paws. Her skin tingled sharply as a coat of dappled silver fur was thrown over it. Strength poured into her every muscle as she grew pointed teeth, a lustrous thick tail, rounded ears, and whiskers. She tried to concentrate on the feeling of her muscles growing, her body lengthening, pushing herself to be larger, stronger.

Too late, she felt her magic stutter as it lost its grip on the form. Her bones began to scream at her again; an aching protest that they couldn't go any further. It only lasted a moment before panic took over, like snatching her hand back as it brushed a hot stove. She crashed back into her true body, heaving a breath, then another, dizzy from the exertion.

Oren shifted too. He watched her catch her breath, hands on her knees, and nodded in understanding when she straightened.

"You're not hurt?" he asked.

"I'm fine. I tried to go too big, is all."

"Don't," he said. Ilsa made an exasperated sound at that "advice", and Oren raised a hand to halt her protests. "That is to say, do not focus on growing at all."

"But how am I s'posed to get bigger?"

"If you can maintain the transformative state, you will grow to the limit of your magic quite naturally, if you wish it. Cede control. Your magic knows what you want. Your only focus should be the form."

"I din't know that," said Ilsa, though it sounded obvious now. She let her magic lead when it came to the form – it was the breakthrough that had finally let her escape the orphanage all those years ago – but she still exhausted herself by forcing other things. She wondered what else she was getting wrong.

"Do you want to try again?" Ilsa nodded. "Envisage the animal with the size and strength you desire, but remember to let go of it all when you begin to shift. *Keep* letting go, and see what happens."

He stepped back, giving her plenty of space. Ilsa commanded her body to shift, and once again, her hands flew out to catch the ground as she changed shape. She tried not to think of completing the transformation; she simply kept the form in her mind without tugging on it as her magic did its work.

It was a matter of a second, then at the moment she knew the leopard was complete, years of habit compelled her to push the transformation further or shut it down. She resisted, holding her calm, not stoppering the magic as it continued to work. Her paws spread under her; strength poured into her legs and shoulders. The second she braced for the pain that told her she'd gone too far, her magic cooled. She didn't choose to finish shifting; her body did for her.

"No pain this time," said Oren, smiling in that reserved way of his.

Ilsa padded over to the mirror, a thrill of success rushing through her at what she saw. The menagerie snow leopard Ilsa had seen in the flesh was no larger than a dog. The beast looking back at her was twice the size at least, and built to kill.

She sat back on her hind legs, extended her claws, and took a vicious swipe at the air. She could feel the weight of her paw, the power of the strike. If she had to fight for her life again, she would be ready.

"You must practise," said Oren as she shifted human again. "Do not let your grasp of the animal grow stale."

"I won't," Ilsa promised, beaming. "Thank you. That mean you practise a snow leopard too?"

Oren took his glasses from his pocket again and began polishing them. It appeared to be a force of habit. "I practised a great number of animals for a great number of years. I practised until the forms were stuck in my mind and my muscles."

"Can you do reptiles?" Ilsa said eagerly.

"An unimpressive lizard or two," he said with a small smile. "I believe Eliot can accomplish a serpent. The marine science faculty of Lenarth College are known to swim the Thames as dolphins two Fridays a month."

Dolphins. Ilsa had always suspected she could push her magic that far, if only she knew the form better. If it took the knowledge of a marine scientist, she probably never would, but now that she was in the Witherward, surrounded by other Changelings and their wondrous talents, so much more was possible. She felt a buzz of excitement and awe; of pride in her magic.

But the feeling was followed by the memory that there were those who reviled what Ilsa and her people could do. Who believed the Changelings to be base and beneath them for the shape their magic took.

Oren must have seen the dark direction of her thoughts in her expression, as he looked at her quizzically.

"Cassia told me 'bout the Fortunatae. 'Bout the night my parents died," she explained. Her bones hurting from her poor attempts at shifting, Ilsa sank down, her back against the wall. "She said you was the one what took me to Lord Walcott."

Oren smiled wistfully. "The last one of us to see you for seventeen years," he said. He shot an unsettled look at her fine

223

dress, then at the chairs against the far side of the ballroom. He gestured at them. "Would you not prefer a chair?"

Ilsa smirked. These rich people were awfully proper, and she would have been lying if she said it didn't tempt her to scandalise them. "I'm perfectly comfortable, thanks."

"Well. Alright." He went to the far wall and returned with a chair for himself, the exact position of which he fussed with fastidiously before sitting down.

"I had been a wolf for less than a year, but I would have done anything for your mother. I owed her a life debt, and that night she gave me the chance to repay it. I hope she died trusting that I did. Trusting that you were safe."

The truth of what happened to Ilsa's safety in the years that followed hung between them, unspoken. "What happened that you owed her?"

Oren laced his fingers together, unlaced them, laced them again. For a long moment he was silent and contemplative.

"I'm not from this starsforsaken city," he said eventually.

"You ain't?"

Oren shook his head. His fingers continued to fidget. "I came from Brema. It was a city a two-day voyage from here, to the northeast. I believe on the world map *you* know, Brema would fall somewhere in Denmark, if that's helpful."

The things Ilsa didn't know about the Witherward were becoming a source of headaches, and she hadn't even begun to contemplate geography, but she nodded all the same.

"You said Brema *was* two days' voyage from here?"

"I did. The city was not built to suffer earthquakes," he said. "Most of it is in the sea now. The rest is ruin. That was the year my parents brought me to London. I was a little younger than you are now."

Ilsa screwed up her face. "They came here *on purpose*?" she said.

"London was founded to be a utopia," he said. "Five magical peoples living in harmony. We heard tales of the experiment's dramatic failure, of course, but we did not understand the extent. There was a war going on in Brema at the time, and my mother and father believed London would be better. That there would be real opportunities to build their fortune here."

A shadow crossed Oren's face, and Ilsa knew what she had to ask. "What happened to them? Your parents?"

Oren sighed. In different circumstances, Ilsa would have mistaken it for a sigh of contentment. "We had paid a fair price for passage from Brema. High, but fair. But it was a cheat. When we docked in London, the captain told us we owed him more. Much more than we had. He brought a Sorcerer named Lazaro Tilley on board and told us Lazaro would buy our debt, and we would work for him until it was paid. My mother and father tried to refuse, but we were given no choice. They kept us on the ship until they relented. So we became indentured servants." Oren spared her a weak smile. "But at least we were together, my father would say."

Ilsa tried to smile back, but it felt false.

"Lazaro was an antiques dealer. He would buy furniture from all over London which he needed to transport back to his shop. He worked my mother and father to death as horses," Oren continued mildly, but it was like dropping a stone in Ilsa's stomach. She didn't know how to react. "Might I ask, Ilsa, what is the longest you have continuously held an animal form?"

It sounded like a strange question at first. When Ilsa understood why he was asking, she was afraid to answer; afraid to hear the rest of the story.

"A few hours, p'raps," she said. "No more than that."

"But I daresay you've experienced a little of the feeling of your mind growing more animal. Changelings who have spent weeks as animals take time to recover. Those who have spent months, without respite, have been known to suffer permanent damage to their minds. Lazaro told my mother and father the work they were to do for him if they were to repay their debt, and when they transformed, he bound them in Changeling leather; bonds which, upon contact with Changeling skin, suppress our ability to transform. They cage us within whatever form we are in."

Ilsa resisted the sudden urge to touch her wrists. She was familiar with Changeling leather, she realised. It was what Captain Fowler had used to foil her escape in the fish market.

"I wasn't permitted to see them, of course. Lazaro guessed rightly that I would unbind them, and damn the consequences. But there was a very small window in the room where I slept that looked onto the stable in which he made them live. Every night, once he shut me in, I would open it, and my mother and father would come to the window, and I would talk to them. I would see in their eyes the man and woman they truly were.

"As the years went on, sometimes it would take longer to encourage them towards the window, and it was plain that they understood me less and less. But still I talked to them. I would tell them stories about our life back in Brema in the hopes it would keep something of their old selves alive."

He paused, gaze on something in the middle distance; on his memories.

"One day, when I opened the window and called to them, they came immediately. I reached out to touch my mother's face, as I always did, and she began lipping at my fingers. When they saw I had nothing for them, they lost interest. Lazaro had neglected to feed them again, you see, and they thought I was bringing their feed. Like horses. I could see it in their eyes. I should say, in fact, it was what I couldn't see. It's a small comfort, but... by the end, they no longer remembered they were human at all."

Ilsa could only nod. She had no words of comfort for such an unimaginable fate, for Oren's parents and for their son. To lose them slowly, over years, when they were right there.

"I was luckier, of course," he went on. "I'd been apprenticed to a merchant back in Brema, and I had skills Lazaro could use me for in his shop. I knew better than to ask him for much, but I was foolish enough to hope my mother and father would receive a proper burial. But they did not. 'They were animals,' he told me. 'They are worthy of no such thing, and neither will you be.' I was unaware of the existence of the Fortunatae at that time. I knew only that Lazaro attended a salon once a week, hosted by someone who called themself the Sage." He looked down at his hands. "He had been devoted to the ethos for decades, and he had not only bought our debt, but helped others bring Changelings into forced servitude as well. It was a practice banned by the Principles." He looked up at Ilsa and smiled. "By your mother."

"So after the Principles, Lazaro had to let you go?"

Oren shook his head. "Unfortunately, it was not quite that simple. Lyander could not get the other faction leaders to agree to write off debts some citizens felt they were owed, but she did convince them that all debtors be forced to sell the debt to her. She came to the shop herself one day. I knew nothing of the Principles; Lazaro kept current affairs from me as much as he could. I could see in her eyes what it cost her to give the man who had stolen everything from me a fair price for my life." He looked around at the ballroom. Ilsa saw the reflection of the specks of rainbow in his eyeglasses. "She brought me here. She fed me at her table, with her husband and her son, and told me there was a position for me within the wolves should I want it, and money to start my life over should I not. I have been a free man ever since. The debt I will forever owe your mother is not servitude or money. That debt is my privilege to bear."

He stood, and returned the chair to the exact spot from which he'd taken it.

"What the Fortunatae did to my family is personal for you too, ain't it?" Ilsa called as he was leaving.

Oren smiled, but shook his head. "It is personal to every Changeling, Ilsa. Questions of one's humanity always are."

16

Ilsa wanted nothing more than to spend the following day in a quiet spot deciphering Lila's riddle but, as Fyfe had warned her, the afternoon was to be taken up by a different activity: defence lessons.

The two Whisperers in the drawing room were more like Ilsa than an Oracle or even a Psi – in fact, they looked entirely like the Londoners of the Otherworld – but still Ilsa shivered in trepidation as she looked upon them.

The woman was fair-skinned with greying hair pulled into a severe bun. Her eyes were unusually large, unfocused, and golden-brown in colour, and had pronounced wrinkles fanning from the outer corners. They reminded Ilsa of an owl's eyes, rimmed with feathers. She was tall, and even though she looked weakened by age, she stood straight, and had a commanding presence that told Ilsa she was the more senior of the pair.

Her companion was younger – in his thirties, perhaps – with chestnut hair grown long and severely slicked back. He wore a thick moustache above tight, bloodless lips, and his eyes were sullen. He stood like a military man, with stiff posture and his hands behind his back.

"Ilsa, this is Alitz Dicer, my astrology tutor," said Fyfe, indicating the woman. "And her assistant, Pyval Crespo. Alitz is very respected among her faction and has negotiated with the

Lord of Whitechapel – their leader – on our behalf for decades. She's a valued friend."

"How do you do," said Alitz Dicer, coming forward to take Ilsa's hand.

Her heart pounding, Ilsa reached to shake her hand, but her arm fell uselessly to her side as a knowing smirk spread across the Whisperer's face. It had seemed like such a great idea to learn to protect her thoughts that she hadn't considered the price: exposing them to this stranger. Now her bones were threatening to melt; into a starling, or a fox – something fast.

Eliot had called the Principles an exercise in finding the loophole, and Ilsa suddenly understood why. She couldn't shift in plain sight without raising suspicion, and a Psi certainly couldn't use psychokinesis secretly. But one of the Wraiths' skills was their senses, and they were using them all the time. And what of Whisperers and Oracles? If a Sorcerer cast a glamour outside the Heart, would anyone even know?

She should have objected to this meeting when she had the chance. What did this woman already know about her?

Alitz, seeing Ilsa was not going to shake her hand, lowered hers. Her absent gaze seemed to look through Ilsa, not at her. "Don't look so alarmed, Miss Ravenswood. I have been invited into your home, not your mind."

Fyfe mumbled something about Ilsa being new to all this. But if Ilsa had insulted Alitz, she didn't mind much. She could breathe again. Pyval stayed where he was, and only inclined his head by way of greeting.

"Another living Ravenswood," said Alitz. "Is Camden hiding any more surprises in the Otherworld? A second treasury to pay for its Wraith hirelings? How many of this city's poorest could the Zoo have fed for Cadell Fowler's fee?"

Ilsa glanced hesitantly at Fyfe, who stuttered something about negotiating a good price.

"Do forgive me, Miss Ravenswood, for not exulting in your return. But our friends are there to keep us honest, are they not?" Her voice had a flat, unreadable quality, but the arch of her brow made her look amused, if not warm.

"So Whitechapel's got a lord, does it?" said Ilsa.

Alitz considered her. "His Honour is self-styled."

"And you answer to this Lord…"

"Voss," said Alitz bitingly. "Lord Jericho Voss."

"That mean Lord Voss knows I'm here? And… all the rest?" She looked to Fyfe, unsure of what she could say in front of these outsiders.

"You refer to your brother's most recent exploits. Missing, they tell me, though I hardly agree with that assessment. Children and cats go missing. Gedeon Ravenswood is up to something." Alitz dipped her chin and levelled her gaze at Ilsa in a way that made her feel reprimanded. "And I answer to no one. But it seems Whitechapel and Camden have a common problem."

"The Fortunatae."

Alitz nodded. "We don't believe its members are exclusively Whisperers, but we know they are based in Whitechapel, and that creates problems for the faction. We are enjoying a period of prosperity, and His Honour is tasked with upholding the Principles. He fears retaliation from both Camden and the Heart if he fails to suppress the Fortunatae, since we too suspect the secret society of having a hand in the Sorcerer rebellion. Their interests align so closely with those of the rebels that I doubt the Sage would have to lift a finger. So His Honour has been made aware of your existence, and the murder of your friend in the Otherworld by a member of the Fortunatae, whom Mr Tarenvale identified as a Whisperer.

"As for your brother. He has kidnapped an important Oracle and broken the Principles. Abandoned them entirely, for all we know." Fyfe opened his mouth to object but Alitz silenced him with a hand. "If anyone came to suspect Gedeon Ravenswood was changing the rules, he could start a conflict the likes of which London has not seen in your lifetime. I have made an executive decision. The fewer who know that Gedeon Ravenswood is a loose cannon, the better."

"We're indebted to you, Alitz," said Fyfe.

Alitz smiled. "And we've not even begun." She turned to Ilsa. "We are not here to discuss relations, I trust you know."

"Fyfe said I was to learn how to guard my mind," replied Ilsa, though she wasn't sure it was a question.

"Precisely. Pyval." The younger man stepped forward and Ilsa found herself shrinking back.

"What's gonna happen?"

"To start, I would like your permission for Pyval and myself to access your thoughts. It will better help me guide you and assess your progress."

"You ain't listening to my thoughts already? How d'you even stop yourself?"

Alitz's smirk was condescending. "Any Whisperer who has trained can protect themselves from the onslaught of unwanted mental chatter. We have closed our minds to yours, and to Fyfe's."

Ilsa shot Pyval a glance and wondered if Alitz truly spoke for both of them. "And if I give permission…"

"Then we will explore. Certain aspects of your mind will be more apparent to each of us. Myself, I read emotions well. Pyval is skilled with memories. The further we venture into your psyche, the more we will learn. But since we're strangers, we shan't go too far."

Alitz's words were reassuring, but her cool indifference put Ilsa on edge, Pyval's unreadable silence even more so. But what choice did she have? Expose herself to two trusted Whisperers now, in the safety of the Zoo, or risk coming face to face with a hostile thought-bender without a shred of defence.

"Very well," she said. "Do what you got to."

Alitz laced her fingers together. "Just relax. You won't notice a thing," she said. Her watery gaze sharpened, like a veil had been lifted, and she stared levelly at Ilsa. Pyval, by contrast, relaxed his posture, his gaze hovering somewhere near Ilsa's feet, his head inclined as if he was listening.

For a few seconds, the only sound was the ticking of the standing clock, and Fyfe, creeping quietly to the nearest couch.

"Well," Alitz said after a spell. "This ought to be straightforward. You're rather guarded; that's a good foundation for those seeking privacy from the likes of a Whisperer. Though, as Pyval points out, it is a hindrance in matters of love and friendship."

Ilsa glanced to Pyval, certain he hadn't said a word. But before she could open her mouth and make a fool of herself, it struck her: he did not need to speak aloud. Alitz and Pyval had permission to use their magic now, and they were conversing through their thoughts. She shivered.

233

"But you *were* able to read her?" said Fyfe.

"Of course," said Alitz. She glanced Pyval's way occasionally as she spoke, perhaps hearing his input. "It takes more than a careful heart to conceal oneself from our magic. We read enough. A frigid mistrust of ourselves, for a start." When Ilsa opened her mouth to explain, Alitz raised a hand. "No need. We cannot take it personally, having seen who you are. Your thoughts and feelings are buried deep, Miss Ravenswood. Your memories even more so. But your nature is plain to see. You're wary of others; their motives, their influence... their prejudices. It's who you are."

Fyfe cleared his throat, leapt from the couch, and started buttoning his jacket. "Perhaps you'd be more comfortable if I left," he said to Ilsa.

"No, stay," she replied, her eyes on Alitz. Fyfe had guessed correctly that if she was going to be dissected, having him there would be uncomfortable, but it was also another line of defence. She didn't want to be outnumbered. "Go on."

"Very well. You present a front," continued Alitz, "because you find it advantageous to be appealing, and you're not afraid of a little dishonesty, if it gets you what you need."

Was it any defence that she had needed these qualities to be a magician's assistant? Ilsa didn't get the chance to find out before Alitz continued.

"You feel misunderstood, and you fear it is your own doing; perhaps a product of your propensity to conceal yourself, and to withhold trust. And yet you have the vulnerable heart of the young woman you are." Alitz paused. Perhaps Ilsa couldn't *feel* the Whisperer's magic, but she knew Alitz was reaching deep into her psyche all the same. She wanted to slam the door and shut her out. "Whatever made you so thoroughly cynical has not destroyed you yet."

Fyfe averted his eyes, but Alitz and Pyval extended no such courtesy. They had stripped her of her armour of charm and confidence, laid her bare, and were watching her like a specimen under glass. The heat of scrutiny burned Ilsa to the core, and she threw water on it the best way she knew how: she squared her shoulders, slipped on a mask, and forced herself not to feel.

"You ain't told me nothing I don't already know," she lied.

"Good," said Alitz happily. "To know one's own mind is the first defence against telepathy. As for your more immediate thoughts" – she turned to Fyfe – "your little princess is remarkably hard to read. And her current state of mind is an utter mystery to me."

"How d'you know I ain't just dim?" said Ilsa. "Hypothetically speaking."

"She's not," said Fyfe quickly, but he was ignored.

"The same way I know you have a rich imagination. I cannot see your thoughts very clearly but I know they are there. Imagine the mind as a spider's web. Everything in it is connected and held together by the silk of the self; your identity, if you will. When I venture into your mind, I land in the centre of the web. If I reach further I can see towards the edges. Your mind is large, Miss Ravenswood, and the imagination has a distinctive pattern. These are things one cannot learn to obscure from a Whisperer; only what the web holds."

"And as for... the rest?" said Fyfe, rubbing his unruly hair.

"I'm getting to that. Miss Ravenswood, I'm now going to try and place a thought in your mind. I'm telling you so that you might recognise how it differs from your own, organic thoughts." Her lips twitched. "At least, you might be able to look back on it and tell, though I'm sure it will feel genuine at the time. Like a dream."

Ilsa, caught halfway between her eagerness to learn and her feeling of being violated, tried to relax. Perhaps if she thought of something else, she could both distract herself and notice when the usurper thought snuck in. She went straight to a faithful daydream: her supper.

"It's not as easy as one may think," said Alitz abruptly, "to notice when one's thoughts have been tampered with."

"But—"

"You were thinking of roast beef, yes?" She raised an eyebrow.

Ilsa scowled. She had liked it better when she was good at this. "My thoughts go to roast beef just fine on their own. Try another one."

"Very well. Pyval."

Pyval's expression glazed over as before, but what he did next, Ilsa couldn't say. She was suddenly absurdly distracted by a beautiful vase on the console behind him. She stepped past Pyval, intent on touching it, perhaps picking it up. Her fingers were about to brush the glossy china when something stopped her. It felt wrong, this distraction that had tugged on her from nowhere; ridiculous even. How did a vase hold any sway over her? Was it a trick? Would something happen when she touched it?

She looked over her shoulder at Pyval, who had given up and was watching her with a stony expression.

"Was that better?" Ilsa asked smugly.

Alitz was appraising her too. "Very good, Miss Ravenswood. Your caution serves you well yet again, I daresay…" She trailed off, head inclined.

Ilsa glanced at Pyval as he spoke to Alitz. The man had an uncanny stare, as if he were looking at her and through her at the same time. It was full of intent and indifference all at once.

"I suppose it cannot hurt to try once more," Alitz said in answer to an unspoken question. "Something a bit more challenging this time."

Ilsa had no chance to object, because the room around her vanished into darkness.

It was like stepping under a spotlight; everything beyond was a void. Dread seized her like a hand gripping her throat; suddenly, completely.

"Fyfe?" Her voice echoed off walls that were far too close, but when she flung her arms out in panic they met with nothing on all sides.

Fyfe made no answer, but something was there. She could *see* it moving closer – black against black, vast, ethereal – and yet there was nothing to see. She could *taste* it – fear, rot, blood, static – and yet she tasted nothing at all.

And something else flickered in and out of existence, always in the corner of her eye, no matter where she looked: Pyval. If he was doing this to her, where was Fyfe? If none of this was real, why could she feel the air dance as the thing in the void surrounded her? She opened her mouth and heard a cry from far away.

And then the light rushed in. Hands were gripping her

shoulders. Wide brown eyes were inches from her face. "Ilsa? Ilsa?"

Fyfe. The drawing room. The void was gone. The formless dread loosened its grip and Ilsa braced herself on Fyfe's arm to stop from sinking to the floor.

"What the *bloody hell*—"

"Are you alright?" said Fyfe.

"I'm fine. No thanks to *him*." Ilsa shot her best dirty look at Pyval, who gave no reaction. Alitz's lips were a thin line as her eyes bore into her companion.

"You screamed. What did he do to you?" said Fyfe.

Alitz turned to them. "I apologise on behalf of Mr Crespo, Miss Ravenswood," displeasure dripping from every word, "I don't think it was necessary so startle you so. Not yet, in any case. But you've been gifted valuable insight nonetheless."

"You can take your insight back for all I care," snapped Ilsa, memories of the cold, peculiar dread still echoing down her spine.

Alitz's lip quirked into a sardonic smile. "There's no need for dramatics, Miss Ravenswood. We're here to help you." She turned to address the room, and Ilsa knew the subject was closed. "There are some weaknesses. I'm afraid an active imagination is inconvenient when it comes to resisting thought manipulation. The more varied the pattern of thought, the harder it is to notice anomalies. But we will address it in our lessons."

"Lessons?" said Ilsa.

"I require all my students to acquiesce to hard work and daily practice. If you apply yourself, Miss Ravenswood, I think you can secure your mind in a fortnight or so. We'll start tomorrow."

Alitz gave a cordial goodbye and took her leave, Pyval behind her. As the man passed by, he slowed, and Ilsa caught his scent. Organic. Coppery. The dread rose up again, and she pushed it back and met his eye. He spoke just once as he left, his voice reedy, but every syllable precise.

"If you're going to live in the world of Whisperers, you ought to be prepared for the worst of what our magic can do."

17

It was late, and Ilsa was in the library. She was wrapped in a dressing gown, her hair twisted into a long plait over one shoulder, and the Oracle girl's riddle written out on the paper before her in her own wobbly, unenviable handwriting.

Lila had alluded to *two* worlds that Ilsa didn't know, and a street that didn't exist in the other London. Much to Ilsa's dismay, when she consulted a map of the city, she discovered it didn't exist here either. There was no Marin Street off Moorgate, nor anywhere else.

Not the street, the station, Lila had said. The only trouble being, Ilsa had scoured the map a dozen times and there wasn't one of those either. There was no Metropolitan Railway in this London. The one thing Ilsa had recognised in this new London was the lay of the land; it was frustrating to find that even parts of *that* were unrecognisable.

The more she turned Lila's riddle over in her mind, the more its meaning eluded her, until she let out a string of profanities, scrunched the paper into a ball, and threw it across the table, where it scattered the pieces of a chessboard like skittles.

"If one has an impulse to spend some violence," said a smooth, resounding voice, and Ilsa looked up to see Aelius in the doorway, one hand resting on his cane and a smirk on his face, "there are plenty in this city who would be happy to oblige you."

"I think I got it out of my system," Ilsa replied with a weak smile, and the man chuckled.

She was unsure of Aelius. He was charming, quick to laugh, and had an amiable way with almost everybody, but something about him reminded her of a magician on the stage; all dazzling lies and misdirection.

"Cassia tells me you plan to help us find young Gedeon," he said, coming into the room. As Aelius began leisurely righting the chess pieces, Ilsa retrieved the balled-up riddle and scooted it into her lap, out of sight.

She had kept her word to Eliot and not told anyone of the stolen vemanta or Lila's incomprehensible claims. Ilsa still didn't trust his motives, but having him on her side had been a help so far, and her instincts were telling her to keep the secret. In her experience, more harm was done by loose lips than by discretion.

"I take it you're at a dead end?" said Aelius. "Learned that we're not as incompetent as all that?"

"Competence got nothing to do with it," said Ilsa, matching his condescending tone with her own. "I reckon you need a pair of fresh eyes, is all."

Aelius smirked and pointed his cane past her shoulder. "Well, Ilsa my darling, if you mean to find out what we know, you ought to cast your fresh eyes right there."

Ilsa followed the line of his cane to the window and peered into the gloom. In the garden, beyond the halo of light emanating from a lamp left aglow on the terrace, a black silhouette stood rigidly by the roses, looking out towards the park.

Cassia appeared so absorbed in her melancholy that the dark

241

did not bother her, nor was she wearing a coat to ward off the nighttime chill.

"Actually, I got a question for *you*."

"Delightful!" He settled himself in the chair across from her and toyed with one of the chess pieces like a cat toys with a mouse. "I will endeavour to be of the utmost use."

"Cassia's a Sorcerer, ain't she? So, how come she's with us?"

"The most excellent of questions," Aelius said with mock seriousness. "You may find your mark after all with that sort of gumption. Our Miss Sims is Jupitus Fisk's granddaughter. She may bat for the Ravenswoods, but she has loyalty to the Heart too, I assure you."

Ilsa frowned. "Who's Jupitus Fisk?"

Aelius grinned. He clearly liked being the one to hold all the cards.

"Allow me to set the scene," he said, nodding at the chessboard. "Do you play?" Ilsa shook her head. "It's a marvellous education, chess. And no coincidence your mother was both a masterful chess player and an effective leader. The game is defence and attack in perfect measure. This" – he picked up a piece from the centre of the white formation in front of Ilsa and held it up between a thumb and forefinger – "is the king. The deciding piece. The game is lost when he falls. His position informs every move one makes and yet, alone, he is helpless."

Ilsa nodded, grasping the analogy. "He's the alpha," she said. Aelius smiled and replaced the king on the board. "And I s'pose these small ones all in a line are the wolves, right?"

"Right you are," said Aelius. "The pawns. Often undervalued by less seasoned players, impossible to ignore at a crucial

242

moment. A well-placed pawn can frustrate, agitate, distract, plug a weakness. But they demand a player astute enough to wield them to their full force."

"Like Eliot?" Ilsa said. She had heard the way Aelius spoke of, and to, the former commander of the wolves. As she anticipated, his expression hardened at the mention of his name. "He was the player wielding the pawns in all this, weren't he?"

Aelius was still but for the hand twisting his cane as he no doubt contemplated the cleverest response. "Quillon's father was a gifted strategist, may the stars keep him," he said eventually. "It stands to reason he would pass some of that flare onto his son. It also stands to reason Gedeon would give as firm a friend as Eliot Quillon a position of such esteem, and that Hester would see fit to remove him from it. The lad is eighteen, lest we forget."

Was there jealousy in his tone? Aelius was clearly ambitious, and leading the militia was a great deal of power.

"So who's going to command the wolves now?" probed Ilsa, compelled by her hunch.

Aelius smiled convincingly, but then again, all his smiles were convincing. Ilsa doubted all of them were true. "With any luck, Hester will recognise that taming wolves and taming foxes is not so different."

Is that why Hester had removed Eliot? To give the role to Aelius? Ilsa wasn't convinced it was that simple. Something else hung between Eliot and her cousin.

"So which of these pieces are you and the other lieutenants?"

Aelius tapped the three pieces to the king's right and named them in turn. "Bishop, knight, rook; the pieces that shape the game. They lay elegant traps. They move in beautiful and complex formations, always linked. They claim the victories in battle that win the king his war." He flashed his wicked grin. "But don't mistake me, even those pieces closest and most valuable to the king can be sacrificed when the game demands it."

"Sacrificed by who?" she challenged, the double meaning of his words not lost on her. Was it a pledge to die for his faction and his alpha, or a willingness to give up his comrades for his cause?

"By the *game*, my darling." He met her eye unwaveringly, in that way that told her he was assessing her reaction. That was the real game, Ilsa realised, so she refused to give him one.

There was a piece in the centre, next to the king, that Aelius had not yet mentioned. "And who's that one?" she said, pointing to it.

"Ah. The queen." Aelius picked up the piece and put it in the empty centre of the board. "That, dear girl, is Jupitus Fisk. The leader of the Sorcerers. When the Fortunatae massacred the Ravenswoods, Fisk was the one who stood at Hester's side while she demanded merciless retribution for those who killed them. Every other faction was willing to face the other way as the Sage amassed support, and who could stop them? The Fortunatae took pains to keep their members anonymous. Hester Ravenswood may have cried that she watched a Wraith plunge a dagger into her father's heart – but did she have a name, the North replied. Could she identify the Psi who cut her cousin Lyander's throat, said the Underground. What were they to do?"

Had Hester really seen those things the night her family had been killed? Ilsa couldn't bear to think about it. "So what did Fisk do?"

Aelius's expression turned grim, but he couldn't keep the glimmer from his eyes. "What he had to," he said. "As with our recent troubles, the Sage had found support among rebel Sorcerers, so Fisk gutted his militia in search of the renegades. At Hester's behest, he interrogated and executed any of his people with so much as a *sympathy* for the Fortunatae and their backward little philosophy. Meanwhile, Hester presented the other faction leaders with an ultimatum: follow Fisk's lead, deal with their Fortunatae sympathisers in kind, or she would do it for them. And with the might of Fisk and the Sorcerers at her side there was nothing anyone could do to stop her."

Ilsa smiled. "'Cause they'd just signed the Principles. Camden had a right to retaliate."

Aelius pointed at her, white teeth flashing. "Precisely."

"But why not let Hester deal with the Fortunatae herself?" said Ilsa. "What was in it for him?"

Aelius smiled slowly, eyes sparkling. "It seems you have the measure of this city already. Fisk's ruthlessness put rebellion in the Heart to rest for seventeen years. He saw a convenient opportunity to flash his teeth at anyone who challenged the way he chose to rule, and bought himself a reputation. And reputation, ah, Ilsa. One wears one's reputation either as armour or as chains. Remember that." He chuckled. "It may be that Jupitus Fisk never truly cared for the plight of the Changelings, but the man was one of the best weapons Camden had in her arsenal."

"Had?" said Ilsa.

Aelius flicked the queen and she toppled over. "He's dead.

245

He passed in his sleep at a highly respectable age, may the stars keep him. A man named Samuel Lucius has taken control of the Heart. And herein lies our recent problem."

"Let me guess." Ilsa reached across the board and picked up the black piece that matched her king. "He's this fella."

Aelius spread his hands in a gesture of defeat. "That, even *I* cannot tell you. Sam Lucius, we might say, is not on the board."

Ilsa frowned. "What d'you mean?"

"The man is an unknown. He has made vague overtures to continuing the Heart's alliance with Camden, but when confronted with questions about how he plans to handle the rebels, he has no answers. Perhaps he is simply not the leader Fisk was. Perhaps he lacks the stomach for quashing dissent in the manner of his predecessor. Or" – Aelius leaned back and elegantly crossed one leg over the other – "perhaps the High Sorcerer is no longer the ally Camden needs. It is my ongoing project to find answers. I fear they are growing more pressing by the day."

Ilsa looked at the chessboard; at the gaping hole next to the king, and the fallen piece in the centre. Sam Lucius might not be on their side, but the mastermind of their opposition – the king across the board – was the Sage. With fewer pieces, Camden needed to make cleverer moves.

"I can teach you, if you like," said Aelius, watching her. "I wager there's a sharp chess player in you."

"P'raps I ought to learn. If it's such an education. But you ain't answered my question." Aelius raised an eyebrow expectantly. "You ain't explained why Cassia's with us."

A mischievous smile spread across his face. "Have I not?"

"Did Cassia work for her grandfather and the Zoo at the same time? Like a go-between?"

"One could say that. But even allies have their differences. It's a complicated business, this diplomacy lark, and one can never know when one's comrades are plotting to stab you in the back."

His light brown eyes brimmed with mischief as he studied Ilsa's frown and waited, unblinking.

"Cassia's a spy?" she said eventually, and Aelius's brows shot up in a show of happy astonishment.

"Well, aren't you full of pleasant surprises? Your father was just as fiercely shrewd. You must get it from him," he said, and he tapped the side of his nose.

Ilsa feigned her best shy smile, but she wasn't fooled by his flattery. She had deduced only what he wanted her to; no more, no less. And if anyone asked about it later, Aelius had never said Cassia was a spy.

She tucked the scrunched-up riddle into her pocket and stood. "This don't look nothing like diplomacy to me. In the Otherworld London, it's street gangs what got territories and recruits and a hundred ways to get killed by their enemies. This ain't nothing but criminal warfare."

Aelius had no snide answer for that, but she could hear him chuckling as she turned on her heel and went upstairs to bed.

*

Ilsa had not closed her bedroom door behind her when a shout went up in the park. Then another. She peeked carefully through the curtains to see torches shining from the park, not far from the garden wall, and they were advancing. Cassia had apparently been roused from her reverie and was forming the wolves into a front line on the lawn; an array of snarling, clawing giant animals ready to defend the Zoo.

Ilsa's bedroom door swung open. She spun, prepared to defend herself however necessary, but the one who stumbled in and grabbed her by the wrist was Eliot. His feet were bare, and his shirt was wrinkled and open at the collar. Did he sleep in his clothes? She was momentarily distracted by the image of Eliot sprawled across tousled sheets, and before she knew it, they were hurtling down the corridor in the direction of Hester's chambers.

"It's the rebels again, ain't it?"

"There are acolytes with them," replied Eliot. "It looks like the Docklands have allied with the rebels. The enemy of my enemy, and so on."

The sounds of fighting were coming from the garden; the raider-assassins had breached the wall. "Where're we going?"

"Hester's room. There's a trick wall with a—"

Ilsa dug in her heels and brought them to a halt. "There's no way I'm going in no hole in the wall."

A window broke nearby, and Eliot drew her closer, but Ilsa was more afraid of this plan than another bout with the Oracles.

"I don't want to go in no wall, Eliot," she said again, louder, as he dragged her on. "Eliot—"

"Please, Ilsa." He had the sense to look apologetic, but not enough to relent. They arrived at the door of Hester's bedchamber and Eliot knocked. Several locks turned and Fliss appeared on the other side, looking harried.

"She won't let me lift her," she whispered as they passed.

Hester was sat on the bed, her fingers clinging to the sheets. A narrow door had been opened in one wall, and a lamp glowed inside. Ilsa's chest tightened.

"This is my house," Hester said through clenched teeth. "Take me downstairs so I can defend it."

Eliot groaned and ran a tense hand through his hair. "You know, in a better moment, you approved of this plan," he said as he approached the bed. Hester only glared. "You can't defend us today, Hester, but you can stay alive. *Please.*"

Slowly, her fingers relinquished their grip on the sheets, and when she let out a relenting sigh, Eliot swept her up and placed her in the hidden space behind the wall.

Then it was Ilsa's turn. There was a chance she would be sick.

"No. Eliot. Please don't put me in there," she rasped.

He and Fliss exchanged exasperated looks. Ilsa took a step towards the bedroom door, but Fliss shifted in front of it.

"Forgive us," she said, "but you're the acolytes' target, Ilsa. We can't protect the house while we're trying to protect you."

"You don't need to protect me, I can hide! I'll shift into a mouse. They won't see me." She backed away as Eliot approached, shaking his head. "*Eliot—*"

But Eliot lifted her clean off the floor and, before she could shift and skin him, deposited her next to Hester.

"I have to," he said weakly, backing her further into the hidden room. Bare brick met her back less than three feet in. "It's what we decided if they attacked again. We can't risk your murder."

What we decided. Anger lanced through her.

"*I* din't decide. Let me fight!" The words spilled out in a jumble. "I've been practising! I've got a combat form—"

"This isn't practice!" he yelled. He glanced over his shoulder at the sound of another window breaking. "I'll be back before you know it."

"No—"

As the panel slid into place, its edges vanishing against the seams of the wooden wall, Ilsa's knees buckled. Her vision was blurring around the edges, perhaps to save her from seeing the dimensions of the "room". But she could feel them; feel four solid walls within arm's reach.

She closed her eyes and drew her knees to her chest, not caring if Hester was watching and judging her. She wasn't at the orphanage, she told herself. She wasn't trapped, not forever. The wolves would fight off the invaders and then she would be freed. She just needed to survive until then. She needed to breathe.

But the memories were coming with startling clarity. The screams of the other children as she became one of them by mistake. Bruising her feet as she was dragged up the stairs, begging. The iron scrape of the lock on the attic door. The taste of dust and rot on the air; the cold whisper of a draught kissing her hairline. The hides of dogs and birds and horses prickled across Ilsa's skin, but the harder she grasped for them, the more their full forms eluded her. She couldn't do it. She would never be able to change at will; to get out of here. Miss Mitcham would open the door again, and Ilsa would perform her penance, shaking, because she knew that within days, her ungodly curse would erupt again, and maybe this time the matron would tie her up. Ilsa made her do it, she said. She had to protect the other children from this devil she'd been cursed with.

Ilsa heard herself moan. How could she hurt the other children when she was barely allowed to spend time with them?

Something cold and hard pressed against her arm. Ilsa covered her mouth to stifle a yell and opened her eyes. Hester was staring opaquely at her, her arm outstretched. In her hand, against Ilsa's arm, was a metal flask.

"I'm sorry we don't have a magic potion for misery, but whisky laced with vemanta has always worked for me."

Focusing on nothing but the flask, Ilsa took it from her and hastily unscrewed the top. She took two long gulps, relishing the burn as it barrelled through her. The sensation that followed was unexpected. It was like sinking into a feather bed when exhaustion was about to claim you. The wall and floor grew softer. Her limbs felt loose. It occurred to Ilsa that this lack of control was why she had vowed never to drink as Blume had, but the corresponding emotions were blunted. She wasn't content, she wasn't comfortable, but she wasn't going to vomit either.

"Better?" said Hester, taking the flask.

Ilsa only nodded, and Hester let out a humourless chuckle and frowned at the flask. "The effects get weaker with constant use, but this small dose just about keeps me sane. Most of the time." She sighed. "I hate to state the obvious but this box would be larger if you were *smaller*. A rabbit, perhaps."

Ilsa only shook her head. She couldn't be smaller, weaker. If anything, she wanted her snow leopard. But she couldn't explain that to Hester; she could barely explain it to herself.

But Hester didn't press, and they lapsed into silence. Ilsa tuned out the distant sounds of violence and focused on the feeling of the vemanta.

"I'm sorry you got hurt."

Hester's eyes snapped to hers. "You grew up in an orphanage,

251

yes?" she said with no hint of sympathy, as if she were asking where she could buy nutmeg. Ilsa nodded. "And you ran away. Why? And don't lie. I'll know if you're lying."

The memories felt so real that Ilsa wondered if Hester could see them too. The older she got, the more her magic grew, and the longer she spent suffering for it until, by the end, she forgot what the rest of the orphanage looked like.

"They were 'fraid of me," Ilsa said, her eyes on her hands. "They... did things."

With frightening speed, Hester shifted within reach of Ilsa and snatched her wrist. With her other hand, she pulled back the sleeve of Ilsa's nightgown. "Show me."

Ilsa didn't have the wits to disobey, nor to question how Hester knew. She had mastered this one deception so flawlessly that she could literally maintain it in her sleep, but she grappled at its edges now and tore it down. The scars rose from her skin like phantoms from the grave; white, ugly, and with gruesome stories to tell. Coils upon coils of them around each wrist where chains, wires, whatever Miss Mitcham could get her hands on had bitten into her flesh all those years.

"They must have thought you an abomination," Hester said conversationally, pushing herself back against the wall and toying with her long braid. Ilsa vanished the marks from her wrist and leaned away from her, or tried; even with the alcohol and vemanta calming her nerves, the room was definitely shrinking. "Did they bleed you? Try to exorcise you? Flog you holy?"

"All of it. 'Til I ran away." Ilsa tentatively reached for the flask and Hester gave it to her.

"And then – what luck? I lose everything and Gedeon goes

rogue. He kidnaps the Seer's apprentice, the Seer puts a bounty on you, and my lieutenants whisk you home like—" She snapped her fingers. Cruel amusement sparkled in her eyes. "Now you have a house full of wolves fighting to protect you, and your biggest worry is a few minutes in here with me. Don't be sorry I got hurt, cousin dearest. It was the best thing that ever happened to you."

Perhaps she was right. But curled up in that closet-sized hole in the wall, in a house under siege from two kinds of enemy, Ilsa learned to be careful what she wished for. She took another long drag of the spiked whisky, squeezed her eyes shut, and prayed to the Witherward's damned stars that everyone would make it out of this alive.

Especially Eliot. He had a whole other kind of hell waiting for him when Ilsa got free.

Slowly, the sounds of fighting died away, and not long after, the hidden door slid open. Fliss's hair was falling from its pins, and she was breathing heavily, but she looked unharmed.

"The Zoo is secure," she told Hester.

"Then get me out of here," said Hester through gritted teeth.

Ilsa scrambled gratefully out into Hester's bedroom and gulped down several large breaths. The cocktail she had taken to survive the box was resurging with the fresh air in her lungs, and as she climbed to her feet, a soothing tingle spread through her.

But she was not too afflicted to gasp when a familiar black panther padded into the room, dragging a wailing Oracle man by the arm. Then with one fluid, lightning-quick motion, Eliot was before them. He lifted the man by the collar, and tossed him at Hester's feet.

"I brought you a gift to make up for hiding you."

At the sight of the Oracle, something came alive in Hester. "Stars, how many of you people have we killed this week?" she said. "Keep coming at her like this and you'll be an endangered species. Any others?"

Eliot shook his head. There was blood on his shirt, and it had torn down the arm where he'd been cut. "The Sorcerers were all wearing homing charms. They were vanishing to wherever they came from as quickly as we could wound them. There were only half a dozen Oracles. The rest are all dead."

"Sorcerers and Oracles?" Eliot nodded. "But the Fortunatae have members in every faction—"

"They're not here," said Eliot. "They don't need to be. They've got this rebellion on a string, I guarantee it, and now they have the Docklands too. They're all working together."

"So Gedeon has made this easy for them." Hester tutted and added scathingly: "Well done, little cousin."

Oren entered, looking just as battle-weary. There was a glint of violence and bloodlust in his eyes as he said, "Three wolves down. The raiders formed groups and fanned out around us. It was a sweep. Or would have been, if they had gotten very far. Aelius was right, they're looking for something."

The Oracle on the floor was clutching his arm where Eliot had bitten him and was moaning in pain. Eliot lifted him to his feet. "I think we ought to make the most of this audience, don't you?" he said, grasping the man by his hair.

Ilsa swallowed. She was about to witness something horrible, but perhaps it would tell her something about her brother, so she was going nowhere.

Hester levelled her lethal glare at the Oracle. "Have you allied with the Fortunatae?"

The man was breathing heavily. He mustered a cruel smile. "The enemy – of my enemy – is my friend."

"Yes, yes. Oren."

It was then Ilsa noticed that Oren, pacing like a caged animal, had a knife. "Hold him," he said in his ever-genial tone. Ilsa tensed as Eliot tightened his grip on the Oracle and tilted his head back. Oren brought the knife up to rest on the man's cheek.

"I've always wondered," said Hester. She wasn't even looking at Oren or the knife, but searching her braid for split ends and plucking them out. "If you take an Oracle's eyes, can they still See?"

Without further preamble, Oren drove the knife into the soft flesh of the Oracle's eye socket. The man screamed; a high-pitched, agonised sound that sobered Ilsa a little. But the acolytes had attacked her three times now, and they had murdered Martha. She felt surprisingly little urge to turn away as Oren hooked his bloodied fingers around the man's eyeball and tore it out.

The man trembled and wilted like he would faint, but Eliot forced him upright as Oren calmly wiped his hands on his handkerchief then wrapped the eye in it.

"Please!" cried the Oracle, blood pouring in a steady stream down his face and onto the floor.

Hester looked incredulous at his plea. "You attack the Zoo, you pay the price," she intoned, as if this was simple arithmetic. "No riddles, no lies. And if you utter the words *yours not to know* I will have the other eye. The Fortunatae are making your rebel friends dance, are they not?"

"Yes," the captive whimpered. Hester shot Eliot a look that was almost approving, and he nodded.

"And you have allied with them too."

"Yes."

"There's a good man. Though it's awfully bold of the Docklands to anger Camden *and* the Heart in one fell swoop, I can't fault the Seer's bravado. So. Where is Gedeon Ravenswood?"

"I d-d-don't know," the man gasped. "I don't have enough power. Please—"

"Stop your begging," Hester snapped. "Did he really kidnap your Seer's apprentice?"

"Yes!"

"Oren." Oren brought his knife down above the Oracle's other eye.

"Please, understand!" he shrieked. Oren paused. "The apprentice belongs to the Seer. They are not free to leave."

"Is he making sense to you, Eliot?" said Hester.

"Not much," growled Eliot.

"Oren?"

"Sounds like a riddle to me." Oren pressed his blade nearer the Oracle's eye socket.

"The Changelings came for the temple! We were ready for them but the apprentice was not there!" His words fell over each other. "The apprentice met them on the border of our lands. They went willingly but they were not free to leave."

"I see," said Hester acidly. "What a neat little deception."

"Where're they now?" said Ilsa, stepping in front of the Oracle's remaining eye.

The man recognised her as his target, and unmistakable

256

violence flashed across the visible part of his face. Eliot noticed it too, and it earned the man a blow hard enough to double him over.

"No one can See Cogna," he gasped when he recovered. "Cogna is different from the rest of us."

"Different how?" said Hester.

"No one can See Cogna." His words were slurring together. He was going to pass out.

Hester sighed. "Send him home," she said. "See that he doesn't drop dead on the way. I want the Docklands to see for themselves what this vendetta will cost them. Fliss, fetch me another bottle of whisky."

As Eliot and Oren hauled the now unconscious captive from the room and Fliss peeled off to the pantry, Ilsa made straight for Fyfe's lab, hoping desperately to find it whole and Fyfe unharmed.

She was relieved to find not just Fyfe, but Cassia and Aelius in the lab, none looking too worse for wear. As for the room itself – Ilsa had forgotten the clutter. It was difficult to tell at first glance whether it had been spared a ransacking, but after a moment, it was clear the raiders hadn't been there.

"They din't get in," Ilsa said, and for Fyfe, she managed a smile – but he didn't return it.

"Well… actually, it appears they did," he said, scouting about and rubbing his hair absent-mindedly. "Everything's undamaged and where I left it. Nothing's missing – except the pocket forge."

Cassia was eyeing the clutter disapprovingly. "You're certain it's not… somewhere here?"

Fyfe pointed to the desk full of holes. "It lives right here, between this inkwell and this bookend. I was showing it to Ilsa just yesterday and I put it back there as always." He shrugged despondently. "I know the place is a mess, but it's organised mess."

"These damned raiders have been making the odd visit since the spring," said Aelius. "They couldn't possibly have been looking for a… what did you say this thing is, Fyfe? A torch of some kind?"

"It's a" – Fyfe sighed and rolled his eyes, like he'd explained it a thousand times – "the pocket forge can melt *anything*, Aelius, don't you see? One could, I don't know, rob a bank with it."

"Or destroy a magical artefact," said Cassia ponderously.

"Precisely!" agreed Fyfe, before frowning. "Although, what artefact exactly, and how destroying it would help their cause, I haven't the faintest."

They lapsed into silence. To have the thing the rebels were looking for finally taken, and so quietly, felt like a perverse anticlimax, especially given what the Zoo – and Hester in particular – had suffered in obstructing them. But something about it didn't feel right. If the thing the rebels had been searching for was here all along – then what was Gedeon doing?

Ilsa's gaze met Cassia's, and she could tell the other woman was thinking the same thing.

"I don't see any catastrophic outcome in the rebels having this pocket forge," Cassia said, but there was no relief in her tone.

"P'raps one of the Oracles took it," said Ilsa. "They'd know where to find it without turning the place over. And I s'pose they'd know if they might need it at some point in the future. And I wouldn't put it past any of the Oracles I've met to rob a bank if they could."

Aelius chuckled. "Yes, indeed. I'm sure one of our forceful guests simply took a shine to the thing."

"Either way, we can't relax," said Cassia, turning and heading for the door. "I'll pass this on to Oren and the wolves, but I recommend we prepare for more raids." She paused at the threshold. "I've a feeling this isn't over."

Ilsa followed after her and found Eliot lurking in the corridor. The Oracle had been unloaded on someone else, but his blood still mingled with Eliot's in patches on his shirtsleeves.

"Walk me to my room?" said Ilsa.

Foolishly, Eliot obliged. The second everybody else was out of sight, Ilsa turned on him, arms folded tightly across her chest to stop herself throwing a punch. Eliot must have seen the fury burning in her eyes as she did so, for he stepped back warily.

"Next time you pull something like that, I will hammer the living daylights out of you, you hear?"

"Pull something like what?" choked Eliot.

"You shut me in a three-foot box!" said Ilsa, voice rising with every vicious syllable.

Eliot groaned and looked heavenward. "Stars, Ilsa, I was following orders," he said tiredly. For a moment Ilsa watched him in stunned silence as he picked at a bloodstain on his shirtsleeve, not even looking at her. After everything she had lived through that evening – the attack, the hidden room, watching a man be tortured – Ilsa finally felt her very last nerve snap.

She placed her hands on Eliot's chest and pushed him into the wall.

He stumbled. He was looking at her *now*. "What the—"

"How do *you* like being pushed around, Eliot?"

"I—" he cut off, mouth snapping shut, the indignation wiping clean off his face and leaving it blank.

"I *begged* you not to lock me in there." Ilsa was trembling, and she prayed that her words wouldn't do the same, but she could feel the angry tears building behind her eyes. "P'raps I can't… fight off rebels as well as you or… or make a plan if we get attacked. But that don't give you the right to lock me up like I'm the fine china you don't want the rebels to break. So you can hang your orders! You think Hester's got a bite? Well I can still shift, and I'll rip your bloody throat out the next time."

For a long moment the only sound was Ilsa's breathing as it came in jagged pulls of air. Slowly, Eliot leaned back against the wall and buried his face in his hands.

"Stars help me," he whispered between his fingers. When he looked up at her, bleak remorse shone in his eyes. "I've grown so used to doing as Hester orders," he said softly, "even when it feels wrong." He rubbed his eyes and rolled them heavenward. "Though now I think on it, I would have forced her into that room too. I panicked. Ilsa, I'm so very sorry."

Ilsa nodded tightly, the violence that had been coiling inside her like a snake loosening. Given time, it would melt away.

Eliot straightened his ruined shirt and fixed his hair, all the while watching her guardedly.

"I didn't realise the hidden room would be such a… an ordeal for you."

"It weren't," said Ilsa automatically, tilting her chin proudly.

"Really."

They were near a window seat, and Ilsa dragged herself to it and sat down. Only when she tried to fold her hands in her lap did she notice they were still trembling. There was a spattering of the Oracle's blood near the hem of her robe, but when she closed her eyes, it wasn't the image of his bloodied, empty eye socket that assaulted her. It was the door to the hidden room sliding closed. Better to open her eyes and look at Eliot. She concentrated on the sharp lines of his jaw and cheekbones, more elegant than she had first thought; on the fathomless intensity in his eyes as they searched hers with something like concern.

"I'm sorry I shut you in a three-foot box. I ought to have listened." With the tentativeness of a nervous wild animal, he lowered himself onto the seat beside her. "May I ask something?"

The only safe answer to that question was *no*, but Ilsa saw an opportunity. "I'll trade you. You answer one first."

A muscle fluttered in Eliot's jaw. "Alright."

"Where's Gedeon?"

Eliot's breath left him in a rush. Ilsa thought it might be relief. "I'm still offended by that question."

"Then why'd he leave?"

"I don't know that either."

"But you might. You might have clues at least." He was shaking his head, but she pressed on. "What was his mood like? What did you talk about? He do anything strange?"

"No," snapped Eliot, surprising them both, and Ilsa remembered who he was: the boy no one trusted. The boy with secrets.

"I see they din't teach you manners in the Witherward," she parroted, holding his cold glare with her own.

"Oh, they tried." Eliot leaned his forearms on his knees and rubbed his eyes. He groaned and relented. "Between the attack and Gedeon leaving, I barely saw him. And we didn't speak once."

"Weren't that strange itself?" challenged Ilsa.

"Well, yes, but his cousin had nearly been killed, and as alpha, Gedeon felt responsible." He paused, then added stonily: "As any of us would."

"What 'bout... meetings and that?"

"There were none."

This would get her nowhere. "I s'pose he wanted to be with Hester, din't he?" she said weakly.

At this, Eliot tilted his head. "Well, no. He barely saw her either."

"What? How'd you know?"

"Because I hardly left her side," he said, looking at his hands. The right one clenched and fidgeted, toying with a pocket watch he had no doubt left in his room during the commotion. "I heard him talking with Fliss in the lounge once or twice, but he never came to her bedside. Not when I was with her, at least."

Ilsa grappled to place this in the growing picture. Hadn't she decided there was bad blood between Eliot and Hester? Had he sat at her sickbed because he cared for her? Ilsa's boldness nearly got the better of her, but she bit back any more questions. She had the sense she would scare the honesty out of him if she got too close to the truth.

"Look." He cleared his throat. "Talk to Cassia. If any of us have been privy to some clues they didn't recognise, as you say, it'll be her. Perhaps Gedeon let something pertinent slip during their pillow talk."

"Their – oh."

Ilsa marvelled at her own obliviousness. The impenetrable sadness behind her eyes; the cracks she couldn't hide when someone mentioned Gedeon; the brittle shell she had donned to keep herself upright.

Cassia's heart was broken.

"I din't realise," said Ilsa.

"So you got some information from me after all. Now it's my turn." He straightened and eyed her curiously. "You fight with your fists. I hear when you woke up in the Zoo you threatened Cassia with a statue."

"That ain't a question."

"You're a Changeling, Ilsa. A capable one, I hear. But you don't use your magic on instinct. Why?"

Ilsa pretended to rearrange the folds of her dressing gown. "I use my magic," she said. "I used it to sneak and get places and that before, when people weren't looking. It ain't like you can bust into a leopard in the street in the Otherworld."

"You're not in the Otherworld any more."

"I *know* that, I just… it's habit, is all."

"Did any Otherworlders ever see you shift?"

"Plenty. But the only one who knew it weren't a magic trick was Mr Blume."

"No one else?"

He knew the answer. She could tell from the way he looked at her like he'd believe anything she told him.

"And how d'you think them Otherworlders would react if they did see it?" she challenged. "They don't know 'bout magic through the portal but they know 'bout God and the devil. Anyone knew the things I could do, they'd think I was possessed by something from hell. They'd think my magic came from the devil."

"There's no such thing as the devil," he said.

"Oh yeah? You can tell that to—"

She stopped herself too late. The liquid quality of Eliot's eyes turned to ice.

"Who?" The word rushed out like a breath. Was he truly angry for her? And did it mean anything, when he was angry about everything else?

"It don't matter. Point is, p'raps I had good reason to learn not to use my magic." Ilsa shifted to look out the window. The chaos of the attack still hadn't been righted. Someone had sent for more wolves to reinforce security, and they were receiving orders on the lawn. A body lay near the wall. Someone had covered it with a sheet, but the blood was seeping through.

Helpless to stop it, Ilsa snorted out a laugh. Eliot eyed her with a new kind of concern.

"Least no one wanted to run me out of London in the Otherworld. And your damned Principles mean I can't use my magic for nothing a mile east of here, or they'll kill me." She shook her head. "Captain Fowler told me this weren't the bad side of the portal. He said there's worse horrors where I'm from."

Eliot's scowl returned in full force, and when he spoke, his voice was cold and hard as marble. "Cadell Fowler lives and breathes for blood. Carving up his enemies is his idea of bliss."

Ilsa shook her head. "He said there'd be peace one day. Everyone's just got to decide they want it."

"Do you believe that? That it could be so simple?" It wasn't a rhetorical question. He tilted his head, studied her mournfully and waited.

"I don't know. I can't get my head 'round nothing 'bout this damned city."

"Then allow me to explain."

He stood, offering a hand to pull Ilsa to her feet before steering her in the direction of her bedchamber.

"London is nothing but a battleground *disguised* as a city. The Callicans founded it to assert their dominance and when the empire fell, domination was for the taking. This city is *designed* to court hatred, Ilsa. It's in its bones. We'll fight and we'll die, and then our children will fight over our bones, and so on."

"Trying to protect yourself ain't the same as having hate for those what threaten it. That ain't what Camden's doing."

"Fight for long enough and you'll stop seeing the difference."

"Then why do it at all?" said Ilsa, throwing her arms wide. "Why not leave?"

They had reached her bedroom door. Eliot opened it but didn't go inside. There was an intensity in the way he regarded her that was nothing like the fierce malice he so often wore. It was determined and passionate.

"Because there are ordinary people in this city who are just trying to live. Who keep their heads down and don't attract attention; who follow the rules to the letter to buy themselves as much peace and safety as they can scrape together; who are trying to be happy. You said it yourself – they have lives here. And it's not the choice I would make, but they're entitled to it. So as long as there is a single Changeling living in London – an *ordinary* Changeling; a chimney sweep or a schoolmaster or a laundry woman – then the Zoo will protect their right to be here. *I* will protect that right. If we stop fighting, we condemn them all."

Occasionally, a person had a different kind of tell. Lying made people feel vulnerable, but the truth – when that truth really, truly mattered to them – did the same. It was hard to disguise, just like a lie.

For a moment, Ilsa didn't care what Eliot's concern for her meant, or what his secrets were. There was good in him, she could see it, and it was noble and self-sacrificing. He hated this city – this battleground – and he was here anyway. Without second-guessing herself, she took Eliot's face in her hands – inhaling the scent of fresh linens and rain – stood on tiptoes, and lightly pressed her lips to a fresh bruise blossoming on his jaw. He stiffened, but he didn't stop her. When she didn't immediately pull away, his hand drifted tentatively to her waist.

Ilsa hadn't meant to linger; hadn't planned to crave more of this. But she couldn't take her hands off him, so she let them drift down his neck, across his shoulders to his chest. He drew in a sharp breath.

"Ilsa…" There was no mistaking the reproach in his voice, the warning, even as his hand tightened on her waist and his breath hitched. And he was right. The part of her she still controlled didn't want to kiss Eliot this way. If she fell into him now, when all her other thoughts were of prisons and chains and people who wished her harm, she might want to get lost.

Maybe that wasn't Eliot's concern. Maybe he was thinking of a pocket watch with another girl's name on it.

She let her hands fall. She put some distance between their lips.

"Your people are lucky to have you, Eliot," she whispered against his shoulder.

Then she stepped through her bedroom door and closed it behind her, with Eliot staring dazedly after her.

18

As the Zoo's master of "communications", Aelius was the one to face the Seer in the Docklands and request they drop their vendetta now that the Zoo knew the truth. It was not a long visit. The Oracles were stalwart; Gedeon Ravenswood had broken the Principles, and they would have Ilsa's life in compensation. Nothing Aelius said could talk them out of trying to claim it.

"But I suppose there's good news," said Aelius wryly. "Their own stubborn traditionalism means the truth of Gedeon's misdeeds still remains between us and the Docklands. Theirs to know, everyone else's not to, and all that nonsense."

"Great," Ilsa whispered to Fyfe. "So the rebels are looking for we don't know what for we don't know what purpose that probably involves revenge and overthrowing us, the Oracles only want to kill me – guess that's something to be thankful for – and the Fortunatae want to wipe out my family and dissolve Camden, and have done a champion job of getting the rest to put their differences aside and work together to destroy us. But least no one's worried Gedeon's gonna kidnap them too. Then we'd really be in trouble." Fyfe didn't laugh and Ilsa didn't blame him. It wasn't funny. "I don't get it. We got wolves and barricades all 'round the border, right? So why let any Oracles in at all? Why let anyone in?"

"Trade," said Fyfe. "It's the only thing that's sacred in this city. The threat of losing it is perhaps what keeps the Principles working. We're free to close our borders, but if we did, the Docklands would almost certainly close theirs to us. And the Oracles have possession of the docks, of course. They don't have the numbers or, ah… care to manage them, so the rest of us pay them a share to do our own business. It's how they stay solvent despite the vemanta crisis. We trade with all the factions." He smiled wryly. "We're all doing so much violence, swindling one another at the Trade House is almost a good-natured pastime."

When they weren't trying to get a step ahead of the rebels or bargain with the Docklands, it was mainly trade that kept the lieutenants busy, because just weeks before, it had been Hester's job. There was still a faction to manage, and the unfortunate irony was that managing it without Gedeon left little time for *finding* Gedeon, even if they hadn't exhausted all their ideas.

They were so stretched that they even begrudgingly called on Eliot, if only for the most menial and innocuous tasks. It left Ilsa truly on her own in her search for clues to Gedeon's whereabouts, but Eliot had given her a new lead.

It was many days after learning of the Sorcerer and her brother, that Ilsa finally cornered Cassia. Fyfe had told her that she had a small laboratory of her own, and that she had been spending a lot of time there recently. Unfortunately, its location did not appeal. The hidden room in Hester's chambers was one type of horror, but it wasn't where Ilsa's fear came from; it wasn't an attic.

Cassia's lab was a narrow, bare space in the servants' quarters, with dark floorboards, white walls, and a small lattice window looking onto the roof. On a wooden bench along one wall was a neat succession of flasks and beakers, and opposite, two shelves of orderly, labelled jars. A glass-fronted cabinet at the far end housed what looked like completed concoctions. There was none of the clutter, or the appeal, of Fyfe's larger, eclectic space downstairs.

Cassia was stood by the open window, frowning into a book. A breeze was making a lock of black hair dance across her shoulder, but if she had noticed, she didn't mind. Ilsa fixed her eyes on that window – through which she could fly away if she needed to – and rapped lightly on the open door.

"Oh, hello," Cassia said. She looked neither pleased nor uncomfortable to see her, but instead folded her book closed and turned to a large round flask on the bench. It contained a transparent liquid of the palest green, and underneath, a tiny flame bloomed from thin air.

"D'you do that?" Ilsa gasped.

"Hmm? Oh, that." Cassia snapped her fingers and a small flame erupted at her fingertips. She shook it out like she would a match. "I've been slaving over this potion for four days, and everyone who has come up here has marvelled at that *flame*, perhaps the most basic bit of corporeal magic. Changelings."

"What is it?" asked Ilsa.

"It's supposed to be a truth serum. Hester asked me to try and make one up after that Oracle Eliot captured was so uncooperative, but even a specialist potion master would struggle with the formula, and I'm nothing of the sort." They shared a glance at the fact that Hester had asked anyone to do anything other than wheel her back to bed. "I've been testing it on myself and all I've managed to do is induce hallucinations. Oren came by this morning and found me arguing with an empty chair." Her

270

words became quieter and more mumbled as she spoke, and Ilsa wondered who Cassia had thought was with her.

"D'you make all them potions?" she asked instead, gesturing to the cabinet. One of them was the syrupy magenta sleeping draft Cassia had once given her. A crate on the bottom shelf read ANTIDOTES, which struck Ilsa as wise.

"Well, the Zoo could hardly let a Sorcerer into their ranks and not put her to work. I prefer corporeal magic to this stuff, but I like to be of use."

"But Fyfe makes potions too, don't he?"

"He does," Cassia said with a pensive tilt of her head, "and he's a remarkable chemist, but he always needs a little of my help. I imbue my potions with something Fyfe can't replicate on his own. Certain substances and ingredients are strong receptors, but they do very little by themselves. They can only perform magic" – Cassia pressed the very tips of her fingers to the bowl of the flask, and a barely discernible ripple shot through the liquid within – "with the right nudge."

Ilsa toyed absent-mindedly with the worn corner of the cabinet as she worked up to her reason for being there. "Eliot said you might be the one to talk to 'bout what happened with Gedeon just before he disappeared," she said, and Cassia blanched. "He said something 'bout pillow talk."

"Oh." Cassia turned back to her potion.

"I ain't judging. I've known lots of girls what've lain with men what ain't their husbands."

"It's not that. The Witherward is different to where you grew up. Our laws are concerned with far graver matters than our flesh. Our deities don't condemn us for what we do with ours.

271

Hester and Fyfe's mother was married to neither of the men who fathered her children, you know, and she was held in the highest esteem by all of Camden."

Perhaps Ilsa should have suspected something like that when she first learned a woman was in charge in Camden. Things were not as she had known them in the Otherworld.

"It's just that… Eliot doesn't approve of me."

"Why's that?"

Cassia's voice quivered as she answered. "My parents and yours were good friends. They wanted to strengthen the Heart's alliance with Camden, and raising us without the biases of their generation and my grandfather's was a way of accomplishing that. So they sent me here. I've known Gedeon since we were five years old. I lived here in the Zoo with your family. Eliot's father was a lieutenant to your mother so Eliot grew up here too. We played together. We shared a governess and took lessons together. Camden is my home and it always has been." Her voice broke. Indignation flared in her lovely, wide eyes. "But I needed a Sorcerer's education too. I wasn't entirely unversed in how to use my talents, but they did suffer because of my upbringing, so when I was fifteen, I went home."

"Was that before you and Gedeon were…?"

A faint, humourless smile appeared on Cassia's lips, but her eyes became even more desolate. "I always loved him. He has this way. He made all our differences feel like puzzles he wanted to solve. Even as a child, I knew that whatever I told him, he would make me feel clever or interesting or special for saying it. He just has this… curiosity for everything and everyone." She blinked, suddenly self-conscious. "I knew that he felt for me too, but I was shy. It was the hardest decision I ever made; to leave just as he was coming of age and meeting so many girls. I thought, without a doubt, he would fall in love while I was gone, and if I ever came back, I would be just this girl he knew once, deserving of his kindness and attention the way everyone is, but nothing more. But I wasn't a Changeling, I was a Sorcerer, and I wanted to be a talented one." She shrugged, a small smile creeping onto her lips. "And now, I suppose am."

Ilsa blinked. "But you weren't going far! You din't have to be separated."

"It wasn't the distance. There were those in the Heart already suspicious of my return. To split myself between the two would have meant belonging neither here nor there. It was hard enough being the only Sorcerer in Camden." There was an understanding between them then that only experience could bring. Cassia flashed that painful smile again. "I needn't have worried. The night I came back to the Zoo, everyone was looking for him. He was about to become alpha and he wasn't ready. Hester and Oren were putting him through hours of instruction every day. They were frantic that he was missing. I was about to join the search, but when I got to my room, I found a note on the bed telling me to meet him in the park. He had stolen away with pockets full of the sweet buns he had known I would miss – like a child. He wanted to know everything. It was as if no time had passed at all."

Cassia's eyes met hers with a sudden intensity. "He spoke of you often, Ilsa. They used to tell him as a child that you were out there and he would have his little sister back one day, before that woman told us you were dead. It was an unbearable sorrow to him. He never stopped mourning you."

As if from a distance, Ilsa marvelled at how she was still capable of feeling such pain. Gedeon had mourned her. He mourned her still. It was too much; she pushed the feeling down and cleared her throat. "And Eliot?"

Cassia sighed. "We were never the *closest* of friends. We were both quiet and introverted. We were both too serious to relax around one another. I always thought *I* was difficult to get to know, but Eliot couldn't make a friend if he were shackled to a willing volunteer. We needed Gedeon to bring us together. But that wasn't the problem." Her eyes glazed over and she turned to the window. "In the years I was gone, everything changed for Eliot. His father disappeared. Did you know?" Ilsa shook her head, her mind flashing back to that first night in the park. The torment she'd seen when she asked about Eliot's father. "Oftentimes, when someone is assassinated by the Order of Shadows, that's all that happens."

"Assassinated? You mean for money?"

Cassia nodded. "The Order of Shadows is the Wraith guild of mercenaries that Captain Fowler belongs to. They're as powerful as any of the factions. They might even be as large. They never act against anyone unless there's a fee involved but... well, one can't fault them for playing to their strengths as Wraiths.

"Anyway, assassination was the verdict, but sadly Eliot and his family will never know for sure. And we've no clue as to why. I understand how hard that must be, but he's been taking it out on all of us ever since. Myself, especially. He's mistrusting of everyone. I think he must believe the contract was from someone within the Zoo, and as an *outsider*" – she hissed the word – "I'm an easy target for his suspicions."

Ilsa's sudden sympathy for Eliot was uncomfortable. She

couldn't excuse his making Cassia feel like an outsider, but she knew what not knowing was like; how it had permeated her being and led her to keep others at a distance. If she had been like Eliot as a child – shy, quiet, instead of outgoing and charismatic – would she have grown to be just like him?

When Cassia continued, her voice was cold and brittle. "He's been a miserable thing since losing his father. Impossible to reach. I tried at first, but it was no use. The little goodwill Eliot ever extended, he reserved for Gedeon, and it vanished with him. I suppose it takes no great stretch of the imagination to see Eliot's keeping his secrets."

Ilsa suppressed a sigh. Cassia had told her to talk to Eliot, then Eliot had told her to talk to Cassia, when really it was clear they needed to talk to each other. "P'raps he is," she said. "But there's only one person whose fault this definitely is, and that's Gedeon. I know I don't know him, but it don't seem a very honourable thing to up and vanish when he's got all of Camden relying on him."

Cassia blinked at her, shaking her head. "You've got him wrong," she said, turning her attention to the flask. Ilsa waited for her to go on, but whatever defence Cassia had in mind, she couldn't muster the words.

"Put me right then," said Ilsa. "Help me understand it. Did he say nothing to you just before he left? Anything that seemed... I don't know, strange?"

Cassia was silent as she dipped a thermometer into the potion and watched the mercury rise. "Everything about those days was strange. Gedeon wasn't himself. But I'm sorry, Ilsa, I'm not the person to ask. Gedeon and I... we argued a couple of days before the attack, and he barely spoke to me after that."

Ilsa's heart sank. Had no one spent time with him before he left? "What'd you fight over?"

Cassia's hand shook as she removed the thermometer. Her eyes were glassy. "The stupidest thing." She sighed. She tried to gather herself, but failed, and the tears began falling. "He had planned a trip to Millwater. It's a Changeling town an hour or so upriver. He said he wanted to recruit some new wolves. He was taking a lot of the wolves on guard rotation at the Zoo. It seemed foolish to me that we should be left so poorly guarded when the rebel Sorcerers had been attacking. That was all. And in the end, it all came to nothing because" – she turned her back on Ilsa, and dried her tears with her handkerchief. When she turned around, it was with renewed composure – "well, the trip was cancelled at the last minute. We'd argued for nothing. And when the rebels *did* come two days later, it made no difference how heavily guarded we were. The worst still happened."

"But it was days after the attack that Gedeon left, weren't it?"

"A week, I believe."

"Din't you make up?" Ilsa didn't add that it sounded like an awfully petty squabble to hold a grudge over.

Cassia sighed. "I thought we did. He came to my room one night, very late, and apologised. He told me I was blameless. When I fell asleep, all was well between us, but when I woke up…" Her gaze stretched towards an invisible distance. "I haven't seen him since that night."

Ilsa's heart hurt for her. The Sorcerer fell silent, her gaze on the window, and Ilsa suddenly felt like she was intruding. She was about to take her leave when Cassia spoke again.

"Which is worse, Ilsa? To be bereaved, or abandoned? For a person you love to be taken from you, or for him to leave, without a word, of his own accord?"

"I thought I knew," said Ilsa with a weak smile. "Then you brought me here, and I don't know how I feel 'bout none of it."

As Ilsa made to leave, she brushed past the other girl. Cassia's fingers reached for hers, squeezed ever so lightly, and let go.

19

Cassia's tell was more subtle than Eliot's, but she too, was hiding something.

It was the slightest hitch in her voice – a feigned lightness – that had raised the hairs on Ilsa's neck. It didn't take a card player to spot the lie; the picture Cassia painted of her argument with Gedeon didn't add up. She hadn't heard the full story, but what she had learned from Cassia suggested a new and potentially crucial conclusion:

Something had been eating at Gedeon *before* the attack.

But did Cassia know what it was? It was hard to even glance at the girl without seeing the pain of the things Gedeon had done. If he hadn't broken her heart with his secrets – if Cassia truly knew more than she was letting on – did that mean it was all an act?

And if it wasn't, how could Gedeon do such a thing? To disappear before morning like a dream. Even one of the wolves had left word for the girl he loved, but their leader hadn't. Did it show the strength of his dedication to whatever secret plan was in motion – or was it only thoughtless cruelty?

You've got him wrong.

On the way back to her room Ilsa paused by the last portrait in the long gallery. The slant of the setting sun fell across the Prince of Camden's golden hair.

He looked every bit the beatific, charismatic young man Cassia had painted him to be. To imagine him as cruel was unthinkable.

Ilsa cast her eyes over the rest of the benevolent and earnest faces peering back at her from along the length of the corridor. The Ravenswood dynasty. The founders of Camden, saviours of the Changelings. Each one was immortalised like royalty, with a red silk sash draped from shoulder to hip, jewels and satins and gold buttons immaculate and gleaming. Her mother, her grandfather, her great-grandmother. All the way back to Morgan Ravenswood, russet-haired and hawkish. Even the Fortunatae believed that to bring down the Ravenswoods was to bring down Camden. Looking at their portraits, Ilsa could almost believe it too.

But could she believe she belonged to them?

It was unfathomable to her. The history of London Ilsa knew was of William the Conqueror, the Great Fire, the Gunpowder Plot. That her own ancestors had a place in the history of *this* London, that such a thing could be true of a former street urchin, was so far removed from her own life that she may as well have been looking at illustrations in a storybook.

But were these likenesses any more truthful? That's all they were; just paintings. Vanity pieces commissioned by their subjects to cast them in the flattering glow of glory and renown. She scrutinised the portrait of Gedeon again. Nowhere in those clever, courageous eyes was a reckless nineteen-year-old who had fled from his post and left chaos behind him. The first time she had stood here, looking upon her brother's face had made her feel he was just beyond her grasp, a hair's breadth from her fingertips. Now he felt remote, unreachable.

Ilsa turned on her heel, spurred by a sudden flair of frustration and an inkling of how to solve it. An oil painting hanging in a gilded frame of a marbled hallway could not bring the real Gedeon closer. And as sharp and sensible as Cassia may be, she wouldn't be the first girl to be blinded by love, so neither could she.

No one in the Zoo could.

The sun had dipped below the horizon when Ilsa cracked open the window of a deserted corridor above the terrace. Venture downstairs, and she would certainly be seen, so she shifted into a sparrow, slipped through the window, and dropped into the hydrangeas at the edge of the terrace.

The wolf on the perimeter was nowhere in sight; the one by the west gate was about to turn south. Technically, Eliot had been telling the truth when he said the wolves weren't there to keep anyone in, and Ilsa knew that now. But she also knew she wasn't supposed to leave the safety of the Zoo without a guard, and being cossetted like a princess of Camden was the last thing she wanted tonight. She wasn't a princess; she was a Changeling who had survived alone for seventeen years. So, with a glance back at the house to check no one was watching, she scuttled across the lawn before either wolf could see her and launched herself over the wall.

She would head northeast, she decided, towards Camden as she'd known it in the Otherworld. Perhaps away from the Zoo and the volatile south tip of the quarter – by the Trade House, the river, and the abbey – there would be fewer militia. So she flew in a wide circle around the Zoo, occasionally taking cover in a tree to check no wolf was watching. But dusk had descended like a sheet of black gossamer, and a single sparrow was near invisible in the gloom. Buoyant from her seamless escape, Ilsa glided over the canal and landed on her human legs just beyond the northeast corner of the Zoo, a sly smile on her lips. She looked back towards the house – just as three off-duty militiawomen eating supper by the canal looked up and froze in surprise.

"Oh bloody—"

"Muh whaydee?" said one around a bite of her apple.

Ilsa took off again, this time on falcon's wings. She heard her name being called, the splash of something that might have been an apple thrown into the canal. They were following her, three trained wolves, maybe more by now. Speed wouldn't help her. Only anonymity would give her a chance, so she nose-dived between two rows of houses on the High Street.

It was a mistake; the High Street was not quiet, as she'd expected at this time of the evening, but bustling with people. Vendors and shoppers, performers and dancers. A street party was in full swing, and in the thrill of the chase, Ilsa hadn't even heard the music. Now she was plummeting into the thick of it, with no time left to change course.

She shrank herself, slipping impossibly between the party-goers and landing hard, but on her feet, in the form of a tabby cat.

"Look out!" Somebody's tankard of ale followed her down as he tottered to keep his balance without stepping on her. A woman shrieked as he grasped her skirt for support, and as they both went tumbling – she changing into a bird and neatly missing the ground, he landing face down in his spilled ale to a roar of approving laughter – Ilsa darted away on light paws.

She made for the edge of the street where the crowds were

thinner, slipping between feet and hooves and paws. She caught flashes of black and white stripes, rainbow feathers, long, chestnut fur. Every once in a while, a cheer swelled up from somewhere else in the crowd, part shouts and clapping, but also made up of howls and whinnies and growls. Ilsa felt the buzz in her bloodstream kick up a notch as she hopped up onto a barrel to see if she was still being followed. But there were too many people. It would be impossible to tell if the wolves were coming, and a tabby cat disguise wouldn't save her from discovery. They would be scanning the crowd – human and beast alike – for her distinctive hazel eyes.

Ilsa scanned about for a better vantage point, ears pricking when her eyes alighted on it. She grew wings again, dodging other Changelings in the carnival forms of tropical birds: scarlet and golden and green. Past the bunting and strings of lanterns, up onto the rooftop of a butcher's shop, where she crouched low, shifted into a human disguise – with mousy hair and a face to match – and gazed down at the scene below her.

Changelings, it seemed, were their own entertainment. Interspersed with the feasting and dancing, the revellers joined in all sorts of games. Shrieks of laughter were coming from a circle where a precarious sculpture of counter-balanced monkeys was forming, each new joiner climbing over the heads and limbs of the others to form the next row. From the numerous spectators nursing small hurts, Ilsa could guess this wasn't the first attempt.

At the visibly drunker end of the street, two hulking gorillas wrestled as bets were placed among the spectators. Ilsa's eyes grew wide. No party she had ever attended had included competitive fighting among the entertainments, but then again, no party she had ever been to had been held among Changelings. The mind became a duller, more instinctive thing in the body of an animal. Ilsa conceded that if she were a gorilla – a drunken one at that – she might find it fun to wrestle someone too. She wondered what Alitz would make of it.

But the biggest event was unfolding in a space in the middle of the street. Revellers were taking turns to walk into the centre of the circle and showcase their most impressive transformations. As Ilsa watched, a hooked-nosed, greying woman stepped forward, and with a surprisingly wicked grin, folded in on herself until she was a tangle of smooth scales on the floor. Amidst the shrieks of delight and alarm, the tangle writhed grotesquely, and from its folds emerged the black eyes and triangular head of a python. As she raised her head, swaying uncannily and flicking her black tongue, she began to unfurl. The murmurs grew louder and turned into gasps as coils of the snake kept revealing themselves, like scarves out of a magician's cuff, until all twenty feet of her was uncoiled in the middle of the street. She raised her emerald head higher and took a serpentine bow to the raucous applause of the party-goers.

Next was an unassuming man who cracked his neck one way, then the other, screwed up his face in concentration, and transformed himself into a pure white peacock, unlike any Ilsa had ever seen.

Since coming to the Witherward, she had confirmed much of what she'd learned for herself about her magic, including the fact that a Changeling could only become an animal as it existed in nature. Bigger, if they were gifted with their magic, and as beautiful and fast and strong as they could muster, but they could not create, or amalgamate, only imitate. The albino peacock below wasn't just a showcase of the man's magic, but of his history and experience; the things he'd seen and learned. He drew an awed gasp from the mesmerised crowd as he spread his tail feathers in an arc, and was mobbed with questions when he stepped out of the circle.

The crowd began to rumble with thunderous shouts and applause as they parted to make way for a third competitor. Into the circle, arms raised in pride as she played the crowd, stepped a stocky, matronly woman of about fifty. She did a lap in front of the spectators, shouting encouragement as they chanted her name.

"Millie! Millie! Millie!"

Ilsa couldn't help but lean forward over the edge of the roof to get a better look as Millie took her place in the centre of the circle. A few of the onlookers encouraged the rest to step back as they pressed in, kids pulled into arms and behind legs to keep them from approaching.

And then Millie shifted. She fell to all fours as she swelled with a motion like bread rising. At the point Ilsa thought her skin might burst, it hardened and darkened to a wrinkled, grey hide. The lower part of her face appeared to melt and drip as it elongated, all in a flash.

Within a single second, Ilsa knew what she was witnessing. Within two, Millie was an elephant.

The roar of the crowd couldn't drown out her trumpeting as she raised her trunk triumphantly. Ilsa barely suppressed the urge to join in the applause, but she could see them now – six large hunting dogs with noses to the ground. The wolves were on the street, combing their way through the crowd, and they knew her scent. She wouldn't be safe on the roof for long; they would have hawks in the air soon, if they didn't already. But between sneaking out and finding the party, Ilsa was on too much of a high to be escorted home now. She still had a mission to fulfil before that happened.

She turned back into a sparrow, flitted to the other side of the roof, and dropped into the next street in her mousy human disguise. She only had to evade her pursuers long enough for them to realise she was no longer on the High Street and then she planned to double back. She'd had her eye on a tray of iced cakes that were circling.

But Ilsa had barely moved before a prickle on the back of her neck made her turn around. There was nothing there but a deserted corner where two houses met, but Ilsa hadn't picked pockets for years without learning when she was being watched. Music and laughter drifted from the High Street, amplifying the silence of where she stood – or masking the sound.

A strange instinct struck her.

"Eliot?" she called down the street, a vivid image in her mind of a panther stalking from the dark.

But there was no reply. If one of the wolves had found her, surely they wouldn't be playing this game. Not waiting to find out, Ilsa picked up her skirts and headed in the opposite direction, poised to sprout wings if one of the myriad threats of the Witherward emerged from the shadows. She pushed down her fear. There were wolves nearby, here precisely for her protection, wanted or not, and a whole community of Changelings, at least one of whom was strong enough to shift into an elephant.

But then, there it was again. The nagging sensation that

someone's eyes were on her. It was strong, more than a learned mechanism or a relic of her pickpocketing days. It was tugging her gaze to an alley across the street, a barely there space between terraced houses. Ilsa squinted into the dark, but didn't stop. If she made it to the end of this street, perhaps she could take to the skies without a militia hawk sighting her.

But now the presence was ahead of her. For a split second, Ilsa was tempted to face whatever watched her head-on, drunk as she was on the half-dozen foolish things she'd already done that night. But she tamped down the reckless instinct and retreated to the only place left to go: another alley, this one leading back towards…

At the end of a tunnel of black was the multicoloured glow of a thousand lamps, the carefree flicker of wings flapping and skirts twirling. She was being herded towards the party. Back towards the militia who were seeking her. Another instinct, this one more sure, made her stop in the tunnel and put her hands on her hips.

"Captain Fowler."

A black form flickered at the very corner of her vision, and when she turned, there was the Wraith, arms folded, impassive expression belied by the glint of humour in his eyes. He was dressed head to toe in black, the hood of his long coat thrown back and a bandolier of knives strapped across his broad chest. More weapons dripped from his belt. Ilsa couldn't recall what the Principles had to say about walking about armed, but she doubted it was good.

"How'd you recognise me?" she huffed.

"Your eyes, of course." He nodded towards the High Street.

"My eyesight is far stronger than a Changeling's. I saw you on the roof from across the street."

"And I s'pose they've roped you in to bring me back home?" she snapped, knowing better by now than to try and make a break for it.

Fowler looked over his shoulder, back in the direction Ilsa had come. "You were about to cross paths with your bloodhounds. They're on the scent trail of a pair of gloves that have mysteriously found their way up a tree half a mile west of here." He reached into his coat and produced something Ilsa recognised. It was her bag, the one she'd been carrying the night Martha had died. The night he'd saved her life. It had had her gloves in it. "You're in the clear. For now."

He held the bag out and Ilsa took it, fingers closing on the worn, faded velvet. She ran a thumb over the repair she had done on one corner with the red cotton thread she used for alterations on her stage costume. It was all she'd had. Funny, how she only noticed how tattered it was now.

"So you just went and broke the Principles, all over me sneaking out?" she said, holding the purse behind her back, where she couldn't see it.

"Which Principles did I break?"

"You ain't allowed to use your magic outside the Wraith quarter." Ilsa shot a glance at the party. A group of men with tankards of ale were joking and laughing mere feet from her and the Wraith, but shrouded as they were in shadow – and drunk as the men appeared to be – they hadn't noticed them.

The flash of humour returned in the captain's grey eyes. He reached a hand into the collar of his shirt and drew out a chain. On the end was a silver coin embossed with a bird's skull and crossed arrows. "I belong to the Order of Shadows. We're exempt from the Principles, *and* from their protection."

The Order of Shadows. Mercenaries. Assassins. Ilsa was reminded that Fowler had only saved her life because he'd been paid to do so. If the Docklands had hired him first, would he have slain her in that fish market alongside Martha?

"You're saying if I clawed your chest open, right here and now, no one would stop me?"

"No one would stop you," he conceded. He took a step closer, shifting so that his body filled the whole tunnel, and slipped a blade from his wrist into his palm. It was a pathetic, dull-looking thing compared to the weapons decorating his belt and chest. As he held it up, Ilsa saw why: it was *her* blade. It had also been in her bag. "Just as no one could stop me cutting your throat in time. But the Zoo would have its vengeance, and likewise the Order take care of their own."

Ilsa reached out and snatched the knife from him. He let her; she was under no illusion that she'd been quicker than him. "Go through *all* my things, did you?"

"Curiosity is a force of habit."

Ilsa folded the knife and put it away. She had drawn it several times in the Otherworld, and used it once – against a lecherous drunkard who had flung her against an alley wall and let his hands roam where they pleased.

"And you ain't gonna ask me what a Changeling's carrying a blade for?" she asked, thinking of that night. She hadn't been afraid of the man, she'd been afraid of her urge to shift and of what might happen if she did. Her gaze drifted out to the party,

288

where Millie was still enjoying the attention showing off her magic had earned her.

"Something to do with her impeccable foresight?" said Fowler. "A blade is only as good as its backup. The same is true for claws, I imagine."

Ilsa glanced at the Wraith's dozen *backup* blades, remembered him throwing one at an Oracle's chest with lethal precision. "And what're you doing at a Camden street party, so well prepared?"

"Nothing bloody, I assure you. Let's get a drink."

Ilsa blinked in surprise as he slipped past her and out onto the High Street. She hurried to catch him up as he made for an open-fronted tent that had been erected on one side of the street.

"What's the occasion?" Ilsa asked the captain as she dodged a gentleman with a tray of beer.

Fowler glanced over his shoulder at her. "Camden's foremost astrologer told them to."

"Come again?"

"Every lunar cycle, she reads Camden's stars. This month, she told them to throw a party."

Ilsa shot a bemused glance at the scene around her; streamers, dancing, heaps of food on giant platters, all because someone told them the stars willed it. "Do people here do everything astrologers tell them?"

"Some do," said the captain. "Most probably discard whatever asks too much of them and keep what they like. As guidance from the stars goes, I doubt *throw a party* rustled many feathers." He glanced at one of the rainbow-bright birds still dancing through the air, then at her, his eyes sparkled at his own joke. "Do the people in the Otherworld not take their fun where they can find it? Life is trying here sometimes. We like to remember that it can be good too."

That much was clear. Ilsa saw no trace of the violent chaos that threatened every moment of her life among the lieutenants and militia. She wondered how well these people understood what the Zoo did to protect them.

Inside the tent was a long table in front of a rack of ale casks; a makeshift bar. The Changelings shot the captain glances as he accepted two mugs of beer and handed one to Ilsa, but no one challenged his presence. Ilsa also drew attention just by being beside him. Perhaps they thought she'd invited her assassin beau to drink and dance with them. She checked her disguise was still in place and averted her eyes from all who glanced their way.

Fowler found a spot near the entrance of the tent, right in a corner. It would have been an inconspicuous place to stand if he hadn't been a six-foot-two Wraith clad in black and accessorised with a small armoury.

"How'd I know you was there?" Ilsa asked. Fowler quirked a brow in question. "Back in the street, I knew you was watching me. I knew exactly where you was."

"Ah. Something about slipping through solid objects creates a feeling of unease in those nearby, if they're attuned enough to their surroundings. That sense of being watched. You wouldn't have noticed it when we first met. You had, ah, other concerns at the time."

Martha. The acolytes.

"I did in the theatre though," Ilsa said, suddenly understanding the prickle on the back of her neck the moment before she'd first seen the captain.

"The sensation's not often so acute," said Fowler, studying her. "You knew precisely where I was."

"Caution's a force of habit too," Ilsa shrugged. She took a long sip of her beer and studied Fowler over the rim of her mug. He had fixed his gaze intently on the dancing outside the tent. Ilsa followed his line of sight to a smiling, dimpled young man, his waistcoat unbuttoned and his neck scarf askew as he spun his pretty dance partner in his arms.

"Who's that?" said Ilsa, an inexplicable thrill of fear coursing through her at the way Fowler watched him.

"His name's Edgar Dawson," said the captain, his eyes still on the man. "He's a con artist."

"We're Changelings," she said. "Ain't we all con artists after a fashion?"

Fowler pursed his lips, and Ilsa got the impression he was trying not to smile. It made her oddly proud, to draw a reaction from the stone-faced assassin, and she swallowed more beer to hide her own smile.

"This *particular* con artist," said the Wraith, "has a lover in the Underground, a wealthy merchant's son, who's packing his belongings and his considerable fortune and preparing to leave on a ship tonight with our man here. All Dawson's taking with him is a single suitcase and a vial of poison."

Ilsa's gaze snapped back to the dancing; to the laughing, carefree Edgar Dawson. He didn't look like a killer, but for all Ilsa knew, he didn't look like that at all.

"His lover's friends have pooled their gold to have me put a stop to the affair. They suspected foul play. I doubt they suspected a murder plot."

291

"You gonna kill him?" Ilsa whispered, though she was afraid to know the answer.

Fowler tore his eyes from his mark and looked at her wryly. "If I have to. But I won't. Tonight will be the second time Dawson's seen me. He'll get the idea."

Sure enough, after a few minutes of Fowler's eyes burning into the back of his head, Edgar Dawson glanced towards the tent, and his smile, his dimples, his carefree glee all dropped from his face. He careened to a halt in the middle of the dance. His partner tripped and caught herself on his arm, but Edgar didn't notice. Ever so subtly, Fowler raised his cup to his mark and nodded. With his bewildered partner staring after him, the man stumbled away, looking like he might be sick.

Studying the captain – his predatorial stare, the casual way his hand rested on the hilt of his long knife – Ilsa wasn't sure she blamed him.

"You really would kill him, wouldn't you?" she said, though she already had the answer.

Fowler nodded. "If my contract required it," he replied nonchalantly. He turned that stare on Ilsa. She could feel him reading her every reaction. Not wanting to appear cowed, she met his stare.

"I s'pose it might be the right thing to do, if it saved another's life," she said, though she wasn't sure she believed that. She only wanted to see him react too.

He downed his beer in one long swallow. "My job this time is not to save anyone's life," he said to the bottom of his cup. "It's to end the affair. One way or another."

"Oh."

The heat drained from her at the finality of his tone. Fowler signalled a barman with a tray of cups and swapped his empty one for another. "And what's compelled you to slip away this evening?" he said quickly, and he took a deep drink of his second beer. "The people of Camden often extend their invitations to the Zoo, but only one person is known to regularly accept them. And I was under the impression he was missing."

Ilsa felt that kick, the one her heart gave whenever she gleaned the slightest detail about her missing brother. Gedeon mingled with his people. That was something real. Not a portrait made to flatter, or the contradictory testimony of his lover.

This was why she was here.

"D'you know him?" she asked Fowler. "Gedeon?"

Fowler shook his head. "By sight. That's all. The Prince of Camden's never been a friend to the Order. Your brother has lofty ideas that a society of mercenaries and killers should not have so much power."

"Outrageous," muttered Ilsa.

"They could have told you everything you wished to know about him at the Zoo. Had you not run away."

"I din't *run away*," said Ilsa, fingering the worn velvet purse still clutched in one hand. "And they can't tell me everything. Or they don't want to. He's gone missing when he's s'posed to be running things, and still no one's said a bad word about him. It's like they're afraid he'll hear or something."

"It is not that type of fear that stays their tongues, my lady. Gedeon Ravenswood holds the hope of a whole people on his shoulders. To topple him is to dash that hope."

"So it's wilful ignorance?"

"Who's to say he's not deserving? Have you uncovered his whereabouts? Do you know what made him leave?"

Ilsa huffed a sigh. "No."

Fowler fixed her with an earnest look. "Let your friends' trust inform your own," he said slowly. "They know him as you don't."

That was the truth of it, and it cut her to her core. She was angry with Cassia, with all of them, because they had something she didn't. No number of truths gleaned or stories told could compare to real memories of her brother, and she hadn't been there to make any. She had been struggling to survive alone in the Otherworld.

You belong here.

Ilsa wished it were that easy. It still wasn't the Zoo she pictured before she opened her eyes in the morning. It was the attic at the orphanage.

Ilsa's thoughts were interrupted by a word plucked straight from them: her brother's name.

"Gedeon!" came the call again.

Her stomach lurched. She stepped out of the tent, pulled as if by a string to whomever was calling that name. Could Gedeon be here, miraculously, suddenly? Why not? No one knew why he was gone, so no one could say when and why he might return.

"Gedeon, it's time to go home!"

Ilsa came to a stop when she found the caller, her hope snuffed out. It was a man summoning his son. The little boy, three years old at most, was shooting his father mischievous, defiant grins as he continued to play with the other children.

Ilsa felt foolish. Perhaps she had had too much beer.

Fowler appeared at her shoulder. He could probably have told her that her brother wasn't here if she'd given him a chance. With a Wraith's senses, he could probably hear every single person at this party.

Little Gedeon's father gave up with a groan and looked up, startling when he saw them standing there.

"Can I help you, miss?" he said, shooting uncertain glances at the captain, who took a couple of steps back and kept his hands far from his weapons.

"No. It's nothing," said Ilsa, arranging her face into a gracious smile. "It's a lovely name, is all."

The man smiled proudly. "After the alpha, thank his stars."

"Oh, spare the poor girl, Bren!" A woman came running from the dancefloor, breathless and red-cheeked. She ran right into the man's arms, and his smile widened as he wrapped an arm around her. "He'll talk your ears off if you let him," she said to Ilsa, rolling her eyes. She too looked the captain up and down, and kept her distance.

"Gedeon almost didn't make it into the world," said Bren. He spared an affectionate look for the woman, but a hardness had crept into his eyes. "Diana and I were taken for ransom by a gang of Wraiths when she was eight months gone."

Ilsa swallowed a gasp. "That's… horrible."

"And common," Fowler cut in. "It's one of the citizens' preferred ways of terrorising one another."

Bren nodded. "Snatch someone from a neighbouring faction, make their leader pay to get them back. It's one way to make money if you're desperate, or just ruthless, and if you don't get caught, you can't get punished. We lived right by the border to

295

the North, but far from the nearest guard point. No militia about. They slipped in through the walls while we were sleeping. I woke in the dark to cloaked phantoms all around me. Diana was too far along to shift, and I suffer the Changeling's bane something terrible. We had no hope against them."

"S'cuse me," Ilsa cut in. "Changeling's bane?"

Bren and Diana exchanged a look, and Ilsa realised this must have been a stupid question. Diana's eyes drifted to the twitches along Ilsa's right cheekbone; the proof she was a Changeling too. "That feeling when you shift?" said Bren. "The stretching or squeezing, the pain in your bones?" He shuddered. "That… burning feeling of feathers or fur growing on you."

Ilsa nodded. "Right. Used to make me really sick at first."

"That's Changeling's bane. The price of using our magic. Some of us don't ever overcome it. I wish it weren't the case but I never learned to use my magic all that well. I never got used to the pain." Bren shook his head. "So I couldn't even put up a fight when the Wraiths came for us. And once we were taken, we thought that was it for us."

"Hester was alpha back then," Diana said. "She didn't strike deals with kidnappers."

Ilsa could believe it. Hester would have considered it a show of weakness to cave to someone's demands; a weakness others would seek to exploit.

"We were trussed up in a disused stable for two days, barely fed or watered, left in our own waste." Bren shot a glance at his son, who was still playing rough and tumble with his friends, and lowered his voice. "Can you imagine it?

"But the wolves came," Bren went on. "And he was with

296

them. He didn't send his militia to do the job, he wanted to see for himself that we were rescued."

"Gedeon?"

Diana nodded. "We were blindfolded," she said. "We didn't see what happened, but he'd brought a small squad of wolves with him from what I could make out. Not enough to seem threatening, just enough to look like he was thinking of his own protection. But he was the distraction. While he stalled the Wraiths, a second group of wolves surrounded them. Next thing I knew, we were pulled to safety, out of the way of whatever happened next."

"Gedeon was just a lad," said Bren. "But not a tremor of fear in him. I owe him my life, and my wife's and my son's." He laughed. "He said his cousin's wrath would be worth it."

To save a family from slaughter? Ilsa would go toe to toe with Hester too. But could she walk into a stable full of Wraiths – men and women as fast and strong and deadly as Captain Fowler – on the fool's chance of walking out again?

"Camden's stars-blessed to have a leader like that," said Diana, and Bren pulled her into a hug and kissed her forehead.

Ilsa turned to where the couple's son was still playing with the other children; they were taking turns shifting into lion cubs.

"You want to see a real lion?" called a voice through the crowd, and Millie the elephant woman approached.

"Millie! Show us!" squealed the children. "Show us, Millie!"

The children squealed and cheered and Millie became a massive roaring lion. They climbed on top of her and Millie let them pull her to the ground. Bren and Diana watched with fond smiles, their brush with death relegated once more to the past.

This was who Gedeon was, Ilsa realised. Trusted. Admired.

Courageous. Someone who made people feel valued whether they were the woman he loved or the people who looked to him to unite them. Perhaps it wasn't the whole story – the full portrait – but Fowler was right: it was important.

The Wraith spoke by her shoulder. "Your hounds will be on their way back. Shall I set them another game?"

Ilsa shook her head. "No," she said quietly. "I'm done now."

They cut a path through the party heading south, stopping only briefly when Fowler's curiosity was tugged by the wrestling.

"D'you think they'd let a Wraith in the ring?" teased Ilsa. "P'raps you can take your chances."

Fowler pulled his gaze from the spectators laying bets and raised an eyebrow. "Unlikely. That's not a fair fight," he said, and abruptly continued past the circle.

The High Street spat them out on a quieter road not far from the park.

"So Wraiths are the strongest of the magics, ain't they?"

"What makes you say that?"

"You said it wouldn't be a fair fight, between you and a Changeling. I've seen you fight," said Ilsa, skittering quickly over the memory of the fish market. "You're unstoppable."

"I'm strong," Fowler conceded with no hint of humility, "but the same can't be said for every Wraith. Learning to transmute – to pass through something solid – is an acquired skill, like learning any magic. Some aren't as fast or as strong. Plenty are immensely fast and strong and have never trained for combat. Power isn't black and white. Some Changelings shy away from the pain of using their magic, some Oracles cannot tame theirs. The Sorcerer ability to transport – the move from place to place in an instant – never comes to some, however learned they are. They believe it to be an inherited trait."

"And you having strong magic," said Ilsa. "That something you inherited too?"

Fowler's grey eyes slid to hers, then to his feet as he walked. "I've belonged to the Order since birth. I can't say if my strength was inherited but that is often the way of things. As for being unstoppable – do you want to try me?"

Ilsa came to a dead stop in the street, mouth hanging open in shock. "You want to wrestle?"

"You say I'm unstoppable," he said, unbuckling his bandolier and tossing it aside, "but in the Order we learn that's never true. No one is unbeatable. And you say Wraiths are the strongest of the magics. So fight one and see for yourself."

It was an awfully elaborate way of deflecting, but Ilsa was intrigued. She put her purse down next to his bandolier. "Alright."

"No gorillas," said Fowler. "That's child's play."

Ilsa wouldn't dream of a gorilla when she had a snow leopard in her arsenal. Fowler watched her shift the way he'd watched Edgar Dawson dance: like she was prey. It set the same thrill racing through her blood, but she wasn't afraid of the Wraith.

He circled her, fifteen feet away. "I might be faster, but to score a strike I still need to get under your guard. I need to get close. That gives you a chance to be stronger."

Quicker than lightning, Fowler closed the space between them and tapped Ilsa on the shoulder. She snapped at him, but he had already danced out of reach. Then he was on her other side, hitting again. Ilsa turned, jaws primed, but he had moved again.

"You're on the defensive," he said, stopping out of reach and looking for all the world like he hadn't lifted a finger. "You don't need to wait for me to strike."

Then he attacked again, scoring featherlight touches one after the other. Ilsa launched herself at the places he appeared time and time again, but she was never quick enough.

Exasperated, she shifted human. "How am I s'posed to strike when I can't bloody keep up with you?"

In answer, Fowler came at her again. Ilsa didn't have time to shift before he caught her by the arm and pulled it behind her back. It was perfectly judged; he didn't hurt her, but she could never have twisted free.

"You have more than one blade, my lady," he whispered in her ear.

He loosened his grip and stepped back, and when Ilsa shifted again, it was into a kestrel. She launched herself beyond his reach.

"Better," said Fowler, keeping his eyes on her even as she moved soundlessly through the dark above him. When she slowed to hover, he averted his eyes, like a challenge. Attack how she wished, he would hear her coming.

She picked a spot behind him and dived for the ground. Predictably, Fowler spun, and was there before she was, ready to strike. But he had expected Ilsa to grow into something fierce and battle-worthy, not shrink as she did into a mouse. She freefell under his guard, and when she landed, a leopard once more, it was with her jaws closed around flesh.

Fowler stilled. Ilsa had him by the forearm.

"Ah," he whispered, the ghost of a smile on his mouth. He tugged experimentally on her grip and almost broke free, but

Ilsa held tighter, a growl reverberating against his skin. "That's it. You almost have me."

She didn't want to hurt him, so she only bit down a little harder. Fowler's smile grew. "You can do better than that."

Ilsa did as he asked, and again Fowler almost slipped her, but he nodded his consent, and she tightened her grip again, planting her feet like in a tug of war. Fowler hissed in pain, but the glint of humour in his eyes told Ilsa not to let go. He tried to pull free again, putting his weight behind it, and though Ilsa was pulled off balance, she held on.

"Do you see? A Wraith may be inhumanly strong," he said, struggling against her vice-like grip and losing, "but a Changeling is more than human."

As if to prove his point, Ilsa applied a flash of more pressure, and Fowler gasped.

"Alright, I yield!" He laughed.

Ilsa released him. She still doubted it would be so easy in a real fight with a Wraith, but she would take the win. She shifted human, a victory quip on her tongue, but Fowler's expression stopped her. His eyes were on the sky, cynical and weary. Ilsa's bravado faltered. "Did I hurt—"

A black shape descended between them, fluttering wings obscuring the captain. Ilsa jumped back in surprise, and Fowler didn't, as Eliot appeared where only a raven had been before.

"Back away, Wraith," Eliot growled.

"*Eliot!*"

He started at Ilsa's scalding tone, spinning to face her, incomprehension forming a scowl.

"Quillon," said Fowler by way of greeting. His expression

was shuttered, a tension in his narrowed eyes.

Eliot's glower swung between them. "What's going on here? Did he hurt you?"

"No, he din't bloody hurt me! It was playfighting."

The tension in Eliot's shoulders eased, but his snarl didn't let up as he shot another look at Fowler. "Well do forgive me for not trusting a merciless bit of steel."

Ilsa placed herself in front of him, between Eliot and the captain. "What are you doing here, Eliot?"

Eliot made an incredulous sound and gestured wildly. "You slipped the wolves to spend a stolen evening with an assassin while the Seer and all her acolytes are baying for your blood, where *should* I be?"

"Take a breath, Quillon," said Fowler lazily. He strolled to where his bandolier lay and picked it up. "She's been with me all evening. She was safe."

Eliot pointed an accusing finger at Fowler. "That's a damned lie and I think you know it," he said, danger dripping from every word. He turned to Ilsa. "Please trust me when I say members of the Order of Shadows do not make good friends. Just because he saved your life, don't fool yourself into believing he wouldn't end it *just for coin*."

Ilsa wanted to shout that he was being unfair, but hadn't she had the same thought earlier that evening? She hesitated to answer as she wondered how she'd come to be playfighting with an assassin, and Fowler answered for her.

"We can talk money if you like, Quillon," he said, and Ilsa heard a darkness in his tone that had never been there before. "Do you have another job for me?"

Somehow, that did it. With a *snap*, Eliot was a panther. Ilsa barely had time to react; she had seen him several shades of vicious, and she had seen him violent, but the rage rolling off him as he snarled at Fowler was something new. He reared as if to strike at the Wraith, who stepped back with a hand on the hilt of his blade. But Ilsa was still between them, and she was about as scared of the panther as she had been of the Wraith. She crowded Eliot until he dropped to all fours. When he tried to dodge her, she opted for rank insanity and grabbed him by the scruff of the neck. Eliot growled as she dug her fingers in, blue eyes turning on her. Then he was human again, pulling away with an outraged glare and massaging his neck.

"Next time, I'm going to let him gut you," said Ilsa, her own anger bleeding through in the tremor in her voice. "Now, I bet the wolves are still looking for me, so let's go."

Eliot stared Fowler down with the full force of his cruel, cold eyes, then wrenched himself away and leapt into the sky. Ilsa looked back at the Wraith. She opened her mouth to apologise for Eliot, but Fowler shook his head and sketched a paltry bow. "My lady."

Ilsa waited until he was gone and shifted into a falcon to chase down Eliot. He was stood in the forecourt when she reached the Zoo. The darkness cast him in pallid, ghoulish tones, but it did not account for the haunted look in his eye, the dull way he stared at the white knuckles of his clenched fist.

"What the bloody hell was that about?" Ilsa snapped.

For an endless moment Eliot didn't move or say a word. Then he sank his hand into his pocket with aching slowness.

"I'm sorry," he whispered.

Ilsa's anger was dampened under a worse feeling. She didn't know what it was about Eliot's anguish; why it always felt fresh, like virgin snow, like she was the first to brush up against it. She reached out a hand to touch his arm and his head snapped up in surprise, like he'd forgotten she was there.

"It was nothing," he said. He removed her hand, but squeezed it before he let go. "I'll round up the wolves, tell them we found you."

Before Ilsa could blink, the raven was lost to her against the vast night's sky.

20

Ilsa's escapade into Camden had taught her a great deal, but provided no clues to the whereabouts of her brother. She continued to pore over Lila's riddle to no success and to turn Cassia's account over in her mind, but she feared she was hurtling towards a dead end.

To combat her frustration, Ilsa had taken to practising her snow leopard form every morning with Georgiana and Rye. It left her feeling a little less useless to see her mastery of the leopard's most lethal qualities improve day on day; to know that, if her life was threatened again, hiding wouldn't be her only option. Plus she suspected that, for Georgiana and Rye, putting Ilsa in her place when they sparred took the sting out of losing to her whenever they played cards in the guard room.

Progress was also being made in her lessons with Alitz. The Whisperer and her assistant came to the Zoo for two hours every day to run drills with her. They began with some breathing and relaxation exercises that Alitz said allowed her better control of her own mind, and which Ilsa riled against with a passion.

"Why've I got to relax my mind to protect it?" she challenged, arms folded. "I've got to be sharp and concentrate, not half asleep and picturing a calm sea and that. I won't do it!"

"Tell me, little expert," Alitz said, "what were you thinking about when I saw you in the rose garden just now?"

"All kinds of things," Ilsa said loftily.

"Recount them for me. Every one." Ilsa was silent, and chewed the inside of her cheek. "No? Your *sharp mind* got away from you, and you don't remember. You chose none of those thoughts because you are not in control. So, you will start at the very beginning, as if you had never once used your brain before, which I am tempted to say you have not."

So Ilsa reluctantly submitted to Alitz's methods, and by the end of their first week of lessons, Ilsa could perform card tricks, hold a conversation with Fyfe, or play "Three Blind Mice" clumsily on the piano while guarding her mind.

"You will never be able to hide everything from a Whisperer," Alitz declared. "Decisions to act, observations, impressions of the present moment – these things appear so close to the surface of your conscious mind, it is not much different to reading them on a person's face." Her owl's eyes wandered Ilsa's face. "I understand that is how non-Whisperers make sense of one another."

Tone of voice too, said Ilsa in her head, with a pointed glare, so that Alitz would know her derision hadn't gone unnoticed. Alitz smirked knowingly. The Whisperer was fond of such speeches; assertions of her own power, thinly disguised as warnings. It was the price she exerted for her wisdom.

She was particularly insistent about the relative weakness of Changelings against Whisperers, as was the focus of one afternoon's lesson.

"As an animal, a Changeling's mind is different, is it not?"

Ilsa shrugged. "A little. And it depends on the animal. Generally, everything's sort of… clearer, but less deep."

"Blunter," said Alitz unequivocally, though it wasn't what Ilsa had been trying to say. "Smaller. And far less capable of resisting telepathy, regardless of one's training. You must remember this." Alitz's mouth quirked smugly. "Your particular brand of magic makes you weak against a Whisperer. Allow us to demonstrate."

"Us?" said Ilsa, glancing pointedly at Pyval.

The younger Whisperer had limited his part in their lessons to consulting privately with Alitz, and he and Ilsa had not exchanged words since the first incident with his nightmarish manipulation. As much as she was loath to admit it, and never would out loud, the experience had kept her on her toes and made her sharp.

"Manipulation is Mr Crespo's speciality, not mine," said Alitz. "But you have no reason to be afraid. Nothing you will experience is real, after all."

Ilsa almost asked whether Pyval had ever thrown *her* into a dread-filled void, but she bit her tongue.

"Now, if you would, become an animal."

None of it was real. That was true. She clung to this knowledge as she dropped to all fours, as the coat of dappled fur prickled across her skin and her bones grew and shifted with exquisite pain, until her body was that of a massive snow leopard.

Pyval wasn't the only one who could show off.

He took in the size of her as she stalked closer, her ears twitching in warning, but he wasn't cowed. No, for the first time since entering the Zoo, he smiled.

And then he seized her. The darkness rushed in. The sentient horror in the void made the impression of sound this time too; an unearthly clicking all around her and moving ever closer. The sound, the smell, the sight of it; none were real, and so she could block none of them out. They were things she knew without sensing them, like in a dream, and they burrowed incessantly into her mind. They brought with them a feeling that slipped past the *true* things she knew and the thoughts she recited and pierced her anyway: dread. Cold and consuming.

Ilsa growled, and the sound reverberated off walls that weren't there. She pawed in a circle, thrashing her tail, tracing the void with her eyes and finding nothing, but knowing all the same that unimaginable horror lurked there.

Then a light fell on her. Looking up, Ilsa saw a hole. A gap in the void where the sky above London poked through, rafters and broken roof tiles around its edges. She stepped back, a sinking suspicion taking hold. And beneath her paw, where before there had been nothing, the loose floorboard of the attic creaked.

A ribbon of darkness lashed out and struck her in the side. She roared, her legs buckling, pain burning across her ribs. Another hit her in the back, agony racing up and down her spine as her nerves sang from the blow.

Demon, said a voice. *Devil's get*. The darkness shivered, and Ilsa knew what lurked there.

She pulled herself into a ball as she took another blow to the head, tail tucked tight to her body, ears flat against her skull. She would never be free. She would never be safe. She screwed her eyes shut, but she could still see it all; the attic, the woman with the switch.

And there, at the corner of her vision, Pyval, flickering like a flame. Was he doing this to her? Or had her own terror taken over?

Another lash. Another sting of pain. But she could make it end. Pyval danced in the void, never in one place, but if she

308

focused her gaze, she could hold him in the corner of her vision. Then, maybe…

She pulled herself onto four legs. She couldn't see the drawing room, couldn't even convince herself it was there, but she could picture it. She could *imagine* this horror wasn't real. Pyval had been stood beside the couch, opposite the French windows, and if she kept her gaze elsewhere, he always hovered in the same spot in the void. She had nothing else to go on, but she leapt. Pyval raised an arm in defence, but Ilsa was defending herself too. It was instinct, and she struck without a thought.

Someone roared. Miss Mitcham, the pain, the attic all vanished, and the light rushed in. Ilsa was on the floor, her skirts pooled around her, her back to the wall. She felt her ribs, her face. She was uninjured, but the heedless dread wouldn't vanish.

Pyval hissed. He was clutching his arm, blood seeping through his fingers. Alitz was watching him impassively. Fyfe appeared at the door of the drawing room, eyes wide with horror at the scene within. Ilsa pushed herself up on shaking legs, and Fyfe dashed to help her.

"I din't mean to bite him," she murmured, stunned. "I was just trying to make it stop."

She had only wanted to knock him out of his concentration. She didn't even remember opening her jaws.

Across the room, the Whisperers were engaged in a fierce, silent exchange. Alitz tore her seething gaze away from her assistant long enough address them. "He needs stitches," she said, her tone as unreadable as ever. "Would you be so good as to fetch a healer?"

Fyfe hesitated, a supporting hand still on Ilsa's arm and a distrustful frown aimed at Pyval. But when the Whisperer removed his hand from his injured arm, and blood gushed from the wound onto the floor, Fyfe snapped to his senses.

He dragged Ilsa from the room with him.

"Are you alright?"

Ilsa nodded. "Fine. Go find a healer." She smiled weakly. "My lessons with Alitz will be really awkward if he bleeds out."

"I'll be right back."

But Ilsa didn't wait for Fyfe to return. She made for her room – the sounds of servants and wolves responding to the emergency echoing around her – locked the door, and lay down on the bed.

Only then did she let the tears come.

*

Ilsa woke gasping for air, fistfuls of bed linen gripped in both hands.

Night had fallen, and she hastened out of bed to turn up the lamps; to reassure herself she wasn't still dreaming. But though the nightmare faded with the light, the memory of the waking moments she had spent in that void continued to assault her.

The Zoo trusted Alitz, and Alitz trusted Pyval. And whatever it had cost her, she now had a crystal clear idea of the worst things a Whisperer could do to her, and how helpless she was to stop them when she used her own magic.

But did that make terrorising her a kindness? Had Pyval even meant to conjure the worst memories Ilsa had, or had she done that herself? Did she need to stop being a coward and confront her training head-on, or was it right to put her foot down and refuse to be taught by him?

310

She couldn't trust her instincts when it came to Pyval; they were muddied by fear.

The lights weren't dousing her persisting sense of unease, and if Ilsa just sat she would descend into panic, so she decided to take a walk. If no one was in the kitchen, she would make herself some tea.

But she didn't get as far as the kitchen. At the top of the stairs descending to the entrance hall, a different room – a different idea – ensnared her.

She had not set foot in her brother's chambers since that first time; the day she'd realised so much of what she'd hoped for was already gone. The same stillness permeated the room; the same uncanny sense that someone had just stepped out and left their life behind only a moment before.

Though it was clear someone still came in here to clean, no one had drawn the curtains, and another clear night filled the rooms with soft moonlight. Ilsa trod lightly through the sitting room and the study, into the bedchamber, her footfalls whispering on the wood floors and a strange calm finally fighting back the dread.

These rooms had been her parents' once, and then her brother's, and they enveloped her in a feeling she couldn't work out. All she knew was that the memories she'd seen in the void couldn't reach her here, that nothing the likes of Pyval Crespo did could hurt.

So she pulled back the covers, climbed into bed, and fell into a dreamless sleep.

2 I

For several days, the incident during Ilsa's lesson haunted her. Spikes of panic would creep up when she least expected them; flashes of being back in that void.

But Ilsa hadn't survived the traumas of her childhood just for a reminder of them to bring her to her knees, and she had found a way to quash the panic. She would go to the master chamber, the room that belonged to her brother, and lie on the four-poster bed, and let the scents of furniture polish and gardenias fill her nostrils.

Without deciding to, she had started treating the rooms as her own. Cassia had refused to step foot in them since Gedeon had vanished – which explained why she had stood stiffly beyond the door the day Aelius showed Ilsa around – so after the first night that she'd slept there without anyone stopping her, Ilsa gathered a few belongings from her chamber – Bill's scarf; the tattered velvet bag she found herself unable to throw away; and her folding knife and playing cards from inside – and arranged them on top of Gedeon's dresser. She scooped up the small stack of books she had pilfered from the library and put them next to the four-poster, in easy reach when she was lying there at night.

At first, she resisted the urge to open drawers and peruse shelves, but by the second day, she had talked herself out of such restraint. She had heard so much about her brother, but the space where he lived; it would be like hearing about him in his own words. More importantly, it might even hold some clues.

She began in his study. If there was anything in the rooms that would help her track her brother, this struck Ilsa as the best bet, so she went straight to the desk, where a number of letters, receipts, and a heavy ledger still lay. As she rifled through them, Ilsa imagined Gedeon sitting where she sat, and going about his duties thinking she was dead. Cassia had said it was an unbearable sorrow to him, and even as she upturned nothing useful at his desk, she found renewed purpose in her mission; she was on the trail of what she'd been missing, but Gedeon still didn't know it yet. She had to find him for his sake as much as her own.

When she was certain there were no clues at the desk, she poked through the bookshelves, pulling each volume out by the spine to see if anything fell from the secret spaces between, or from inside the pages. When she had exhausted that possibility, she went through the drawers of his bedside table – he slept on the left – then the liquor cabinet – he favoured an imported rye – then the shelves of his wardrobe. She dipped her hands into the pockets of his jackets – noting the lingering scent of grass and apples, of him – and though she learned a great deal, she found nothing.

Nothing, until she lifted the lid of a chest beside the bed. Its contents were a mess of unremarkable bric-a-brac, but on top was an object Ilsa felt rather than saw; a wooden toy in the shape of a wolf.

It had been eight years since Ilsa had seen her toy wolf, but she recalled it clearly enough to know that this one was identical.

Had Gedeon known, perhaps, that she had one like it? Reverently, she tipped Gedeon's wolf upside down to hear that familiar rattle – but there was no sound. The wolves weren't quite identical: Gedeon's didn't appear to be hollow. She imagined a scene: matching toys presented to the little prince and his newborn sister. One for a growing boy, one to make appealing noises for a baby.

Someone who had loved her before she was born had dreamed of such a thing. They probably didn't imagine their gifts would be received in a shop cellar, or that everyone present would soon be dead or fleeing for their lives; that the twin wolves would be in different worlds before the day was out. Ilsa shook her head to scatter the thoughts and gently placed the wolf back on top of the clutter, closing the lid.

Such sentimentality would get her nowhere. She stood in the centre of the room with her hands on her hips. "We all got secrets, Gedeon," she murmured. "Where d'you hide yours?"

When she had lived with Mrs Holmes, Blume's landlady, the woman had made the mistake of teaching Ilsa how to read. She was forever after pinching volumes from Mrs Holmes's small collection of fiction and reading them by candlelight when she was meant to be asleep. She couldn't disguise the scent of a candle just extinguished, but she stopped the books from being confiscated by stashing them hastily beneath the mattress. So, with dwindling hope, she got down on her knees and sank her arms as far as they would go between the mattress and the bedframe.

She swept her arms back and forth, feeling for something, anything, and thought she must be imagining things the first time her fingertips brushed a single sheet of thin paper. Gedeon was no doubt taller than her, with longer arms, and she had to reach to close her fingertips around the paper, but she managed it.

It was a page torn from a notebook, stained with blotches of ink and folded in half. On the inside, a diagram had been untidily scrawled.

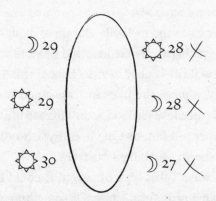

Ilsa's hands shook and she fought to tamp down the surge of excitement.

How could she be sure Gedeon himself had written this? And even if he had, was it relevant to his disappearance? But, most importantly, what could it possibly mean? The numbers weren't in order. The suns and moons, clumsily drawn, didn't appear to be either. And what was the shape in the middle? It didn't look like it was intended to be a circle. Was it a map of some kind? And why did the numbers and symbols on the right-hand side have crosses beside them?

Ilsa found a use for Alitz's damned calming exercises; she needed to clear her mind, to think her thoughts one at a time. So she counted her breaths until she felt her heart rate slow, and focused on what was in front of her.

For a start, it must have been under the mattress as a way of keeping it hidden, and it was under *Gedeon's* mattress, so she would do the sensible thing and assume he wrote it. It must have been here since before he disappeared. He left it behind, so he must not have needed it anymore, and he had hidden it, so he didn't intend it for anybody.

Ilsa lost her calm and methodical train of thought. This was a secret. A thing perhaps only Gedeon and Ilsa knew. She couldn't tamp down the thrill it gave her, to hold a small piece of her brother's story, a piece the likes of Cassia and Eliot had never seen. But why? Because Gedeon hadn't trusted them? If she took this slip of paper to Eliot, or Cassia, or Fyfe, would her brother have thought she was making a mistake?

Perhaps it wasn't that type of secret. It could be something innocuous, like a prop for a game. Or something intimate, like a thing he scribbled down in the night when it came to him in a dream.

Or perhaps it could tell her where her brother was.

Even as the possibility danced in her mind, Ilsa didn't truly believe it. Gedeon had been gone for weeks. There was no telling how long it had even been there; perhaps it had been years. Perhaps it was good for nothing but kindling.

But that didn't mean Ilsa couldn't discover what it meant.

If she took it to one of the others, and they explained it away with some memory or story of Gedeon, Ilsa would only be reminded of how everyone knew her brother but her. And perhaps it was childish that that had started to hurt, but she couldn't help it. She wanted a secret of Gedeon's that was only hers to know.

So when someone knocked on the sitting room door and entered, Ilsa hastily folded the diagram again until it was about the size of a playing card, and, with an unnecessary but nonetheless perfect flourish, she secreted it up her sleeve just as Fyfe appeared in the bedchamber.

He looked from her hands to her face and back again, expression blank with confusion. "What did you just do?"

"Magic."

Fyfe narrowed his eyes, the natural investigator in him unsatisfied.

"Stage magic," Ilsa conceded with a shrug. Hoping she could fool him, she did the trick in reverse. "See, nothing up my sleeve," she said in her stage voice, and with a little sleight of hand, her handkerchief appeared between her fingers.

Fyfe's face lit up. "Remarkable! Can you show me?"

Ilsa crossed her arms. "Not if you ain't going into the business. Magician's code. But I can show you something else. Want to learn to make yourself invisible?"

Fyfe's scepticism returned, but it was mixed with curiosity. "No one can make themselves invisible. Not even Wraiths."

Ilsa flicked a curl over her shoulder. "Well I can. Come here."

She took him by the hand and led him out into the hallway – away from the scene of her snooping – where she let him in on the secrets of being a good magician's assistant that she had shown Eliot; like how to hold yourself so you appear unremarkable, and how to move without attracting attention. They pretended the hallway was a street, and Fyfe practised following Ilsa while looking like just another pedestrian when she turned around.

"But you need to make yourself shorter too. And plainer."

He smiled at her and puffed up. "I knew you thought I was handsome." Ilsa punched him in the arm. "Shorter. Plainer." He shot her a sheepish look. "You might want to stand back."

Fyfe shifted like he was being attacked by bees. He flinched and jerked like every changing muscle was a nasty sting. Ilsa had never imagined it could be necessary to *move* so much. It was like the form Fyfe was searching for was a suit of overalls three sizes too small, and he had to thrash to concertina himself in. His features cycled through a hall of mirrors, no face quite right and each wearing a frown of concentration. Ilsa let out an involuntary yelp when his limbs elongated and he shot up by two feet, arms windmilling for balance.

She smothered a giggle with everything she had. "Wrong way, Fyfe."

"I wasn't finished."

He almost fell again in the pandemonium of shrinking, his hair flashing alternately bright orange and silver blonde. He kept muttering something that sounded like *ouch*, and Ilsa couldn't blame him. It was uncomfortable to grow too extremely short – or too extremely anything – and Fyfe was now no more than four feet. With another dangerous flurry, he stopped shifting at around Ilsa's height, planting his feet and holding his arms out like he couldn't be sure his body was through with its games.

For all his face had been put through, it looked the same. His nose was rounder where it had been pointed and his forehead had shrunk so that his black curls fell into his eyes, but that was it. He was wincing, and Ilsa worried he was still in pain, but on closer inspection, it was just several severe, incessant twitches.

"Well," said Ilsa, tapping her lip to hide her smile, "it's the sneaking bit what's more important, anyhow."

"It's alright. I know I'm an awful shifter," said Fyfe, breaking into a grin. "You can laugh."

Ilsa did. She laughed like she hadn't done since Martha had died, until her stomach hurt and she was crying. She did impressions of Fyfe shifting until he was laughing through tears too, and begging her to stop.

It turned out Fyfe didn't need his magic to master Ilsa's trick. For a conspicuously tall and frenetic boy, he was a natural talent at being invisible. He had tricks Ilsa had never even thought of; a faraway look to appear lost in thought; a way of holding his hands that made an onlooker forget they were useful for anything. Where Fyfe fell behind, he changed the game to make up the difference.

When Ilsa had nothing left to teach him, they wandered in the direction of his lab. There was a question threatening to bubble out of her, and she knew it wasn't entirely about finding Gedeon that she was compelled to ask it.

"Fyfe, what d'you think of Eliot?"

He caught a blush so quickly Ilsa wondered if he had lost control of his shifting altogether and was becoming a flamingo. "What do I think of him?"

"You know, d'you like him? D'you think he's a good person?"

Fyfe's shoulders were suddenly very tense and Ilsa's suspicions were piqued. Had she discovered his tell? The thought of Fyfe being untruthful with her was so much worse than Eliot or Cassia; he had always seemed so unguarded.

"Yes, I think he's a good person. Being reserved doesn't make him a villain."

"Reserved is generous," said Ilsa, even as she thought of the flashes of warmth and playfulness she'd seen when the façade cracked. There was a side to Eliot the others didn't know, and it gave her a peculiar jolt of happiness to have what felt like a particularly precious secret. Ilsa hadn't even known secrets could be happy.

"Well, Gedeon's disappearance has been difficult, but especially for Eliot. You would never guess, knowing Eliot and knowing Gedeon, but—" Fyfe cut off, forlorn. "Oh. I suppose you don't know Gedeon. But they're unlikely friends to say the least. Gedeon is outgoing and easy with everyone. He's likeable. But being likeable isn't the same as being good. I mean, of *course* Gedeon's good. I just mean that Eliot..." He noticed he was rambling and his blush spread to his ears. At least Fyfe had seen the good in Eliot too. That part didn't feel like it should be a secret. "I know the others think he's in on this Gedeon business, especially Cassia, but... well, even *I'm* not sure I believe Gedeon would do something like this without telling Eliot. He leans on him. He always has. All Gedeon's best ideas are Eliot's. But if it's true, if he does know where Gedeon is and he's not saying... well, I believe he has his reasons." He seemed to think better of himself, and added quietly, "I don't mean any disrespect to Cassia. She's entitled to her opinion of him. But I think she's wrong."

Sweet Fyfe, who would protect Cassia against the feeblest of harsh words. Perhaps there was nothing suspicious about the same boy going out of his way to be kind about Eliot too, but his discomfort was strange.

"What 'bout Hester? She think he knows where Gedeon is too?"

Fyfe held the door of his room open for Ilsa. "She must.

She made him give up command of the wolves. And she's been particularly frosty towards him since the attack. And whenever I mention him her face does this—" He did an impression of Hester's sneer that, while uncannily true to his sister, was twice as unpleasant to see on him.

"But she's always making that face."

"Well." Fyfe scrubbed absent-mindedly at his hair. He was still hurting over Hester's pain. A perverse part of Ilsa wanted to prod and poke at him until she understood the feeling exactly, until she knew just what it meant to love a sibling, but instead she changed the subject.

"What d'you remember 'bout the attack?"

"Ah, well." He hopped the arm of his oversized chair and dropped down, his nervousness over Eliot and melancholy over Hester gone. "It was early in the morning. The smash of glass woke me. I ran to Eliot's room but he was already downstairs in the fray."

Ilsa studied the desk full of holes where Fyfe's pocket forge had lived. "And they came for the lab?"

Fyfe threw up his hands in a dramatic shrug. "They came for *everything*. In one of the raids they turned the greenhouse over. In another they slashed the upholstery in the library." His shoulders dropped. "A couple of weeks before that attack I told Hester I was losing sleep over the lab and everything they might destroy, but it never seemed like a *target*, until…"

"'Til the pocket forge got took." Fyfe nodded. "Who knew 'bout it? Anyone outside the Zoo?"

"I share ideas with some Sorcerer contacts of Aelius's sometimes. When my experiments go beyond Cassia's purview."

321

Ilsa straightened in excitement. "Then p'raps they're with the rebellion!"

Fyfe grimaced. "I don't recall mentioning the forge."

She deflated again. Aelius – and probably Gedeon too – believed the raiding Sorcerers had come looking for something, and on their last break-in, something had been taken. It wasn't a complicated chain of events to follow, yet nobody was convinced it was that simple.

They both jumped as the door burst open and Eliot stalked in without knocking.

With a jolt, Ilsa thought against reason that he must have heard them talking about him, and she found herself rifling her memory for anything she wouldn't wish for him to know. But Eliot registered the pair of them with nothing more than a moment's glance. His cold gaze swept the lab like the room had displeased him somehow.

Fyfe shot out of his chair and started to say hello at the same moment Eliot's attention snagged on something across the lab, and he stalked past Fyfe towards it. It was the map with the overlay of the underground. He took in the frame, the stand, the wheels, looking at it from several angles before moving to the far side and pushing it towards the door. Fyfe scooted out of his way. Ilsa made him go around.

"I'm borrowing this," was all Eliot said as he reached the hallway.

"Don't you got enough maps already?" called Ilsa, but the door was already closing behind him.

Fyfe let out a long breath and collapsed back into his chair.

2 2

Following the incident in which Pyval Crespo nearly lost an arm, it was decided by all involved that he should cease attending Ilsa's lessons. So Ilsa was unprepared to step into the drawing room and find him standing there, hands behind his back like a military man, sullen expression staring through her as if she were nothing.

But she refused to show him any weakness. She folded her arms and looked only at Alitz. "I ain't doing jack with him here."

Alitz raised a placating hand. "Pyval is here at my request to ask your forgiveness."

"He can't have it."

"Let him swallow his pride, anyway. You might find it amusing."

Gritting her teeth, Ilsa let out a slow breath and faced Pyval.

"I apologise that my teaching methods are too much for you," he said in his reedy, delicate voice.

Incensed, Ilsa turned back to Alitz. "That ain't an apology!"

Alitz's eyes bored into Pyval, and Ilsa could imagine the scathing content of her reproach. But Pyval did not relent.

"I was under the impression you wanted to learn to protect yourself," he said, "not play children's games. So I *apologise* that I misconstrued your intent."

"Go to hell and burn there, you hateful—"

"Alright!" said Alitz. "I see this may not have been the best course of action to take."

Pyval was dismissed without another spoken word and stalked from the drawing room like nothing in the world could keep him there. *Good riddance*, Ilsa thought, as she glared daggers at his back. She hoped to never see him again.

"What are we doing today?" she asked Alitz.

Alitz almost smiled. It must have been a relief for her too that Pyval's loathing would not mar their lesson. "I'm quite satisfied that you are able to guard against mind reading as well as you ever will, as long as you maintain your practice. So we are turning our attention more thoroughly to the second matter: this afternoon I am going to test what you are capable of."

Someone had laid out tea for them as always, and Alitz poured. "You and I are going to talk," she said, "and as we do, I will attempt to manipulate your thoughts. You have fared well since the first time Pyval tried to control you, but be warned, I shan't make it easy to resist."

Ilsa eagerly accepted a cup and saucer. She knew how to make the most of a good prop, and sipping and stirring would buy her time to concentrate. She piled in four lumps of sugar – a move that usually earned her a look of unrestrained disgust from Alitz, but today resignedly amused her – and took a long drink to fortify herself, relishing the heat as it singed down her throat.

"Now." Alitz arranged herself in a chair, straight as a rod, and stirred her tea. "Tell me, how are you acclimatising?"

"Slowly, I s'pose," said Ilsa. "What with discovering there's a whole other universe under Westminster Abbey, and that some people can walk through walls or magic themselves from place to place, and that all them times I felt like the fortune teller in the theatre across the street was reading my mind, well, she just bloody might've been. S'cuse my French."

Alitz smiled restrainedly. "I meant, how are you acclimatising to being a Ravenswood?"

"Oh." Ilsa had been cracking jokes because she was nervous about the exercise, but a new anxiety crept in, unbidden. "Fine, mostly. It ain't like they expect all that much of me. 'Cept that I don't run off and get myself killed."

"I understand the wealth and privilege they enjoy here at the Zoo is starkly different to the life you used to lead. It's somewhat jarring, I imagine."

Alitz watched her with patient, probing eyes, but Ilsa let the silence linger, a weight sliding off her as she realised what the Whisperer was doing. It was a classic pickpocket's trick; draw the mark's eye with one hand and pilfer their pockets with the other. Alitz knew enough of Ilsa's mind and memories to unsettle her with just the right question, and if Ilsa got lost in her thoughts – thoughts about learning to be part of Camden's ruling family, for example – she would not notice Alitz slipping in.

Ilsa smiled sweetly. Alitz could borrow a pickpocket's tricks, but Ilsa had *been* one, and she knew how to watch her back without looking like it.

"Well, I can't say I find it ordinary that when I leave my petticoats and stockings all over the floor, someone comes and puts them away."

There it was. An errant thought. The sudden and inexplicable urge to look over her shoulder, like someone might be standing right behind her. Ilsa caught it, bent it until it broke. The corner of Alitz's mouth twitched before she could disguise her surprise.

"And I'd prefer to dress myself than have a maid help me. Call me old-fashioned, but I just think it's a valuable skill."

Another: the glint of metal in the mirror above the console. Ilsa's intellect told her it was Alitz's magic. Her instinct still made her look. There *was* someone behind her, stepping away from the wallpaper where he had been camouflaged, drawing a blade. Ilsa felt her skin prickle as the leopard begged to be let out. She felt around the edges of the image and found the seam where it had been stitched in between her senses. But could she be sure? He could be a Wraith…

No, the Zoo was warded against such intrusions, and Ilsa's own thoughts were stronger than these. The image was *wrong*; when she focused, she knew it was. She tore her eyes from the mirror and held Alitz's stare with stubborn resolve. Only when her tutor let out a small, dissatisfied sigh did she dare to look back. The man behind her was gone.

Ilsa smiled to hide her growing nerves. "Other than that I can't complain. There's an awful lot of leisure time when you're rich and no one trusts you to help run the place. Aelius is teaching me chess. And I play cards with the wolves some nights and batter all of them."

Alitz's eyes narrowed in question, whatever game she'd been playing forgotten. "And you think it wise to befriend the militia?"

Ilsa frowned. "What d'you mean?"

"Three of them perished in the last attack on this house. Ten altogether in the raids, and four in other altercations in recent months. That is the role the faction rulers have given them. It's unwise to find value in the expendable, Miss Ravenswood."

Ilsa choked on a mouthful of tea. "*Expendable?*"

Alitz was raising her cup to her lips, but she put it back down. "If I sound callous, understand that that's not my intention. I have lived in this city my whole life, and you, a matter of weeks. Wolves will die. Whitechapel stewards will die. Disagreements and skirmishes are in abundance, so bitterness and bloodlust are as well. They fuel one another and dauntless men and women run headlong into the fire."

As much as Ilsa didn't want to hear her go on, the fact *she* had managed to distract *Alitz* had brought with it a welcome reprieve. And knowing the Whisperer, there were plenty more opinions where that came from. Ilsa only had to ask the right questions.

"I s'pose some of them wolves and stewards die fighting *each other*, don't they? What with us sharing a border."

"His Honour would have otherwise if he could make it so. He believes being border fellows brings with it the responsibility of good citizenship, not opportunities for war." She had fallen into the disapproving tone she usually reserved for Ilsa. "But, unfortunately, you are correct, Miss Ravenswood. Stewards and wolves die on our border every year." She brought her teacup nearly to her lips, frowned into it, and continued, compelled to talk on. "I remember one particularly vile incident some years ago. A Changeling woman was crossing into Whitechapel, fleeing her husband, who had beaten her. Not for the first time, from what I understand. So the stewards denied him entry. They protected her, as one should under such circumstances."

Ilsa nodded warily, but Alitz didn't see. Her eyes were clouded over.

"He grew enraged. The wolves involved themselves, futilely.

They failed to subdue him, so when he became a bear and charged the guard point... one of the stewards shot him dead." Alitz blinked and turned her newly sharpened gaze on Ilsa. "Do you think that's reasonable, Miss Ravenswood?"

Ilsa hesitated, but it was clear Alitz expected her to answer. "If it was the steward's life or the Changeling's... then yes, I s'pose. I think so."

"Hmm." Alitz was silent a beat, her lips pursed. "The wolves did not. Evidently, they considered the steward to have drawn first, and they attacked. Do you think *that's* reasonable, Miss Ravenswood?"

"They're s'posed to defend Changelings," said Ilsa uncertainly. "P'raps they thought—"

"While defending themselves against the wolves," Alitz went on, "no one thought to defend themselves against the dead man's wife. She slaughtered the steward who shot him, while his comrades were looking the other way."

Ilsa gripped her saucer in both hands. Alitz asked her no more questions. Her features were tense, but after a long moment of silence, she turned to Ilsa with accusatory, narrowed eyes. She had noticed they'd stopped the exercise.

"As I said, a veritable inferno of bad blood. But enough of this talk. I prefer a brandy in hand when discussing such things. Tell me, what success in the search for your brother?"

Ilsa was glad Alitz was trying to manipulate her thoughts rather than read them, but she still clamped down hard on any memories of the search; Lila's riddle, the diagram she had found in Gedeon's room. She was keeping these things from most of the Zoo because she couldn't decide whom to trust. She would keep them from outsiders as a matter of course.

"I ain't had all that much success," said Ilsa, though the lie was painful and Alitz's narrowed gaze said she didn't believe it anyway. "I'm still trying to understand what made him leave in the first place."

"Discontent, perhaps?"

Ilsa could suddenly see her brother with stark clarity. It was night. He was alone in the library, slumped forward in a chair by the fire, face lost in troubled thought. A sound disturbed him, and he turned to face her, wiping clean his expression.

"Concentrate, Miss Ravenswood."

Ilsa's eyes snapped to Alitz's. She had been aware, distantly, that the Whisperer was still putting images in her head, but stopping her had become unimportant. Ilsa was fully back in the drawing room, teacup in hand, and she wanted the daydream back. Alitz must have read this on her face or in her mind, because she pursed her lips and scowled.

"You would rather not focus on the present, as I have taught you," said Alitz acerbically. "Very well. Why don't you tell me about your life in the Otherworld instead?"

"I was a magician's assistant," said Ilsa. "Like on the stage. Guess you don't have that here."

"Theatre?"

"Stage magic." She thought of Fyfe's awe when she had magicked her handkerchief into her hand. Then she thought of the diagram that had been hidden up her other sleeve – and wrenched herself immediately back to the present. She shot a glance at Alitz, taking a long sip of her tea to hide her anxiousness.

"Well, we have exhibitionists," said Alitz primly.

There was Gedeon again in her mind's eye, younger than

329

his portrait; fifteen, perhaps. Ilsa looked down on him from the balcony over the entrance hall, where he was sizing up a familiar black jungle cat and laughing. Eliot was ready to pounce. Gedeon cracked his neck arrogantly and transformed into a gigantic lion just as Eliot collided with him—

"Miss Ravenswood," snapped Alitz.

"What am I seeing?"

"If you were trying but at all, you would be seeing very little," said Alitz.

"I mean, are you making these thoughts up, or are they memories? You know him, don't you? My brother?"

"Oh yes," said Alitz, lifting her cup to her lips. "I've known Gedeon his entire life."

Ilsa was hit with another image: a boy of seven or eight, fair-haired and red-cheeked, running across the park with the string of a kite in his fists. Another boy with black hair and blue eyes – Eliot again, as an untroubled child – was tossing the kite in the air, trying to get it to catch the breeze.

"You've seen all these things!" gasped Ilsa.

"And you are failing at your task, Miss Ravenswood," said Alitz, putting her cup back on its saucer with a clatter. She was losing patience. "If I wanted to distract you from the present moment, of course I would show you things you wished to see – and then perhaps I would slit your throat while you were daydreaming. Do not underestimate my magic, Miss Ravenswood. A Whisperer can incapacitate you with nothing but your own mind the same way a Wraith would with blunt force, and they would leave less evidence."

"Right," said Ilsa. "It's just—"

"It's just that you're yearning," said Alitz, like the idea bored her thoroughly. "Want is a weakness, Miss Ravenswood; a weakness any half-skilled Whisperer would be able to exploit. Show someone what you desire and they can use it to control you."

"It ain't a weakness."

"Speak up."

"I said it ain't a weakness," repeated Ilsa, hearing her own uncertainty. Perhaps Alitz was right, but her whole life had been about want, and she was loath to think of it in Alitz's terms. Want was Ilsa's driving force.

Had it been Gedeon's too?

Ilsa disguised her thoughts by bringing her cup to her lips again, but missed, sloshing tea onto her white lace summer dress.

"Oops," she said, but it came out in a slur.

"Miss Ravenswood?" said Alitz, quirking a disapproving brow at Ilsa's ruined dress. "Are you well?"

Ilsa didn't know. She held her teacup with both hands to stop it slipping from her lax grip. She felt drowsy. No, not drowsy. Her mind was sharp, it was just her body that was losing strength. She tried to tell Alitz this but her lips wouldn't cooperate. They had gone completely numb. It was happening to her fingers as well.

Alitz nodded, but she didn't understand. She wasn't reading Ilsa's thoughts. "The heat does get to one this time of year," she said, though her tone was as unsympathetic as ever. "I find an afternoon nap the best remedy."

Alitz raised her teacup to take another sip, and Ilsa summoned every drop of her failing strength to launch herself from her chair and swing one dead hand at the cup, which went flying and shattered on the floor. Ilsa landed in a heap on the rug.

The tea. Someone had poisoned the tea.

Indignation replaced Alitz's usual coolness, but only for a second. She was no fool. She turned her scrutiny on Ilsa, and her unfocused gaze finally sharpened.

"Earth and stars," she hissed when she saw what Ilsa had understood. She pushed herself to her feet – only to collapse back into the chair. When she tried to speak again, only a jumble of sounds escaped.

Alitz was old. She would be taken by the poison quicker. Ilsa needed to be the one to summon help.

The crash of china hadn't brought anyone running. Ilsa drew breath to scream but the sound died in her weakened throat. The numbness was spreading up her arms. She could still feel her legs, though they trembled like blades of grass whipped by the breeze when she forced herself upright. Could she make it to the hall, where someone might see her? *Might* wasn't good enough, and one step sent her crashing to her knees. She tried a bigger form – her trusty leopard who might withstand poison longer than small, human Ilsa – but she couldn't hold the shape.

Ilsa half-crawled, half-dragged herself to the console, rage and determination propelling her forward. She hadn't survived Miss Mitcham, winters on the streets, Oracle assassins and Sorcerer rebels to die drinking *tea*. To never even see the face of the cowardly bastard who had ended her.

Alitz tried to speak again; she said something that sounded like *what*, but Ilsa knew what she was doing; she knew what was on top of the console. She used one of its legs to haul herself into a standing position and balance. There was the vase; the beautiful, probably hugely expensive vase Pyval had tried to compel her to pick up on the Whisperers' first visit. And above the console was a mirror.

With one useless hand, Ilsa knocked the vase towards her and scooped it into her arms like a baby. She needed a little distance. She only needed to hold herself up for a moment. Even her lungs were struggling now, and Alitz's unmistakably frightened visage swam and doubled in the mirror as she raised the vase carefully. She couldn't drop it; she couldn't botch the throw. She had one chance to summon help or they would both die here.

Ilsa put all her weight into her shoulder and threw the vase at the mirror with a pitiful cry. She pitched forward and hit the floor. She didn't see what she'd accomplished – but she heard it. An immense, ringing crash hailed a shower of glass and pottery all around her.

All the fight went out of her, replaced by relief, when shouts went up across the house and garden. Feet pounded the floors. The door burst open with a crack of wood and the French windows to the garden shattered as wolves and bears and big cats piled into the room, ready to protect the Zoo once more. At their head was a sleek black monster Ilsa recognised.

Eliot. He shifted, eyes sweeping the room diligently for the threat, even as he made straight for Ilsa and knelt beside her. He scowled at the shattered glass like *it* was his enemy, but his touch was gentle as he scooped an arm around Ilsa to lift her out of it. Ilsa tried to gesture at her throat, then at the teapot, but her motions were too sloppy. Panic made them worse.

"Poison." It was Aelius, who had transformed from a ragged, battle-worn mountain lion into his elegant self. He was stood above Alitz and the shattered teacup.

Eliot's fierce, livid gaze met that of the nearest wolf.

"Liesel, find Cassia," he ordered. "The rest of you secure the perimeter. No one leaves."

Liesel didn't move. She looked between Eliot and the pack, her ears flat to her skull. Eliot growled. "I don't give a damn who you answer to. Do as I say or I'll make you the first to pay for this."

The wolf didn't dare argue. She dispersed with the rest of the animals but two. One, a bear, became Oren. The other cycled through several increasingly small, increasingly ugly dogs before revealing itself to be Fyfe, who stumbled to Alitz's side and took her hand seriously. He inspected the tips of her fingers, her mouth, her eyes, felt her palm and pinched the skin between two nails.

Only a moment had passed before Cassia appeared from thin air, the whole crate of antidotes Ilsa had seen in her lab cradled in her arms. "Fyfe?"

"It's a smokeweed draught," said Fyfe. "Paralysis, numbness. No taste or odour. Do you have the antidote?"

Cassia was already fumbling with the stopper of a clear bottle of milky liquid. She knelt among the shards of glass and porcelain, shoving Eliot aside, and tugged Ilsa's limp head onto her lap. Ilsa tried to tell her to give it to Alitz first, which Cassia understood, but she only made a tutting noise and opened Ilsa's mouth with surprising roughness.

Ilsa choked on the first dribble of the liquid, but the feeling came back to her throat instantly, and she was able to swallow the second sip. It tasted like sloe berries, bitter and dry, but as Cassia trickled more of the antidote between her lips, the pressure on her lungs eased. A tingling told her the sensation was coming back to her hands too.

Cassia moved on to Alitz, who evidently had not drunk as much of the poisoned tea as Ilsa, but whose breathing was also laboured. Eliot pulled Ilsa to her feet and supported her to the couch, calling for someone to fetch some iodine for the cuts the broken glass had made. Now that Ilsa thought about it, getting feeling back had brought with it a lot of pain.

"Who brought the tea?" said Oren.

"It was out when we got here, like always," said Ilsa, her voice thick. Someone handed her a glass of water, but Oren plucked it from her fingers.

"Aelius, you round up the servants, I'll deal with the guard," he said, already sweeping towards the door. "We question everybody. Someone who knows about this is still here."

"No, they ain't," said Ilsa. Oren turned. She gestured with a freshly mobile hand for him to give back the water but he didn't move.

"And what do you mean by that?"

"It was Pyval."

Every eye was suddenly on her, but Ilsa was looking at Alitz. The Whisperer was testing the effects of the antidote by curling and uncurling her fingers, but her hands fell into her lap at Ilsa's words.

"I beg your pardon?" she rasped.

"Ilsa, why would Pyval hurt Alitz?" said Cassia, shaking her head.

"P'raps he's done helping you help Changelings." Now that Ilsa had her voice back, she couldn't keep it down.

Alitz's mouth fell open. "That is absolutely—"

"Tell me he was ever happy to come here and teach me," challenged Ilsa. "Tell me he don't resent every second he's in the same room as one of us."

Alitz's lips were a thin line. Her previously rod-straight posture had collapsed with the poison, and she had too much dignity to struggle to right herself. She looked spent, and older than her years. "Pyval has his reservations about my aligning myself with the Zoo, yes."

"*Because?*" pressed Ilsa. She knew she wasn't wrong. She'd known that kind of hatred before, at the orphanage.

Alitz hesitated. "He is, unfortunately, a separatist at heart. His prejudices are not reserved for the Changelings, I can assure you, and they have never caused him to do harm. He was not compelled to do *this*."

"He's with the Fortunatae."

"Miss Ravenswood, please!" Alitz snapped. Even half-prone, she had that way about her that made Ilsa feel reprimanded, but she wouldn't be cowed. "Not everyone who would wish you dead is aligned with that group, or do you forget the world you have become a part of?"

"What kind of enemy is he, then?" shot Ilsa. "We have tea here every day with our lesson. Pyval knows it. And the one day we get poisoned, he ain't here. Gedeon's gone, p'raps forever. Hester don't leave her room. The Fortunatae want my family exterminated like rats, right? And I'm the only one left standing. It don't take a detective to figure it out."

Alitz didn't reply. Now she was the one who wasn't sure of herself. Ilsa looked to the others, who were in various stages

336

of disbelief and hard understanding. Eliot met her gaze, his expression harsh but not judgemental. He believed her.

"Professor Dicer," began Oren in his unnervingly even tone. He handed the glass of water back to Ilsa and poured a second for Alitz. "We will speak to every wolf, servant, and resident of this house to develop a picture of what has happened here, but here is what I expect to find: that a kitchen maid we trust made tea. That a butler we trust delivered it. That wolves who have proven themselves to us have guarded our walls vigilantly, and the only outsider to have been allowed to come and go from the Zoo this afternoon is Pyval Crespo."

"We take vetting our people very seriously," added Aelius, but Ilsa didn't miss the way his eyes settled on each person in the room when they weren't looking.

"I understand that," said Alitz petulantly, but the fight had gone out of her. She had been betrayed with the rest of them, by someone she had trusted, and there was no denying it.

"If you ever see him again," said Oren, "though I doubt you will, tell him he has broken the Principles. Tell him the Zoo will have his life."

*

Ilsa trembled slightly as she unfastened her tea-stained dress, and nausea threatened in waves, but otherwise the antidote had done its job; she would live to teach Pyval Crespo to poison her.

She would start by making him tell her who ordered her family killed.

Ilsa's dress had slipped down over her hips and pooled on the floor of the chamber when a sound like the squeak of wheels came towards her down the corridor. Then came a knock.

"Wait – one minute!" It was probably the maid she'd told not to bother helping her change. She threw a robe around her shoulders, not even fastening it over her chemise, and opened the door.

"I said I'm alright—"

But it wasn't the maid. Eliot was there, the tight set of his jaw the only evidence that he was *trying* to keep his eyes on hers. Ilsa felt her skin heat everywhere his eyes touched her. When his gaze fell on her arms – bandaged along the length of both to cover a dozen glass cuts – its molten warmth froze over.

"It ain't that bad," said Ilsa, turning away from the door and hastily pushing her arms into the sleeves of her robe. She tied it closed and turned to face him. "The cuts are shallow."

Eliot shut the door behind him. The sun had dipped behind the houses and the chamber had been plunged into a low, pink light, the kind that muffled sound and made a voice soft and low.

"You're alright?"

"I'm fine," Ilsa replied automatically. "Little weak, that's all."

Eliot came close – close enough that Ilsa could feel the warmth of him – and lifted a hand to her cheek. Ilsa held her breath as his thumb grazed her jaw with a featherlight touch. When he withdrew it, it was bloody. "You missed one."

He stepped away abruptly, leaving Ilsa bereft, and picked up the iodine and a cloth that lay next to a bowl of warm water gone pink with her blood. He soaked the cloth with some iodine, and came back to her, eyes wary.

"It will sting," he warned softly.

"I've survived worse today."

Gently, he tilted her chin up with one hand, and carefully

cleaned the cut on her cheek with the other. It did sting, but Ilsa had grown used to it over the course of cleaning dozens of scratches. Eliot was waiting for her to wince, but she didn't, and it took some of the tension out of his shoulders. A grin pulled at one corner of his mouth.

"Was that your first time being poisoned?"

Ilsa raised an eyebrow. "Was that your first time making a joke?"

The grin widened. "It's possible to build up a tolerance to smokeweed, if you don't mind a tingling sensation in your hands." He flexed his fingers, eyes straying to her mouth as he added, "And your lips."

"You do that? You take poison on purpose?"

"The only way I could persuade Gedeon to do it was to join him. He didn't see it as a threat. He used to say he hadn't survived the Sage's massacre to die by poison."

Ilsa's mouth fell open in surprise. She had had just as stubborn a thought when the smokeweed was working on her. She had a sudden, fierce wish to speak to her brother; to tell him the thing they had in common. Eliot studied her expression and must have seen her longing shift elsewhere, for he stepped away, tossing the cloth aside.

"I didn't come by to check on you."

"Oh."

He smiled again, and Ilsa hoped her disappointment hadn't been too telling. "Not *just* to check on you. I think I've solved our riddle." He opened the door, and in the hallway, of all things, was the map he had liberated from Fyfe's lab. He pulled it into the room and stood it before Ilsa.

"You and this map have got a weird thing going, you know that?"

Eliot ignored her. "I've been getting in my own way trying to work it out," he said. "The Oracle girl said the shop was on Moorgate, so I started with Moorgate. I've been staring at a dozen starsforsaken maps of the street, histories of the area, directories of chemists in a mile radius, trying to work out what the rest of the riddle meant, but nothing fit."

"Alright…"

"I didn't put the rest of it together. The station, Marin Street, and she said over and over that you didn't know the city, yes? But you do. This London is the same."

"Well, *I* know that."

"But it wasn't what she meant. She called it a city, but she meant the quarter. The only place you're not familiar with because it's entirely different in the Otherworld."

Ilsa stared at the map, finally understanding what Eliot was waiting for her to grasp. The transparent overlay was pushed over the top of the frame, but she reached up and brought it down to cover the London of the surface. Her fingers traced along the new lines, nose close to the paper as she read the tiny street names.

There it was. Marin Street, a long, curved road in the Underground.

"We just need to work out where—"

"Shh." Ilsa was a step ahead now. She didn't need to work anything out. She just needed to remember. Because Lila had told her *exactly* where she would find the chemist… if she was in the Otherworld. She lifted the overlay, her fingers hovering over where she would find the Moorgate entrance if the station had existed here. She brought the overlay down, then up again. Moorgate on the surface map and Marin Street in the Underground weren't that close at all, except at one point where they bent towards each other and almost kissed. Ilsa jabbed a finger at it, success lighting up her face in a grin. "You know what's here in the Otherworld?"

"Moorgate station," said Eliot. "Ilsa." His voice curled around each syllable like it was the best thing he'd ever said. "I believe you've found our chemist."

23

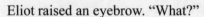

Eliot raised an eyebrow. "What?"

He had taken the first half-dozen steps of the entrance to the Underground, looked over his shoulder to find Ilsa hesitating at the top, and come back.

Though she was not simply *hesitating*. The real reason she clutched the post at the top of the rail was to maintain her balance, and she would never admit it to Eliot, but she feared she would keel forward if she let go.

Ilsa had been under the streets of London before; everyone had. But the furthest she had ever got was the platform – just once, and she had stayed for all of four seconds. Boarding a train, and disappearing into the tunnels, had been a work still in progress. Whatever was underneath *this* London, Ilsa was unprepared for it.

The Psi militia who had approved their passing – *cloaks*, Eliot had informed her they were named, so called for their capes in various shades of pink – eyed her like they might change their mind, and Eliot reassured them with a smile. Ilsa didn't see that smile head-on, but she doubted it looked very reassuring.

"It's just… I don't like confined spaces," she murmured.

"I never would have guessed." When Ilsa shot him a look, he was watching her with cruel amusement. Was he actually enjoying this? Had he been waiting for the moment Ilsa buckled? "I can do this alone, you know."

She scrutinised him. There was a truth that had become so shamefully obvious to Ilsa that she couldn't deny it any more: she liked Eliot. She liked when he touched her. She liked when he looked at her. She liked trying to work out what he was thinking. And she was cursing the fact that she had had him alone in her room and missed another opportunity to kiss him. She was going mad wondering whether, if she ever got his mouth on hers, he would be as sharp as he looked.

The worst part was, every time her thoughts went to kissing Eliot, she remembered he was carrying a torch for someone else. There was no Athena at the Zoo – she had checked. Neither Eliot nor anyone else had ever mentioned her, but he kept that damned pocket watch and it had to mean something. It stung her.

She *loathed* it.

But Ilsa's feelings didn't stop her being suspicious of Eliot. Now he was offering to seek out this chemist alone, and she didn't trust it. Was he being kind – unlikely – or did he feel Ilsa closing in on his secrets?

"No, I—" *I don't know whether to trust you? I think you're keeping things from me? I need to work out if we're actually doing what you told me we're doing?* "You're helping *me*, remember? I got to come with you."

From the look that crossed Eliot's face, Ilsa thought she might have said any one of her rejected thoughts by mistake. Then he flashed her that smile – the one that was the *opposite* of reassuring – and she shuddered.

"The familial resemblance is stunning," he drawled. "Gedeon thinks everything is about *him* too." He angled his head towards the stairs, and then he had vanished down them.

Ilsa let the retort on her tongue propel her after him, not stopping to think as the curved, tiled walls of the tunnel greeted her on all sides. Eliot was waiting at the bottom, hands in pockets.

"I s'pose you'd rather I was like you?" she said.

He grinned wolfishly. "Absolutely not. If you were like me, you would have taken the information I handed you and come down here alone." He joined the flow of bodies heading further into the tunnel, and Ilsa gathered every ounce of her courage to follow him. He brought his lips close to her ear – close enough that his breath made her shiver – and added in a taunting whisper, "Although perhaps you needed someone to catch you when you swoon."

It was true that she had lost her colour, and her breath was coming in jagged little gasps, but she would not swoon. She'd be damned if, of all the things about the Witherward that might terrorise her, this utterly unthreatening tunnel would be the one to best her – and in front of *Eliot*.

"Remember, you'll bring the wrath of the Psi down on us if you shift in their territory. Don't so much as spring a second dimple. We're going to find out who's been in contact with Gedeon, swap some money for his whereabouts, and be back on the surface by teatime."

They descended another set of stairs and the tunnel split – one avenue for those descending and another for the blessed souls about to break the surface. Then she was being swept along on the downward current like a pebble being dragged to the bottom of the sea. Was there any air down here? A pressurised blast of it was swelling from below – stale, suffocatingly warm, and smelling faintly of a thousand strangers' skins – but it refused to be drawn into her lungs, no matter how deep she breathed.

344

Another set of stairs. Bodies surrounded her on all sides but no one said a word. With no other stabilising force to cling to, Ilsa reluctantly grasped for Eliot's arm and entwined it with hers. He must have felt her fingers tremble as they brushed his shirtsleeve, as instead of mocking her, he threaded her arm tighter through his and pulled her close to him. Ilsa resigned herself to her fate; he would have to catch her when she fainted.

She had just reached her limit, pulled Eliot almost to a standstill, and opened her mouth to beg that they turn back at once, when the tunnel before her opened up.

They were at the top of another set of stairs, but these ones weren't bracketed by polished tiles. Instead, they looked down on an entire city.

"Oh my…"

Ilsa instantly forgot that she was underground. The Psi quarter wasn't formed of a warren of train-track tunnels like she had imagined, but of broad, cavernous boulevards, the height of which stretched several storeys above and below. Enormous turrets carved from the stone acted as supports, and wrapped around them were staircases leading from the surface. Some of the buildings – also carved from the cave and taller than Ilsa had ever seen – also reached to the roof, and bridges cut between them at every level; some so wide they were streets themselves, with shops and houses along them.

It could have been an oppressive mess, but every bridge, every turret, and every winding set of stairs was so thoughtfully, perfectly placed, like the pieces of a three-dimensional puzzle, that this city beneath the city was nothing short of a wonderland.

"Not what you were expecting?" said Eliot, tugging her down the broad spiral stairs.

"No," was all she managed, her relief hitting her so hard that her head spun.

The stifling staleness of the tunnel was gone, and by some magic, a cool breeze tickled her skin. Golden light hovered over them, like low clouds, but she couldn't make out the source, and above that the ceiling of the cave was doused in translucent sky blue. The effect was that of a perpetual dawn; the pale stone all around her was tinged pink and orange and dappled in long shadows. If she couldn't feel free and unbound in a place like this, could she ever?

Eliot released her to hail a cab as a wondrous kind of magic went on around them. The Psi, it seemed, used their talents for everything. Crates and baskets of goods and deliveries soared through the air above her; mothers pushed their prams ahead of them with the power of their minds; and the carriage that pulled up in front of Ilsa and Eliot had no horse. A driver sat in the usual place above and behind the cab, but the axle extended before the passenger seat, bearing a second smaller pair of wheels.

As the cab pulled into traffic, so did another twenty yards behind them. Eliot didn't notice it, but Ilsa sat at a slight angle to keep it in the corner of her eye.

"This must be the biggest quarter of them all," she said as she watched the Underground go by, her view unimpeded by a horse's backside.

"I believe it is, but not by much. It doesn't span the entire area of the city above."

"I hope these people catch the sunlight every so often."

Eliot let out a small laugh. "Don't worry for them," he said. "The Psi are the most employable people in this city *and* the one above. They get about."

They instructed their driver to make for the Moorgate entrance to the Underground, and once there, it didn't take them long to find the only chemist Lila could have meant. It was a corner shop called Brecker & Sons, on a junction bustling with the commerce of a farmer's market.

Eliot was about to enter the chemist's when Ilsa took his arm. "What're you doing?"

"What we're here to do, of course."

"And what's that? March into the place and demand to know where Gedeon Ravenswood is? He probably ain't going to know jack. We need the *customers*, not the chemist." Eliot was scrutinising her, his expression stuck part-way between irritated and impressed, but he didn't argue. Ilsa nodded across the street. "Look, there's a café right there. We can get out of sight and keep an eye on the place. The thing 'bout a habit is it's regular, right? I bet you someone's gonna come along any minute."

So they went to the café as Ilsa suggested. As Eliot went to the counter to order tea, Ilsa took a seat by the window and sat on the left-hand side, where she would be able to see both the chemist's and the street in the direction they had come. The cab that had been following them had dropped its passenger an inconspicuous distance from them; inconspicuous for anyone less observant than Ilsa. She only looked in quick glances, so as not to be seen noticing, but she realised their tail had followed them from the surface. She decided not to mention him to Eliot.

When their tea arrived, Ilsa's also came with a huge slice of a cake she had been delighted to discover in the Witherward; a spiced sponge with sour cherries and buttery icing.

"You ordered this for me?" she asked, blinking.

"You're always hungry," said Eliot, his eyes on the corner shop. When she continued to stare dumbly at him, he glanced over, and his face fell. "I thought it was your favourite. Orlagh said you're in the kitchen two or three times a day asking for some."

"It is my favourite." And, yes, she had started wondering about her elevenses on the cab ride.

"Then what's wrong?"

She forced a flirtatious grin. "You asked Orlagh 'bout me?"

Eliot's expression hardened. "I *overheard*. She likes feeding you."

When Ilsa continued to study him, he rolled his eyes and went back to watching the shop.

She picked up her fork. "Thank you."

The cake was rich and moist and even better than Orlagh's. A little sound of pleasure escaped her lips as she took another bite. And another. She had all but forgotten where she was and what she was meant to be doing when she looked up and found Eliot's attention was no longer on the chemist's.

He watched her mouth as she brought the fork to her lips, her throat as she swallowed, her fingers as she brushed the crumbs from her lower lip. She had never seen anything fascinate him like the sight of her enjoying her cake.

Ilsa had spent most of her life diligently controlling when people did and did not look at her, whether she was slipping wallets from men's pockets or distracting them stupid on the stage. But she hadn't forced Eliot's attention – she just had it, and it made her feel bare.

"Does it take so little to make you happy?" he murmured.

She shot him a smile and took another bite. "You ain't tried this cake," she said with her mouth full.

In a flash, he stilled her fingers between his and liberated the fork. Ilsa made a playful sound of protest as he speared the cake and popped a forkful in his mouth.

"Hmm. We should get their recipe for Orlagh."

"I ain't gonna be the one to try and give it her."

Eliot's smile widened, and he took another bite of the cake they were now sharing. Ilsa felt a kind of giddy pleasure flow through her. Some part of her mind must have decided she didn't deserve it, for before she knew it, she was asking the question she had been trying to avoid.

"Who's Athena?" Her voice held a lightness she didn't feel.

"Sorry?"

"The girl what gave you that watch you carry."

Eliot gave her a look she couldn't read; intense and probing, but not as cruel as she expected him to be for prying. "Ilsa…" He said it like the beginning of a question, but he trailed off.

Ilsa had never been one to blush, but she could feel it happening. Her eyes found her teacup. "Don't say no one," she warned. "It's in your hand even when you don't need the time. It's precious to you." When she dragged her gaze back to his, she knew she was right. "So?"

In answer, Eliot produced the watch and put it, engraving up, on the table. *With all my love, your Athena.* All her love. *His* Athena. Ilsa could still feel his eyes on her as she flipped it over, revealing a second engraving: *E.Q.* His initials.

"You're right," said Eliot, leaning back in his chair. His voice had taken on an edge. "It is precious to me."

He was gauging her reaction, that wicked amusement pulling at one corner of his mouth, his eyes alight and liquid in a way Ilsa had never seen them. She schooled her face into indifference and pretended to be concentrating on Brecker & Sons. Without meaning or wanting to, she found herself imagining what Athena looked like – tall, immaculate, devastating – when Eliot cleared his throat.

"Elijah Quillon," he said.

"Beg your pardon?"

"E.Q." He sipped his tea. "Athena is my mother."

The beautiful penny dropped. Ilsa's mouth fell open in indignation. She wanted to say something mean – to put them back on equal ground – but first, she was too absurdly relieved to stay angry, and second: "Elijah was your father." He raised his head when she said *was*. "Cassia told me…"

Eliot swore. "Of course she did."

Ilsa shifted in her chair and toyed with her teacup. "I know what that's like. The not knowing, I mean. I din't know what happened to my family 'til a couple weeks ago." She meant to go on, but when she looked up, Eliot had closed back up. He was staring out of the window – or perhaps just *at* it – with that mask of unforgiving ire she had first seen him in.

"I don't want to speak of my father." His tone left no room for negotiation, and Ilsa flinched.

"Alright." She shouldn't have asked him about the pocket watch. She should have dealt with her jealousy without prying.

She was about to apologise when Eliot's hard mask cracked, revealing a sliver of aching sadness.

"It's just" – he let out a long breath; carefully, like he was struggling to control it – "I don't know how to mourn somebody I—" He shook his head.

"You don't need to tell me," she said softly.

Eliot nodded stiffly, and Ilsa felt a pang. He didn't need to tell her, but she couldn't help wishing he would. She wanted to know it all. Instead, they fell into silence. While he kept his eyes trained on Brecker & Sons, Ilsa leaned close to the window, tilted her head up, and gaped at the majesty of the cavern above her.

"I wish I'd known it was like this," she said.

"You were afraid to come down here." Ilsa nodded, her eyes still on the window. "And you were afraid of Hester's hidden room. Why?"

Ilsa stiffened, but as Eliot watched her patiently, her discomfort began to wane. He had declined to talk about his father, and looking at him then, she knew she could do the same. He wouldn't push. He wouldn't pry.

"I don't want to feel trapped," she heard herself breathe.

Eliot frowned. "Trapped?"

"I know it's in my head, but sometimes… it feels like I'll be stuck forever. It's alright if I can see the way out, and I can get to it if I want, but…"

"And yet you came down here, imagining it was a warren of tunnels." He shook his head, but smiled. "You're something of a masochist, aren't you?"

"A masochist?"

"You court pain. You like to hurt."

"Who *likes to hurt*?" replied Ilsa, a little louder and a little higher than she had intended.

Her incredulity made him frown. "Plenty of us."

"I can see why you'd think that, but it ain't true."

"No?"

Ilsa paused, and rolled his words around her mind. "If I don't like to hurt, but I do it anyway and don't complain, that still make me... what you said?"

"A masochist?" The humour in his eyes was rapidly dimming.

"Right."

"No," he said softly. "That makes you something else."

"What?"

"I suppose the word is courageous."

Ilsa scoffed. "Courageous people don't get scared because the room's too small."

"Evidently, some of them do," said Eliot. Ilsa rolled her eyes. "Fine, don't believe me. But I know plenty of courageous people, and they're all scared of something. Hester goes white as a sheet at the smallest drop of blood, but she's never let it stop her. Don't tell her I told you." He nodded towards the window and the underground city beyond. "Look around you, Ilsa. We're all scared. It's only a weakness if you give in to it."

"And what matters to you?" she said, leaning across the table. "What d'you fear?"

Eliot's jaw clenched. "Hurting the people I love."

"And who—"

She cut off as Eliot's gaze snapped suddenly towards the chemist's.

352

"Here comes someone," he said.

"Told you." Ilsa turned in time to see a skinny, sluggish Oracle man approaching Brecker & Sons. His hair was a ghastly shade of orange and his pale face was spattered with freckles. His upturned button nose was familiar too. The family resemblance was uncanny.

"That's got to be Lila's brother!" Ilsa hissed.

Hardwick's gaze swung towards the café like he had heard them. His eyes widened as he tapped into the power he tried so hard to smother with a pipe. He had Seen them, and he ran.

"Oh no you don't." Ilsa's chair tottered on its hind legs as she leapt up.

"Ilsa—" Eliot reached for her elbow as she passed but he was too slow. "*Damn it.*" There was a rattle of change as he tossed some coins down and chased after her, but by the time they were out on Marin Street, Hardwick had disappeared among the market stalls and their patrons.

"He went that way," said Ilsa, and they dodged through the shoppers after the Oracle. But the lane beyond the market was barely any quieter, and Hardwick was at the next corner, vanishing again. Eliot made to chase after him, but Ilsa stopped him.

"We ain't going to catch him like this. We got to shift."

Eliot laughed, eyes wide. "No thank you. Do you have any idea what they'll do to us if we're caught?"

"Will it be any worse than what the Zoo'll do to you if you arrive back alone?" Ilsa took from his hesitation that he knew he couldn't stop her. "I'll herd him into an alley. You fly above and block him off."

Before Eliot could speak further to the recklessness of the plan,

Ilsa shifted. Her leopard wouldn't do; she needed a canine's nose. She dropped onto all fours, relishing the sting in her muscles as they moved to support four long, sinewy legs. She shivered as a bloodhound's long ears sprouted from her skull. The colour definition leached from her vision, and her world exploded in a chorus of shrieking and a maelstrom of scent. A second round of screams told her Eliot had taken flight, but she was already bounding to the door of Brecker & Sons to catch Hardwick's trail. Some of the Psi grabbed their children; others shouted abuse at her. It was already a scene, and it was about to get much worse.

She tore after Hardwick, following the ripple he'd created and throwing everyone she passed into even more chaos. She had him back in her sights in no time. Hardwick was casting his eyes upwards. He knew Eliot was there – a swallow haunting his movements – and he would do his best to lose him. As Eliot swooped lower, Hardwick made a hard right, diving down a passage covered by a bridge; a bridge Eliot nearly collided with trying to keep Hardwick close. The Oracle had known; he'd baited Eliot to come lower so he could slip him.

Ilsa couldn't see him either, but she still had the scent, and she barked to direct Eliot as she dodged a horseless cart and plunged after him. Eliot picked up speed as he chased and then overtook her. With her eyes on the swallow and her nose to the street, Ilsa caught up with Hardwick as he tried to cut an evasive path through the maze of streets. She was practically on top of him, her hound legs an impossible match for his human ones. Looking ahead to the next turning, she came up on her prey's left flank, steering him right, and that was when Eliot saw his moment.

It made no difference what the Oracle did and didn't See.

He was in an alleyway: Ilsa at one end, steps ascending to a footbridge at the other. He made a break for the steps, but Eliot was faster. He became human again as he landed; big enough to block Hardwick in. Hardwick skidded to a halt, instinctively doubling back, but Ilsa – a girl again – was behind him and had closed the distance. Before he could rush her, Eliot threw an arm around the Oracle's chest and put a knife to his throat.

"Let's make this quick and painless," Eliot snarled, but there was as much urgency behind the words as threat. Ilsa resisted the urge to glance over her shoulder for advancing Psi cloaks. "We know you've been trading information for vemanta. Tell us what he wanted from you and we'll let you live."

"Long as there's no riddles," amended Ilsa. Eliot flashed her an approving smile.

Hardwick stared venomously at her, spittle spraying from his lips as he regurgitated the mantra: "Yours not to—"

He was cut off as the back of Ilsa's hand met his cheekbone sharply. She didn't revel in making a man fear for his life, but she had a real lead on her brother and nothing was going to stop her. "Would you keep to your oath if you were choking it out through your own blood?"

Hardwick just continued to stare.

"I s'pose you don't value your life then" – unable to resist a little showmanship, she wiggled her fingers and showed him up both sleeves before she magicked back the vemanta tin she had lifted from his pocket when she hit him – "how 'bout this?"

Eliot's eyebrows shot up, and he pressed the knife harder to the man's throat. "We know how to cut off your supply. Die or don't die, it'll be a long, painful wait for your next pipe."

He continued to struggle, but his heart was no longer in it; they'd found his real weakness, and it was the same as Lila's. "He had us visit the temple and pay our respects to the Seer," Hardwick blurted, "but it wasn't the Seer he was interested in."

"It was the apprentice, we know," said Ilsa.

Within his limited range of motion, Hardwick shook his head. "No. Cogna wanted *him*. He did not want Cogna."

Eliot's and Ilsa's eyes met, and each saw their confusion mirrored.

"What'd he tell you to do at the temple?" said Ilsa.

"Find the crypt," choked Hardwick. "He needed to know if it was true what he heard. That there's a crypt under the temple."

"Is there? A crypt?" said Eliot. Hardwick hesitated, so with a flash Eliot slashed the blade across his cheek. The crimson blood was especially chilling against the pale sheen of his skin. The Oracle howled.

"Yes! There's a crypt, yes! The alpha went to break in and found Cogna instead. Whatever the alpha wants, it isn't there."

Ilsa wanted to ask what Gedeon had been after, where he was, anything, but their time was up. On the footbridge above them, quick footfalls were approaching. She spun; men and women, all in capes of various shades of pink, were looking down on them like spectators around an arena.

The cloaks had them surrounded. It was a good job they could grow wings.

Eliot shoved Hardwick away from him. His eyes swept the cloaks above despairingly, but he spared a glare for Ilsa. "Too late for diplomacy now. Think small," was all he said before turning into a sparrow.

Ilsa followed suit, but couldn't help questioning the wisdom of Eliot's words; *fast*, not small, was usually her first rule of escape.

But she quickly learned why small was better, when the first missile came at them. It was a dustbin lid, lifted psychokinetically from the street below and used to herd them in the direction of another missile; a basket of mushrooms stolen from a cart. On all sides, whatever objects their hunters could find filled the air and manoeuvred to trap them, and only their diminutive size allowed them to evade capture. They moved erratically, around buildings, over and under bridges, back on themselves, until the Psi had lost sight of them amidst their own enchanted jumble. Ilsa hung on Eliot's tail, determined not to find herself alone down here.

A horn sounded, then another. A cacophony of brass notes sang out, alerting more cloaks to their presence. Before they were out of range of the first wave of Psi missiles, more magenta capes flashed below and a wall of nets rose above them, fine enough to catch even a sparrow. Ilsa beat her wings in a frenzy, straining for a gap, but there was nowhere to escape to but below, where the cloaks waited with restraints that looked alarmingly like the ones Cadell Fowler had used to stopper her power.

If Ilsa could only fight in one form, it wasn't going to be a sparrow. As the small, walled-in square below got near, she commanded her muscles to change again, and she hit the ground on the four massive paws of a giant snow leopard. Eliot changed too, becoming his favourite panther. They were surrounded on three sides by magenta-clad Psi, a wall at their backs. Ilsa's hackles raised. They could shred a dozen cloaks each, but they would still be in their territory, surrounded.

They had broken the Principles by using their magic outside

the Changeling quarter, but they had only *shifted*. They hadn't hurt or threatened any Psi. Hardwick had used his magic too. A Whisperer could do so without ever being detected. Ilsa's righteous anger burst out of her in the form of a snarl. She flexed her claws, daring the Psi to come closer or ensnare her with their ropes. What would they do to them once they were captured? If they were slaughtered, would the others ever find Gedeon?

But before anyone could move, birdsong sounded above them, and the Psi gaped as a third bird swooped low above the square.

In the chaos of one chase and then another, Ilsa had forgotten their tail. He had been trained in stealth by the very best, had stuck close to their heels, paws and wings, and it seemed he was shadowing them still.

The bird was a nightingale – then a macaw, then a swan, then not a bird at all but something in the fox family, its gangly limbs flailing in thin air as it fell to earth.

Fyfe landed in an inelegant human heap with a defeated sigh, but when he pulled himself up it was with a slow, methodical motion, like someone trying not to provoke a growling bulldog. He half-turned towards them, locked eyes with Ilsa, and brushed back his coat to reveal a sort of toolbelt, loaded with coloured pellets.

Dampeners. They were getting out of here after all.

Ilsa snagged Eliot's attention with a soft growl. She couldn't tell him to do as she did, but he understood all the same, and followed suit when she turned back into a sparrow.

"Now!" yelled Fyfe, as he launched a pellet in either hand and plunged the Psi into a magenta fog.

Above the roofs of the square, nets were still waiting to

enclose on them, but as three birds took flight, they began to sag in place like roses wilting in a vase, before fainting out of the air. Footsteps chased them and horns sang out their direction, but no enchanted obstacles rose from the magenta smoke. As they darted back towards the safety of a Camden-bound staircase, the snares of more cloaks came to greet them. But each time they did, Fyfe crash-landed on a rooftop, briefly became human, and launched another handful of pellets. The soldiers were unharmed, but robbed of their powers. Ilsa laughed – it came out in a gleeful chirrup – to think she'd once thought of Fyfe as a golden retriever. For all his boyish gawkiness, his sweet humility, and atrocious shifting, he might have been one of the most dangerous people in the Witherward.

Suddenly, every Psi in the Underground was powerless to stop their escape. They shrieked as Ilsa, Eliot, and Fyfe swooped low above their heads to aim through the tunnel that would take them to the surface. When they finally burst into the waning evening sunshine and left the Psi border guards far behind them, Ilsa was so giddy on adrenaline she botched her landing, turning human too soon, and went sprawling onto the pavement.

24

Fyfe helped Ilsa up, a cocky grin pulling at one corner of his mouth, but an alarmed glint in his eyes.

"Do I want to know what that was about?" he said.

Before Ilsa could reply, Eliot stepped between them, gaze searing into Fyfe. "You followed us," he said darkly.

"I think the words you're looking for," snapped Ilsa, hands on hips, "are 'thanks for saving our hides'. We'd be throw rugs by now if it weren't for him."

"If anyone recognised Fyfe or me, that future is still not beyond the realms of possibility." He had turned his ruthless fury on Ilsa now, but that was fine with her. At least she deserved it. "If the Psi hesitate to skin us, Hester certainly won't. You broke the Principles."

"Well the Principles are *stupid*," said Ilsa, the injustice fresh and still burning.

Eliot rolled his eyes melodramatically and rubbed the bridge of his nose. "Stupid," he intoned.

"We din't hurt no one! Well, no Psi, anyhow. And we got what we needed."

"Which was what?" Their heads snapped to Fyfe, and Ilsa could see his investigator's mind picking through every detail of the afternoon. There would be no keeping anything from Fyfe any longer. "Tell me what you're up to and I'll take the blame," he added when no one answered. "If this comes back to bite us, I'll say I was conducting some field research, I set a dampener off by mistake and it escalated. Hester's never been able to shout at me."

Ilsa and Eliot exchanged glances.

"Of course, the business with that Oracle will be hard to explain." Fyfe's expression was exaggeratedly grave. "But with the details I'm sure I could make something of that as well."

His eyes darted between them as they stared it out. Something in Eliot's expression revealed layers of unease Ilsa couldn't account for.

"He saw everything," she said. "And we owe him. And we ain't getting nowhere fast just the two of us."

Eliot closed his eyes, and let out a long sigh. "That's a double negative," he muttered, stalking past them in the direction of a drab-looking pub.

*

The Screeching Hen sat on another "weak spot", and just like its equal in the Otherworld, it was particularly grim. The saloon was in the cellar; a narrow space little wider than a corridor with too few windows and too-dark wood. Even the necessary presence of a roaring fire did little to brighten the room, so on heady, late summer evenings such as this, it was inevitably deserted.

They took a table in the corner furthest from the bar, ordered a carafe of wine, and sat with heads close together.

"Why are you carrying an arsenal of dampeners?" began Eliot.

"Fail to prepare, prepare to fail," said Fyfe. "When I saw you were sneaking off together, I assumed it was out of Camden. That, or a love affair."

Fyfe seemed to regret the words as soon as they left his

mouth. The awkwardness leached around the table from one pair of eyes to the next, like a round robin.

So Ilsa jumped in and explained everything she and Eliot had been doing. She started with Eliot's discovery that Gedeon was using the city's vemanta supply to control its Oracle users for information.

"That's awfully clever," said Fyfe, eyes cutting to Eliot. "It sounds like... well, it sounds like something you'd come up with."

Eliot stiffened. Malice flashed across his features, but Ilsa kicked him under the table and he calmed himself. "I don't know where Gedeon is, Fyfe."

"I believe you," Fyfe mumbled, and he swallowed a long gulp of his wine. "I just meant that it was very well done."

Ilsa went on with how they had used a little bribery themselves to find Brecker & Sons, and what they'd managed to get out of Freddie Hardwick before their time was up.

"Gedeon din't go to the Docklands to get that apprentice at all. He was trying to break into some crypt."

"One would assume a crypt at the temple would be for dead Seers," said Fyfe, frowning. "But disgraced Seers are executed by fire and their ashes are poured into the Thames."

"And we know how well the Docklands like to execute their leaders."

Fyfe nodded. "They've done away with two in my lifetime, if memory serves. If a crypt existed for the remains of the honourable ones, it would be no surprise if we'd never heard of it. It would be practically unused."

"Lucky for us," said Eliot. "The less that's down there, the less Gedeon could have been looking for."

"But Hardwick said whatever Gedeon was looking for weren't in the crypt," said Ilsa. "So what would he do next? Where's he gonna look?"

Fyfe shook his head. He was chewing his lip, lost in thought. "That's not a good question."

"Pardon?" said Ilsa, affronted.

"No. I'm sorry. I mean… of course it's a good question, it's just not the one we need to answer. Eliot, that acolyte you interrogated. He told you Cogna met with Gedeon at the border of the Docklands."

"That's correct." Understanding dawned in Eliot's eyes. Ilsa reached it too. "Because Cogna saw him coming."

"Hardwick said Gedeon din't want Cogna. Cogna wanted Gedeon."

"So the question's no longer what Gedeon would do next," said Fyfe grimly. "It's what Cogna's going to do."

There was a silence as they all came up short. Ilsa couldn't anticipate her brother's next move with so little information, let alone some Oracle's.

After a long, aching moment, Eliot shook his head and downed his drink.

"Gedeon has abandoned the Zoo, robbed from half the city, and broken the Principles. It wasn't all for nothing." He turned to Fyfe. "He has a goal. Would the Gedeon you know be persuaded away from what he wants by some runaway Oracle with their own agenda?"

Fyfe shook his head. "He's stubborn. And persistent."

"Exactly. If Gedeon was after something he hoped was in that crypt, then he's after it still. We need to know more about this apprentice, you're right. But we also need to know who's entombed in that crypt."

When Eliot looked at Fyfe again, Ilsa was relieved to see his wrath had been subdued. "I suppose thanks is due again, Fyfe."

"You din't thank him the first time," Ilsa muttered.

"I should have trusted your intelligence weeks ago."

A furious blush spread up Fyfe's face all the way to his ears.

"And for another thing too," he added, "if you'll oblige me. The acolyte said Cogna was different; that they couldn't See him—"

"Or her," interjected Ilsa.

"—or her. So coercing random Oracles has reached the limits of its usefulness. We're going to have to tap another source for information, one outside of the Docklands." Fyfe nodded his understanding as they stood to leave. "I'll research this crypt, you two – Cogna."

"What other source of information?" Ilsa murmured to Fyfe as they exited the pub into a dwindling warmth. "What's he mean?"

Fyfe grinned, his eyes alight. "He means you and I are going to Whitechapel."

"The Docklands want to kill me."

"Yes," said Fyfe.

"It ain't just an empty threat."

"Oh, they're committed."

"And it ain't some rebel unit or secret society – it's the whole bloody faction."

"Seer's orders."

"Then tell me again," said Ilsa, crossing her arms, "why we're 'bout to go *knock on some senior Oracle's door and ask for a chat*?"

This was where she and Fyfe were headed. In order to find a neutral, cooperative Oracle beyond the Docklands – one who might tell them more about the Seer's apprentice without hoarding secrets or bartering for vemanta – they needed to visit the Whisperer quarter.

"You don't need to be afraid of Jorn, Ilsa," said Fyfe, grinning.

"Who said afraid?"

Fyfe grinned wider. "He's important to the Docklands, yes, but Jorn isn't the ambassador in Whitechapel because he cares. He's the ambassador because he gets to live the life he wants away from those he answers to. Not standing up for your people is messy morally, but fighting for them is messy literally." Fyfe held his hands palms up like he was weighing the two, and his grin became a grimace. "And Jorn just bought an expensive Belugian rug."

Ilsa narrowed her eyes, but she hadn't made it to seventeen by questioning people's reasons for *not* wanting to kill her. "Well I wouldn't want to mess up his new rug, neither. Long as we're agreed."

The mid-morning sun was already sweltering when Fyfe tugged her out the door, but Ilsa was dismayed to find there was no carriage waiting.

"We're walking?" she whined.

"It's not far," said Fyfe. "Besides, it's better to avoid the fanfare of a carriage and guard detail on a mission like this." He delighted on calling the trip a *mission*, and had done so thrice already. "Whitechapel is unlike anywhere else in the city. When its people can conduct all their business without ever breathing a word out loud, the smallest of disturbances could attract unwanted attention. Eliot was very insistent that if I take you with me, we slip in and out."

They came to the edge of the park and peeled east towards the Whisperer quarter.

"He don't think I can handle myself against a *Whisperer*?"

Fyfe rolled his eyes, but smiled affectionately. "Sometimes, you've got too much fight in you. Try not to *handle yourself* against anyone."

Ilsa pantomimed cracking her knuckles. "It's the street urchin in me. Can't help myself."

King's Cross marked the boundary of Camden Town and Whitechapel, so it wasn't long until the border loomed and Ilsa was trying not to stare at another breed of soldier.

The Whitechapel stewards were dressed in their faction's midnight blue. Their double-breasted coats with gleaming silver buttons, black gloves and patent leather shoes gave them the appearance of Otherworld constables, if not for the matching half-capes cascading from one shoulder. They were more elegantly dressed, and more fearsomely disciplined in appearance, than any of the militia she had met.

And, to her surprise, they were armed. Not with claws or spells or hovering nets, but with more metal and fire power than any man would ever need if this was the Otherworld. Here, they were probably still weak against the likes of a Wraith.

The stewards squared themselves as Ilsa and Fyfe approached.

Men in police uniforms and good old-fashioned guns; finally, some fears Ilsa was accustomed to. It made her homesick. Almost.

"We need to state our purpose for coming," Fyfe murmured in her ear. "Telepathically, I mean. Hold meeting Jorn in your mind and keep the rest locked away."

Ilsa had a moment of panic and started skimming through all she remembered from her lessons. But that was exactly what Fyfe had told her not to do. How would a Whisperer react to a blow-by-blow of how she learned to best them? With those pistols at their hips and a bandolier of blades gleaming on each chest, Ilsa didn't want to find out.

Wordlessly, the steward in charge placed himself in their path, so that they met him face to face. He exchanged a nod of recognition with Fyfe, who crossed the border often, then looked Ilsa up and down. His eyes weren't vacant the way Alitz's were, but they still took on a new sharpness when he focused his gaze on Fyfe, who remained still and stared back at him. After a moment, the Whisperer nodded and turned to Ilsa. She pushed aside her thousand curious questions and tried to speak directly into the soldier's mind. *We're going to the Oracle embassy to meet with Ambassador Jorn*, she tried to tell him, but the background hum refused to die down. *What do you see? What does it feel like? Do my thoughts have my voice? If I thought only of your face and your eyes looking into mine would you see anything at all? How can you tell if I'm lying?* It felt like they were staring at one another for longer than he'd stared at Fyfe, the steward's brow knotting with irritation, until at last he blinked away that unnerving sharpness and shook his head.

"The same way you can tell if *I'm* lying," he said, surprising both Ilsa and Fyfe. "You read my tells."

He signalled for them to continue and they hurried past. When they were out of hearing range, Fyfe said, "I think he liked you. Ceric doesn't open his mouth for anyone."

"I did terribly! He knew I read people's tells."

"He let us through, so he can't have seen the worst of it." He frowned. "Do you read *my* tells?"

"Let's just say you wouldn't win a penny 'gainst me at cards."

He led them through the streets of Whitechapel. Rows of sagging mews on narrow cobbled lanes; tree-lined streets of immaculate white townhouses; and featureless terraces of red brick, all among one another like a shuffled deck of cards.

Fyfe was right; a relentless hush filled the air like a smog of its own. It got thicker as they ventured deeper into the quarter. Birds still sang, leather soles still struck the pavement, a child's pull-along train still grumbled along with a wooden churning. But the sounds didn't harmonise to become the signs of a living,

368

breathing city. Each pierced the ear-splitting silence like an intrusion, no matter how small and soft a sound. Ilsa couldn't shake the feeling they were being watched, or heard, and she doubled her efforts to protect her thoughts.

"There's something you ought to understand about Oracles," said Fyfe, rubbing his hair. "You're about to learn that despite all your training with Alitz" – he hesitated, before evidently deciding against mentioning Pyval – "coming face to face with a skilled Oracle isn't all that less invasive, and there's no protection to be had. You see, even talented, trained Oracles, like Jorn, have the whole knowledge of the universe to contend with when they See. It can make searching for what they're after a long, exhausting process, unless they have an anchor. A starting point. Like a person for example. In Jorn's presence, anything he wishes to See relating to you or me will be at the forefront of his divination."

But that wasn't true of the Oracles Fyfe had told her she would meet in Whitechapel. Sure enough, an Oracle man bearing a tower of parcels to the post office came into view. He wore a servant's clothes and had the lazy, fluid gait of a typical pipe-smoker, but something was different. His steps were sure and didn't drag. His fingers gripped the parcels without fidgeting. But his head did loll forward like a guilty dog's, and as he drew closer, his face had an alarming vacancy about it. Ilsa had thought of all Oracle's eyes as expressionless chasms, until she was looking into this man's. They had none of the life of Lila or Freddie Hardwick's. The only people who appeared as absent as this man were dead.

Some Oracles spent years mastering their skill so that it

369

wouldn't drive them mad. Some dulled the onslaught of eternity with vemanta. And a third group, like this man, gave up their minds to a Whisperer. They lived as slaves, mindlessly compelled to do their master's bidding in exchange for the peace it brought them. The only thing an enslaved Oracle was capable of thinking of was their work. Their histories, their families, even their own names, all ceased to exist for them.

"But the Principles banned slavery," Ilsa had said when Fyfe explained.

"And the arrangement between the Whisperers and the Oracles was *part* of the Principles," said Fyfe. "Whitechapel wanted it. The Docklands wanted it. They installed Jorn to administrate and guard against abuses and let them get on with it." He laughed. "That part was your mother's idea. I believe she said the sure-fire way to know a person is serious about what they're after is to put a bureaucrat in their way."

Ilsa tried not to shudder as the Oracle man passed by them, but she recognised it as a death of sorts, and this man was a corpse. All the same, she could understand his choice.

Ilsa had imagined the ambassador's home as an official-looking building on a well-to-do street; perhaps bearing a flag of the Docklands, if such a thing existed. But while there were poorer districts in London – and Ilsa had lived in some of them – the cobbled street Fyfe led her to was far from upper class. It was permanently shaded by the colourless, three-storey terraced houses crammed too close together on either side. The terrace end sagged, like someone had removed a bookend and the whole row was about to slide. A glance at several windows revealed that most of the houses had been partitioned into flats. If this was the level of luxury that could distract an Oracle away from the faction war, Ilsa wondered what the Docklands must be like.

When they rang Jorn's doorbell, a bashful servant girl – not an Oracle; probably a Whisperer, thought Ilsa – answered the door and led them to a parlour. At least inside, the house was exceedingly comfortable. The parlour was hung with colourful fabric, and a cluster of ornate brass lanterns hung from the ceiling. Under foot was, indeed, a reassuringly expensive carpet in an intricate pattern of colourful flora and fauna. The room was thick with the cloying scent of rose.

"Is Jorn Moroccan?" muttered Ilsa.

"I believe some of his ancestors were, but Jorn's as cockney as they come." Fyfe frowned. "You meant Marauccan, didn't you?"

"Ain't that what I said?"

Before Ilsa could wedge the unlikely image of a cockney ambassador from a country she still believed was Morocco into her already shaken expectations, a bead curtain rattled behind her, and an Oracle entered the room.

"Well, if it isn't Hester's baby brother," he said. He was a cockney alright, but a better spoken one than Ilsa. "And this is…" He studied Ilsa, and the corner of his mouth twitched. "So, this is a family affair."

"How'd you do," said Ilsa uncertainly.

Jorn was short and broad-shouldered, with lumpy features set into a wide face. His skin was medium brown, but with a cold, blue undertone. Like every Oracle Ilsa had met, he looked like he needed a jug of cream. His gunmetal hair was fine, and thinning on top, but his eyebrows were unconcerned, cutting across his face like unkempt hedgerows in the throes of spring.

He was dressed in a burnt orange robe of a luscious material, and he repeatedly pushed up the sleeves as he crossed the room and scooped Ilsa's hands into his. She sucked in a breath but didn't pull away, even as Fyfe's lips tightened.

"How lovely you are, Miss Ravenswood," Jorn purred, his white eyes roaming over her. "Truly the fairest young lady I have met in a long while. It would be a crying shame to deliver your head to the blessed Seer."

Ilsa snatched her hands back, her every muscle tensing, ready to shift. Fyfe warily drew her behind him, but the action only made Jorn laugh.

"I jest, Master Whitleaf. We both know you wouldn't be here if I concerned myself with the petty interests of the factions." He crossed to one of the silk-upholstered chairs, spread out in it like a cat, and sighed theatrically. "I cannot abide all this pretence. It makes me weary. So let's not pretend my people's fictitious quarrel with you is anything but."

"Why?" said Ilsa before she could think. "Why're they pretending we kidnapped someone when they know it ain't true?"

"Because you do nothing for them and need nothing from them. In this city, fairest, that makes you their enemy. Please." He gestured to the chairs, and Ilsa and Fyfe sat. "How may I be of service?"

"It's a rather delicate matter," said Fyfe.

"Boy, breathing is a delicate matter in this starsforsaken city."

"I'm finding that," muttered Ilsa.

"We'd like to know what you can tell us about the missing Seer's apprentice Cogna."

A slow smile spread over Jorn's face. "That's not cheap information," he said, greed flashing even in the emptiness of his gaze.

Fyfe frowned. "We're not asking for your divination. We hoped, as a fellow Oracle of influence, you would know them, or about them at least."

Jorn's expression hardened. He jerked his chin at Ilsa. "You're new to this city," he said to her. "Your friend does you a disservice by not leading by example; by trying to grift me. So take it from me instead, fairest. Learn the value of everything, and do not give it away if it can be sold."

He spoke the last to Fyfe, who narrowed his eyes right back at the Oracle. "I should have known," he said.

"We din't bring no money," said Ilsa.

"Coin is cheap," Jorn replied scornfully. "Tell me, fairest... who is your most powerful friend?"

"I ain't sure I know that."

Jorn laughed again. It was a grumbling, spiteful sound. "It is dangerous to spend too much time with Whisperers," he said, leaning so far towards her that Ilsa was sure he would fall from his chair. "They'll tell you all knowledge is theirs for the taking because they can peer inside your weak little mind. It flatters them and it flatters you. Your very own history is vaster than what you're keeping up here." He tapped his temple. "It lives after you die. It survives your children's children's children and everyone who knew them. And I can See it all. If I want to know who your most powerful friend is, I will search your life and the lives woven with yours, and I'll decide the truth for myself. You only need to give me your hand."

If this was the price to be paid, Ilsa wasn't fooled; it was more costly than Jorn was letting on. His power was formidable, if his own assessment was to be believed. What else might he See while riffling through Ilsa's history, and her future too, if he chose? Was it dangerous to give so much away? Ilsa's instincts told her yes, and her past agreed unequivocally. This wasn't a questions and answers game – it was a piece of herself in exchange for a chance to find her brother. She cast a glance at Fyfe, who shrugged non-committally. It was Ilsa's call.

"If coin's so cheap, what's the information worth to you?" Ilsa looked pointedly around the room. "You din't do this place up so nice with secrets."

Jorn gave her an assessing look that dragged on for an age. "You'd never hear an Oracle ask such a question. *What is information worth*," he scoffed. "*What is knowledge worth*. You have no idea how little you understand, girl. You want to know what *I* will earn from your information? Something to pay for my silk and tobacco? For all my heart's desires? Lovely" – he spread his hands wide – "knowledge *is* what I desire. It's the most valuable thing on this earth, and here I am, giving it away for free."

"So you ain't gonna tell nobody what you learn from me?"

Jorn sat still as a cat, and he smiled. "I make no such promises." Ilsa let out a sigh of exasperation, which Jorn dismissed with a hand. "I've given you my terms. And I'm very close to concluding that you're here to waste my time. So what'll it be?"

Ilsa was less sure than ever, and yet she knew what she would do. She had known it before Jorn set his terms; before she stepped through the door. Jorn was calling her bluff, because nobody needed an Oracle's Sight to see how she was growing desperate to catch up with her brother.

"Alright."

Jorn took her offered hand and bowed his head in concentration. There was silence as he pried through her life; a silence in which Ilsa and Fyfe tried to wait patiently, but soon resorted to making mocking faces and rolling their eyes at one another.

"Well?" said Ilsa when Jorn's gaze re-met hers.

"Illuminating."

"Who *is* my most powerful friend?"

"Young lady, do you want the answers you came for or the answers to my questions? We will be here a very long time and learn a great deal about one another if it is both."

She bit back her exasperation as Jorn resettled in his chair. "So, you want to know about Cogna."

"We don't even know if they're a man or a woman," said Fyfe.

"Cogna is a child." He left a long pause to relish in his guests' surprise. "Neither a male nor a female child. They were born with a sex, like all of us, but they shed it like a snake sheds its skin. No use of it."

"How old?" said Ilsa.

"Thirteen, I believe."

Fyfe furrowed his brow. "How could a thirteen-year-old have mastered their talent?"

"Steady now. I have a question for you, boy." His mouth curved cruelly as he studied Fyfe. "I would like to know about your first kiss," he said, his tongue darting out to wet his lips.

"And what's the use in you knowing that?" said Ilsa.

"Pay or don't pay. That's my price."

Glowering, Fyfe extended a hand to Jorn. The touch was brief; the smile that spread across Jorn's face, feline. "No? A dashing boy like you?" Fyfe let out a slow breath, but it did nothing to calm the blood rushing to his face. "You're young. There's time. Don't despair."

"Cogna," prompted Ilsa. The word came out more forcefully than she intended.

"Yes, yes. Some think Cogna's a god; others, a mere genius. We all develop early mechanisms to control our Sight to some degree; the strong of mind have more success than the dim, of course. Cogna's control was powerful from the first. They sailed through the training. An unusual choice for the seership, I must say, but I believe it was thought to be the only way of controlling the child."

"What do you mean?"

Jorn turned his attention to Ilsa. "What is the closest you have ever been to death?" Jorn asked. Ilsa was already holding out her hand.

He took it, and the wait was even longer this time. To distract herself from thoughts of days on end without a morsel of food or lashings that cut too deep, Ilsa hazarded a glance at Fyfe. His blush was giving way to a look of irritation to rival Eliot's.

Jorn's brow creased; it might have been sympathy. "Death is a dear friend of yours, it seems."

"I like to think of him as an unwanted admirer."

A laugh. "He'll win you eventually," the Oracle said. His gaze roamed over her again and she shuddered. "Cogna is an omnic."

"A what now?"

Fyfe shook his head. "I've never heard of an omnic."

"Because they are incomparably rare. Cogna is the first born in the city, or in Albia, or on the whole continent I would wager. An omnic Sees not only the future as it might be, but all possible versions," said Jorn, spreading his arms wide.

"Don't that defeat the purpose of a plain old Oracle?" said Ilsa. "Multiple futures and all that? I mean, *I* can see multiple futures. In one, Fyfe and I leave here happy because you've been helpful. In another, I smash your face in." She smiled. "All hypothetical, 'course."

Fyfe leaned towards her. "Didn't we talk about not handling yourself?"

"It's philosophy, Fyfe, it ain't fighting."

"No, she's right," said Jorn. "Put an omnic among the rest of us, and our Sight becomes laughable."

"But you can still know the future, even as it changes, and Ilsa and I can only guess at it. What use is it to see all the outcomes that never come to pass?"

Jorn raised a hand and slowly curled it into a fist. "Control. An ordinary Oracle Sees only an eventuality, malleable and abstract. They cannot say what will change that eventuality, nor how. But Cogna – Cogna knows how to bring the future they want into being."

Ilsa resisted the urge to glance at Fyfe. What eventuality was Cogna seeking by joining forces with Gedeon?

"It is why other Oracles cannot See the apprentice. The world around Cogna – its possibilities – shifts as Cogna does," said Jorn, his white eyes narrowed at Ilsa. "It is the reason you are alive, fairest."

Again, Ilsa's mind went to her many brushes with death. "I weren't even in the Witherward 'til a few weeks ago. What does Cogna know of me?"

"A good question. Perhaps your companion can help me answer it." His gaze snapped to Fyfe. "Tell me, what were the last words spoken to the one you love?"

Ilsa snorted. "Bleeding hell. That's really what you want to know most?"

"What can I say? I appreciate a mess."

She didn't know what to say to that, but Fyfe stared levelly at Jorn.

"There isn't anybody," he said. It was a lie.

"Let me be the judge of that." Jorn extended a hand and, reluctantly, Fyfe took it.

Ilsa wondered idly, if she could look through all of Fyfe's days and nights, whether she would be able to tell who it was he pined for. Yet it didn't matter. Whatever was in Fyfe's heart, he hadn't shared it freely, so Ilsa didn't want to know. She was just about to intervene, to propose some other secret, when the men disconnected, and Jorn raised his head. His grin was gleeful.

"You're not his type."

"Is this the price? Amusing you?" snapped Fyfe. Abruptly, he was on his feet. Ilsa followed. "If you would answer our question we'll be on our way."

Jorn continued to grin, and casually crossed his legs. "We have always known of you, Ilsa Ravenswood," he said, even as his eyes stayed on Fyfe. "It would take more than the fabric between dimensions to keep you from the Oracles. It was Cogna who triggered the series of events that led to your attempted murder that night, as you know. But it was also Cogna who told the Changelings you were alive."

Ilsa's eyes widened. "Cogna sent the messenger."

"Yes. The apprentice moved you out of harm's way before fleeing the temple with your brother. The only question you should be concerning yourself with is why. What use are you to them? That, I cannot help you with."

"Then we're done here," said Ilsa. "We won't take up no more of your time."

Before they could depart, Jorn sighed heavily and rose from his chair. When he locked eyes with Fyfe, his expression was mercifully kinder. "Don't be afraid of love, boy. It can wound deeply, but it is also a salve. You can have that one for free."

Fyfe, with his unfailing good manners, seemed to take this as an apology, and offered his hand to shake Jorn's. But when their fingers met, Jorn's clamped tightly around Fyfe's as if by their own accord. His eyes moved as if he were dreaming; his features slackened. It was only for a second before Fyfe pulled away in alarm, and the Oracle gasped.

"The avarice of men!" Jorn said fiercely. "Do you think you're the first to want what was never yours to claim? Every few centuries your ilk abandon your experiments when you learn the truth. Transference is a forbidding and dangerous magic, Master Whitleaf. Your alpha cannot wield it!"

"Transference?" said Ilsa. Jorn was talking about Fyfe's experiments; the machines designed to replicate Wraith and Whisperer magic.

"It is what the Prince of Camden seeks."

Ilsa saw her own startled alarm in Fyfe's wide eyes. They had stumbled on more answers than they had hoped for, but Ilsa felt only fear, not triumph.

"What d'you mean he can't wield it?" Ilsa couldn't stop herself from asking. "Will it hurt him?"

Jorn's whirling eyes settled on her, his mouth pinched into a cruel smile. "More questions?"

"Please." Ilsa extended her hand again, even as Fyfe made a move to protest. "Is Gedeon in danger?"

"I want a part of your future," breathed Jorn. "I want your next mistake."

"Take your pick," muttered Ilsa.

Jorn's words about transference still hung in the air, yet what she wouldn't give to see inside his mind the way a Whisperer could; to pluck her next mistake from the future and squash it under her heel.

Even more so when Jorn looked up, his unruly eyebrows pulling together. He tried to begin several sentences before settling on one. "To be like you," he said. "To be so helpless and so unburdened... how does it feel? Regret?"

"You got your question," said Ilsa. "Now answer mine."

"The price just went up," said Jorn, grinning.

Ilsa let a sharp breath out through her nostrils and considered. How could she describe regret to someone who had never felt it? "It's like you're travelling, but you can't ever visit the same place twice," she said slowly. "You had a different future in your suitcase, a better one, but you left it on the platform. You want to jump off the train but it's moving too fast."

Jorn's white-eyed gaze bore into her as he pondered her answer, but he was satisfied. "Gedeon Ravenswood's desires will do only harm," he said. "To himself. To the city. You must do everything you can to stop him."

*

Ilsa wanted to beg Jorn to save her from her next mistake. There were some things she knew she could never go back and change – things she would get just one shot at – and this thought weighed heavily on her psyche as they left the ambassador's house.

Thankfully, an impression was not one of these things.

She had been suspicious of Fyfe when they had talked about Eliot; she had told herself he was hiding something. Now, she knew what it was. Knew why Fyfe had defended Eliot when no one else did. Knew what had caused him to tense and blush at the mention of the boy's name.

Fyfe was in love.

And Ilsa was skimming through her memories of every interaction between Fyfe and Eliot like some would-be, amateur Oracle. Did Eliot know? Should *she* have known? Would she have done anything differently if she had? She imagined Fyfe witnessing those moments she and Eliot had been alone and close enough to breathe each other's breath, and her stomach cramped.

When Ilsa dragged herself back to the present moment, Fyfe was several paces ahead of her and walking at a furious pace, and she tensed. Perhaps Fyfe *did* know. Perhaps he had caught Ilsa looking at Eliot when she thought he wasn't watching, the way Jorn must have seen Fyfe looking at him too. Was he avoiding her now because he couldn't pretend ignorance any longer?

"Fyfe…" said Ilsa tentatively, and she hurried to catch him up. "Fyfe, wait."

When she reached him, Fyfe was chewing his lip and muttering under his breath. He didn't acknowledge her. She tugged feebly on his sleeve.

"Fyfe?"

"Yes!"

He stopped suddenly, and Ilsa ran into him. His mad gaze landed on her, and Ilsa realised he wasn't thinking about Eliot at all, nor was he answering her. She'd seen that light go on before, in the Screeching Hen, right before he said something brilliant.

"I know why they tried to break into the crypt," Fyfe said. "I know what Gedeon's looking for."

2 6

While Ilsa and Fyfe were in Whitechapel, Eliot had apparently been in the library.

"Eliot," Fyfe called breathlessly. He was propelling himself up the spiral stairs to the balcony where Eliot was leaning on the rail, tome in hand. Ilsa was on his heels, struggling to contain her impatience.

She had given up trying to get Fyfe to tell her what he'd worked out. To his credit, he had tried, but they were nearly home before he had calmed his excitement, and even then, few of the words he had gasped at her – *transference*, *legend* and something about Wraiths – meant much to Ilsa.

"Did you find out who's buried in the crypt?" he asked Eliot, so quickly the words tumbled together.

Eliot snapped his book closed. His curious gaze slid from Fyfe to Ilsa, where it lingered. She shot him a glare that said she knew what she looked like; cheeks red as apples, sweat trickling below her neckline. She lifted her hair off her neck, took a journal off the shelf and fanned herself with it.

Tall, excited Fyfe had walked home. Ilsa had jogged.

"I think so," said Eliot, barely disguising a smirk as his eyes travelled over her. "There are about a dozen Seers down there."

"Is one of them Hetepheres Emeryat?"

These were two of the words Ilsa had failed to understand

the first and second time Fyfe had said them, but Eliot's gaze snapped to Fyfe. He raised an eyebrow. "The seventh Seer?"

Fyfe made a wild gesture Ilsa thought was acquiescence. "*Yes!*" he said vehemently, and turned to Ilsa. "The seventh Seer's amulet. That's what the legend's called. That's what I was trying to say."

Ilsa nodded. She was still catching her breath. "Right. What legend?"

"It's a folk tale, really. Hester used to tell it to me when I was little, which means she probably told it to Gedeon too. Nearly two thousand years ago, when the city was founded, the Oracles built their temple by the river and brought the Seer of Esfa Kala to live there. She was only the seventh Seer to rule in the modern age, which is when Oracle customs changed and the Seer went from a leader to a slave. The previous six had all been denounced by their people in a matter of years and executed, so she was considered to be doomed to an untimely death.

"But when the different peoples of London were brought together, the Seer met a Wraith general who fell in love with her. Back then, the Wraiths were feared and even worshipped by the people of the other factions and he was the wealthiest and most powerful leader in all of London. He waged war on the Oracles to try to free his lover from her indenture, and slaughtered hundreds of them. Ironically, this bloodshed is what eventually brought a death sentence on the Seer. Her people blamed her for failing to protect them from the Wraiths.

"But before the sentence could be passed, the Wraith general's grief and anguish led him to swallow his pride and turn to a Sorcerer who was able to help him. He paid the Sorcerer in land and gold and anything the Wraiths had, making his people nearly destitute, and the Sorcerer crafted for him an amulet that would protect his lover when her people came to execute her. All he had to do was unfasten a clasp and put a drop of his blood inside the amulet.

"So he did, and he smuggled the amulet to his lover. The moment she let the chain fall around her neck, she was imbued with the Wraith's power. She was still an Oracle, but with the unstoppable speed, strength, and senses of a Wraith."

The hairs on Ilsa's arms stood on end. An amulet that could replicate a Wraith's power, just like Fyfe's experiments.

"What the general failed to learn until too late," Fyfe went on, "was that the amulet took the power of the person whose blood it held and gave it to the wearer. In making the Seer practically invincible, he had been made helpless. When she tore apart her prison with her bare hands, her people thought her a goddess, and she was restored to her position. When she learned that her new-found powers were stolen, she betrayed her lover, kept the amulet for herself and wrought vengeance against the Wraiths for the slaughter of her people to win their favour. The helpless, mortal general was burned at the stake, a sacrifice to the Oracle gods, but when he died, the amulet's power was lost. The Seer grew sick and died as well." Fyfe rubbed his hair. "Hester used to tell me the cosmos brought it on her as punishment for her sins. But, then, Hester also told me Wraiths eat Changeling children who misbehave. Who knows what happened."

"Gedeon must have thought the amulet was buried with the Seer," said Ilsa.

"It was," said Eliot, turning both their heads. He had listened to Fyfe tell the story with stoic patience. "I mean, it might have been." He ran a hand over his face, frustrated. "An hour ago, I would have said there was no way Gedeon would be acting on some fairy tale."

"Legend," corrected Fyfe.

"But… well, come with me."

By a chair in a hidden nook up on the balcony, there was a pile of books. The top few lay open, and Ilsa picked one of them up. It was a history of magical artefacts, open on a page about the supposed existence of the legendary seventh Seer's amulet.

"I saw some sections of the history shelves had been pillaged, including all the books I needed," said Eliot. "At first I thought some raiders had helped themselves, but then I found them all here. All of them reference the legend or Hetepheres Emeryat, or the amulet itself."

"How d'you know it was Gedeon what had them?" said Ilsa.

"Because he folds the pages when he reads." She let out a small sound of disapproval as Eliot showed her the mangled corner of a page. "I know. Never lend him your books. Or anything, for that matter. The man is a bull in a china shop."

"Please don't use that phrase," said Fyfe, a haunted look coming over him. "It was such an expensive dare."

Eliot gently smoothed the page corner and put the book down.

"The question is," said Fyfe, "what does Gedeon even *want* with this amulet? From a scientific standpoint, it's an intriguing piece of magic, and certainly powerful but… it can't be worth all this trouble."

"Well." Eliot shifted some of the books and held up a tome bound in green leather. "This fellow says that if the amulet could be studied, it would be a simple matter for another Sorcerer to replicate its magic." He flicked through the book, glowering at it in a way Ilsa wouldn't want to be on the receiving end of. "Somebody must have hurt him, because he goes on for several pages in *near impenetrable* prose about an unstoppable army equipped with artefacts that could bestow the owner with the magic of all six peoples."

"But the amulet *steals magic*," said Fyfe, eyes wide with horror. Ilsa wondered if he was thinking of Hester. "Would Gedeon do such a thing?"

"For an unstoppable army? Even a single unit of unstoppable wolves to fight the rebels?" Eliot shook his head grimly. "He would be a fool not to. Tell me about Jorn."

They filled him in, minus any details of Fyfe harbouring unrequited feelings for him.

"We got no way of knowing what Cogna's up to," Ilsa concluded. "I know you said Gedeon is stubborn, but this kid knows how to manipulate the present to get the future they want. P'raps Cogna and Gedeon ain't looking for the amulet no more. P'raps Cogna's steering Gedeon in a different direction."

Eliot shook his head. "So we don't know where Gedeon is, and even the Oracles don't know where Cogna is, and they can't find Gedeon either because he's with this omnic, and they may or may not be after something that may or may not exist and either way, is also missing."

"That's about the crux of it," said Fyfe. "You don't know if the amulet even *exists*?"

Eliot tossed the book in his hand onto the pile with enough frustration to send them all toppling. "Like I said, there is probably *an* amulet, one that was entombed with the seventh

Seer, but whether or not it's a magical artefact, every historian claims something different. A lot of Sorcerers have said it isn't possible, but I also found half a dozen insisting this crafter or that crafter was the one who made it. Most of them are claiming it was their own ancestor though, so who's to say."

"But that Hardwick fellow said whatever Gedeon was looking for wasn't in the crypt," said Fyfe.

"No, it isn't. The only thing every account agrees on is that the amulet hasn't been seen in over a thousand years. Gedeon must have gone to the temple purely because it was the only lead he had. I would have done the same."

"But how'd it get out of the crypt?"

Eliot let out a breath. "There's no saying. The Oracles have claimed at various points that the amulet was destroyed, that it never existed, and that it was stolen, probably according to whichever makes the least sense to the person asking."

They fell into silence.

"So what do we do now?" said Fyfe, slumping against a bookcase.

Eliot glanced at Ilsa, who realised with a bittersweet pang that he was deferring to her. But she was spent. She could feel her brother slipping away from her with every idea they used up, and she wasn't sure how many more she had left. When she didn't speak, Eliot said, "We work on the assumption that Gedeon and Cogna are still looking for the amulet. Gedeon knew no more than we do when he tried to break into the temple, but he's with a powerful Oracle now."

"Then don't they likely have it already?" said Ilsa.

Fyfe shook his head. "I doubt it. If the amulet has had a

complicated history, it would take any Oracle a very long time to locate it, even an omnic. Jorn was able to find details of our past quickly because we were touching, but Cogna's shooting in the dark."

"Besides, Gedeon can't stay hidden forever," said Eliot. "Once he's got what he wants, he'll have to come back."

Fyfe was encouraged by this, but Ilsa raised an eyebrow defiantly. "*Why?*"

Eliot scowled. "Why?" he said indignantly. "Because everything he has is here. We're his home and his family."

She wanted to remind him that Gedeon abandoned them all without so much as a note, but instead, she voiced the thought that had been circling since Fyfe first mentioned the amulet. "Aelius said Gedeon had worked out what the raiders were looking for here at the Zoo."

Eliot gestured tiredly. "It's the most plausible explanation."

"But the raiders took Fyfe's pocket forge. If it's transference they were interested in, there's plenty more tempting inventions in that lab."

"Perhaps Aelius was wrong," said Fyfe, though he didn't sound convinced.

"And if he ain't – why'd the Heart rebels think *we* got the amulet?"

"Ah," said Eliot, a smile tugging at one corner of his mouth. "It's occurred to me that there's a way to find out. Fyfe, if you were a Sorcerer and you were looking for something, what's the first—"

"I'd use a locating spell," blurted Fyfe, eyes lighting up. "It's hit-and-miss magic, but if someone knew what the amulet looked like, or what it was made of…"

"It was probably silver," said Eliot, gesturing to the books Gedeon had collected. "And there are drawings in some of these books. They're all similar."

Fyfe shrugged. "It would be a start. If there was a connection between the amulet and something in the Zoo, a locating spell might be sending them here. Something made with the same hand, or the same material, or owned by someone who had the amulet. I've collected all kinds of Sorcerer spells and objects that I wanted to work on. I'll comb through the lab."

"Good idea." Eliot glanced at Ilsa again, but she still wasn't having any bright ideas. "You keep talking to everyone here," he told her. "Ask them about the attack. I suppose I'll comb through our correspondence with the Heart for anything that hints at the amulet; perhaps they got their information by non-magic means. But if there's a chance they know something we don't, it could help us find Gedeon. We have to find out what it is."

They left the library and Fyfe skittered away to his lab. But as Ilsa turned to leave, Eliot grasped her by the hand. It was a gentle pressure, but her reflex was still to swing around and sock him. He caught her by the other arm.

"Easy."

"Sorry. Old habits, and all."

"So I remember you telling me," he said, with a pointed glance at her clenched fist. "Still working on that, are you?"

Ilsa peeled her wrist free. "What d'you want?"

"To know what's wrong." Though his voice was soft, his gaze was stormy as ever. This time, all that intensity was on Ilsa's side. It was for her. She toyed with the lace sleeve of her dress.

"Nothing's wrong."

"Is that so?" He ducked his head to try and catch her eye, but she stepped away from him. "If you've lost your enthusiasm for this chase, I might understand. But you declined an opportunity to start an argument. It's out of character."

"You can talk."

Eliot smiled. "That's better. But something's upsetting you."

She was about to speak when a servant appeared from the lounge opposite. Catching onto her wariness as he passed, Eliot angled his head in the opposite direction. "Come with me."

She followed him through a set of glass doors and into the garden. They wove between the orderly lines of flower beds, in which roses of every colour were perpetually in full bloom, thanks to a spell Cassia had cast on them. The scent was heavy in the late summer warmth; it was rising from the velvety rose heads like heat haze. She had never seen blooms as vibrant and large until she came through the portal, and she came to a stop among them, entranced.

Eliot was still and patient as he watched her lower her nose to a crimson flower.

"Cogna knows 'bout me," she said.

"Yes. You said Cogna sent the messenger who told us you were alive."

A fist clenched around her heart as she forced out the next words; the thought that had been festering in her mind like a disease since Whitechapel. "Cogna's with Gedeon now. They're working together. So Gedeon probably knows 'bout me too. I think p'raps Cogna told him I was alive and back here and he... doesn't care."

391

Eliot's face only registered surprise for a heartbeat before it melted into something else. Fearing it might be pity, Ilsa looked away.

"Gedeon doesn't know about you."

"Hmm. You and him are trading secret messages, I s'pose," she teased.

"Who told you?" She could hear the smirk in his words.

"Just a guess."

"Well, you guessed wrong. If I knew how to contact him, your being here would be the first thing I'd've told him. He deserves to know his sister is alive, and that she's clever and capable and brave. That she's someone he would be honoured to know."

Ilsa glanced up to find Eliot standing closer than she had thought, his face betraying how ardently he meant every word, and her pulse kicked. Eliot swallowed, blinked, but mastered his nervousness.

"I *know* Cogna hasn't told him you're alive. Because if Gedeon knew the first thing about you, if he had any idea how… he would be back in a heartbeat."

Despite the sun, a wave of cold trembled down her spine. Her body wanted her to close the gap between them, was pushing her forward with an icy touch. She gave into it at the same moment Eliot did, her mouth meeting his halfway, her fingers travelling up his neck to tangle in his hair. He tugged her closer desperately, until their bodies were flush against one another – Ilsa's every nerve singing – and deepened the kiss.

Ilsa had been kissed before; a handful of clumsy fumbles that had done nothing to answer the question of what all the fuss was about. But kissing Eliot was like hearing her call in the dark answered. She swallowed his breath like this was the air she should always have been breathing. His fingers kneaded the nape of her neck in a way that travelled down her spine and knocked every muscle along the way out of action.

It was only when their lips disconnected, both of them breathing hard, that there was any space for another thought to push its way into Ilsa's mind: Fyfe.

She gasped and stepped back, out of Eliot's embrace. He was startled back to his senses. His hands went into the air.

"I'm sorry," he said. "I didn't mean to—"

"No, it ain't you. I—" Ilsa shook her head. She didn't have the words to explain. She wouldn't have told him even if she could. The truth of why she didn't want Eliot kissing her like his life depended on it – even though she really, really did – in the open of the garden, with everything she had learned that day, wasn't hers to share. So she murmured an apology, slipped past him – at a safe distance – and practically ran back to the house.

27

Ilsa was a coward.

She might also have been a bad friend. It was difficult to know for sure when her head was still spinning from the feeling of kissing Eliot.

The fact was, Fyfe couldn't have him, and nothing Ilsa did or didn't do could change that. *You're not his type*, Jorn had said. What was more, Jorn knew what Ilsa's next mistake would be, and he had made it seem a lot more dire than an ill-advised kiss, meaning that she was as confident as any non-Oracle could be that kissing Eliot was a good decision. Perhaps she should have kept doing it while she was still protected by that knowledge.

Then again – what did *not his type* mean? Was Eliot Ilsa's type before he'd flirted with her in the chemist, or let his fingers linger on her skin, or his eyes linger on her face? If Eliot had never thought of Fyfe that way, how was anyone to know how he might feel about him? And if Eliot was busy kissing Ilsa, when would he ever find out?

But no, Eliot deserved more credit than that. He had made his choice. In fact, it was all his fault. He was the one who had started soliloquising about what an honour it was to know her. He was the one who had come just a little too close, and muddled his words, and let his eyes flicker to her mouth like he had never noticed the soft, full shape of it before. *She* hadn't started whatever was happening between them.

As Ilsa stalked through the house, cursing Eliot to keep from cursing herself, the sickly scent of flowers she had left behind in the garden returned. She was outside Hester's rooms, and the door was ajar. Tentatively, she pushed it open. A faint breeze was tickling the lace curtains and wafting the strong aroma of too many floral arrangements – and an undertone of whisky and stale cigarette smoke – throughout the room.

It had been nine weeks since the attack that had injured Hester, and she showed no signs of wanting to re-join the world beyond her suite, let alone lead the Changelings. She was stretched out on a loveseat by the open window, a book balanced in one hand. She didn't look surprised to glance up and see Ilsa in the doorway.

"You got a lot of flowers in here," said Ilsa, wrinkling her nose.

Hester glanced around at the arrangements – some fresh, some browning – with mild disgust. "Fliss keeps bringing them. I roll my eyes every time, but I can never bear to have her toss out the dying ones."

Ilsa raised an eyebrow. "You can't bear it? I don't mean no offence, but you don't strike me as the sensitive sort."

"Why on earth would that offend me? I'm not. But I can't help thinking of how much life they have, how much character. And yet they're just dying things. It's sort of pathetic."

Her voice never faltered, but her face gave her away. She scowled at Ilsa like she had forced a confession from her. As if to change the subject she gazed pointedly out of the window, and quirked her brow. "But what am I saying? You're very fond of flowers."

She was only on the first page of her book, and her reading glasses lay abandoned on the end table. She must have been looking out the window – at her view of the rose garden. Ilsa cleared her throat to change the subject.

"P'raps I should ask you 'bout Gedeon too," she said, lowering herself into a chair. "'Bout him leaving."

Hester sighed. "Cassia warned me you would come creeping." She pulled herself into a more upright position, warning Ilsa with a severe flick of her hand not to dare try and assist her. "But as far as insight goes, I can say only that I don't share in the lieutenants' shock. This is not as out of character for Gedeon as they wilfully believe."

Hester's tone – sure and superior – riled her. "You sure 'bout that? 'Cause it ain't the impression I got from everyone else. They say he's selfless. And caring."

"Oh, very. And do either of those traits preclude what he's done, whatever that is? I'm certain he believes fully that it is right. Selfless and caring, just as you say." She paused, and shot Ilsa a patronising look, like the conclusion was obvious. "But there's no denying it's also foolish. That, cousin dearest, is why I am unsurprised. It is well within Gedeon's nature to act first and think later."

"But he planned to leave, din't he? Aelius has got that note from one of the wolves—"

"Yes, he *planned it*," said Hester with an impatient wave of her hand. "Yes, it would have taken time and organisation. But reflection? A modicum of doubt? Do not underestimate the fools like your brother. They can achieve a great deal without *thinking*."

It seemed unfair, but it was also unfair for Ilsa to tell her she was wrong; she couldn't vouch for someone she had never met. And yet…

"Well the Changelings love him," she said. "I was in Camden the other night, and the kids were playing games where they pretended to be Gedeon. They tell stories 'bout him."

"Of course they love him. He's their kind, smiling prince. He remembers their names and sympathises with their concerns. Gedeon makes people feel valued. He makes people love him. It's his gift." Her lip curled cruelly and she looked away. "It's a nice touch in a leader, but a useless one."

Ilsa doubted it was useless, but she wasn't about to tell her cousin that. "That ain't why. It's because he's brave. He saved a pregnant woman and her husband when they were kidnapped."

Hester laughed. "Bren and Diana Luckett. They campaigned to have Gedeon replace me before he came of age after his little stunt."

Her voice was bright, her smile was wide, and still Hester couldn't disguise the edge in her words. Ilsa didn't think she was trying to. "They din't mention that," she said weakly.

"And did they mention how many more people their brave alpha-to-be saved before he killed five wolves in a rescue gone wrong?" Now the pretence at humour was gone. Her voice cut like a hot blade, fury burning behind her hazel eyes. Ilsa felt her stomach sink lower in her abdomen. "Did they mention that the alpha they wanted so desperately pays his ransoms now, and only sometimes succeeds in finding the culprits later? Did they mention how many more of our people have been snatched from their homes since Gedeon started *rescuing* them? Ask Cassia how much his caring and selflessness costs us, how much less the wolves earn while dying for him."

"But he's the alpha. It's his *job* to help people," said Ilsa stubbornly, even as the doubts piled down on her.

"This is London. Death and hardship are built into it like the stones in its streets," Hester said, determination in her features. "A faction leader's job is to swing the pendulum in her people's favour as often as she can, with as little damage as possible and as much of her conscience as she can afford to keep." She sighed, softening. "Your brother's heart is always in the right place. But one does not lead two hundred thousand people with one's heart, cousin dearest."

As brutal and dispassionate as it was, what Hester said made sense. There would always be difficult choices. A leader with too much heart – someone vulnerable to letting those choices tear them apart – was no use to anyone.

"But Gedeon's grown hardened, of course," said Hester, as if she'd read the direction of Ilsa's thoughts. "He makes better decisions every day. With each dire mistake he changes, and he listens. I've learned how to make him listen to *me*. I may not be the true alpha any more, but I'm his voice of reason." She gave a brittle laugh. "Or I was. I thought he listened. Perhaps our young alpha has tired of making better decisions."

"So he din't ask you 'bout this?" challenged Ilsa. "Nothing that might be a clue?"

Hester sighed. "I can't be of any help. I spent a week in a healing potion haze, and when I came to, they told me my back was broken, my magic was gone, and I was in charge. That's all I know."

"And before the attack?"

"Before?"

Ilsa shifted in her chair. "I been thinking p'raps something else got Gedeon worked up. Cassia said she and him had a fight…"

"Yes, about Millwater."

Hester said no more, and a weighty silence fell between them. As Ilsa studied her cousin for potential tells, she had the unshakable feeling that Hester was doing the same. The gaze that met hers was bold, unwavering, and cut straight through her in a way even Alitz Dicer had failed to do. Ilsa had forgotten who was interrogating whom by the time Hester tossed her braid over her shoulder and sighed.

"I suspect Cassia came down a little too hard on his decision, and it riled him. Powerful men often like to think they can take advice from us, but it's seldom the case."

"D'you know why he cancelled the trip?"

"*Cancelled?* That was the day of the attack," said Hester matter-of-factly, her eyebrows raised.

"But I thought the attack weren't 'til after."

Hester opened her mouth, and closed it again, frowning. She made a small sound of displeasure. "You're right, I'm sure. I'm afraid I don't remember much about that either. I don't know if I hurt my head or what else, but it's all a bit of a blur."

Hester shook her head regretfully, then pushed her obvious frustration with herself aside. Her hands lay calmly in her lap. Her shoulders were straight but relaxed.

"Memory loss?" Ilsa probed lightly.

Hester, so obviously loath to admit to weakness, narrowed her eyes. Then that cruel smile curled the corner of her lips. "And what of it? I would give up *all* my memories and start afresh in exchange for my legs and my wings back. Wouldn't you?"

Hester had seen her scars; she knew the answer. But Ilsa whispered anyway, "I'd give up mine for a lot less than that."

Her honesty took Hester by surprise, and the cruelty evaporated. She cocked her head to one side. "You know, perhaps I would too," she said, in a tone that suggested lamenting the horrors of their pasts was a delightful way to bond.

Now that her heart had stopped skittering from Eliot's touch, she remembered a dozen reasons, besides Fyfe, that she should have thought twice. She believed that Eliot didn't know where Gedeon was, but he was definitely hiding something.

"What d'you think of Eliot?" Disdain flashed across Hester's features, and Ilsa added, "Need I ask?"

Hester gave a short, forced laugh.

"Have you always detested him? 'Cause he thinks really highly of you."

"I know he does. I was his alpha for sixteen years before little Gedeon came of age, and a loyal soldier will always love his queen."

Ilsa shook her head. "If Eliot was a good soldier, why'd you remove him as commander of the wolves?"

Hester faltered, her expression pained. Her attention roamed to the window. Eventually, she took a shaky breath. "Eliot is loyal to a fault," she said, almost to herself. "To a hopeless, impossible fault."

If Hester was being dishonest, she didn't have a tell. Her memory of the attack was missing. Her knowledge of Gedeon's behaviour was as Cassia had told her. And her opinion of Eliot wasn't muddied by resentment like Cassia's, or infatuation like Fyfe's – and yet it was more damning than anyone's. The way Hester said it, loyalty sounded like a curse.

She wouldn't meet Ilsa's eye as she said, "I stripped him of his command because I was angry. And paranoid."

Whether that was anything close to the truth, Ilsa couldn't tell. "You don't hate him, then?" she probed.

A slow breath. "I don't know."

Another loaded silence settled between them, and when it became clear Hester wouldn't be the one to break it, Ilsa stood to leave. "May I speak plainly?"

"It would be an utter blessing if *somebody* would."

"I just can't decide what to make of you, Hester."

"And I know just what to make of you," she said, her bitterness spent. When their identical hazel eyes met, Hester was looking at her like an old friend. "I know you, cousin dearest. You're drawn to the damage in others; to their darkness."

Ilsa opened her mouth to argue, but she couldn't form the words. Was Hester right? Was that the real reason she had never severed ties with Bill Blume? Why, of all the sorry cases in her boarding house, the orphaned and abused Martha had been her ally of choice?

"It's alright," Hester said lightly. "You're not a monster. We respond to the parts of ourselves we see in other people, whether we realise it or not. It's what makes them real to us. It's why you're here, in my room."

"I was just passing."

"The room you've claimed is the other way."

"I—" Ilsa realised with a thud that she was right.

"On a personal note, cousin dearest." Hester inclined her head towards the window overlooking the rose garden. "A word of warning. Eliot's darkness runs deeper than you believe. He is a ticking time bomb, and if you are too attached you will be obliterated."

She said the last almost triumphantly, and even as a shudder ran through her, it took all of Ilsa's strength to tear her eyes from her cousin and leave.

28

Ilsa sat on her bed, the diagram she had found under Gedeon's mattress open in her hands.

She had looked at it at least a dozen times, hoping that some meaning would pop out at her. She had memorised the numbers and symbols, and read them every which way; from left to right; clockwise and anti-clockwise around the shape in the middle, and kept them in her mind all day long, in case she discovered them elsewhere.

But nothing could make the diagram make sense, and unless it related somehow to the amulet, it didn't even matter. But something kept her from giving up her fascination with it. It was an irrational fancy, but a little voice inside said Gedeon had left it *for her*. She clung to the diagram and its secret meaning like it was the tether with which she would reel her brother back home.

*

It was the following evening, and Ilsa was barrelling down the main staircase, her eyes on her feet, when a second pair of shoes came into view.

Eliot was stood in her path at the bottom of the stairs. As she reached the last step, they met eye to eye.

"Hello."

"Hello."

Ilsa was sure she had put together a watertight argument

concerning something Eliot had done wrong, but now she couldn't retrieve any of it, nor was she sure it had been truly watertight in the first place.

It appeared Eliot, on the other hand, had his argument all sewn up.

"Hmm. It looks a little like you regret running into me," he said with a sardonic tone and a frightening smile.

Ilsa squared her shoulders – like that would help her hide the riot of feelings; nervousness, irritation, and still, worst of all, desire. "I don't know what you're talking 'bout."

The smile widened. "Don't worry. Your sprint from the garden yesterday was a big enough hint."

It had been bold to think Eliot would let her get away with that, yet still, it was a little unfair. She had kissed him too, and at the time she hadn't been shy about how much she wanted to. Short of a way of reminding him of that and still keeping her dignity, Ilsa said nothing.

Eliot studied her, then his eyes fell away. He straightened his shirtsleeves like the conversation was boring him. "I was kidding myself, I know." He was still trying for malice, but despite the ice in his tone, it wasn't coming off. "Sooner or later you were going to see what everybody else does."

Somehow Eliot's self-pity was even worse than his wrath. "Have you always got to think the worst 'bout everybody?" Ilsa snapped, throwing up her hands. "You really assume I wished I hadn't, even after them other times I almost—"

"Almost what?" His gaze snapped to hers, part thunderstorm, part wariness and hope. Ilsa so rarely struggled for what to say, but nothing felt adequate, or allowed.

In the silence that fell between them, a carriage pulled up in the forecourt.

Eliot broke their gaze. "I thought it might be about Fyfe," he said.

"Fyfe?" So he did know. That meant he also knew how awful she was for kissing him in the first place.

"It's difficult to miss how close you two are, and—"

"Wait, what?"

"—well, Fyfe's a saint. And a gentleman."

And Eliot was neither of those things. He was also an idiot. And Ilsa needed to tell him.

"Eliot—"

The carriage door creaked on its hinges and they both turned at the sound of a familiar drawl. The front entrance had been left open to let the breeze in and cool the rooms, and through it, Aelius was disembarking from a carriage that was not the Zoo's. He turned and tipped his hat to the man who had given him a ride; a man wearing a yellow tie, and a large gold pin on his lapel.

"Who's that?" Ilsa muttered.

"The pin means he's an enforcer," said Eliot curtly. "Heart militia. Aelius has been trying to feel out Sam Lucius and find out if he's an ally." Eliot sank his hands into his pockets; the right one closed around his father's watch. "We're not sure yet what keeping our relationship with the Heart will cost us, but if we don't find Gedeon... Aelius will be the one to negotiate it."

Ilsa took in the tight set of Eliot's jaw, and his wary glower. "You think he bets too high."

Eliot's gaze found hers again, and in it, Ilsa saw something that unsettled her deeply. Vulnerability. Perhaps even fear. Ilsa knew, as sure as she could read Eliot's tells, that whatever he said next would be the truth. "I think he's gambling without all the information," he said quietly.

Ilsa shook her head. "What do you—"

"Ilsa, my darling." Aelius shot her a smile as he crossed the hall towards them. "Whatever your reasons for hiding away indoors on a day as glorious as this, I'm sure they are spectacularly wise."

Ilsa was about to shake Aelius off – to drag Eliot somewhere private and make him tell her whatever he had been about to say – when a realisation hit her like a steam train.

She had been going about this all wrong.

"Aelius," she said, blinking. "Aelius, you and I need to talk. 'Bout Gedeon."

Eliot shot her a warning look, but she ignored him, and led them both into the empty drawing room and closed the door.

"So," said Aelius, tossing his hat onto a nearby loveseat. He still gripped his cane. "What's this about our errant alpha?"

"We think Gedeon is looking for the seventh Seer's amulet—"

"*Ilsa*," hissed Eliot.

"—because then he can make a bunch of them and use all six magics to protect Camden. We also figure it's what the rebel Sorcerers are after with these attacks, and I reckon if anyone knows 'bout that, it's you."

Aelius blinked, his wide, amiable smile frozen in place and slowly souring. Eventually, he laughed. "Is that so? Do tell."

"You were the one what said the rebels were searching for something, weren't you?" A moment's hesitation told Ilsa he'd been caught out. She didn't need to decipher Aelius's tell; she had caught him entirely off guard. Despite his myriad compliments, he had underestimated her this whole time. "The day I got here. You said Gedeon left of his own volition and took a dozen wolves. Then you showed me the letter what one of them left for his sweetheart. *Then* you said you reckoned Gedeon had discovered what the Sorcerers were after and gone looking for it himself. The first clue 'bout what Gedeon's up to came from something you said. So tell us what gave *you* the idea."

The flush that had arisen when Ilsa began had leached away. Aelius narrowed his eyes at Eliot. "You can't seriously be indulging this."

Eliot didn't appear to know what he was doing. His gaze swung from Ilsa to Aelius and back again. "She's right," he said. "You did say something like that."

Aelius glared. Eliot opened his mouth to fill the crackling silence, but Ilsa put a hand on his arm and shook her head minutely. Let the silence linger. She wanted the other man to break it. Aelius's knuckles were pale on the grip of his cane.

Finally, he met her gaze. "Have you been interrogating the others this way?"

"Din't have to. Everyone else was forthcoming," she lied, then softened her voice as she continued. "Please, Aelius. There's something I should know, ain't there?"

"I tried, you understand?" he said abruptly, his voice cracking. "It was just a rumour, one of a dozen I hear every day, but I tried to prevent it nonetheless."

"Prevent what?" coaxed Ilsa.

"Anybody getting hurt."

Eliot had gone very still beside her, but Aelius turned and paced to the empty fireplace.

"There has been so much unrest in that starsforsaken faction since Fisk died," he said, "it's hard to move without brushing up against a Sorcerer with grand ideas of revolution. The foxes have had their ears to the ground. I've chased every whisper, including those of another raid."

Ilsa had never heard him speak with so little theatre, so little swagger. He took a shuddering breath before he went on.

"A Sorcerer contact informed me that the rebels knew of this expedition to Millwater, and would use the opportunity—"

He was cut off by a strangled noise from Eliot, whose face was a mask of horror. He looked like he was choking from poison, and Aelius had been the one to spike his drink. "You knew when they were planning to attack again," he said in a voice like a blade. "You damned traitor, you knew."

Ilsa braced to spring between them if Eliot erupted into violence, but his posture was terrifyingly calm, like he would sway and fall if she nudged him.

"You have no idea what I do for this family!" Aelius hissed, each word spilling into the next. "No idea of the sacrifices I make—"

"That we all make," said Eliot, his voice soft. "You make those sacrifices for all of us. Do you think the foxes are the only ones among the militia who can spy? Do you think we don't know why you're so secretive about your methods?"

Aelius laughed uproariously. "So it all comes out! You've been gathering intelligence on your intelligence man, is that it?"

"You serve up our secrets, our resources," Eliot went on, as if the other man hadn't spoken. "You siphon away a piece of every valuable innovation Fyfe has ever created – don't you dare look surprised. Everyone knows why you take so much interest in him. You sell our *safety* to forge contacts, over and over, because at heart, you're out for no one but yourself." Aelius opened his mouth to retort and Eliot raised his voice. "You knew they were coming and you *let it happen*."

"*I thought I knew!*" Aelius boomed. One moment, his anger was like a fire engulfing the room. The next, it crumbled. He spared Eliot one last disdainful glare, sighed, and collapsed into a chair with his head in his hands. "I thought I knew. Thought that I could… but my information was bad. I lied and misled and pressed on the squad leaders to get twenty extra wolves here that day. This house was guarded to the nines, even after the trip was cancelled, so that I could be *sure*. And then – then they didn't come. It wasn't until after, when the wolves had all gone home and the place was quiet, that they…

"My information was bad," he repeated. "Do you understand, Quillon? Nothing I could have done, no one I could have told would have made a difference."

He put his face in his shaking hands once more, and Ilsa's gaze slid to Eliot.

That icy reticence was as present as ever, but something else was going on underneath; something he couldn't disguise. She stepped closer; perhaps now he might share something: with a glance, or even a word or two. But it was as if he had forgotten she was there. Aelius too. He stared into the middle distance, a haunted hollowness in his storm-blue eyes. Then, he dragged himself back to the present, and slipped from the room.

Ilsa quelled the unease he had sparked in her belly and turned back to Aelius. "Why didn't you tell no one?" she snapped.

Aelius laughed derisively and raised his head. "That Gedeon's confidential plans had reached the Heart? You can work that much out yourself, can't you?"

Ilsa bit the inside of her cheek. She wanted to scream at him for never saying what he meant – that the rebels had a spy in Camden – but something stopped her. They were alike, she and Aelius. He had kept his information about the attack quiet so it wouldn't leak back to the Heart and give him away, but valuing secrecy was second nature. He played his cards close to his chest, same as her. He had thought he had a strong hand – until he'd fallen for a bluff. How close was *she* to being in over her head? She had played on her own team for so long that she had learned to accept the risk as part of the game. But she had grown to trust Fyfe, hadn't she? She didn't have to play that way any longer.

"You know of the amulet, don't you?" she said.

"I believe I've heard of it. It's a children's tale."

"Well them Heart rebels ain't breaking in here every chance they get because of some children's tale. We think they got information that it's here at the Zoo." She had edged closer as she spoke, so that she stood over him. "I think Hester'd probably cut your throat if she knew you din't stop that raid, don't you?"

"And I suppose you're going to tell her," he said. There was fire behind his eyes, and it struck Ilsa that she would never want to make an enemy of this man.

"'Course I ain't gonna tell her. It's done. She won't never

walk again. Never shift." She let the words hang in the air until they weakened him again, and he sank back in his chair. "But you can find Gedeon and you can stop these bloody raids."

Aelius's hand tightened on the top of his cane.

"If anyone can find out what the rebels know 'bout this amulet, 'bout where it is, or where they *think* it is, it's you. Whoever your contacts are, go back to them."

A flash of his usual condescension flickered across his face. "Do you think I haven't considered it? There is more at stake here than some mythic relic, dear girl. If I don't tread carefully along my channels in the Heart we may never make an ally of their new High Sorcerer. We may find ourselves at war on several fronts." His fingers toyed with his cane in an uncharacteristically bashful way. "Besides, one can never be certain who one's friends are. To pull the wrong string would not just be dangerous, it would be suicide."

Coward, was the word on Ilsa's tongue, but she bit it back and sighed deeply. "Fine. If I can't convince you to redeem yourself, least I can say I tried, right?" She made to leave, then turned back again. "Oh, by the way, Fyfe's helping me now, so I should probably tell him everything you said, but I'll make sure he don't repeat it to Hester, promise. And Eliot knows, 'course, but who's he gonna talk to?"

She had her hand on the doorknob before a muttered *for pity's sake* sounded from the hearth. "I'll do what I can," Aelius called morosely. When she turned he was rising from the chair, something like a smile playing on his lips.

"You're only half as clever as you pretend to be, you know" he said, "but pretending is three-quarters of the game."

"By my count, that makes me pretty unstoppable."

He chucked her under the chin as he passed her. "Pretty unstoppable indeed."

29

The metal clang of something awkward and heavy crashing against stone called Ilsa into the garden.

It was late. The air was balmy and pleasant, and crickets were calling to one another. Someone had hung lanterns above the terrace, and their warm yellow light illuminated Eliot.

He stood at the top of the steps to the lawn, a wrought-iron chair on its end at the bottom. All his uncanny calm had dissipated. He drew heaving breaths, and ran both hands through his hair.

Before Ilsa had a chance to speak, he turned and saw her. Fury swathed him like mist, and echoed in the tempest of his eyes.

"Enough," he growled. "Enough of this damned game."

Ilsa folded her arms. "This ain't a game, Eliot."

"But it *is* to you! You have nothing to lose, nothing to grieve. You think you can win if you find your brother, like he's some kind of prize." He was pacing, his voice rising with every acid word. "You have no idea what you're meddling in."

Their eyes met; Ilsa's flaming with indignation, Eliot's desperate and angry and afraid.

She took a step forward. "Then *tell me*," she said, her voice breaking.

He shook his head. His fist closed around the back of another chair, and Ilsa braced herself for him to throw it too. "We can't find Gedeon. We can't go back to *before*. The family you think you're looking for is already torn apart."

"And I'm telling you no. I don't need your help if you've given up, but I ain't gonna." Ilsa felt tears well up. She took a breath to try and rein them in, but it was little use. "How can you say this is a game to me? A family what's torn apart is still damn better than anything I ever had."

He turned on her, disgusted and shaking his head. "You don't know what you're talking about."

Ilsa brushed her tears away calmly, as if pretending she hardly noticed she was crying would stop Eliot from noticing too. It didn't. His iciness cracked, and he took a tentative step towards her.

"P'raps," she said. "P'raps you know better. I still want to know for myself. I can't help it."

"Ilsa…" Eliot came closer – too close – until Ilsa felt that tug that had pulled them together in the rose garden. But he was shaking his head. Whatever war he was fighting inside, he was losing. "I can't… Gedeon's gone, Ilsa. Please listen to me—"

"He's not." She knew she sounded petulant and stubborn, but she didn't care. Eliot was wrong. She would keep fighting him until he understood. "This ain't over. I told Aelius everything we know. He's gonna go back to the Heart and—"

"You did what?" Eliot's tone was ringing with danger, hard and resonating and utterly merciless, and Ilsa swallowed.

"You heard," she said. "I think you're right, in a way. We ain't gonna find Gedeon like this, without trusting no one. We need his help, and Fyfe's, and probably everyone else's too."

He stepped back slowly, his chest rising and falling with

laboured breaths. "You're a fool," he hissed. "You're a stupid, naïve fool."

Ilsa snapped. "And you're a hateful bastard but everyone else seems to know that already."

The blow landed. Eliot reeled back, hurt flickering across his face before vanishing again.

"You hate me too, then."

Ilsa opened her mouth to deny it, but backtracking in the middle of a fight felt like weakness. In the end, nothing came out.

Eliot drank in her silence with diamond-hard indifference. Then that vicious, dazzling smile fell into place. "Gedeon is never coming back. The sooner you realise he wants as little to do with you as he does the rest of us, the better."

The words stung like a blade missing its mark; searing one moment as they grazed her flesh, and gone the next, leaving her stunned, but still on her feet.

Eliot was storming back towards the house, and she swung around. "P'raps I should just go back to my London, then."

"Perhaps you should," he said without missing a beat.

Then he was gone, and despite the crickets chattering and the breeze tickling the leaves, the garden was suddenly far too quiet.

30

Aelius wasted no time.

When Ilsa went down to breakfast the next morning, the carriage was already gone, bearing him south to the Heart. It was little surprise that Eliot was absent too, but she'd be damned if she'd ask after him, and when Fyfe did as much, she shrugged and crammed another slice of toast into her mouth.

She'd fought with Bill Blume dozens of times, and when he was drunk, he sometimes said vicious things. She had hardened herself to the point of not caring – from the theatre that had told her once when she overheard, it wasn't about her.

And as she had lain in her bed for several long hours, unable to sleep, she had reasoned that the same was probably true of Eliot. It did nothing to cool her anger, or stop her rehearsing all the comebacks she wished she had thought of at the time, but it did make her wonder.

Eliot felt betrayed. He was losing hope over something that mattered desperately to him. But the shades of undulating horror that had crossed his face as he absorbed Aelius's confession had felt like something more. This suspicion is what she chewed over to keep from wishing she could go back to the garden and hear him tell her that he hadn't meant it, he was just trying to hurt her, he didn't want her to leave. Suspicion felt better than all those other things.

Her brain foggy from too little sleep, she drank nearly as much coffee as Fyfe before setting about her mission for the day. She was on the stairs, heading bravely for the small laboratory in the attic, when a shot rang out from the park.

Ilsa's blood chilled. Fyfe bounded from the dining room, eyes wide, but Oren emerged behind him, polishing his glasses.

"We're not under attack," he said. "It's only Cassia. She's nurturing a new... passion."

As another round was fired, Ilsa pushed down her hackles and followed the sounds past the garden and into a grove of trees beyond the duck pond.

Cassia stood in a side-stance in the unkempt grass, one arm at a perfect right angle to her body and a revolver in her hand. A target had been rigged up ahead of her, a spattering of nicks already clustered around the centre.

And a boy Ilsa only knew from his portrait was with her.

Gedeon.

Ilsa clapped a hand to her mouth. It was him, here, back. But how? She'd taken two stunted steps forward before she understood the truth, a split second before her brother shifted with a jerky movement akin to shrugging on a coat. It was a movement Ilsa recognised, and all her giddy alarm rushed out of her.

It was Ferrien, one of the wolves who frequently guarded the bridge. He cringed, gaze darting hesitantly between the gun and the target, as Cassia let off another round. But Cassia didn't wince, or blink, or give an inch to the kickback. The shot landed three rings shy of the bullseye.

"Drat," she said, her arm dropping. "One more time, please,

Ferrien. And could you hold it just a moment longer?" The wolf mumbled his dissent. "*Please*, Ferrien?"

Ferrien's shoulders sagged, but he did as he was asked, and the chestnut-haired, stocky young man ceased to be, replaced once more with the taller, leaner form of the boy Ilsa had never met. It was no less jarring the second time. Ilsa's mind wouldn't quite believe he wasn't who she wished he was.

He saw her and shrugged apologetically.

"What the bloody hell," she began, swinging towards Cassia, but the Sorcerer's face made her halt.

Normally so distant and fragile – a living porcelain doll, who would sooner shatter than smile – Cassia's expression had taken on an alarming degree of passion. The mist in her eyes hardened to ice; the tension in her mouth turned hot and feral. She dipped her chin and trained her eyes on Ferrien like an animal coiled to pounce.

Looking at Gedeon was making Cassia *furious*.

She lined up the revolver again with a graceful, chilling surety and fired off three rounds. They all hit the bullseye.

When Ilsa turned back to Ferrien, he was already shrugging back into his own skin. Ilsa shook off the twinge of longing as Gedeon disappeared. She wanted a moment to be with her brother in the flesh; wanted to hear his voice for the first time. But it wasn't him – it was some perverse copy, a violation – and she daren't ask.

She turned to Cassia. "How long you been practising?"

Cassia reloaded the gun. "A little every day this week. I have a knack, it seems."

"You planning on shooting some poor bastard?" She tried to

keep her tone light, despite fearing Cassia already had a target in mind.

"It wasn't my first objective, but perhaps it's crossed my mind." Her gaze fluttered to Ferrien, who blanched. "It's just the most incredible release. I suspected it when I shot that Oracle, circumstances aside. Mechanical weapons are awfully fun."

Ilsa had never imagined Cassia to indulge in fun – she was far too serious and contained – but there was a liveliness to her as she held the gun. While Ilsa had more than once worried that Cassia had died in place – or at the least nodded off – the girl in front of her was undeniably both breathing and awake.

"Here," she said, offering the gun, "take a shot."

"I don't know if that's a good idea," said Ferrien to no one in particular, as Ilsa accepted the gun and let Cassia mould her into a forward-facing stance, the revolver in both hands. Bracing herself for the bang, she squinted at the bullseye and pulled the trigger. A moment of focus, a spike of adrenaline, and then the sudden, ferocious burst of power from between her fingers.

She clipped the edge of the target. Letting her arms fall, she let out a stream of creative curses, and raised an eyebrow at Ferrien. "Think you could be Eliot?"

Cassia made a noise that might have been a laugh. Ferrien lowered his brow and, declaring that he'd had enough, stalked back to the house. When they were alone, Cassia cocked her head and asked, "Eliot?"

"You've met him, ain't you?"

"I torched a pillow once when he made me angry," she replied, taking the gun. She studied it in her hand, then added, "Gedeon always took his side."

Ilsa barely had time to step out of range before Cassia was shooting again; three quick shots found their mark.

"I'm sensing he's been on your mind," Ilsa said so drily that Cassia almost looked proud.

"Am I awful?" she said. "For being so vexed with him for the way he left? He must have had his reasons, and yet I can't stop going over everything I want to say if... if I ever see him again."

"Vexed? Vexed is when you're playing chess and Oren watches your move and makes that tutting noise. I'd say you're closer to murderous. And I'd rather a friend what was murderous than mournful any day. Anger makes you useful. Sadness just makes you tired."

Cassia considered for a moment, her fingers rhythmically squeezing the handle of her revolver. When she looked up, neither mist nor ice reflected in her bright green eyes, but warmth. "Thank you, Ilsa."

Ilsa hesitated, nervously straightening her skirt, but there would never be a good time to say what she needed to. "'Bout that fight what you had with Gedeon," she blurted. "I think I know what you din't tell me."

Abruptly, Cassia's painful stillness returned, and Ilsa regretted the change in topic. "Oh?"

There was nothing for it now. "I think when you pointed out his trip might be a bad idea, he was suspicious of why. I think he accused you of leaking information back to someone in the Heart. Of being a spy."

Silence. Ilsa held her breath to disguise all the uncertainty in her claim. But she'd had a hunch. Aelius said the rebels had known about the trip, and maybe Gedeon had feared that;

420

suspected it. His lover was a Sorcerer, after all.

Some of the fire was back as Cassia took a deep breath and faced her. "I'm not, you know."

"I think I believe you, even though no one's being honest, it seems." At least she could fill in the blanks about Cassia. Maybe she could forget about Eliot's secrets for a few hours.

"I still can't for the life of me understand what gave him the idea." Cassia had put the gun carefully in the case that rested open atop a small folding table. "It's common sense, isn't it? That if he and all his strongest wolves were elsewhere, we would be weak at the Zoo. The rebels were cropping up frequently enough that of course I was worried. But Gedeon said as long as the rebels didn't know, there wasn't a problem, and that if I thought otherwise, perhaps there was something I needed to tell him." Her fingers traced the edges of the revolver case that still stood open. "I'd made my peace with it. The fight, I mean. The way he accused me of betraying him, of playing him for a fool, of never... never loving him at all. I forget sometimes how young he is to be dealing with all this. Before my grandfather died, he'd never truly faced any of the difficulties of being alpha, and then suddenly things were getting worse and worse. I'd chalked it up to pressure.

"But then he left," she said, her fingers reaching for the crutch of the revolver again, "and I think it's me who's been a fool." She frowned, turning on Ilsa. "I'm sorry I didn't tell you everything, but I really didn't see that it mattered why Gedeon and I fought. It was only a lie by omission. Why do you bring it up?"

"Because I discovered something. I think the rebels what

421

attacked you *did* know 'bout the Millwater trip, and I was wondering who could've told them."

"You think there *is* a spy," Cassia said faintly. She shook her head. "It's not possible. The rebels must have been in league with the Oracles longer than we thought. That's how they got the information."

"I already considered that," said Ilsa carefully, "but it don't make no sense. Cogna hadn't been kidnapped when the rebels first came. The Oracles had no reason to get involved."

"Perhaps one of them did. Or there's another explanation. Everyone who knew about the trip to Millwater has proved their loyalty to Gedeon." She shook her head again, and the frown deepened. "Eliot put this idea in your head, didn't he?"

"What? No, I—"

A twig snapped beyond the grove and Ilsa's head snapped to the source of the sound. But there was no one there. Ilsa was letting herself get wound up for nothing. She shook her head, shaking off the unease still prickling her neck. But when she turned back around, Cassia was pointing the revolver at her, that sad, distant expression on her face. Without hesitation, she pulled the trigger.

All Ilsa knew was the bullet hit her.

She was on the ground. The force of the shot had spun her around and thrown her to her stomach. Cassia fired again and she covered her head, perplexed and enraged, a slew of curses on her lips, but when she raised her head, everything came into focus.

A cloaked figure was sprinting to the west boundary of the park. As they ran, their hood fell away.

Pyval Crespo.

He ducked but didn't slow as another bullet came at him from over Ilsa's shoulder.

Cassia wasn't aiming for her any more. Pyval had relinquished control of her mind.

Before Cassia could shoot again, a snarl tore through the clearing, and Ilsa turned to see a wolf tackle the girl to the ground. They were pouring into the clearing and surrounding her. They hadn't seen the real threat, but it didn't matter. Ilsa was on her feet, and then she was in the air.

That was when she felt the bullet. Pain lanced through her shoulder and her every muscle seized in protest as she tried to spread her wings. She careened towards the ground, catching herself at the final moment with one excruciating push. Then another. She could run on all fours, but it wouldn't be any easier. Momentum. Only momentum would keep her flying through the agony.

Pyval was far ahead now, beyond the Outer Circle and into Camden proper. But Ilsa was a falcon. His human legs could not carry him fast enough to get beyond her sights. She just had to catch him up before he hit the border. Just needed to get close enough and—

And what? In animal form, she was too vulnerable to Pyval's magic, and as a human she was unlikely to outmatch him. In the Otherworld, she would have had a pocketknife in her purse, but the Ilsa of the Witherward had no weapon but her claws.

And wolves. She shot a glance back at the park, where they were bursting through the trees on her heels. She wasn't alone, not this time. Pyval wouldn't know she was upon him until it was too late. She just needed to knock him out somehow and let the wolves come.

She just had to be fast.

He had cut a deft path through the streets, straight for the nearest point of the border, but Ilsa was closing in. She was directly overhead now.

But she had misread his destination. As they reached a corner, a carriage came speeding from the adjacent street. A rendezvous. The driver hauled on the reins and the horse banked hard to come level with Pyval, who leapt and grasped the open carriage door, and a pair of hands hauled him inside. Ilsa might have had time to dive and knock him off his feet, but the hands that caught Pyval had wrested her attention. She would never have seen it without her falcon's vision. As it was, the seal ring on the right middle finger was clear as day:

424

a cog, containing a cross-section of the human mind.

The Sage.

And Ilsa, out of time. The border loomed. The stewards raised weapons and shouted orders at the carriage, but there was nothing they could do but leap aside. Ilsa could not attack a Whisperer in front of them all, and she could not wait until they passed into Whitechapel.

But perhaps she could look. She could identify who killed her family.

She dived for the speeding carriage. As her talons made contact with the vehicle, she shifted into a leopard and brandished her claws. The second they knew she was there they would take control of her mind. She would have the briefest moment's grace, if that. Steeling herself, she dug a claw into the roof and tore a window large enough to see inside.

Two heads snapped up, two pairs of eyes went wide with shock. And Ilsa knew them both.

She shifted again and pushed the pain of the bullet to the back of her mind to spread her wings as far as they could go, letting the force of the air push her off the roof.

The carriage sped on, but if Pyval had got to Cassia in the park, then her fragile animal mind was still vulnerable from here. She was eight feet from the ground – close enough to live – so she shifted again, her shoulder screaming but her mind strong and human, and plummeted to the street.

*

Wet noses nudged at her. Growls and raised voices filled the air.

By some evil magic, it felt like every single part of her had hit the ground.

Someone said her name; *begged* her name. She knew them, but not like this. Not begging.

She tried to open her eyes but nothing happened. Every bit of strength had left her, but the pain remained.

"Ilsa, wake up." The voice again. Male. A warm hand slipped under her neck and raised her up. She had liked that hand on her neck, she remembered that, and she instinctively leaned into him. Another hand went under her knees, and then she was off the ground, cradled against his chest, her head on his shoulder. The wolves had come.

Then she smelled fresh linens. Rain. She drew a painful breath and found her voice. "But... I'm cross with you."

Eliot's relieved laugh reverberated against her cheek. His muscles loosened, then held her tighter. "Good," he said against her hair. There was more, and Ilsa wanted to hear it, but Eliot's words faded as the world went dark.

*

She couldn't have lost consciousness for long, because her shoulder was still streaming blood when she came to, and someone was lowering her onto a table top.

As someone cut her arm free from her dress, she rolled her head listlessly to take in the bustling room. She was in the kitchen. Most of the household staff and wolves on guard were crowding around the doorway, their fearful eyes gazing back at her. Oren and Ferrien were arguing in low voices. Fyfe was by her head, chewing his lip, and Fliss was next to him, busy with an array of potions and tonics, pipettes and bandages.

Eliot was gone. Perhaps she'd only imagined him.

"You need the clear one," said a shaking voice, and Ilsa

426

pivoted towards the source. It was Cassia. She was sat against the wall, her hands lying limp in her skirt, two wolves stood over her.

"She din't do it," said Ilsa again, with enough strength to startle the room.

Oren was at her shoulder in an instant. "How close did you get? Are you certain they were a Whisperer?"

Cassia made a scoffing noise. "Ask Ferrien," she said, eyeing the wolf dangerously. "He's seen my aim. If I wanted to hurt Ilsa, I wouldn't have shot her in the shoulder. But mind control doesn't lend itself to good hand-eye coordination, it seems."

Ilsa lifted herself to a seated position, ignoring the protests from Fliss and Fyfe, and swung her legs over the side of the table. The pain in the shoulder was incessant and fierce, but the shock that had made her swoon had passed, and her injuries from falling revealed themselves to be a collection of dull, innocuous aches.

"It was Pyval," she said.

"You saw him?" pressed Oren.

"*Yes* I saw him. He…" Ilsa summoned everything she had to go on. It felt like a confession. It felt like her fault. And it was. She should have known. "He was working for Alitz. He's always been working for her. She was with him in that carriage." She swallowed hard, wincing as Fliss pressed something to the bullet wound. "It's her. Alitz killed my family."

Failing to hold back tears of rage, Ilsa explained about the carriage meeting Pyval as he fled the park; about the insignia on Alitz's ring, worn proudly for anyone to see in a city that didn't care who hated whom, or why.

As Ilsa spoke, the blood drained from Fyfe's face. He shook

his head throughout her explanation. "But" – he looked from Oren, to Cassia and back to Ilsa – "but Pyval poisoned her too. She can't be... she can't be the *Sage*!"

"One can build up a resistance to smokeweed," said Oren. He gripped his glasses so tightly in his fist that they were bent out of shape. "She may have used this method on her enemies before."

"P'raps but—" *If I wanted to distract you from the present moment, of course I would show you things you wished to see.* Ilsa cursed her own stupidity. "I ain't sure she drank the tea at all," she confessed. "She was using my thoughts to distract me. She said it was the lesson."

Cassia pulled herself to her feet. "The antidote probably made her sick for a few hours. Nothing more. It would be a small price to pay for such a convincing alibi." She gasped and turned wide eyes on Ilsa. "Alitz knew about the messenger from the Docklands. The one who told us you were alive. I – I told her. I didn't think anything of it. She must have sent someone to find you when we sent Fowler."

"And they found Bill and decided to wait for me," said Ilsa. The hot burst of hatred felt like a knife twisting in her chest. Alitz had played at being, if not Ilsa's friend, then her ally. She had taken tea with her in her house. All the time, she was the reason Bill was dead.

"She's been the Zoo's intermediary with the Whisperers for decades," said Cassia, breathing hard. "She's had access to all our sensitive information to use as she pleases, not to the benefit of Whitechapel, but the Fortunatae."

The fewer who know that Gedeon Ravenswood is a loose cannon, the better.

"The Fortunatae have known all this time that Gedeon's gone!" said Ilsa.

"And she knows that Hester's not leading us," said Fyfe, catching on. "She could have made a push by now, tried to dismantle the Zoo entirely. Why hasn't she?"

"Alitz Dicer has demonstrated the utmost patience," intoned Oren. He was pale, and his eyes drifted without taking anything in. "Years of it. A faultless front. If she is biding her time, there must be a reason."

There was so much death and terror in the history of the Zoo that Ilsa barely had it in her to process it all, and she realised then that Oren, like Hester, had witnessed some of their worst times. He had smuggled her through the portal the day she was born. He had left his alpha and his people and returned to find them slaughtered. By Alitz.

"Oren," said Cassia, reaching a hand towards his shoulder. But before she could touch him, Oren lurched abruptly for the door and vanished.

"Where's Eliot?" said Ilsa, trying to sound casual. Fliss had applied some numbing concoction to the wound and was extracting the bullet with expert surety. "I thought I saw him, but…"

"You did," said Fyfe. "He saw you chase after Pyval and followed you. He brought you back here, then took some wolves after him again." Fyfe rubbed his hair. "The stewards will never let them cross the border, Principles or no Principles. I don't know what he was thinking but… well, he was angry."

"He's always angry, Fyfe," said Cassia, then turned to Ilsa. "Ilsa, I'm so sorry."

"You din't do nothing," Ilsa said, biting back a wince as the bullet came free.

"Precisely. I've trained to block out Whisperers. I just didn't see it coming. I thought we were alone."

"Ilsa!"

Eliot burst into the room with all the force of the monstrous cat he sometimes was. His shirt was stained with Ilsa's blood. When his gaze fell on her, it was stormy and frantic, and her heart twisted. Suddenly, inexplicably, she wanted to sob, and she thanked residual shock for helping her keep it in.

He was in front of her in three long strides. His hands drifted up like they would cup her face or touch her hair, but changed their mind. Instead, his eyes swept her face and body, lingering on the bullet wound. He frowned at the neat little puncture Fliss had gotten to stop bleeding.

"I swear it looked way worse five minutes ago," Ilsa muttered.

"You're alright." It was equal parts relief and irritation.

"I'm fine, and I'm sure I won't get shot no more once I'm back in the Otherworld where I *belong*, so don't concern yourself."

Eliot shot her a glare and turned to Cassia. "What happened?"

Cassia's face resembled the one Gedeon had earned. "Ilsa called me a spy, and I shot her."

"That's the short version," Ilsa swiftly added. "I know you don't like me all that much, Eliot—"

"I beg your pardon?"

"—but you could do me the courtesy of taking the worst of your accusations up with me personally."

"Cassia, it weren't him who—"

"It's hard enough feeling like I belong here without fearing some belligerent dolt like you is undermining everything I do. You know, I don't have to—"

"I like you," said Eliot.

Cassia blinked. "Sorry?"

"Less, having been called a belligerent dolt, but" – he rolled his eyes, like it pained him to repeat it – "*I like you*. I'm aware I don't show it, but… come on, Cassia. We grew up together. And I never called you a spy. It would be ridiculous to think so. You're better for the Zoo than any of us, not to mention more intelligent – with the exception of Fyfe, perhaps. You" – he swallowed his chagrin a second time – "of course you belong here."

Cassia probably didn't blush like regular mortals. She just stared at him with an unnerving vacancy. Fyfe, meanwhile, had turned beet-red at Eliot's throwaway compliment. But despite the meaningful glance Eliot cast her as his speech ended, Ilsa did nothing but glare.

Eliot cleared his throat. "Tell me everything I missed."

Ilsa couldn't repeat her awful discovery, and Fyfe didn't look like he would ever be able to say the words aloud. But Cassia looked Eliot square in the eye, the way Ilsa had never seen her do. "Let's you and I talk," she said, almost pleasantly. "I'll tell you everything."

Eliot stiffened at the proposition, but followed Cassia from the room, leaving Ilsa with Fliss and Fyfe, who stood fixed to a point right by Ilsa's shoulder, and was uncharacteristically quiet. His expression was solemn.

"I'm sorry 'bout Alitz, Fyfe," she said.

"Oh." He brushed it off with an unconvincing hand gesture. "I need a better astrology tutor anyway." Ilsa eyed him quizzically.

431

Fyfe managed a smile. He took one of her curls between his fingers and tugged it playfully. "If she was any good at reading the stars, she ought to have seen Ilsa Ravenswood coming."

*

Ilsa didn't want to sleep, but as soon as the curtains were drawn, sleep took her. The cocktail of healing potions and pain tonics dragged her under, and when she finally struggled free of the fog and blinked awake, the world outside was dark.

She dragged herself into a sitting position and tested her shoulder. The pain ran deep – a dull ache echoing through layers of tissue and radiating to her chest and arm – but it was manageable. Being shot in the Otherworld couldn't possibly be this easy, she thought as she struggled into a robe. She found a fierce bruise on her right hip from her fall, and an intimidating collection of cuts and scrapes – including those from her altercation with the drawing room mirror – but for two assassination attempts, Ilsa had to admit, she wasn't doing half bad.

The clock in Gedeon's sitting room said it was a little after nine thirty – still early – but an impenetrable quiet blanketed the Zoo. Ilsa wondered at being left so alone. Where was Eliot? Had Fyfe or Cassia come to check on her? Had Aelius returned from the Heart and heard what had happened? Her feet carried her down the hall to Hester's rooms; the one place she could be sure of finding someone to quell the strange unease the quiet brought her.

But the door to Hester's sitting room gaped wide, the bedchamber visible beyond, and neither her cousin nor Fliss was anywhere to be seen.

Something's wrong, said a voice inside her.

She hurried for the stairs, the only sound the soft pad of

her slippers on the hardwood floors. Had they been attacked again? Had all her friends been rounded up and slaughtered by vengeful Oracles?

She didn't know where to search for them. The thud of her own racing heartbeat rose in her ears as she swung around a corner – and walked right into Cadell Fowler.

32

The captain looked, at first glance, like he had come in from the rain. His sleeves and the front of his shirt glistened with moisture. It wasn't until he caught Ilsa puzzling over his appearance and self-consciously shook out a sleeve that the stains revealed themselves.

Blood.

It spattered to the floor in several fat droplets and trickled from his coattails onto the marble floor behind him.

Ilsa backed away. Her brain still lagged from sleep and medicine, and the confusion put her on edge. Cadell Fowler had saved her life and restored her to her family. He had listened to her concerns and offered advice like a friend. He'd helped her crash a *party*, just for fun. But he was a mercenary – an assassin – and he was covered in blood. Perhaps he wasn't an ally tonight.

Sensing her alarm, the captain raised his hands.

"Whose blood?" Ilsa challenged.

"Several people's. Aelius Hoverly among them," he said, and Ilsa's stomach lurched. The captain nodded in the direction of Aelius's chambers. "That way."

She started running, but didn't get far before Fowler called her name. When she looked back, he was glancing around.

"The washroom?" he said.

"I—" Why was this killer in her house, covered in Aelius's

blood, asking where he could clean it off? "By the stairs."

As she reached Aelius's rooms, her pulse was thrumming so fast it was making her dizzy. It was a repeat of the scene from that morning; the entire Zoo crowded around, tense and silent with fear. The door was closed. Oren leaned against the jamb with his head bent to the wood, like he was trying to hear inside. Eliot sat opposite, his head in his hands. It was Fyfe – slumped against the wall, chewing on his nails and bouncing his leg – who noticed her. There was blood on his shirtsleeves.

"What happened?" she whispered when he pulled her aside.

"He got into some trouble in the Heart," said Fyfe. "Some Sorcerers turned against him. Aelius thought they were loyalists, but they had connections to the rebels. He was double-crossed."

Ilsa paled, and braced herself against the wall. It was as she had feared. Aelius had told her it was dangerous, and still she had pushed. Still she had threatened to smear his past mistakes across the Zoo if he didn't do as she asked.

It's my fault.

Her hands curled into fists as she imagined them closing around Jorn's throat. So this is what he had Seen when he looked ahead to her next mistake. He had known, had Seen her send Aelius to his near-death, and he had not warned her.

"Is he…" she began weakly, but she was afraid to say the words.

Fyfe swallowed. "He took half a dozen cutting curses," he said. "Fliss and Cassia are working on him. We sent for more healers and they went in there an hour ago, but… there was blood everywhere, Ilsa."

There still was. A crimson footprint had smeared across the floor. A bloodied rag lay crumpled next to Ferrien where he was

435

slumped against the wall. Aside from Fyfe, three or four others had traces of blood on their clothes, presumably from hauling a man near death to his bed.

"How'd he get back here?" Ilsa asked. Her voice was hoarse. *My fault my fault my fault.*

"The Wraith," said Fyfe. "He showed up at the door with Aelius over his shoulder. He's been quiet but I think... I think he intervened. When Eliot tried to dismiss him, he said that he'd slaughtered three Sorcerers tonight and could he clean up first."

Fowler. Fowler had undone Ilsa's mistake – or tried to. Gratitude doused the toxic, writhing guilt inside her like cool water.

She thought about seeking him out, but at that moment Aelius's door opened, and the crowd keeping vigil leapt to attention.

Fliss emerged, darkening bloodstains marring her blouse, followed by the extra healers. One carried a mess of surgical instruments and gauze on a tray; the onlookers leaned away from him and his macabre burden as he passed.

Then Cassia appeared, looking pristine, and closed the door shut behind her with a gentle click. Her eyes turned enquiring when they landed on Ilsa, flicking between her face and her shoulder. Ilsa mouthed that she was okay and pressed forward.

"He's very weak," said Cassia, "but if he can find the will, he should live." A collective exhale deflated the atmosphere. "All of you to bed. You have duties in the morning."

The wolves dispersed sleepily, still muttering about Aelius's injuries. When the last of their footsteps had faded through the house, Cassia turned to the four of them who remained: Ilsa, Oren, Fyfe, and Eliot.

"Hester's in there," she said. "Neither Fliss nor I could get her to leave. The rest of us should get some rest."

She made towards the stairs, but Ilsa blocked her path. "I want to see him."

Cassia shook her head. "In the morning. He needs to heal."

"No, now. This is my fault, Cassia. He went to see them Sorcerers because I asked him to, even when he warned me." She could feel the curious glances of Cassia, Oren, and Fyfe; Eliot's eyes were trained on the floor. "I'll go mad if I don't see him myself."

"If Ilsa's seeing him, I am too," said Fyfe, squaring his shoulders.

Cassia scowled. "No, Fyfe, I—"

"I know the spells and potions used to heal. I wanted to help but you told me I would be in the way. You said—"

"I said you could see him as soon as he was stable," finished Cassia resignedly.

"Well, if Ilsa and Fyfe are going in there," said Oren, stepping forward.

"And if everyone else is," added Eliot.

"Heaven and earth," muttered Cassia, opening the door, and they all poured into the room. "Just for a minute."

Hester turned stony, tired eyes on them as they entered. There was a sheen of sweat across her brow and she sat angled towards one of the windows that had been thrown open. Her fingers trembled on the arm of her chair, and Ilsa remembered what Eliot had told her: Hester was afraid of blood. She was there throughout, all the same.

"Quite a day," she said lightly, but the humour didn't touch her features. She roused herself to roll her chair across the small sitting room. The strength and grace of her thin arms as they turned the wheels was surprising; Ilsa had never seen Hester move for herself, but she made it look easy.

At the door to the bedchamber, she turned to Ilsa. "Prepare yourself, cousin dearest," she said, before leading the way in.

Ilsa quickly smothered her alarm. She should have been prepared; she'd suspected Aelius wasn't wearing his true form. This version of him was smaller, less muscled, with bones and tendons carving depressions and ridges along his arms. His narrow shoulders seemed to fold around his chest protectively, and his skin was lighter, greyer, like sun-bleached fabric. Two folds of weakened skin hung heavy under his resting eyes. The glossy black hair and moustache he normally wore were complete works of fiction.

The Aelius Ilsa had come to know appeared to be around thirty. The real man was fifty years his senior.

Unsure of herself, Ilsa glanced around, and found that everyone looked as awkward as she; everyone's eyes sought somewhere to rest other than on him. He wouldn't want them to see him like this, and they all knew it.

But when he stirred and murmured, their qualms were forgotten. Oren went to his bedside and gripped his hand.

"Welcome back old, *old* friend," he said. Aelius murmured again, and Oren got closer to hear his reply; something that sounded to Ilsa's ears like a string of curses.

Oren straightened and smiled. "I think he'll be just fine."

"Aelius," said Ilsa, squeezing past Fyfe to approach Aelius's other side. "Aelius, I—"

438

"Shhh," Aelius managed – an easy word even for the frailest – and stretched a wrinkled hand up to catch hers. Tears had pooled in her eyes before she could stop them.

"Why d'you got to be so brave?" she scolded through her tears. "You should've told me I was a fool, like Eliot does."

She caught Eliot's eye, and despite the tempest of fear and anguish in his features, he managed a ghost of a smile.

Aelius was suddenly gripping her hand with some force, Oren's too, and beckoning their attention again. They both leaned closer as he struggled to force out the words.

"Gedeon," he gasped, his chest heaving from the effort. "You need to find Gedeon. He's in terrible danger."

Ilsa felt everyone stop breathing at once.

"Aelius." Hester said his name like a command. She came to the side of the bed and Ilsa was forced backwards. "Aelius!"

"What does he mean?" said Cassia quietly. Despite her recent penchant for violence towards Gedeon, she looked stricken. "Hester?"

"Cassia," said Oren gently, "he's under the influence of a healing tonic. He might be delusional."

"And he might not," said Cassia, her voice rising.

"Let him speak!" said Ilsa. She had forced her way back to Aelius's side, and could see that he was struggling, but still conscious; still present. And she knew, unlike the others, what Aelius had been doing. "He knows something Gedeon don't."

The frown on Cassia's porcelain forehead was as deep as Ilsa had ever seen. "What are you talking about?" she demanded.

Ilsa shot a glance at Eliot, but all his mistrusts and reasons didn't matter anymore. Gedeon was in danger. "Aelius went to the Heart because I asked him to," she said, her voice breaking from desperation, or shame. "He went to try and find out what the rebels know 'bout the seventh Seer's amulet."

Oren and Cassia appeared confused. Hester laughed disbelievingly.

"To what end?" she said. "It's a fairy tale."

"We don't think it is."

Ilsa told them how they'd tracked Gedeon as far as the crypt at the Seer's temple, and then discovered he had researched the amulet in the library. When she explained their theories about the Heart rebels being after it too, she skirted the truth of Aelius knowing the raid was coming. All the time, she held his hand in hers, squeezing his fingers, willing him to find the strength.

"You were right," he said thinly when she was done. "The rebels think the amulet is here. Their spells tell them that it is." He coughed. "Or was."

"Was?"

"Within the last twenty years. They're certain." He laughed a painful laugh that made Ilsa wince. "They meant to kill me. So they told me everything."

"What of Gedeon?" said Hester. "What did they tell you about him?"

Aelius's humour vanished. "He's been... planning for months. A coup."

"A *coup*?" Hester laughed in disbelief. "He's already our leader."

"Camden's, yes." He paused, struggled. Ilsa could hardly believe what she knew he would say next. "He wants the city."

Oren drew a breath. Eliot toppled something on the dresser he

440

was leaning against. Hester's eyes were on Aelius, but her gaze was far away. Her tight mouth quirked up at one corner.

"That doesn't sound like Gedeon," she said.

"No. It's a peace enterprise," Aelius said, and despite his state, he managed to force some derision into the words.

"*That* sounds like Gedeon," said Fyfe.

"He means to form a conclave. Six members. Each faction."

Ilsa had been in this torn-up London a matter of weeks, and even she knew such a thing was idealistic at best; at worst, delusional. What was more, she thought with a flash of anger, Gedeon had gone about his grand plan without confiding in his lieutenants, the people who supported him; who had been doing his job in his absence, and could have managed a lot worse at it too.

Or had he? Ilsa cut her eyes across to Eliot. Is this what he had been hiding? Everyone seemed to think he knew more than he was letting on, but perhaps the secret he'd been keeping for Gedeon wasn't about his disappearance at all.

Somehow the more Eliot showed her, the surer Ilsa was that there was more she couldn't see. She only had a moment to study him before he glanced her way, and it was inconclusive. He was unsettled, but so were they all.

"Gedeon was the first to mention the amulet... as a tool... for their takeover. They think... he has it."

"So they're not his true allies," said Hester, her tone screaming of long-suffering disapproval. Had Gedeon always been too trusting?

"Not all. I don't know who." He took several long, slow breaths and closed his eyes. "But his Whisperer... Fortunatae."

441

Ilsa knew who. The Zoo had had a high-ranking Whisperer ally for years; an obvious choice. "Alitz."

Incomprehension registered on Aelius's haggard face before he let out a long sigh and fell unconscious.

"That's why she's been waiting," said Ilsa to the room. "She ain't found the amulet here so she needs to see what Gedeon does."

"The closer he gets, the more danger he is in," said Oren, almost to himself.

"Hester, we have to do something," said Cassia. "We can't keep trying to keep this quiet."

Eliot – ever hovering at the periphery – stepped forward and addressed Hester. "Gather the wolves. Let Ilsa tell them everything she's learned of Gedeon's movements and have them try to track him. They know their missing pack members. They'll know how they think."

Cassia made an exasperated noise. "We've already asked the wolves," she said. "We exhausted all of our leads in a day, or don't you remember?"

"But now we know what he's seeking," said Oren, his voice soft, "and perhaps where to find it."

Fyfe shook his head. "The amulet isn't here, Oren. I've been looking but—"

"No, not here," said Oren, toying with his glasses. He turned to Ilsa. Something in his gaze stirred unease deep inside her. "Do you know what the seventh Seer's amulet looks like?"

"Uh…" Caught off guard by the question, Ilsa looked at Eliot.

"Silver," Eliot cut in. "Round. The chain probably attaches to a cap which stoppers the contents."

Oren sighed. "Then I believe it is at the St Genevieve Orphanage on Kennington Road, in the London of the Otherworld." His eyes calmly met those of Hester and the lieutenants, before coming to rest on Ilsa. "Since that is where I hid it, seventeen years ago."

Ilsa's head swam. Her own ribcage tried to smother her. It was the feeling that overwhelmed her in confined spaces, but it was happening right here in the Zoo.

"Oren," said Cassia, aghast. "You—"

"You're telling us this now?" said Hester. Her back was rod-straight, her chin was tilted fiercely, and in that moment, she looked bigger than all of them.

"I hoped not to tell you at all," said Oren unapologetically, "but if Gedeon is truly headed to the orphanage, then we have run out of time."

"Oren," said Hester, her voice low. "If you have kept something from me, I suggest you explain yourself *fast*."

"There is a lot you must understand," he said. "You know, all of you, that I was among those Changelings whose debts Alpha Lyander bought when the newly drafted Principles permitted her to do so. She found me in an antiques shop in the Heart, helping the man who kept me to trade and keep shop, when an amulet fitting Eliot's description came to him in a contents auction. It was in a trinket box with some other jewels. It was tarnished, and the clasp was stuck. When he got it open and found traces of blood, he of course knew at once that the amulet had magic. It was no great leap to work out how to test that magic. Out of caution, he tested it on me."

Oren delicately laced his fingers together. His movements, his speech; he was always so controlled. Hearing what he had suffered, Ilsa wondered *what* he was controlling. "I won't patronise you by labouring the point, but legends are not reliable. If the thing that came to Lazaro was the same amulet you describe, then I doubt the fairy tale tells the whole truth. I doubt that it tells of the way the amulet consumed blood; of its boundless greed. A single drop of my blood would make Lazaro a Sorcerer-Changeling for a day, and then he would take another. And every drop tore my magic from me with an agony I cannot describe. I was not just without my magic. It cost me my strength, my wits, at times my sanity. Working for a Sorcerer, I knew some of what their magic was capable of, but I had known nothing like that amulet, and I've known nothing like it since."

Ilsa shuddered imagining what Gedeon would inadvertently become responsible for if he obtained the amulet. What if he had it already? What if he had tried to use it?

"Lazaro Tilley was not an ambitious man," Oren continued, "nor a particularly clever one. He never understood the power of what he possessed, nor how much the right person would pay for it. It's been nearly nineteen years and still I thank the stars every morning and night that he did not. That he only viewed the amulet as a tool for his... dare I say, his amusement."

Amusement. Ilsa swallowed hard, but the lump in her throat remained.

"Still, I couldn't risk such evil falling into the hands of anyone else. So once I was freed, as soon as I had recovered my strength, I called on Lazaro in the night, and I clasped his throat in my jaws until he suffocated."

"And you took the amulet," said Hester, seemingly unfazed by Oren's murder confession.

"I didn't hold much hope of destroying it, but I did try, many times. I had resigned myself to the burden of hiding it forever when Lyander confided her plan to me; to protect her unborn child should the Zoo face destruction.

"It sparked my resolve. If the strongest and bravest woman I knew would hide what was most precious to her in the Otherworld, then it was the best place for the amulet too."

"Did it occur to you that by hiding the amulet with Ilsa, you put her at risk?" said Hester. Ilsa would have sworn, for just a moment, that the idea made Hester angry, but perhaps it was just that Oren had kept this from her.

"It wasn't my intention," said Oren. "I was young, and I was not as conscientious as I have been forced to grow in serving the Zoo. At the time, it was the only plan I had. It was never supposed to be a permanent fix. But when we returned to the Otherworld and were told Ilsa was dead, I thought, perhaps the amulet would never be discovered there. Perhaps, if it was, the Otherworlders would take it for a pretty bauble and nothing more. So I left it there."

Very briefly, he caught Ilsa's gaze with a meaningful glance. Was she supposed to know something about the amulet? Oren must have been mistaken; Ilsa had forced down her memories of her time at the orphanage, but she was sure she'd remember something like that.

"Hester," said Cassia imploringly, "if we fetch it, Cogna's Sight will lead Gedeon back here."

It's what Ilsa had been thinking, but every time she tried to imagine setting foot back in that place, her mind refused. It shuttered with a violence that sent a physical tremor down her spine. How had the place that haunted her past wrenched itself into her present?

"And then what?" said Hester. She was resting her chin on her steepled fingers, her eyes glazed over in thought. "Alitz is waiting for Gedeon to make a move. And if we interfere, he just might."

"We're connected to Gedeon, ain't we?" said Ilsa, catching Hester's meaning. "So's the Zoo. So if we're the ones who've got the amulet, and we bring it here, we might be making it easier for Cogna to find."

"Then that's precisely what we should do!" said Cassia. The news that Gedeon was headed straight for harm appeared to have carved a manic edge into her. "We could end this."

"*Start it*, you mean." Hester shook her head. "Alitz is, at best, one step behind us, and at worst, a long way ahead. We have to assume she will find out if we take possession of the amulet. The fight will only get bigger once that happens."

"Oren had the amulet," said Eliot. "It was already here at the Zoo. Cogna's bound to hit on that sooner or later. A bigger fight is coming either way, but if we're the ones to force it then at least we'll be ready this time."

"And we will be, but we needn't be the ones to provoke it." She turned to Oren. There was a steel in her gaze that belied the civility of her tone. "Is the amulet safe and hidden where you left it?"

"I have no reason to suspect otherwise."

"Then it'll stay there. We will concentrate our efforts on finding Gedeon before he finds the amulet. Thankfully, he will have a hard time getting to the Otherworld without us knowing. Oren, send a message to the wolves at the portal to be on alert for him. I want to know within moments if he tries to pass through. They are to *stop him*, whatever he says."

Oren shook his head and massaged the frown lines between his eyes. "They won't follow your orders over Gedeon's own."

"Then remind them which of us will punish them if Gedeon's not in the Witherward to stop me.

"Cassia, for all we know, the Lord of Whitechapel is quite aware that Alitz Dicer is the Sage and has chosen not to interfere, but I'm sure it will interest Mr Voss to know that she's planning a coup."

"But Gedeon—"

"—does not need to enter the conversation. Try and spin this to our advantage."

Cassia nodded stiffly, and swept from the room, Oren behind her.

"Fyfe," Hester continued, "draft a letter – I will sign and seal it – asking Lucius to name any and all high-ranking Sorcerers who are suspected of dissent or stand accused of breaking the Principles. These are his people allying with the Fortunatae, and he'll be held responsible. I won't wait for him to lay his cards any longer."

Fyfe, ever eager to be employed, darted from the room, and Hester rolled her chair after him. "Eliot, come with me, we need to talk."

Left behind, Ilsa checked that Aelius was comfortable, then left him to his rest. In the hallway, she allowed herself to fall against the wall, where she gulped down several deep breaths and willed her hammering heart to slow.

Despite the trepidation and hopelessness creeping slowly

through her veins like ice, she had to believe they were finally going to find her brother. They were a step ahead of him at least, and they had what they had truly needed from the start; not Ilsa, but Hester, their alpha. Hester, who could mobilise their militia and make demands of Sam Lucius; who could put an end to her lieutenants' squabbling and make a plan. Even as they had shaken with anxiety and bitten back their retorts, a palpable relief had spread through the others as Hester had come to life. Something had thawed, and she could feel it thawing still, in the very walls of the Zoo. As she gazed out of the window to the front of the house, and saw Oren sending a wolf into the sky and straight for the abbey, she knew: they were the family she had been promised when she stepped through the portal.

She was passing the stairs on the way to her room when she saw the tall form of Cadell Fowler slipping silently from the house, and a thought struck her.

"Captain!" He halted, one hand still on the doorframe. "Come with me."

Fowler gazed quizzically at her, but after a beat he turned around, climbed the stairs and followed her to Hester's rooms. She left him in the corridor and let herself in.

The door to the sitting room had been ajar, but Hester and Eliot were ensconced behind the closed door of the bedchamber, talking in hushed voices. With a jolt, she realised this conversation was secret. Naturally, she crept to within eavesdropping distance and deciphered what she could.

"… promise you, Hester, I haven't heard… but listen…"

"… told you to keep an ear… you've been distracted by my pretty little cousin…"

"… please… something you need to know about Millwater…"

At the mention of Millwater, Ilsa crept closer, wincing as a floorboard creaked underfoot. There was an echo from behind the door as Eliot moved to open it. She thought about shrinking herself to a mouse, but what were the chances another Changeling would fall for that? In the end she could do nothing but look innocent and surprised when the door flew open.

Hester and Eliot both frowned suspiciously at her, but her mask was convincing. Hester raised an eyebrow. "Did I neglect to give you an order, cousin?" she said sharply.

"Actually, yes," said Ilsa, and it was probably for the best; she didn't respond well to authority. "But I managed without you. I've had an idea."

33

Fowler was frowning at a painting when the three of them emerged into the hall. He dipped his head to Hester, eyed Ilsa questioningly, then turned an inscrutable gaze on Eliot.

Ilsa tried to recall the words exchanged the night they'd almost come to blows in Camden, but nothing had given away the source of their bad blood. Studying them now, it was clear Fowler was barely any older than Eliot, and Ilsa wondered if there was a love rivalry in their past.

"So," said Hester, "you're Cadell Fowler."

"I am." He rested both hands on the hilt of a long knife at his belt.

"From what I understand, you're one of the most deadly people in the city."

A shadow crossed Fowler's face, and he nodded almost imperceptibly. "Perhaps."

Hester folded her hands in her lap. "What happened tonight?"

"I was in a bar in Chelsea. Your man Hoverly arrived with a group of men I recognised as rebel sympathisers and requested a private room. My interest was piqued, so I followed them to listen in." He glanced knowingly at Ilsa, who scowled. "But things had already turned... bloody."

"So you failed to hear any of their conversation?" said Eliot.

Fowler glared at him opaquely. "My interest was piqued by

a scream," he clarified. "I was engaged before that, too far away to hear anything."

"Ah." Eliot smiled his cruellest smile. "Remind me, what's your vice? Cards, isn't it?"

"Eliot," growled Hester.

For a brief flash, Eliot had got a reaction from the Wraith – a sting of surprise; the most weakness Ilsa had ever seen in him – but then Fowler schooled his features into impassivity. Ilsa marvelled that the captain could have anything in common with Bill Blume, but in that single moment, she knew unequivocally that he did. That was why his attention had snagged on the wrestling at the street party that night in Camden. It wasn't the fighting; it was the money changing hands.

"So you just decided to be a hero?" said Eliot, changing tack. Definitely a love rivalry, thought Ilsa with a sting.

Fowler gazed levelly back at him. "I decided to help a fellow man in need when it was in my power to do so."

"So much for ruthlessness," said Eliot, adding: "it's a wonder the Order are as feared as they are."

"Ruthlessness is not the same as strength, Quillon. You of all people should know that." Eliot ground his teeth, and even Hester opened her mouth, but Fowler did not answer to either of them, and he pressed on. "It's our strength the rest of you fear, and we didn't cultivate it by undiscerningly slaying our way across the city. Mercy can be strength too."

"I'm sorry, was that *mercy* or money?"

"Eliot, enough," snapped Hester. Fowler hadn't deigned to rise to the taunt, and simply smiled. "That's quite some speech coming from a paid assassin," Hester said to him.

He crossed his arms over his broad chest and gestured to Ilsa with a nod. "Paid rescuer too."

"And who paid you to rescue Aelius?" said Ilsa.

He was quiet as he studied her. "It's my night off."

Hester caught her eye, and Ilsa nodded. It was the core of decency she had suspected the captain had, despite Eliot's misgivings. Hester sighed, and obviously decided to trust her.

"I take it you've heard the rumours?" she asked the captain.

"I make it my job to hear."

"Then I suppose it won't hurt if I tell you they're true. Gedeon Ravenswood is missing. The apprentice Seer of the Docklands is with him. And we need to find them both, along with twelve of our wolves, without any more delay."

There was silence. Fowler's brow knotted as he studied Hester. "Your cousin has been missing for nearly two months. Can I ask why the sudden urgency?"

"No, you can't," said Hester. "Do you want the job or not?"

"Why me? Because I'm here?"

"Because my cousin trusts you, and because you found her in three days when we failed to for seventeen years. I want you to do the same for her brother."

Fowler considered each of them, his gaze lingering on Eliot, who had once again withdrawn several paces from the rest of the group. Eventually, he rolled his shoulders and said, "I'll need to know everything."

34

With a blow-by-blow of Gedeon's movements as far as Ilsa knew them, and a manifest of the missing wolves, Fowler disappeared into the dawn with a promise of sending word on his progress soon.

Soon.

It was all they could get from him.

But every minute that they didn't hear from Cadell Fowler felt like an hour, and "soon" became an eternity. When a messenger arrived from the Heart, with a note saying Lucius would "think about" Hester's request – precisely the kind of non-news they had all feared – Ilsa was about ready to snap.

She was restlessly wandering the corridors, playing cards in hand, when she came across Oren in the meeting room.

Perhaps out of habit, he was in his usual seat. He had pulled the chair out and was facing the window, but didn't seem to be looking at anything in particular. Rather, he gazed into space, lost in thought and oblivious to her standing there.

She closed the door with a sharp click and Oren started.

"Hello," said Ilsa.

"Hello." Compulsively, he took out his glasses and started to polish them. After an awkward pause he added, "I expect this seat at the end is yours now."

For a moment, Ilsa thought he meant Gedeon's chair, but he

was gesturing to the other end of the table; not the head, but equally set apart.

She sat, but she wasn't sure what to say, and Oren continued to stare out the window. It was a minute or more before he broke the silence.

"I was told that Captain Fowler bound your wrists with Changeling leather when he found you," he said. His tone was conversational but his face was taut and his fingers played with his shirtsleeves. "You didn't mention it."

"I made him do it twice, actually." Oren blinked in bemusement, so Ilsa demonstrated her deftness with a disappearing card. She tried to sound light-hearted, but her voice came out weak when she added, "I ain't easy to keep tied up these days."

For a moment, Oren just stared, his expression unreadable. Then he nodded, just once, and began rolling up the sleeves of his shirt. "In that case, I am especially sorry that he bound you."

Oren's skin changed, and the markings he revealed made Ilsa's blood run cold. Cords of scarring ran around both wrists. He rotated his forearms so she could see all of it and then, just as quickly, hid it all again. "As you know, Changeling leather is fairly soft, but tie it tight enough for long enough and it will wound as well as anything."

Ilsa wanted to say something comforting but her mouth was dry.

So she put her cards down and pushed her sleeves up to her elbows. "You called London an experiment what failed."

Oren blinked. "Yes."

"But it's still standing, ain't it? So, it can't have failed yet."

She laid her palms on the table, then with a deep breath and

454

half a thought she changed her naked flesh and showed Oren what was underneath; the scars that matched his own. "This place might still be better than the one I left behind," she said. "Or it might not. But please don't say you've given up on it."

Oren stared blankly at her scars, then reached a hesitant hand towards hers, and took them in both of his. He ran the pads of his fingers over her ragged skin, like he could better read its stories that way. When he looked up at her over the rim of his glasses, something had come back to life in his eyes.

"It would be a shame to give you back your home just to see it laid to waste," he said. "Nothing has failed yet," he echoed.

"Well, that's more like it." Ilsa beamed and discreetly vanished her scars again.

"I'm sorry, Ilsa," Oren said. "I'm sorry I wasn't truthful about the amulet. I tied the fate of a dangerous artefact to yours, without knowing where it might lead."

"You did what you thought was right," said Ilsa. "It's all any of us are doing. Was Hester angry?"

"Oh, yes," he said mildly. "On many counts. But I gave her my reasons, and I stick by them. I told her the truth: that the only person I trusted to resist the lure of such power was myself, having suffered at its hands."

"D'you think…" Ilsa hesitated. She wasn't sure she wanted to know, but the truth of her own words made her wonder – they were all doing what they thought they needed to; what they thought was right. "If Gedeon knew what the amulet really was, what it did… d'you think he'd still use it?"

If Oren was taken aback by the question, it didn't show. He gazed into the middle distance as he considered. "The boy I've known him to be would see the seventh Seer's amulet tossed to the bottom of the ocean if he knew the suffering it caused – but I don't know if that is who Gedeon is anymore."

"What d'you mean?" said Ilsa, Oren's uncertainty making her uneasy. "Who is he?"

"Well, I suppose the Gedeon I have known is a lot like you. Determined, forthright, self-assured." His eyes glinted with amusement. "A little headstrong sometimes. But he hadn't been himself for quite some time. He was thinking about his place and his power, and questioning everything."

Ilsa looked up sharply. "How'd you know?"

"Because I am also a lot like you. I observe. I see things others don't care to notice. This inter-faction conclave of his – it doesn't surprise me. I don't believe he wants to rule the way Hester and their forebears did." He paused, shook his head, and fussed with his glasses again. "The only thing I had failed to see was how desperate he had become. He was withdrawn, distracted. I didn't understand it at the time, but... I'm sorry to say, I think he was losing faith in us."

Ilsa felt the sadness in Oren's words wash over her, like Gedeon had turned his back on her too. "You don't think that's why he was going recruiting in Millwater?"

"That's exactly what I think."

"Then why'd he cancel it?"

Oren frowned slightly. "That was the day of the attack."

Ilsa blinked to clear the confusion, and shook her head. "The attack was after. Aelius had only thought it was the same time, but he was double-crossed."

"Aelius is mistaken," Oren said. "The trip was scheduled for that evening."

Ilsa shook her head. "But Cassia said so too."

He regarded her mildly and reached for his notebook. "No matter. I have always believed the secret to a reliable mind is writing everything down. So let's see." He licked a finger and started skimming back through the pages. "Here it is. Gedeon to Millwater, seven pm on the twenty-ninth." He laid the book on the table and turned it to face her.

"That's the day of the attack alright," murmured Ilsa. "But then why…"

The date.

The meeting room.

She gasped and leapt from her chair, startling Oren. "What's the matter?"

"Nothing. I – I have to go."

He didn't try to stop her as she wrenched the door open and hurtled for the stairs. Privacy; she needed privacy.

She was running so fast that when she met Fyfe rounding a corner, they collided hard enough to back him against the wall.

"Ilsa, why are you – gosh, you're pale."

"Fyfe," she gasped, holding onto the front of his shirt. "Gedeon's trip to Millwater. The one what got cancelled. You knew 'bout it?"

Fyfe frowned, his mouth opening and closing. "Well… yes, he mentioned it in passing. He said to keep it quiet."

"What time was it?"

"I'm not sure I remember. Why do you—"

"Was it the morning or the evening?" she pressed frantically.

"Early. Definitely the morning. Ilsa, why—"

But Ilsa was already gone, hurtling for Gedeon's room, where

457

she couldn't be caught by the wrong pair of eyes. She locked the door behind her, and dragged a chair in front of it just to be sure.

Panting, she sank to her knees and reached under the mattress with shaking fingers. She had kept the slip of paper where she'd found it, under Gedeon's bed, folded twice and tucked inside a book to keep it flat.

Stupid. She had been so stupid.

The diagram wasn't about the amulet, it was about Gedeon's cancelled trip.

Oren's notebook told him that it had been scheduled for the day of the attack, approximately twelve hours *after* the rebels broke in. He would have written it down at the time; it was nearly impossible for him to be wrong.

And yet he had to be. Because Cassia and Aelius had pinned the timing of the trip as *before* the attack, and both had a crucial reason to remember it correctly; Cassia because the rebels robbed her and Gedeon of their chance to reconcile, and Aelius because he had arranged for extra wolves at the Zoo.

So Ilsa started matching lieutenants to the numbers and symbols. Oren's, she knew. Cassia and Aelius could be narrowed down to two of three, but if the shape in the middle represented what she thought it did…

Sickness roiled in her gut as she pieced together an answer she desperately didn't want to find; that the real reason Gedeon had fled the Zoo was that he had done some investigating of his own, and this diagram was the proof.

The symbol meant morning or evening, the number beside it was a date, and every one of them had been a trap.

IV

THE GREEN
SEA TURTLE
Chelonia mydas

A marine reptile found in tropical and subtropical seas worldwide. Like all members of the family Cheloniidae, this turtle will only come ashore to mate and lay eggs. They are known to migrate many thousands of miles to return to the beach on which they hatched.

35

A fake trip. Six different times. Gedeon had invented the perfect opportunity to attack the Zoo; a few hours when he would be away, most of the wolves on guard with him. Then he'd quietly fed conflicting dates and times to his lieutenants to see who would leak to the Heart rebels.

And one of them had.

Sitting in the meeting room, staring at the oval table where they all would meet, the shape in the centre of the diagram had suddenly made sense. Hester, Eliot, Oren, Cassia, Aelius and Fyfe. Six lieutenants flanking their alpha. Gedeon's place was between Hester and Cassia, at the bottom of the diagram. He had drawn the table as he saw it, and crossed off his lieutenants, his friends, as the mornings and evenings rolled by. The first had been Cassia, on the evening of the twenty-seventh. Perhaps he'd been most desperate to know, most afraid, that his traitor was the Sorcerer he loved.

Fyfe – who sat in the third seat on his right – had been the morning of the twenty-eighth, and Aelius, who sat next to him, that evening. Then Gedeon had stopped crossing off lieutenants. On the morning of the twenty-ninth, he found his traitor.

There was a *thunk* from the door as someone tried to enter, and Ilsa jumped. Her hands were still shaking uncontrollably as she stashed the diagram under her mattress.

"Ilsa?" came the call. It was Eliot.

She felt herself go to the door, move the chair, and turn the lock. She took several large steps back as he barrelled into the room.

"We've got him," he said.

It was then she heard the commotion in the rest of the house. Footsteps rattled up and down the stairs. Hester was calling orders from somewhere.

But she couldn't form the proper reaction.

"Did you hear me?" he said. "We found Gedeon. He stormed the portal and—"

"You're a spy."

It was little more than a whisper, but Eliot cut off, and they were plunged into silence. The footsteps faded away; Hester's voice stopped echoing. And in that moment, taking in his shock and horror, Ilsa lost the dwindling hope that she was wrong.

"Ilsa—"

"You're a traitor."

"I'm *not* a traitor." His voice was fierce, the denial real. He made to move towards her, but she backed away. He paused, a war raging behind his storm-blue eyes, and when he spoke again it was with new resolve. "It's not like that—"

"You told the rebels when to attack," she said, not lowering her voice when Eliot shot a harried glance at the hallway. "And Gedeon knows, don't he? The other day when we spoke to Aelius, you realised what he'd done. That's why you were so worked up."

The longer Ilsa thought on it, the worse it got. The very night they'd met, he showed her how to leave the Zoo without

461

being seen. He would have designed the guard duty himself. He had engineered that weakness, those fifteen seconds, so that he could meet with Camden's enemies. He had told her everything he'd worked out about Gedeon's movements before he had any reason to trust her, taking her into his confidence to earn hers. He'd tried to persuade her to stop looking for Gedeon – had told her that her brother was never coming back; wanted nothing to do with her – because he'd realised Gedeon knew, and it would cost him his skin. And what else had been a lie? That he was fighting to protect his people? That he ever wanted her at all?

"You" – an unnameable emotion turned her stomach – "you manipulated me."

Rage and remorse hardened Eliot's features. He was shaking his head, but the denial wasn't real.

"You're just like Alitz."

Something in him snapped. The look he gave her was desolate and broken, the accusation one too far. "No," he whispered. "Ilsa, I would never hurt you."

"Right. Just my family."

Before Eliot could respond, Oren appeared at the door.

"Downstairs, both of you," he said, breathing heavily. "We need to move fast or we won't catch him."

Then he was gone again. Eliot made to follow, but Ilsa yanked him back by the arm and slammed the door.

"I should've known sooner," she growled. "You din't want me trusting the others. You did everything you could to stop me involving them, because you wanted to find him before anyone else did, in case he knew."

"I wanted to find him first so I could *explain*!" He heaved a breath but it didn't calm him. He ran a shaking hand through his hair, and when he spoke again, his voice was strained. "All I have ever wanted was to protect Camden. All that's ever mattered to me is serving these people, this house, *your* family. I love Gedeon like a brother but he's never understood. He can never know what I've given."

Pain – the kind carved into his bones and impossible to heal – marred his features. Ilsa wanted to rage and swear at him, but she was too confounded. Was that what he was trying to do – simply confuse her?

"Gedeon needs me right now," he said. Ilsa scoffed but he pressed on. "If we've found him, the Fortunatae have as well. I swear to you, Ilsa, I want to bring him back safe. What you do with me then... I don't care."

Through the fog in her mind, Ilsa tried to clock his tells, but there were none. Still, she took his lapels in her fists and slammed him against the wall with as much force as she could muster. His head cracked sharply against the plaster, but he gritted his teeth and swallowed the pain.

"If I even think you're 'bout to do something stupid," she said into his ear, "I'll kill you myself. I'll string you up by your innards and leave you like carrion for the birds. No trial, no damned *explanation*."

"And if I don't do anything stupid? If we make it through this, will you listen to the truth?" He brought his hand to her face. When Ilsa flinched away, she saw his heart break right there in his gaze. "I don't want to lie to you any more."

She let him go with another sharp shove for good measure.

"If we make it through this, you can tell it to Gedeon," she said, her voice cold and hard as steel. Her heart felt the same. She turned away and wrenched open the door. "I don't give a damn what you got to say."

*

Chaos reigned in the forecourt, and Hester was at the centre of it.

"Lieutenants, retrieve Gedeon and the wolves," she bellowed. "And retrieve the amulet. Arm yourselves. We can expect Pyval Crespo is following Gedeon, and if there are more Whisperers it might be too risky to shift. Don't take wolves, they could just be turned against you. You all know where the armoury is. Fyfe—"

"Science weapons, I know." He flashed his sister a grin and revealed the belt of dampeners slung around his hips.

Hester nodded, already turning away. "Wolves, double the guard at the Zoo and at the abbey. Let's not take any chances."

As the wolves began to organise, Ilsa spotted Fowler at the edge of the forecourt and weaved her way towards him, Eliot following. "What happened?"

"Your brother and his wolves have been hiding out on a cargo boat on the river," said Fowler. "They've been docking for two days, then moving on. I finally caught up with them less than an hour ago, when they docked by the Trade House. I followed them to the abbey. By the time I got there, they had stormed the portal and passed through." He nodded then at a group of wolves talking to Hester and Oren. Some were bloodied, and every one was dripping with sweat. The man at their front was the first person she had seen in the Witherward; the captain of the guard at Westminster Abbey. He seemed shell-shocked. "They say the prince's party numbered thirteen Changelings and an Oracle."

"So his new conclave aren't with him," said Eliot.

"That don't mean they won't follow through another portal," said Ilsa.

"And the guard claim there wasn't a breath to warn him," added Fowler. "They were ready to fight their way through. They knew the wolves would try to stop them."

Ilsa cornered Oren the second he was alone. She glanced over her shoulder, but no one was listening. Hester was across the forecourt, still shooting instructions.

"There's a book what says the amulet could be replicated. It says you could make enough for a whole army." Ilsa felt sick. Would each amulet need a different victim? Or *five*, to give the wearer every magic? Eliot had said Gedeon would be a fool not to use a tool like that to protect the Changelings. Did he still feel that way now they knew what the amulet really did? Her sickness compounded as she realised he might always have known. He had helped the rebels try to steal it. No doubt the amulet would have been passed to Alitz. "D'you think… d'you think Hester would try to do that?"

Oren shook his head. "I don't know, Ilsa. I would like to hope she wouldn't, but…"

He trailed off, and as their eyes met, an understanding passed between them. Hester's orders didn't matter. They couldn't claim such evil magic for Camden.

Ilsa lowered her voice even further. "You said you tried to destroy it already and it din't work. What d'you plan to do?"

"Arm yourself," he said, already stepping away from her. "And don't be concerned. You can leave the amulet to me."

*

465

Nobody thought about the weather.

When they passed through the portal and stepped into the ice-cold downpour of an early March night, the only one remotely prepared was Captain Fowler. The rest were likely to succumb to pneumonia, if they did not succumb to the Fortunatae much sooner.

Four of them spread wings; one took off at a run and quickly became shadow; and the last vanished in place as if she had never been there. All made their way as fast as they could to a place Ilsa had hoped never to see again.

Kennington Road was dark – the gas lamps failing to cut far through the downpour – and quiet but for the groan of the wind and rain against the buildings. Ilsa had directed them to gather in a residential garden, which was walled and hidden, and fifty paces from the orphanage, on the other side of the street. If the owners of the garden were to peer out their window, they might make out six figures huddled in the rain, but some indignant Otherworlders were the least of their worries.

Fowler was the last to reach the rendezvous. "The adjacent streets are all peculiarly busy for this time of night," he said over the rain. "A lot of lurkers."

"You're saying the place is surrounded," said Cassia. Her hair was plastered to her neck and her lips were turning blue.

"It looks that way, but any number of them could be Otherworlders. Unless they make a move there's no telling." He took a blade from somewhere in his coat, inspected its edge in the light of the porch lamp, and put it away again. "Oh, and your man is approaching from the south. He's eighty paces away."

"What?" hissed Ilsa. She craned around the wall as her taller companions peered over and squinted down the street.

Sure enough, a male figure was approaching St Genevieve's. His soaking hair could be any colour, but he had the build of the man Ferrien had impersonated, and as he came into the light of the lamp in front of the orphanage, Ilsa's breath caught.

Gedeon. He was so close.

He stopped with a hand on the gate, his attention snagging on something in Ilsa's direction. Four hooded men were coming the other way, and as they passed their hiding spot, the lamplight flashed across the shape of a revolver.

Eliot spotted it too. "This one's armed. Whisperer. They must be Fortunatae."

Was Alitz one of them? Was Pyval? Ilsa made to step around the wall, but Fowler's hand closed around her arm and tugged her back. She was about to throw her best punch at him when Cassia gasped and pointed down the road.

Prowling silently behind the Fortunatae were four huge wolves. They were gaining with every step, but they weren't fast enough. As soon as the hooded men were in range of Gedeon, the leader raised his gun. Gedeon froze in place. It was too late to run.

The wolves pounced. The gun fired. Ilsa's scream was muffled by the shot. Gedeon fell to his knees and collapsed face first into the street.

36

They burst from the garden into the road, but it was all over. The Fortunatae men were dead, the wolves were Camden militia again and Gedeon was...

Was no longer Gedeon.

Cassia reached him first and hauled him onto his back. "Oh stars. Scotty!" she cried.

He was another soldier, and he was breathing. "Cassia?" he gasped, gripping at his bleeding chest. "What are you—"

An enormous crash sounded from somewhere in the orphanage. "That's the second decoy," said another wolf. "Desmond, with me."

Two of them disappeared through the gates and the door beyond, while the other two hauled Scotty to his feet.

"With all due respect, sirs, Miss Sims, help or get out of the way," said a long-haired wolf. He shot a mistrusting glance at Fowler, then looked Ilsa up and down. "Who are you?"

"I'm—"

"Get down!"

Ilsa's face smacked the cobblestones as Eliot threw himself on top of her. A flash of light filled her vision, the stone wall of the orphanage cracked with a sound like thunder, and then she was being hauled to her feet again.

In those few seconds, everything had descended into chaos.

The flash had been a spell, the first of a flurry now raining down on them from a boarded-up house across the street. Cassia had generated a protective shield, but more Sorcerers were advancing from behind. Fowler was a blur, slowing just long enough to cut each rebel down, then disappearing again. A bird of indeterminate species swooped down onto a rooftop, thrashed like it was having a seizure, landed haphazardly on gangly human limbs, and took cover as he tossed a projectile into the fray. It was as safe a spot as any for Fyfe to defend himself from.

Oren was nowhere to be seen.

"Come on!" yelled Eliot, and they ran for the house. "Be careful when you shift. Keep an eye out for Whisperers."

If there had been time to think, Ilsa would have talked herself out of it. The square, grey-stone structure of the orphanage seemed to reach for her as she drew nearer; the doorframe seemed to narrow even as they passed through.

Inside was a different kind of chaos. Children were pouring from their rooms and running, screaming, down the corridors. Desmond and the other man were trying, and failing, to herd them to safety.

Ilsa and Eliot followed the sounds of fighting to the kitchen at the back of the house. The loud crash, it turned out, had been someone tearing a hole in the high wall that surrounded the courtyard out back. Rebels and more hooded men and women – the Fortunatae – had engaged with the second decoy and were overpowering them. One was Psi, and was using the rubble of the wall as missiles. She could probably take down the whole building if she chose. Another, Ilsa saw with a jolt of terror, was a Wraith. As she watched, he emerged through what was left of the wall behind a cornered wolf, and cleanly snapped his neck.

But several were Whisperers, and Gedeon's wolves were at a disadvantage. The Changelings were less skilled with real weapons, and some were struggling to stay in control of their minds. They became beasts in flashes, lashed out and changed again, but the damage wasn't great enough.

"Bloody hell," breathed Eliot. "This is a shambles."

He drew his own gun and aimed it through the open kitchen door, but missed.

"When your aim is bad," said Ilsa, carefully slipping the knife she had holstered at her waist up her sleeve, where she preferred her tools. *A blade is only as good as its backup*. "You just got to close the distance."

"Ilsa, wait!"

But she had already become a sparrow, and in the chaos, she slipped unnoticed through the Fortunatae's front line. As a bird, it was easy to think about the present moment – and not the things she'd seen Wraiths do, or whether she might lose her knife, or cut her own wrist by mistake – so she concentrated on it as she shifted and landed lightly on the wall behind him. He heard her, of course, but Ilsa had expected that. She had already let the blade slip into her hand; she had already raised it; she was already falling on top of him.

It wasn't until Ilsa opened her eyes that she realised she'd closed them. She was sprawled on top of the Wraith, who had got a hold of her around the ribs, and she gasped as he squeezed, breaking something. But that bit of pressure was the most he could manage, because Ilsa's knife was in his neck, and the light was leaving his eyes.

He went still as Ilsa got to her feet, woozy and breathless, but there would be no respite, because she had attracted the attention of another hooded figure.

The Whisperer glared at her with hatred and disgust. Ilsa was on her knees before she could push him out of her mind. She hadn't thought she would ever want to hurt herself, but a macabre curiosity to learn what the Wraith had felt as she killed him seized her, so she turned the knife to her own neck.

And then the desire vanished. Ilsa stood. A black panther's jaws were closing around the Whisperer's neck. A woman – Oracle – was swinging the butt of her pistol at Ilsa's head, but Ilsa ducked and dragged the knife across her shins. She caught the Oracle's gun as she fell, then finished her with a blade to the neck.

But she now had bigger problems – much bigger. Another Whisperer was smiling viciously at her, and between them, under his spell, was Eliot.

He was stalking towards her on massive paws, claws extended and ready to tear her to ribbons.

"Eliot, you idiot!" she cried, but the cat took no notice. So she fumbled with her stolen pistol and fired off three rounds at the Whisperer. All missed.

The panther pounced. Ilsa tensed. A fourth bullet, fired from the door, found the Whisperer right between the eyes. Soft, wet fur brushed her skin before Eliot became human. The force of his impact sent them flying, but Ilsa hit the ground with one of Eliot's arms banded tight around her waist and the other braced by her head, saving her skull.

They were alright.

Stunned, they both lay there – noses touching, chests heaving – until Ilsa shoved him away and scrambled to her feet.

"I said if you did anything stupid I'd kill you!"

"I didn't realise saving your life counted," he shot back.

"Somebody find Oren!" called Cassia, their saviour, who was still picking off the enemies from the door. She was firing her revolver with her right hand and letting off spells with the left. "Find the amulet!"

She covered them as they re-entered the house and raced back to the entrance hall. The front door had been obliterated, and glass and wood chips scattered the stone floor. The yellow smoke of a Sorcerer dampener was billowing from a doorway to the left, and the singing of a Wraith blade was coming from within. Ilsa hoped it was Fowler and not another Fortunatae member.

The wet sound of flesh tearing made them turn. Five yards away, a man was choking on blood, a blade run up through his abdomen. Ilsa was so utterly horrified she almost didn't notice that his killer was her brother.

"Gedeon!" Ilsa gasped, but he didn't react. He wiped his blade on his breeches and made for the stairs, catching sight of Eliot as he passed them. He careened to a halt, and Ilsa felt Eliot tense beside her.

"Eliot?" said Gedeon, cocking his head. "What are you—"

A nearby window shattered under a spell, and half a dozen Sorcerers poured in. Gedeon cut one down and continued on without a backward glance. Ilsa made to chase him, but Eliot grabbed her arm and shook his head.

"Blue eyes," he said, ducking a spell. "Not him."

They couldn't see any Whisperers, so they both risked their

animal forms to take on the rebels. Eliot moved like water, cutting through air and enemies like a stronger element. Every move was swift, graceful, intentional, like *this* was the body he truly belonged in. He took several hits from a flurry of spells, but each seemed to glide off him like he had a spelled shield of his own. He was just too strong for them.

Fowler joined them, and Ilsa – a menacingly oversized cat in her own right – was left with nothing to do, so she risked letting Eliot out of her sight to find the amulet.

But she didn't have the first idea where to look. When Oren had told them about leaving it here, he seemed to hint to Ilsa that she knew something of it. But how could she? She had been a baby when it was hidden. At a loss, and with enemies in every direction on the ground floor, she decided to try upstairs.

The fighting lessened on the first floor, and as she got further from the stairs, the sounds of claws and guns and magic grew distant. Somehow, the orphanage was more frightening this way. It was more like the place she had known. There was the girls' dormitory where she slept when she was good. There was the stairwell where she had accidentally become Lulu and sent the other kids screaming. Up there, on the second floor, was the door to the attic…

Ilsa jumped as a gaggle of small children burst from the dorm at the end of the hall and ran past her.

"Go!" a Camden wolf called after them, before something caught her in the back and she fell, lifeless, to the floor.

Ilsa ran towards her. She had to step over her body to get into the dorm, where a single remaining wolf was fighting off three men. It didn't seem any of them could break into his mind, but their guns and spells were deadly enough, and the soldier had only a blade. He had barricaded himself behind a cot turned on its end, but he wouldn't hold up much longer.

"Hey!" Ilsa called, and all three men swung towards her.

But she was already a mouse. It was her favourite part of The Great Balthazar's defunct show, her vanishing trick, and she was well-practised in using her surroundings to move unseen. When she grew again, she was in their blind spot, and she shot the first man at close range before he could react. Then the whole room changed. The men were gone. Then they had shifted positions. Then Ilsa was facing the door, not the room. One of them was in her head, pummelling her with confusing images, but she'd been ready for the interference this time. She had already clocked the distance to the makeshift barricade, so she dived blind and rolled behind the cot.

When the Whisperer gave up on her, she found herself face to face with another Gedeon. She was utterly desensitised by now.

"What are you doing?" he said, looking at her like she'd sprouted from the floor.

"Helping."

"Helping?"

"You idiots are surrounded!" she snapped. "Fortunatae, Heart rebels. They got the acolytes on their side too now, so stealing that kid better have been worth it." A bullet hit the cot and they both tensed. "This is a *children's* home, you know. Full of children?"

"We're on top of it," he said, grinning. "No children are getting hurt."

"Yeah, you look really on top of it." A spell; this one hit with a crackle and set the cot on fire. "You take the one on the left,"

Ilsa said, and without giving herself time to reconsider, she stood and started firing.

Or, at least, she tried. She was empty. The wolf had closed the distance between him and the other and was winning, with a little help of his claws, but Ilsa was on her own.

The Sorcerer smiled at her and raised his hand. On instinct, she pulled out her knife again and threw it, and it buried itself in the man's chest. Ilsa took a second to marvel at how many useful skills her former profession had given her.

Across the room, blood spattered across the floorboards. Her comrade shifted from lion to man with a thrashing motion, and grinned; a dashing, carefree grin the portraits never showed.

"Thanks," he said, making for the door. "Now get out of here." He stopped at the threshold and tilted his head, hazel eyes flashing. "It's strange. You look awfully like my mother."

"I—"

But he was gone. "Wait!" She ran, but when she reached the corridor, it was deserted. "Damn it, Gedeon."

There wasn't time to catch up with Gedeon. She needed to find Oren and the amulet, but the house was huge, and it could be anywhere. She kicked the wall in frustration. Why had he been so sure she knew where it was? A floorboard groaned overhead, and Ilsa's head snapped up, something tugging at her memory. The very first time they had spoken, Oren had pressed her for the whereabouts of something, but it wasn't the amulet. It was the wooden wolf, the one that matched Gedeon's.

Only, it didn't. One wolf was hollow, the other was not.

Ilsa's throat went dry. She climbed the stairs to the next floor without difficulty, but when she found herself before the steps to the attic, her feet locked in place like she was under some kind of spell. But the power that had taken over her this time came from her mind; her frightened, fractured mind, scored irrevocably with fifty reasons not to climb the stairs.

She hated that the words that swam up through the depths to soothe her were Eliot's; treacherous, lying Eliot.

Look around you, Ilsa. We're all scared. It's only a weakness if you give in to it.

And so she let herself be scared. Her heart hammered against her ribs, and sickness churned in her belly, but she squared her shoulders anyway, and climbed the stairs to the attic.

37

The attic room was tiny, just as Ilsa remembered, with gaps in the floorboards and roof tiles.

Oren stood warily by the door, his gaze fixed on a spot under the slope of the far wall, between two towers of boxes, where the cot Ilsa had slept on as a child still lay. And sat on it, of all the horrors, was Miss Mitcham herself.

She hadn't aged much, but then, it had only been eight years. Her mousy hair was thinner, and peppered with more greys, but her skin had that same too-soft quality; her face the same shapelessness.

Her hair was messily plaited and she wore a nightgown that had seen better days. The stump of her left arm poked out where she had rolled the sleeve up to the elbow. Ilsa remembered biting her vividly. Her teeth had sunk bone-deep and the wound had gotten infected. That was what you got for cornering a frightened bloodhound. The only remorse Ilsa had felt was over the blood on her own pinafore.

She had been crying, and she shook, but the most striking thing about Miss Mitcham was the knife at her throat.

Her captor was small for thirteen, and round-faced with a round chin; a babyish look that made them seem even younger. Sleek, white-blonde hair was gathered in a tight bun at the top of their head. Small ears stuck out at right angles, and a pair of all-white eyes shimmered like opals.

"*This* is the famous Cogna?" said Ilsa. She kept her eyes on the Oracle to keep from seeing the walls shrink towards her.

"Hello, Ilsa Ravenswood," Cogna said in a light and lilting voice. "We've been waiting for you."

Ilsa glanced at Oren, who said, "The child asked that I fetch you, and only you, or they'd hurt this woman." He gestured to Miss Mitcham. "I told them you would come of your own accord."

Ilsa folded her arms. "You found a bit of jewellery in a different universe with your magic bloody powers, and you couldn't figure out I don't care nothing for that woman?" Cogna's little knife-wielding hand dropped to their side. "You want something from me? Be a dear and cut her throat. Then we'll talk."

Miss Mitcham gave a shriek and cowered, but Cogna gaped, wide-eyed.

"I wasn't actually going to hurt her." It came out like a squeak. "I just needed your attention."

"Then give it here." She held her hand out for the knife and wished that she hadn't left hers buried in a Sorcerer. It wasn't that she *wanted* to slaughter the woman in cold blood, but the sight of her, in this place… something inside her had been stretching since she got here, and had finally snapped. She saw that her outstretched hand was trembling.

"Ilsa," said Oren, and Ilsa felt a hand on her shoulder. She shook him off.

"Ilsa?" Miss Mitcham's bloodshot eyes roamed over her, unsure. It was a look that hollowed Ilsa out in a way she didn't think was possible. "Is it really you?"

The woman had chained her to that very cot, sometimes for

days at a time, had beaten her, bled her, made her believe she was a demon – and now she was looking at her like they had become strangers.

They could never be strangers. Not after what Miss Mitcham put her through. She deserved more. Tears. Screams. *Something*.

"Hello, miss," Ilsa said, somehow rendering a calm she didn't feel. She moved towards them, and Cogna hastily sheathed the knife. "D'you notice I brought some friends with me. They're from the devil's realm too."

Miss Mitcham wept and crossed herself. Another loud crash sounded from downstairs, followed by a groan as the building faltered. They all glanced nervously at the ceiling.

"You better tell me what you want," Ilsa said to Cogna, but she wasn't heard. Cogna's eyes were on Oren, Oren's were on the thing in Cogna's hand – the thing they'd come for. The little Oracle had already retrieved the wooden wolf from the floorboard where Ilsa had hidden it all those years ago.

"S'alright, kid," said Ilsa, "we're all on the same side." But she wasn't sure she believed it. Oren looked like he was readying himself to use force on the child.

"I'm sorry, Mr Tarenvale," said Cogna, one hand twitching towards their knife. Even with the child's Sight, it would not be a fair fight if it came to it. "You cannot have it. The amulet is not for you."

"I don't believe you intended it for Gedeon either," said Oren.

"No, I did not," Cogna sighed, "though I regret that I lied to him. The amulet is for you, Ilsa Ravenswood."

Ilsa started in surprise. "Beg your pardon?"

"I can't say for sure that the amulet is key," said Cogna, "but

479

I have known for some time that you are. When I Saw that the Prince of Camden was coming for the amulet, I took it as a sign."

Cogna cut off as a sound like bending wood resonated from below. The sudden swell of voices was unmistakable; everybody was getting out.

"Gedeon Ravenswood is not the one who saves the city," Cogna told Ilsa, "you are. I have Seen it. Others have Seen it before me. Please, Mr Tarenvale. You mustn't interfere."

Cogna wedged their knife into the wolf and, squeezing those opalescent eyes shut and leaning away, smashed the knife against the wall, breaking the wolf into several pieces.

Ilsa didn't get to see what happened next.

"Cogna!" someone roared from below. "Time to go!"

It was Gedeon. He was on the second floor, mere feet away. Without thinking, Ilsa bolted from the attic and half-ran, half-fell down the stairs.

From the second floor, the extent of the damage was obvious. Part of the exterior wall was missing, and smoke – real smoke, the kind that came from fire – hung thick in the air.

"Gedeon?" Ilsa choked.

"Cogna?" He appeared from through the smoke, his clothes torn, bloody and soaked through from the ceaseless rain. He squinted at her. "You."

"Gedeon."

He frowned at her face, at her sodden, indistinguishable hair. Something halfway between incredulity and understanding crossed his features, and transformed into anger and misery. Before Ilsa could say another word, he had drawn his sword and gripped her by the neck.

"Take it off," he growled. "That disguise. Take it off!"

They both lost their footing as the house shook, and were thrown against the wall. Gedeon struggled to his knees and was looming over her, his grip still around her throat.

"It's no disguise," gasped Ilsa.

She could see him better from nearer the floor, below the smoke, and he could see her better too. The eyes that were a little wider than his mother's; the lids a little heavier, like his father's. The cheekbones that would always be sharper than Lyander's, on account of an adolescence of malnutrition, days without food on the streets of the Otherworld.

Slowly, the hand at her throat softened. His fingers floated over her skin and grazed her cheek, like he had to feel her there to know she was real. The frown never left his face as he pressed back on his haunches.

"You're dead," he said.

"No, she's somewhat hard to kill," said a voice.

Ilsa and Gedeon spun. Pyval Crespo had braved the crumbling stairs and stood behind them, a dagger in one hand and a pistol in the other. The latter was pointed at Gedeon's chest.

Ilsa hardened her mind. She had practised alone daily since the last time she'd gone up against the Sage's twisted assistant. Though she felt Pyval test the edge of her consciousness, felt his nightmare void creeping into the corner of her vision, her mind was sharp and human, and her determination was fierce. She would not let him take control of her again.

"Pyval," said Gedeon, his bravado returning as he shifted himself between the man and Ilsa. "You know, it's hard to stab a man in the back when he has an omnic at his side. Cogna figured you out just in time. You can tell Alitz Dicer all her supporters are dead."

Pyval braced himself against the wall as the house shifted again.

"Yes, we should have realised sooner that you were expecting us." He cast a glance at Ilsa. "We also did not anticipate your friends showing up, since you abandoned them all so heartlessly."

Gedeon cocked his head and looked from Pyval to Ilsa. He didn't know. He hadn't seen any of them.

Pyval's grip on his knife shifted, catching Ilsa's attention. She knew that knife, had seen it before.

No, she had seen one just like it. Its twin.

"Bill," she said through gritted teeth, fury swelling until it threatened to burst out of her. She thought she couldn't hate him any more. "You were the one who killed him."

Pyval's face twisted, halfway between a grimace and a smile. "He was only supposed to be bait," he called over the groaning house. "If you hadn't brought Tarenvale and that Sorcerer bitch with you, I might have spared him."

Gedeon's grip on his sword had tightened the moment Pyval mentioned Cassia. As its blade drew Ilsa's attention, so did the familiar pouch strapped to his belt. Fyfe had one just like it.

"Wait, I'm lost," said Gedeon conversationally. "You tried to kill my sister?"

"The Sage wished not to." With the men fixated on one another, Ilsa went entirely unnoticed as she made her move. "She does not like to act too rashly. When your obliviously trusting lieutenants told her of the message from the Docklands, she thought a Ravenswood pup raised away from the litter might

482

prove a useful tool one day. That is, until she met her." Pyval sneered and cocked his pistol. "Hold it there, *princess*! I said from the first you'd be too hard to control."

Ilsa had crept from behind Gedeon, and been caught. Thankfully, while part of being a magician's assistant was knowing how to go unseen, it was equally important to know how to be noticed. Pyval's gun swung from Ilsa to Gedeon and back again, torn between two targets.

It was just the hesitation she had needed. Ilsa raised her hands so he saw they were empty; that she wasn't a threat. As he levelled his weapon and his attention back on Gedeon, she whispered, in a voice only her brother could hear: "Nothing up my sleeve."

Gedeon glanced her way, as she had hoped he would, and she indicated her formerly empty hand – and the small blue pellet she had lifted from his pouch.

Just like magic.

Gedeon took his cue, falling to all fours and disappearing under a coat of sandy fur and a ragged, golden mane. He was twice the size of a real lion, as tall as Ilsa at the shoulder.

Simultaneously, Ilsa tossed the pellet. It exploded in a swell of dark blue smoke. There was no time for Pyval to notice his magic was missing before one massive paw slashed across his chest, and he was thrown down the stairs.

A scream went up from the attic, and Gedeon transformed again. "Cogna!"

They ran back to the attic. Cogna lay immobile – dead, perhaps – on the floor among the fragments of Ilsa's wolf. Oren stood over them, a pendant of ruby and silver clutched in one hand. Miss Mitcham was cowering from the scene and muttering the Lord's Prayer.

Gedeon knelt beside Cogna and searched for a pulse. "Oren!" he shouted. "What have you done?"

"Forgive me, Gedeon," Oren said, reaching for the back of his belt, underneath his jacket. "I must."

Ilsa expected a weapon – Oren was carrying several of them – and gasped when she saw what he had been hiding underneath his jacket.

All the confusion and second-guessing. All the waiting to see whether the rebels would come again. But they had never stolen Fyfe's pocket forge.

Oren had.

Gedeon must have recognised it, for he left Cogna and launched himself across the attic, toppling a stack of crates. "No, Oren! What are you doing?"

Ilsa blocked his path. His wide, harried gaze swung to her in confusion, and Ilsa shook her head. "It's what's right," she said, hearing the roar of flame as the forge came to life. "That amulet stole his magic and made him a helpless prisoner, Gedeon. It's bad magic. He's got to destroy it."

In a flash, the attic filled with livid red light. Ilsa turned, an arm raised to cover her eyes. The amulet was glowing as Oren held the flame to it, and trembling horribly like a living thing. Even more light burst from the it, blinding Ilsa, and she heard it hit the floor as Oren dropped it. She closed her eyes, but the red light shone right through the lids. A long moment passed before the glow receded, and when Ilsa dared look again, the attic was even darker than before.

"Did it work?" she said. She scrambled forward, her eyes adjusting to the gloom. There on the floor, with the chain still attached to it, was a smouldering pool of silver swirled with ruby. The metal was dull; the ruby clouded. As Ilsa watched, fascinated, it dried to a caked powder.

The seventh Seer's amulet was gone.

Gedeon let out a growl of rage. "I don't understand you, Oren! You have *never* been afraid to do what is necessary." He gestured at Cogna, lying prone on the floor.

Oren blinked at Gedeon like he hadn't understood him.

"Shortly after your ancestor, Morgan Ravenswood, led the liberation and claimed Camden for the Changelings, she had a daughter with a man named Carlin. She chose to name her Ravenswood."

"I know this," said Gedeon, sounding unfortunately like a petulant child.

"But do you know why? Do you know why your name has endured through fourteen generations? Why your mother also passed on her family name to you and Ilsa? Why she took such drastic steps to ensure *someone* in her family survived? It is a pledge Morgan made, to devote not only her life to the freedom and safety of her people, but the lives of her entire line, in perpetuity. Your name is important to Camden because it is an emblem of stability and strength. It is a promise to the Changelings that there is someone who will endure so that they may endure. Who will die, if necessary, so they may live." His voice dropped to a whisper at the end, and he drew a breath. Ilsa did not need to guess what that promise had meant to Oren personally. She understood hope. "Yes, I do what is necessary.

But I do it, Gedeon, so that you don't have to. Your people must respect you and trust in you. And if you became the type of monster this amulet demanded you become, they would not.

"So I *have* done what is necessary." He levelled his sure, steady gaze at Gedeon. "And I would do it again."

Ilsa was knocked off her feet. Not by the shaking house, but by Pyval bursting through the door. He clutched his chest and leaned heavily on the doorjamb, but he was still breathing, and still brandishing his pistol.

"No!" he cried, glaring wide-eyed at what had become of the amulet. He raised his gun at Oren. "You fool! You half-breed fool!"

With a miserable howl, Pyval fired. Oren made the smallest sound of surprise as blood started to seep through his shirt, right above his heart.

"Oren!" bellowed Gedeon as the Whisperer turned his gun on him.

Ilsa didn't think. Thinking was never what she had needed to do; she had been in this very attic when she learned that. This is where fear had drowned out her instincts and stopped her from hearing that power inside her, the one that had always known what she was supposed to do.

She had escaped, but she had never been free. Fear had stopped her from using her magic her whole life. But something about being back here was calling up that power inside her. It was telling her, in a voice she could always hear but had never listened to, to remember what she already knew.

So Ilsa didn't think, she shifted.

Even over the rumble of the crumbling house, the thud of her paws hitting the floor resounded through the attic, as did the roar that burst uncontrollably from her throat as she launched herself at Pyval.

He slammed into the wall, Ilsa's claws at his throat. He howled as she dragged her paw down his neck and slashed open his chest. He thrashed, then slumped against the wall, twitching. Blood was seeping from between his lips when Ilsa shifted, her hands still on his mangled, bloody chest. "That's for Bill Blume," she whispered as she watched the light go out of Pyval's eyes.

Ilsa shoved at him as she turned away, not even looking back as she heard his corpse thud to the floor. He did not deserve her attention. Instead, she crouched next to Oren. Gedeon was on his other side, one hand cradling the man's head.

Oren was breathing rapidly, each gasp ripping from him with a small moan of pain. There was nothing controlled about the abyss behind his eyes now. Ilsa pressed her hands against the hole in his chest like she could hold the blood in, and he smiled.

"Not this time," he breathed.

His hands joined hers on his chest. One closed gently around her wrist as the scars on his own rose like phantoms; he hadn't the strength to hide them any longer. In the other hand was the pocket forge. "A remarkable thing," he said, eyes on hers, before he became still.

"Oren?" His eyes were still open, but there was nothing behind them anymore.

People were calling her, calling Gedeon. She didn't want to look away from Oren's face – serene again, the way she would remember it – but from the corner of her eye she saw Gedeon climb to his feet and lift Cogna over his shoulder. The child must have been alive, at least.

"Leave him, Ilsa!" shouted Gedeon, his tone fierce but his face desolate and tear-streaked. "He's gone!"

She brushed her bloody fingertips over Oren's eyes, closing them, and then she took the pocket forge and let Gedeon pull her to her feet and towards the door. He was descending the staircase when she remembered.

Miss Mitcham was a ball in the corner, her knees pulled up to her chin. She had a rosary, and she rubbed the beads between her fingers as she prayed.

Just like reaching for Cogna's knife, Ilsa didn't *want* to go to her; she didn't *want* to offer her hand. It just happened. Her voice was her own at least, bright and brave, as she said: "Come with me, miss. We got to get out."

Miss Mitcham stared in horror at Ilsa's outstretched hand. "I'm not going anywhere with you, devil!" she cried, and hugged herself tighter.

The floorboards beneath her shifted, Miss Mitcham cowered as the tiles above her came loose, and Ilsa felt something for the woman she would never have imagined possible: pity.

"Your loss, miss."

She retreated to the door and looked back. She searched the loathsome woman's face for any sign of a change of heart, a moment of humanity, even if it only lasted long enough for Ilsa to save her life. But all that was there was pure loathing; a loathing she would cling to through a painful, unseemly death.

"It's all your loss," she said, and she left her there, just as she wanted.

V

THE HONEY BEE
Apis mellifera

The honey bee is but a part of the superorganism that
is the colony. Only the queen is of vital importance;
as such she is fiercely protected.

38

When Ilsa, Gedeon, and the unconscious Cogna got clear of the orphanage – no more than a minute before half of it crumpled to rubble with a sound that shook the earth – there was no hovering about. Kennington Road was swarming with Otherworlders; perhaps two hundred or more. Shivering, wide-eyed children were everywhere. Cadell Fowler stood in the fray, holding a grubby eight-year-old by the collar and scowling. Though the evidence he had any authority over the situation was slim, Ilsa surmised he had been left in charge of the children.

"Wait here," she said to Gedeon, and she became invisible and made a dash for the captain. With the chaos as cover, she put four fingers in her mouth and whistled hard.

"Partner up!"

The orphans filtered through the bystanders towards her and Fowler like water through muslin. In fifteen seconds, they had whipped themselves into an ordered line, two by two and holding hands, just the way they used to in Ilsa's time.

"All present?" Necks craned as they peered up and down the line, then nodded in unison. Ilsa nodded back, just once, and patted Fowler on the arm. "Watch them 'til the police get here, will you?" Before he could protest, she slipped unseen back into the side road where her brother waited.

The rescue mission too, had partnered up.

It had been Ilsa's idea, in case of chaos: once they found Gedeon and the amulet, they were to find their partner and get back to the Witherward. Captain Fowler had scorned Ilsa's system and since his partner, Cassia, did not suffer fools, she appeared to have left him behind. As Ilsa looked back over her shoulder to see the first policeman on the scene put the Wraith in irons, she swore to remind him when they next met.

But Ilsa's partner was dead. It was her and Gedeon now.

On another night, they might have attracted attention as they made their way west and crossed the river; there were certainly enough policemen around, every one of them swarming to the scene they had left in their wake. But a young man too wet with rain for the blood to show, a woman strangely clad in summer attire and shivering and a child who could have been ten years old and sleeping, were the least of the sights in Lambeth that night.

Ilsa was acutely aware at every moment of her brother, and she had the unshakable sense that his thoughts were likewise on her. It made the aching silence between them all the more excruciating. But there was too much to say – some of it she wanted to scream – and she was feeling too much; mournful, confused, bloodied, giddy, horrified with herself, and unbearably cold.

"Where're your wolves?" she asked in a small voice.

"Back through the portal," said Gedeon. After a long pause he added: "I hope."

They reached the fountain in the quadrangle and passed through; the descent, the lurching sensation, the sudden realisation that she was climbing to the surface, then bright daylight and a mild breeze.

"Ilsa!" A blanket was thrown around her shoulders. Cassia's hands pressed into her arms and warmth spread through the fabric, until Ilsa felt like she was sitting by a roaring fire. "You scared the life out of us… where's Oren?"

"Dead." It was Gedeon. He stepped forward and dragged Cassia's attention like he was one of Fyfe's explosives going off.

The quadrangle was teeming with shocked, crestfallen faces. Fyfe was cradling one arm but looked otherwise unhurt. Ilsa didn't have any words of explanation to offer him as she placed the pocket forge in his uninjured hand. He looked at her bleakly, and his mouth formed Oren's name. Seven of Gedeon's wolves had made it back, including Scotty and a badly injured woman who was being tended by a healer.

Ilsa's gaze met Eliot's as he limped into view from the cloisters. It was only for a second, before Gedeon shifted and leapt at him. Eliot's face was pained and wary as he crouched and transformed, just in time to catch the full force of Gedeon as they collided with a roar, shattering one of the arches of the cloisters.

Everyone was too stunned to react. Cassia clapped a hand to her mouth. Fyfe let out a wordless shout. The only witness who knew that this wasn't some petty spat, that Gedeon might just kill Eliot – or be killed trying – was Ilsa.

The cats tumbled into the centre of the quadrangle, oblivious to their friends leaping out of their way. Ilsa dropped to all fours and grew into a great white leopard. She let out a reverberating snarl, but Gedeon and Eliot took no notice, so she saw no choice but to launch herself into the fray.

Her reward was a claw tearing into her shoulder; she didn't know whose. Eliot reeled back, no doubt recognising her, but it took a firm bite to Gedeon's neck to get him to back off. She transformed the second there was space between them, and threw up her hands. Eliot had already shifted, having been ready to end the fight before it begun. Gedeon transformed, looking startled.

"What are you doing?" he said in alarm, eyes drifting to the cut trailing down her shoulder. Her bullet wound had reopened too.

"You can't just kill him," Ilsa said, her breath ragged. Eliot was somewhere behind her. She didn't turn around. She couldn't look at him.

"Ilsa?" Cassia said. Her eyes darted between the three of them. "Gedeon?"

"Eliot's a spy," Ilsa said, loud enough so everyone could hear. "He told the rebels when to attack."

Cassia's fingers stilled. Fyfe lowered himself onto the lip of the fountain. His look of abject disbelief made Ilsa flinch.

"He's a traitor to Camden," Gedeon growled. "Put him in chains and bring him back to the Zoo. I think my cousin deserves to hear what he has to say for himself."

An abbey guard fetched some manacles. Mutely, and reluctantly, the wolves took him prisoner. Eliot didn't resist. He was a faster shifter than any of them; he could have burst from the abbey and been gone. But where? He had told Ilsa that serving Camden had been his whole life. So instead, he offered his hands to be shackled.

Ilsa had once read an article in the newspaper by a Metropolitan Police detective. Something she had been surprised to learn was how many suspects are glad to confess. They want to be caught and cornered. When there is nowhere left to hide, their honesty

493

can finally win out over their self-preservation, and the burden of secrecy is lifted. The weight of running is just too tremendous.

Watching Eliot being led back to the Zoo, Ilsa could have sworn that the mercurial, tormented young man she had come to know was fading. Eliot looked more at peace than she had ever seen him.

*

"Why?" said Gedeon.

He was sprawled in an armchair in the drawing room, with a cold compress to the bruises on his neck where Ilsa had bitten him. The lieutenants, two dozen wolves, and the house staff were arranged around him like satellites.

Ilsa, Cassia, and Hester were the furthest from him; three remote points on the fringes of his influence. He was trying to concentrate on one immediate problem at a time, but his hazel eyes kept returning to each of them; Ilsa the most.

It wasn't Gedeon she was maintaining distance from, but the whole scene. All mysteries had been solved, but something was still tickling the hairs on the back of her neck, and it was putting her out.

Those who had heard Oren's confession put together an explanation of what he'd done at the orphanage. Ilsa did not contribute. She had said her piece in the attic. No one brought up Hester's command that the amulet be brought back to the Zoo, but Ilsa didn't doubt Gedeon would find out later. What he would make of it, she hadn't figured him out well enough to guess.

A long, pressing silence lingered when the story was told. Ilsa never thought she would miss wrapping up a conversation with a thousand pedantic questions and criticisms, but a lump caught in her throat. She could tell everyone else was thinking it too.

At last, Gedeon stood. He was nearly as tall as Fyfe, but broad and muscular. If there was a finite ration of brawn to be passed from parents to offspring, Gedeon had gotten it all. He drew a breath the whole room was waiting for.

"If he wasn't dead I'd be furious," he said, his tone betraying how hard it was to joke.

"Speaking of furious," he added louder, flashing the room a cold, humourless smile. Then he turned to the wolf hovering at the door, waiting to collect his charge and bring him forward. "Let's get this over with."

39

Ilsa's nagging sense of unease grew and grew. A small part of her still believed Eliot was innocent. She tried to catch his eye as he was led into the room, tried to see a glimpse of some unlikely truth, but his attention was on Hester.

Her cousin stared back at him from the edge of the room, and even Ilsa cowered from her look of stoic disappointment. But Eliot didn't flinch. Every apology he had been unable to give was etched onto his face.

Gedeon fixed him with a long, unreadable stare. Then he turned to Ilsa. It jolted her. She couldn't get used to him. His eyes were just like Hester's, just like hers, but gentler. Curious, instead of probing. "How did you know?"

She hesitated. Would he be asking her if he knew what she would expose? It didn't matter; the others deserved to know what he had done. She had the diagram tucked in her sleeve, and she unfolded it and handed it to him. Gedeon stared at her, incredulous.

"You worked it out from this alone?"

Ilsa shook her head. "It started with Aelius. He had his suspicions 'bout a spy at the Zoo, but truthfully, I don't think he was all that serious. I din't think much of it at first, but then Cassia told me what you said when you argued 'bout Millwater." Gedeon flushed, and his mouth moved like he would argue, but no sound came out. Cassia watched him squirm. The upward tilt of her chin was stubbornly fixed. Her arms remained crossed. "And I realised you thought it too. 'Bout the spy, I mean. It weren't until this afternoon, when I talked with Oren, that I understood you din't think it was Cassia who was spying, not in particular. You were suspicious of everyone.

"And Eliot—" She dared to look at him. He met her gaze, but warily, like he wasn't sure how badly she was about to hurt him. Everything he had done to deceive her; everything she could tell them all now. "He said you din't see Hester when she was hurt. But it weren't her you were avoiding. It was because Eliot was always with her, and I knew. I knew it the second before I worked that diagram out."

"Knew what?" said Cassia, though she looked like she didn't want the answer.

Ilsa glanced at Gedeon, but his eyes were on the floor. He folded the diagram away protectively.

"There was never no trip to Millwater," Ilsa told the assembly. "It was a test, to see if one of you'd pass the information along to the Sorcerer rebels, to give them a window to attack."

Cassia's stoniness faltered. Fyfe blinked stupidly at Gedeon, hurt in his eyes.

"Eliot," he said, like a question. "For how long?"

A muscle fluttered in Eliot's jaw, and he swallowed. "For three years." Ilsa didn't realise she was clenching her fists until they weakened in a rush, and she felt the sting of her nails come free from the cuts they'd made in her palms. It was true; Eliot had betrayed the Zoo. "They weren't rebelling at the time. They were merely unhappy with Fisk. And I had no idea, I swear, that they had ties to the Fortunatae."

"Well that's much better," muttered Cassia, and the wolves growled.

"Ten wolves have died at the hands of the rebels," said Gedeon, silencing the muttering. His rage was white hot, but theirs was just as searing. "You're complicit in those deaths. You risked us all."

Eliot was silent. His gaze drifted to Hester again. The weight of remorse seemed to press on his shoulders, and he grew smaller.

"It was an exchange," he told Gedeon limply. "A backchannel. It just got out of hand." The wolves hissed and scoffed. "Last year I warned you someone was trying to obstruct our bakers from the sale of a whole season's crop of wheat. We made an early bid and bought up what we needed. Our people would have starved that year without that tip. I got it from my contacts. And when I told you sixteen of Lucius's people were vying for change?"

"Do you have any names?" challenged Gedeon.

Eliot's expression was as rigid as stone. "I was working on it when the raid happened."

Another rumble of derision from the group. Gedeon sneered. "You could have come to me. I could have helped you. I could have stopped the attack that cost Hester her *magic*!" He gestured at his cousin, who was still glaring coolly at Eliot.

"Hester—" Eliot whispered desperately. He took an unconscious step towards her, but Gedeon blocked his path.

"I should kill you," he said.

It didn't sound like much of a threat – maybe, like Ilsa, he was still expecting some miracle of vindication – but there were a few murmurs of assent from the wolves. Eliot ended them with that venomous look.

"Gedeon," he said firmly, "I'm sorry. For everything." Stirred by the realisation that Eliot was begging for his life, Ilsa found herself pressing forward. "But you couldn't have helped me. Believe me, I have played every decision of the last three years over and over in my mind. Everything I have done… I had no choice."

"Why?" Ilsa said. All eyes turned to her. "Why din't you have a choice?"

She hadn't meant to ask the question, but the longer she pondered the truth, the more wrong it felt. She couldn't imagine an answer Eliot could give that she would believe.

Eliot looked at her for the first time, that rare tenderness melting away the ice, and heaved his shoulders in a lacklustre shrug. "It doesn't matter any more."

"It does to me," said Ilsa, but her small voice was drowned out by Hester's large one. It was the first time she had spoken since they had returned with Eliot in chains and told her the truth.

"He's right," she said. Everyone parted to let her into the centre of the room. "Whatever excuse he has to give, I don't want to hear it." She turned to Gedeon. "Just deal with him."

There were jeers of concurrence from the wolves as Hester wheeled from the room. Eliot's desolate gaze tracked her out. His mouth soundlessly formed her name.

"What does that mean?" said Ilsa, over the dozens of voices.

"It means hang him!" someone yelled before Gedeon could respond.

"We haven't hanged someone since before Lyander's day," said Cassia, but her voice was lost among the growing shouts.

"He's a traitor!"

499

"He's with the enemy!"

"He should hang!"

Gedeon swept a level gaze over his soldiers. He was hearing their piece, Ilsa realised, and it wouldn't do. She stepped close to her brother and spoke at a volume that demanded the rest of them be quiet.

"If you start killing us off," she said, "soon enough there'll be no Changelings left. We lost five wolves today already." She paused, the room having fallen quiet, and looked each man and woman baying for Eliot's blood in the eye, one by one, daring them to argue. "Won't our enemies love it if we start killing each other and save them a job? Ain't there enough death in this starsforsaken city already?"

When she looked back at Gedeon, she was the only one with his attention. He nodded, just once, and put his back to Eliot. Everything in the motion said that he had looked at his old friend for the last time.

"Escort him to the portal," he said. "See that he passes through. Tell the abbey guard he is never to re-emerge. Ever."

"Gedeon—" Eliot began.

"This is mercy," Gedeon growled. "You can thank my sister, and then you can bid her farewell."

He couldn't have known the true impact of those words, but Ilsa felt them like a punch to the stomach. She knew from Eliot's face that he did too. But how did she say goodbye? Wanting him mingled with wanting to hurt him and she couldn't stand it.

In the end she looked away, and Eliot said nothing.

The Zoo was running out of medicines.

Aelius would live, and was growing stronger by the hour, but he was still taking a steady cocktail of pain and healing tonics. Most of those who had been at the orphanage were also in need, including Fyfe, who had shattered his radius, and Cassia, who had never let on, but had taken a cutting curse to her abdomen and lost a frightening amount of blood. Gedeon was frantic when she almost passed out – even more so when she refused to see him.

This was how Ilsa was left to heal from a tear in her shoulder, several broken ribs and a freshly bleeding bullet wound all on her own, with only the Otherworld tools of stitches, iodine, and gauze to aid her. Fliss dictated that there was no medicine either side of the portal more essential than sleep, but between the pain and her troubled mind, Ilsa couldn't manage it.

She was back in her own bedchamber; her belongings had been quietly moved there while Fliss was stitching her shoulder. Sometime in the night, after the Zoo had quietened, she stretched, opened her eyes – and was jolted out of bed by the presence of a short, pale child sitting atop her dresser.

"What the bleeding hell is wrong with you?" she hissed. "Not everyone can See there's a midnight visit from a shady little scoundrel in their future."

"I'm sorry," said Cogna, not sounding it in the least, "but you wanted to talk to me." A little frown of concentration appeared between Cogna's eyes, then was smoothed away again. "No. My mistake. You *will* want to talk to me when you hear what I have to say."

Ilsa gritted her teeth. "Out with it, then."

Cogna hopped down from the dresser. "It hasn't escaped my notice that the only two witnesses of our conversation at the orphanage are dead," the Oracle said matter-of-factly. "I'm sure it hasn't escaped yours either."

They were right, it hadn't, though Ilsa had not decided what to do with this information yet. "So?"

"*So,*" said Cogna, rocking back and forth on the spot, "I have spent the last six months studiously *not* telling people that Ilsa Ravenswood will save the city." Ilsa flinched. "If you like, I can continue not telling people."

Ilsa narrowed her eyes at Cogna. She only knew two things for sure about the little Oracle: they were powerful, and they were devious. It didn't make for a person she wanted to play this game with.

"And what possible motive you got for doing that for me?" she said.

Cogna's expression suggested this was a stupid question. "Because I want to be on the right side of history. Your side."

Ilsa's nostrils flared. "Then you better get comfortable, kid, because I ain't picked no sides. I'll be damned if I let some strangely confident thirteen-year-old with a questionable sense of loyalty dictate my fate to me."

"I'm dictating nothing," said Cogna. The child's imperviousness to insults only made Ilsa want to try harder. "Your fate lies ahead of you whether I See it or not, and whether I tell it to the world or keep it between us. Don't you *want* to be destined for greatness, Ilsa Ravenswood?"

Ilsa turned and climbed back into bed, though she wouldn't have been surprised if Cogna was impervious to social cues too. "What I *want* is a good night's sleep in a comfortable bed, and a meal in the morning, and hot water for my bath, and a little good conversation."

She hunkered down into the pillows and pulled the blanket over her head. Cogna had a hand on the doorknob when she sprang back up. "And on the subject of greatness – I'm a great magician, and I'm a great thief, and I'm a great shifter, and I play a bloody mean hand of three-card brag. And I'm a damned great detective, so believe me, I'll find you out if you breathe a word of this city-saving nonsense to anyone!"

Ilsa settled down again, but she didn't hear Cogna leave.

"We must follow our talents, Ilsa Ravenswood," they said. "They will lead us down the road to greatness."

If that was a riddle, Ilsa was too tired to puzzle it out. She let Cogna leave without another retort.

It was only after the sound of footsteps had faded that Ilsa noticed Cogna had left something on the dresser. Warily, she climbed out of bed to retrieve it.

The toy was as familiar as it was unique; the same size, the same wood, but feline rather than canine, with pinhole nicks to resemble a leopard's spots. It was solid.

It was Ilsa. Impossibly, she would bet good money that it was carved by the same hand, and it made her throat close. Had Oren made this? She had never asked him about the wooden wolf, never thanked him for the only link she'd had to her family and her world. Hadn't she decided the person who made it must have cared for her? She imagined a different future, in which he got to give her the leopard himself. Perhaps she would have understood the gesture, understood *him*, just as well as she did now. Now that he'd died for her family.

She handled the leopard slowly, turning it over in her hands, weighing it, running her fingers over every part of its sanded skin. She wondered, if Oren had asked, what kind of animal she would have liked. This didn't match her brother's, but it wasn't wearing her memories of the attic either. It didn't offer any clues or make any promises, but nor was it a vessel for someone else's secret. It was more hers, and Ilsa liked it better, and she liked it worse.

In the end, she left the leopard on the dresser where Cogna had deposited it – positioning it carefully like she shouldn't have disturbed it in the first place – and returned to bed, so that she might finally get some sleep.

*

But real sleep continued to elude her.

As her addled mind drifted about in the middle ground between consciousness and rest, she felt the pieces of the Zoo settle like a puzzle. Only, whichever way she arranged them, nothing quite fit.

She kept seeing them; Eliot, begging, the desperation etched across his face. Hester, with that look of hatred she reserved just for him.

His queen. Her loyal soldier.

You don't hate him, then.

I don't know.

Maybe she did. Maybe she had hated him before.

Ilsa felt herself climb from the bed, slip her feet into her slippers, and search around for her robe. All the while, a single thought pounded against her skull:

Had Hester already known?

She crept down the dark corridor, one hand against the wall. She wondered foggily what time it was. She wondered what she had failed to see because she couldn't read her cousin's tells.

D'you know why he cancelled the trip?

Eliot, begging. For his life. For forgiveness.

She had heard them whispering, hadn't she? Something about... oh, she wished she'd written it down. It was what Oren would have done.

D'you know why he cancelled the trip?

She couldn't remember. She willed her aching eyes to adjust to the dark. Her head swam with grief and fury and exhaustion, and a cloying fear.

Sometimes a person sees what they expect to see. It was how the Otherworlders remained so oblivious to the flashes of magic that cropped up in their world; the ones Ilsa had spent seventeen years chasing.

She *never* saw what she expected to see. She always looked for the truth. Didn't she?

Eliot, begging. The prickle on the back of her neck.

Something had been wrong. *She* had been wrong. She had seen the obvious, even when her instincts had known otherwise.

That look. The desperation. He hadn't been begging Hester for forgiveness. He had been begging her to defend him. And Ilsa should have known why, because Hester had slipped up.

She was supposed to have believed the trip was happening on the thirtieth, the day after the attack. But something wasn't right about what Hester had told her.

D'you know why he cancelled the trip?

Cancelled? That was the day of the attack.

"Was it you?"

The lamps were out in Hester's chamber, but the curtains were open. Hester was silhouetted in her usual spot overlooking the rose garden. Ilsa picked her way through the moonlit chamber until she was stood before her. She nearly tripped on an empty whisky bottle by the couch.

"Was he acting on your orders?" she said. The words were barely a whisper. "Did you betray the Zoo?"

Hester didn't look at her; didn't change the prideful angle of her jaw. She didn't speak for so long Ilsa began to wonder if she'd said the words aloud. Then Hester shook her head, almost imperceptibly.

Not a denial. Just regret.

"And look what it earned me," she said quietly.

Ilsa did look. At thirty-one, Hester looked alarmingly worn. She was white, sunless skin hanging from a skeleton, all muscle definition having melted away. Her hair was thin and fraying from the compulsive plucking. Her eyes were bloodshot from the drink and the vemanta.

To adjust after a loss like hers was a trial enough. But Hester had caused this herself. Looking at her now, it seemed so obvious.

"You said your memory of the attack was blurry."

"It is."

"So blurry you din't realise the rebels were a day early. So when we talked 'bout the Millwater trip, you told me the way it was *s'posed* to happen. Gedeon and the wolves go to Millwater; the rebels show up. Just like you planned it. Only, I thought you was just confused."

Hester looked at her then; a probing, opaque look that laid Ilsa bare. "I'd been wondering when you'd notice," she said. "You made me think I was losing my mind. Until Eliot who told me what Gedeon had done. We had talked about the trip, but we failed to see the inconsistencies."

Was it a comfort that Hester hadn't *intentionally* thrown Eliot to the wolves? No. She was doing it now. Eliot loved Hester, his erstwhile queen, and she was exploiting that to save herself.

"You had him betray his people." Weak and bone-tired, Ilsa lowered herself onto the couch. "And now you're letting him take the fall."

This last struck like a blade. For a flash, Hester's pride crumbled into guilt. Then the mask slipped back into place. She tilted her head and examined Ilsa with something like disgust.

"You think you know me," she said in a tone of surprise, as if the realisation had hit her over the head. "You think you know what I've done."

Ilsa wasn't sure any more. She had never been able to read the woman's tells, but her pride and her astonishment, her condescension – all felt genuine.

"He has two brothers. Did you know? The younger is twelve. They idolise him, as they idolised their father. Can you imagine the things a person like Eliot would do to protect his brothers from his mistakes? His widowed mother?"

There was something opaque in Hester's words. Ilsa had to turn them over several times before their meaning rearranged itself.

"You ain't talking 'bout Eliot's mistakes. You mean his father's."

"Elijah was a lieutenant to Lyander. He was *here* when we fled. I saw him myself, and yet I never questioned…" She put shaking fingers to her lips.

Two of her mother's three lieutenants had died alongside her, Cassia had said. "Elijah weren't in the cellar."

Hester shook her head and swallowed her emotion. "It wasn't until he was killed that I understood he had told the Sage – had told *Alitz* – where to find us. That was three years ago."

For three years. That's how long Eliot had been colluding with the Heart rebels. There was a connection, Ilsa understood, but she couldn't see it.

"How d'you find out? 'Bout Elijah."

Hester still did not look at her, yet Ilsa saw something shatter inside her.

"I didn't." She shook her head. "I wish I had. I wish I had waited to make lieutenants of them, as I had wanted. Gedeon was only fifteen, but Elijah, Aelius, and Oren were insistent. They said he had to learn my role before it was *given to him*. But I struck a bargain. If I had to have Gedeon, I told them, I would have Eliot too. Yes, he was younger, but he was smarter too. He had a mind for strategy. He understood nuances of leadership your brother is still yet to grasp. Like *accountability*.

"He had been a lieutenant barely a year when he uncovered a plot that someone was trying to usurp me. But he didn't know it was Elijah, only that a member of the Zoo was meeting with Sorcerers. Dissent in the Heart was managed with a firmer hand in Fisk's time" – Hester's eyes flashed with approval – "but it is always there, in every faction. I instructed Eliot to arrange for our traitor to be followed and… dealt with." Ilsa shuddered, and Hester saw. She smiled a vicious smile, but there was no humour behind her eyes. "You have learned for yourself that a mercenary Wraith is a remarkably efficient tool. Pay them to slaughter every person at a clandestine meeting, and they will ask no questions."

Bile rose in Ilsa's throat. She didn't need to hear which Wraith. She had seen for herself that something painful hung between Eliot and Cadell Fowler. She wished she'd never insisted on taking the captain into the Zoo's confidence. She wished she'd never met him.

When Hester continued, her voice shook. Her desolate gaze had drifted back to the window. "I only meant to extend my trust. To give Eliot an opportunity to prove himself. I would never have allowed him to suffer this if I'd known what he was instigating. He was… he was fifteen."

I don't know how to mourn somebody I—

Ilsa thought her heart might break clean in two. Eliot didn't keep his father's watch because he missed him. He kept it because he'd killed him.

"Elijah had courted more allies for his coup than anticipated. Though, perhaps *allies* is not the right word. They saw, as Elijah did not, that they could weaken the Changelings by removing the family who had united them, and when he was gone they saw a new opening into the Zoo. A new puppet. They uncovered Eliot's involvement and threatened to reveal his father's betrayal and murder to the Zoo; to his family."

Can you imagine the things a person like Eliot would do to protect his brothers from his mistakes? His widowed mother?

Ilsa shook her head. "I don't believe you. You're telling me Eliot betrayed Camden to protect his family? To save his father's reputation? I don't believe it."

"The threat of his mother's broken heart was only one incentive," said Hester wryly. "I presented him with a second: make working for the rebels work for us."

This, Eliot had tried to tell Gedeon. How his backchannel had benefited Camden. "The rebels expected a pawn, so Eliot gave them one. They did not know there was a queen behind him. They've never known of my involvement, but together we have fed the rebels innocuous scraps of intelligence while Eliot siphoned off theirs. We have always benefited more than we were hurt. Until."

Until.

"Their first few attempts to raid us, they acted alone," she continued. "But our defences were too solid. Eliot met with them fortnightly. He told me they would hide their faces, but otherwise they appeared to trust in their power over him." She smiled reluctantly. "He must have played a far meeker boy than you or I know.

"One night, he came back and told me their demand: they wanted a window of opportunity to get into the Zoo."

Ilsa's anger flared. "You knew the whole time they were looking for something."

"Looking for something, planting something." Hester waved a hand dismissively. "We decided we could deal with whatever it was later. Eliot believed he was close to identifying some of the highest-ranking rebels; we just needed more time. Gedeon wasn't supposed to be here. Security was supposed to be light. If that damned trip to Millwater hadn't been a ruse, it would never have been the fight it turned into."

"You can't blame this on Gedeon," said Ilsa. "You could have *told him* what was going on but—"

Hester laughed derisively. "No, cousin. I have told you the kind of leader your brother is. He knows *nothing* of hard decisions. Eliot and I are cut from stronger steel. We understand that we must make hard decisions because weaker men and women cannot. That some choices are no choice at all. Your brother believes he can mould the world around him like he can mould himself. But I have learned, as Eliot has, that we can only cut at it. But if our blades are sharp enough, we can leave a scar."

"You let him go through all that," said Ilsa, feeling hot tears on her skin, "you let him carry all that guilt 'round, then you made him take the blame."

Hester faltered, her wicked humour vanishing, and swallowed. "It's better this way."

"Better for you?" growled Ilsa. She didn't know where she was finding the rage. She was shattered.

"Better for Gedeon. Better for Fyfe." She closed her eyes like she could block her own words out. "Better for Camden."

For Camden.

They were not her words; they were Eliot's. Eliot, who had been so accepting of whatever fate Ilsa dealt him when she found him out. Who had left the abbey with his head held high and an air of relief. He had talked her into this, but then he had begged to be saved. He had faltered at the last moment, and Hester had not. Perhaps they were cut from the same steel, but hers was stronger.

Now Ilsa was the one laughing spitefully. "You talk 'bout Gedeon like he ain't a good leader, but you won't even help him be one. You should have told him," Ilsa repeated. "You should have told Gedeon."

Hester shot her a sardonic glare. "You have been lucky again," she said. "When we plucked you from the Otherworld, Aelius wanted to make you alpha."

Ilsa blinked. "But I... that don't make no sense."

"Oh, don't misunderstand me. He never expected you to lead. But I chose, at first, not to oblige their whims when they made me warden, and Gedeon was gone. Aelius wanted a figurehead. A show of strength. He wanted to tell all of London that Camden's lost princess had returned.

"He was overruled, of course, and you were lucky. If they had made you alpha, you would only have had to give it up again when Gedeon returned. Then, maybe, cousin dearest, you would understand why."

"But I don't want that kind of power."

Hester studied her, a tiny crease between her brows, like she saw a lie. "Funny. It seems neither does Gedeon." Then she smiled. She was frightening when she smiled, just like Eliot. Ilsa wondered if she'd ever been that good at reading people. "I heard you today, in front of the wolves, defending Eliot's life. You pulled rank on the Prince of Camden."

"I din't mean to—"

"You pulled rank," she said more firmly, "and the whole pack let you."

Ilsa shook her head, but she wasn't sure what she was arguing anymore. A sort of dreamy calm was overcoming her, and her fear and indignation were disappearing into it like streetlights in the fog. She could barely concentrate on the problem of getting back to her bed. She was making a half-hearted effort to rise from the couch and take her leave when something struck her.

"Ain't you gonna ask me not to tell no one?"

Hester smiled at that, only faintly. "We both know I don't need to. We both understand what sort of a threat I am to Gedeon now." She sighed her dramatic, lofty sigh. "Do not fear, cousin dearest. From now on I shall sit in my chair like a good little girl and be nothing and nobody." She turned her head. Her shaking fingers reached up and brushed the tears away.

Like that, Ilsa could not leave, not if she had all the energy in the world. Somebody needed to stay with her, to be a buoy should Hester need to grab on. Ilsa knew this, even in her shattered, dozing mind. Because despite the devious game Hester had played, a part of her understood the bitter, hopeless woman like she wished she didn't. She wanted to take her hand and tell her that she would always be somebody, she would always matter; that maybe, in time, she would remember that. But Hester had gone back to pretending like her cousin wasn't there, and Ilsa was just too tired. She let herself sink low against the cushions. Some time later, she curled onto her side.

"Go to sleep, cousin dearest," she heard Hester say. "The world will still be as it is in the morning."

4 2

Ilsa wanted to approach Gedeon, but instead she caught herself spying on him from the library. Spying was familiar. Reunions with long-lost siblings were uncharted territory.

Gedeon was in the garden, and Cassia was with him. He had caught up with her there twenty minutes ago, and now he sat on a bench pouring his heart out while the Sorcerer stood rigidly before him. Her arms were wrapped around her like a shield.

It was not going well. Cassia had not thawed one iota since the start of the conversation. And while Ilsa couldn't blame her, she was quietly cheering for her brother, hoping he could transform the doll into the sharp and soft, determined and gentle, dangerous Cassia she liked more.

But it wasn't to be. After nearly an hour – and Ilsa kneeling on the window seat with her nose to the glass the whole time – Cassia turned and stalked back to the house, leaving Gedeon on the bench with his head in his hands.

Ilsa summoned her courage as she scrambled from the seat, straightened her skirt and her hair, and went outside to join him.

He didn't notice her approach, what with his wallowing. It would have been easier if he'd looked up, said hello, started the conversation maybe.

Instead, Ilsa was lumped with breaking the ice.

"What'd she say?"

Gedeon's head shot up. Several emotions – surprise, pleasure, bashfulness – crossed his features before his melancholy frown returned.

"Nothing that should be repeated in polite company," he said.

"Din't no one tell you? I'm as common as they come."

"I'm getting that." A smirk touched his lips. "It's rather charming."

There was a weighty silence. Ilsa wanted to tell him Cassia would come around, but she wasn't sure it was true. She also wanted to ask how stupid he had to be to risk losing her this way. From what she knew of Cassia, pretty stupid, and from what she knew of her brother, it was highly possible.

Gedeon got to his feet and beckoned for her to follow him through the garden. "They tell me you grew up in that place."

"That's right," said Ilsa. She decided to spare him the details for now.

Gedeon stopped suddenly. He took hold of her shoulders, turned her to face him and pressed a tentative kiss to her forehead. Ilsa smelled apples and cut grass.

"I'm so sorry, Ilsa," he said into her hair. Ilsa jolted to hear Gedeon speak her name. She had spent so long imagining this that it all felt a little like she still was. "That I did not find you. That I accepted that you were dead. I should have tried harder. You deserved better than that life."

Swiftly, and very briefly, she wrapped her arms around his waist and pressed her cheek to his chest. She didn't know him; she knew that. She just wanted to know how it felt to be held by her brother. When she pulled away, Gedeon's cheeks had turned pink.

"All them kids deserve better than that," Ilsa said. "It's the way the dice fell. If I start thinking how unfair it all is, I'll go mad."

Gedeon studied her admiringly and nodded.

"'Sides," she went on, "turns out I din't need you to find me. I found you first."

She tossed her hair over her shoulder and Gedeon grinned.

"Before I forget," he said, the smile sliding off his face, "there's a furious missive on my desk from the Underground."

"Ah."

"They're claiming you broke nearly every tenet of the Principles."

"That's an exaggeration!"

"But not a lie?" Ilsa chewed the inside of her cheek. "Ilsa, do you know that they can respond however they choose and the Principles won't protect you? They seem interested in Fyfe's dampener technology so I think I can negotiate, but you could have started a war."

"You're one to talk," Ilsa muttered under her breath.

Gedeon laughed wryly and shook his head. "Please don't take after me. We'll be in so much trouble, you and I."

"I'm sorry," said Ilsa. "I mean it. I ain't had to live by the rules for a long time. I din't take it seriously."

"And now?"

Now? Ilsa had people who would pay for her mistakes. She couldn't pretend the rules weren't hers to follow, however unjust they seemed. "Now I'm gonna. Cross my heart, it ain't gonna happen again."

"I appreciate it," said Gedeon solemnly, and Ilsa saw the leader in him; a man who made her want to make him proud, and not just because he was her brother.

They wandered in silence through the garden until they were among the roses. By the conservatory, Fyfe was explaining something about biology and soil to Cogna. Aelius sat watching. He had healed enough to shift back into his younger body. No one would ever have known.

"Speaking of unfair." She nodded towards the Oracle. "I know they're as good as doomed back in the Docklands, but you need to take Cogna back."

Gedeon scowled. "But I like Cogna."

Ilsa could tell him Cogna had lied to him, but it would raise questions she didn't want to answer. "Enough to have Oracles coming at us 'til we're extinct?" she said instead.

Gedeon slumped onto a bench with a dramatic sigh. "The Docklands do not care about Cogna," he said. "They fear Cogna. As long as the child's not working against them, they'll tire eventually."

"But if Cogna stays here, how d'you s'pect to convince the Oracles—"

"There are some complicated spells involved in glamouring a corpse," said Gedeon abruptly, "but I think Cassia can handle it. And Fyfe's more morbid interests have given him connections at a mortuary."

Ilsa folded her arms. "I don't see how neither of those things helps us."

He grinned. "Oh, we're sending Cogna back, alright. In a coffin. I shall attach a note saying 'sorry' to the lid and I'm sixty per cent certain this whole kidnapping saga will blow over."

Ilsa gaped. She didn't know him well enough to tell if he was

518

serious. "They'll know," she said.

"Ah." He wagged a finger at her. "But they can't See Cogna. They won't even try to check."

"That's still the stupidest plan I ever heard."

Gedeon winked. "But you have to agree it has a roguish charm."

He took in her total lack of amusement and sighed. "We have bigger problems, Ilsa. For all we know, every member of the Fortunatae was at that orphanage, and are now all dead. All but the one who matters."

Alitz. Ilsa hadn't really expected to find her in the fray, but in the night, she had dreamed that she had. She had dreamed it was the Sage's throat she had torn out in that attic.

Then, in the morning, she had found Georgiana and asked her if the wolves kept records.

"What kind of records?" she asked, frowning.

"Like reports of incidents and deaths and that."

"When anything like that happens, we write a written report for the commander." She shrugged. "The alpha sees them weekly, but I don't know what happens to them after that."

She took Ilsa to Liesel, who told them to ask Cassia, who directed them to a corner of the library where Georgiana helped Ilsa search decades of wolves' reports until she found what she was looking for.

Alitz had implied that the incident she once described – the death of an abusive husband and the Whitechapel steward who had tried to protect the man's wife – was recent, or perhaps Ilsa had just assumed. But after learning the Sage's identity, a vague hunch had taken hold.

And she was right. It had taken her the whole morning and three cups of tea, but Ilsa finally found the report from fifty years ago. The wolf who had recorded the incident had been thorough, and perhaps a little emotional, as they described the tragedy. How the woman had approached the border, lip bleeding and nose broken, and begged the stewards to keep her husband from her. How the stewards had refused her husband entry to Whitechapel. How he had appealed to the wolves, but they had sided with the stewards.

But then the accounts diverged. The wolf wrote that the man had indeed shifted into a bear and charged the guard point, but as the wolves had rushed to tackle him, one of the stewards had reached out with their magic and subdued him. Heedless to the danger having passed, a second steward had raised his gun and shot the bear dead.

The author didn't know who struck first after that – the wolves or the stewards – only that the single casualty of the fight had not been at the hands of either militia, but the dead man's wife, who had taken his killer between her teeth and torn his throat out. The wolf's handwriting shook as they recorded that the dead steward's young daughter had been sent to fetch him home for tea. The fighting had stopped when the child ran out into the fray. She had knelt in the street with her father's head in her lap, sobbing as he bled out.

His name was Amadeo Dicer.

Ilsa wondered at how Alitz remembered it differently. In her eyes, her father had been a hero, guilty of nothing but defending himself and the woman who ultimately took his life. Could the wolf who reported on the tragedy be mistaken? Or had Amadeo killed a man who posed no threat to him?

Ilsa couldn't know if what Alitz had suffered as a child

made her choose the path she had gone down – the massacre she had ordered over three decades later – or whether watching her father die like that solidified a hate Amadeo himself had nurtured in her.

But whatever had happened that day, and whatever it had done to Alitz, Ilsa knew none of the people who were dead because of the Sage had been responsible. Not her parents, nor Hester's father, nor the grandfather and aunt she never knew. Not Oren, or Bill Blume. Alitz's quarrel was with a distraught widow who was probably in the grave.

But now Ilsa's was with Alitz.

She decided she would tell her brother what she'd discovered that morning, but not yet. The revelation that Alitz was the Sage had wounded Ilsa, but Gedeon had learned that the person who had slaughtered most of his family was someone he had known and trusted his whole life. She didn't want to inflict what she was feeling on him too; the sense of injustice, the futility of everything that had been lost, and the fear of the way her own hate was eating at her.

Gedeon was staring off across the lawn. No doubt his thoughts were also on Alitz. Perhaps he was thinking not of the past, but of what the Sage's next move would be.

"The matter with the Oracles is done with," he said. "I don't believe the Seer ever planned to shackle themselves to the Fortunatae. They broke the Principles against the Heart when they aided the rebels in the raid, possibly against Whitechapel too for the Fortunatae's part in this. And whilst the Principles are foggy on the legality of allying with insurgents in retaliation for kidnapping, if the Seer has any sense at all, they'll want to call this one even. They can't afford to hold a grudge over a fake kidnapping any more than Camden can afford to worry about it."

Ilsa gingerly perched next to him. "If you're trying to reassure me—"

"I'm not." He braced his forearms on his knees, his levity vanishing. "I want you to know what kind of city you have inherited… so that you will know I understand if you say you don't want it."

She studied him; he was definitely serious now. "You want to know if I want to go back."

"We can find a flat for you. Even hire a housekeeper." He scratched the back of his neck. "You missed out on a life here. You have no obligation to be involved in what's to come."

"Can I take Fyfe?"

"Absolutely not. He's too useful."

"Can we share him?"

Gedeon considered. "You can have him on Sundays." His brow crinkled. "Is that a yes, then? You would like to go back?"

Ilsa chewed her cheek. Gedeon seemed hopeful that she was only playing around and, for the most part, she was. She had found everything she had been looking for her whole life in the Witherward, and she had lost everything she had cared for in the Otherworld.

But she still didn't know who to believe about this broken, violent city; Eliot, who said London was a battleground and a graveyard, or Fowler, who saw the city for what it could be. If she went back to the Otherworld, perhaps she could start a new life there, and never have to kill another person, and never get shot again or mauled by a big cat. But she could visit. She could still have a family.

And she could find Eliot.

A movement in the house caught her eye. Hester watched them from the window. Gedeon said she had no obligations here, but she did. She had made one when she woke that morning on the couch in Hester's sitting room and decided she would not tell anyone what her cousin had done. She would keep her secret, and Eliot's, and Elijah Quillon's. Gedeon had learned of Alitz's betrayal, and that was enough. Besides, with Eliot gone, Ilsa didn't believe that Hester had any means or incentive to do anything more to hurt the Zoo. And if she was wrong about that...

"If I ain't mistaken," she said, "you're down two lieutenants."

Gedeon grinned unrestrainedly and slapped his forehead. "Stars! How could I forget?"

"So you should probably stop promising to let me out of here when it's so obvious you need me."

"You are already proving yourself indispensable." Gedeon stood and offered her his hand. "Ilsa, I retract my offer. I can't possibly let you leave."

And Ilsa couldn't possibly go. Somebody needed to keep an eye on their cousin. For Hester's own sake. For Gedeon.

For Camden.

Because Ilsa belonged here.

Her brother made his way over to Fyfe and the others, and Ilsa watched him crack a joke, watched Aelius chuckle and retort, as if nothing had happened and no time had passed at all. The boy was an enigma – audacious, selfish maybe, blustering through his life and those around him like a tornado – but Ilsa needed a new challenge; a new mystery to solve.

He called her over. The heavens were opening. Aelius, Fyfe, and Cogna were retreating to the conservatory. Ilsa dashed from the garden just as the first raindrops landed on the enchanted roses.

By June, their petals would be laced with frost.

ACKNOWLEDGEMENTS

My first and most heartfelt thanks are to my agent, Zoë Plant, for loving this book as much as I do and being the champion *Witherward* needed, and to everyone else at the Bent Agency for their work and support. Thank you to my editor, Cat Camacho, for adding new shades and surprising turns, but mainly for the note "needs more Captain Fowler"; we all know it was the right thing to do. Thanks also to everyone at Titan, particularly David Lancett, and Julia Lloyd for her beautiful cover design, and to Louise Pearce who copy-edited the book.

To the friends and writers who read early drafts of *Witherward* and helped me believe I was on to a winner: Emma Fraser, Kellen Playford, Troy Balmayer, Sara Crawford, James Lovegrove, and my little sister Ellie (thank you for wrestling with the chaotic energy of your own notes every time we talked about it).

Thank you to my parents. I was unemployed while drafting *Witherward*, and you gave me a place to live and work. It's not a stretch to say this couldn't have happened otherwise. To my brother Sam – people should pay you to cheer them on (I don't mean *me*) – and the friends and family who let me talk at them about my book. I love you all, but I still don't care that you don't care! Thank you, Jack, for always believing I am doing my best, even in the face of overwhelming evidence to the contrary.

Becoming a published author has been a fourteen-year

exercise in how to fail; a skill I have no doubt I will continue to hone. The lesson is tedious and repetitive. On the best days it's uncomfortable; on the worst it's an existential crisis. But most of all it is lonely, and yet it is impossible to accomplish alone. So thank you to every friend, colleague, and passing acquaintance who believed me when I told them this would happen.

ABOUT THE AUTHOR

Debut author Hannah Mathewson has had short stories published by *The Molotov Cocktail* and *The Fiction Desk*, who presented her with the Writer's Award for her contribution to their anthology, *Separations*. She is based in Reading. *Witherward* is her first novel. She tweets @HannahOClock.

For more fantastic fiction, author events,
exclusive excerpts, competitions, limited editions and more

VISIT OUR WEBSITE
titanbooks.com

LIKE US ON FACEBOOK
facebook.com/titanbooks

FOLLOW US ON TWITTER AND INSTAGRAM
@TitanBooks

EMAIL US
readerfeedback@titanemail.com